"COMPULSIVELY READABLE...the terrible beauty of ancient Greece collides with the merciless obsessions of the twentieth century."
—*New York Times* bestselling author Eloisa James

AN ANCIENT
MASK IS STOLEN.
AN AGE-OLD STRIFE
IS UNLEASHED.

AN ANCIENT DEBT COLLECTED

If they were what they appeared to be, this had to be the largest, richest collection of Mycenaean or Minoan artifacts outside the National Archaeological Museum in Athens. Its value was impossible to estimate.

A collection of this size just couldn't exist. Most of the Greek sites had been excavated or plundered centuries before. A collection like this, unknown to modern archaeological science, was unthinkable.

But Deborah knew at a glance that what she was looking at were not copies or reproductions of known pieces. If this stuff was real, it had been stolen, kept secret, traded outside the purview of the archaeological community, squirreled away, its lessons and delights for private consumption. She felt only dread and a disappointment that left her drained and hollow, even stopping her tears with a sudden and emptying weariness.

"Richard." She sighed. "What did you do?"

Why didn't you tell me?

She remembered his old Indiana Jones–esque righteous indignation: *"This belongs in a museum."* Quite. She looked at him again, lying there, pale and unfamiliar, striped and splashed with the garish red of his blood.

You were my friend, my mentor . . .

Richard had been dealing with the worst kind of illegal artifact traffickers and they had turned on him. What other way was there to read the evidence?

THE
MASK OF
ATREUS

A. J. Hartley

BERKLEY BOOKS, NEW YORK

THE BERKLEY PUBLISHING GROUP
Published by the Penguin Group
Penguin Group (USA) Inc.
375 Hudson Street, New York, New York 10014, USA
Penguin Group (Canada), 90 Eglinton Avenue East, Suite 700, Toronto, Ontario M4P 2Y3, Canada
(a division of Pearson Penguin Canada Inc.)
Penguin Books Ltd., 80 Strand, London WC2R 0RL, England
Penguin Group Ireland, 25 St. Stephen's Green, Dublin 2, Ireland (a division of Penguin Books Ltd.)
Penguin Group (Australia), 250 Camberwell Road, Camberwell, Victoria 3124, Australia
(a division of Pearson Australia Group Pty. Ltd.)
Penguin Books India Pvt. Ltd., 11 Community Centre, Panchsheel Park, New Delhi—110 017, India
Penguin Group (NZ), Cnr. Airborne and Rosedale Roads, Albany, Auckland 1310, New Zealand
(a division of Pearson New Zealand Ltd.)
Penguin Books (South Africa) (Pty.) Ltd., 24 Sturdee Avenue, Rosebank, Johannesburg 2196,
South Africa

Penguin Books Ltd., Registered Offices: 80 Strand, London WC2R 0RL, England

This is a work of fiction. Names, characters, places, and incidents either are the product of the author's imagination or are used fictitiously, and any resemblance to actual persons, living or dead, business establishments, events, or locales is entirely coincidental. The publisher does not have any control over and does not assume any responsibility for author or third-party websites or their content.

THE MASK OF ATREUS

A Berkley Book / published by arrangement with the author

PRINTING HISTORY
Berkley edition / April 2006

Copyright © 2006 by Andrew James Hartley.
Cover and stepback art by axb group.
Cover design by Rita Frangie.
Interior text design by Stacy Irwin.

ISBN: 0-425-20913-X

BERKLEY®
Berkley Books are published by The Berkley Publishing Group,
a division of Penguin Group (USA) Inc.,
375 Hudson Street, New York, New York 10014.
BERKLEY is a registered trademark of Penguin Group (USA) Inc.
The "B" design is a trademark belonging to Penguin Group (USA) Inc.

PRINTED IN THE UNITED STATES OF AMERICA

10 9 8 7 6 5 4 3 2 1

To Sebastian,
first revealed to us by cyber-oracle in Delphi . . .

ACKNOWLEDGMENTS

The author would like to thank the following:

People who have supported my writing in the past:

> Jane Hill, David Raney, Jaime Cortez, Alan McNee, Douglas Brooks-Davies, Jonathan Mulrooney, and—especially—Stacey Glick, who never gave up.

People who contributed directly to this novel by reading it or supplying valuable information:

> Gary Hibbert, Kimily Willingham, Cary Mazer, Ron Tipton, Jonathan Brenton, Natalee Rosenstein, and the National Archaeological Museum in Athens.

People who did both:

> My brother, Chris; my parents, Frank and Annette; and—above all—my wife, whose patience with my persistent scribblings defies description and belief.

PROLOGUE

Germany, 1945

Andrew Mulligrew clamped the radio's headphones tighter to his head. He must have misheard. Given the roaring of the Sherman's engine, it was amazing he could hear anything.

"Say again?" he shouted.

"German column heading south fast, directly ahead," the commander repeated. "Armored car lead, then something big, turretless. Maybe a Jagdpanther."

Mulligrew's heart sank. That was what he thought he'd heard. Even over the clank and squeal of the tank's wheels, he could hear the silence in the radio static. Somebody, maybe Williams over in *The Highwayman* to his left—the whole platoon had names stenciled on their hull noses—asked what else was in the convoy. His tone was balanced between resignation and dread.

"Couple of trucks, a half-track, at least two other tanks, probably a panzer four and a panther."

Four Shermans, thought Mulligrew, one of them moving at half speed, and two Stuart M5s armed only with thirty-seven mill canons, against the finest German armor including one tank they couldn't hope to touch unless they got close enough to spit on it. Every one of the German tanks had guns that could stop them cold at five hundred yards. The Jagdpanther would rip them apart at three times that distance.

What in God's name were the Krauts doing sending a prime platoon south like this when they were using every last man and machine to delay the Allied pincer in the north? Berlin was falling, perhaps already had, but a crack unit had been allowed to hightail it south, straight—God help him—into the path of his battle-weary platoon.

Mulligrew's tank and the rest of the platoon had been separated from the rest of the 761st Tank Battalion as they
pressed east through Regensburg on the Danube five days
earlier. They were seventy-five miles or so northeast of Munich, less than that from both Austria and what had been
Czechoslovakia before the Nazi carve-up, not much more
from the Swiss border. It was spectacular country, all wooded
mountains with snow-capped peaks and distant, romantic
castles. One moment they had been rolling along with the
rest of the group, finally starting to believe that their night-
marish slog from Normandy through the Ardennes into Germany was coming to a victorious end, and in the next they
had been pinned down by enemy artillery. Mulligrew's platoon had been ordered to peel off to cut enemy supply lines,
but two days later, they had found themselves completely
alone. The rest of the battalion had been ordered on at their
best speed, rushing with the rest of the army to Steyria on the
Enns River to meet—somewhat anxiously—with the Russians.

Mulligrew and the rest of the company had made the approach north by themselves, and apart from dealing with
roads jammed with refugees, he had started to think they had
gotten the softer deal. Since Regensburg they hadn't fired a
shot and were starting to believe they might fire no more. By
all accounts, the war was over.

Now this.

Mulligrew switched to the tank's internal circuit and
started yelling orders, swinging the nose of the Sherman
around, and calling for armor-piercing rounds. They had just
got off the road when they saw the armored car coming their
way. It was doing at least fifty miles an hour and skidded
badly as it struggled to find cover, its turret guns opening up
so that they could hear the machine gun rounds kicking off
the Sherman's turret. But it was what he could see behind the
armored car that drained the life from his face.

The Jagdpanther was huge, low and menacing like a croc-
odile or a shark, and its frontal armor was well sloped and

several inches thick. Even at close range the Sherman's 76 mm weapon had no chance against it. And if the German tank could get its 88 trained on them, they were dead. Simple as that.

Mulligrew screamed to get the tank into the field and the turret swung round. Their only chance was to slip past the Jagdpanther and hit it—several times and at close range—from the side. The Shermans behind him would have to deal with the other German tanks.

They were coming up out of the ditch by the roadside when the 88 fired, a great blast of smoke and muzzle flash filling Mulligrew's visor so that he winced away involuntarily. It took him two full seconds to be sure they weren't hit. Then he was screaming the order to fire, conscious even as he did so that Williams's turret had taken the full brunt of the 88, tearing a hole the size of a trash can lid in the front, the shell ricocheting around inside . . .

Seventeen long minutes later, Mulligrew stood on the back of the German truck and gazed out over the smoking ruins that littered the road and fields around it. Two of the Shermans and one of the Stuarts had been knocked out; a third had been badly damaged. Williams and all but one of his crew were dead, so were Smith, Jenkins, and Pole. Rogers had lost a leg, and Lumpkin was blind in one eye. Both of them thought they'd got off easy.

The Germans had barely stopped. Instead of repositioning, digging in, and picking them off with their superior weapons, they had tried to just push through, like they were desperate to keep moving. As the Shermans had fanned out to try to hit their flanks, they had done nothing to adjust, still pushing south, exposing even the sides and rear of that monstrous Jagdpanther, a tank that probably could have dealt with the entire platoon if it had hung back and made them come to it.

It made no sense.

And then there was the way that, as the battle had started to turn in favor of the Americans, the Germans had hemmed in this one truck, squeezed together around it as if determined to make sure that if only one vehicle made it out in one piece, it would be that battered little Opel.

"Let's see what was worth all that," Mulligrew said.

Tom Morris, Mulligrew's driver, unhooked the latch on the back of the truck. His face was blank, his eyes wide with the shock of the battle and its strangeness.

Mulligrew swung himself up, climbing over the young German who had tried to hold them off with a machine pistol until they had riddled the truck with .30 caliber rounds. Inside was a single large crate, stenciled with a German eagle and swastika. He took the pickax from the side of his tank, worked it under the top of the box, and leant his weight on it until the pine splintered and tore. Then he pushed it aside and became quite still, staring in silence.

What the hell?

"What is it, Andrew?" said Morris. "What do you see?"

"I don't know," said Mulligrew, his voice hoarse with puzzlement, even fear. "I don't know. Pretty wild stuff."

"What is it?"

"You'd better call the MPs," said Mulligrew. "Right now."

And though they did so, and even in spite of the carnage they had just endured and the grief which pursued the initial horror, Mulligrew never moved from the back of the truck. He was still standing there, staring as if spellbound, when the ambulances arrived to remove the dead.

PART I

OLD BONES

"Furthermore, his wounds, yes, every one he had (and many men cut him with their weapons of bronze) have closed, showing how much the blessed gods still love your son, though he is now nothing but a corpse . . ."
"Respect the gods," the old man replied, "and pity me in memory of your own father—though I am more to be pitied, since I have kissed the hand of the man who slew my son."

Homer, *The Iliad*, Book 24

CHAPTER 1

Present Day

The big man leaned against the wall, his still-substantial weight on the foot he had so casually braced against the doorjamb.

"You're a very striking young lady, you know, Miss Miller," he drawled, his eyes slitting in his piggy face and his tongue showing wetly through his thick, parted lips.

"I know," said Deborah. She was six feet and one inch tall and looked like she'd been assembled out of pieces of pipe. She rarely got called attractive. Never pretty. *Striking,* she heard plenty. In the past she might have been flattered. A long time ago. Tonight, after the weeks of planning and the evening's hours of fixed smiles and indulgent conversation, she was too tired to be polite, even to Harvey Webster, prominent member of Atlanta's League of Christian Businessmen and the head of the museum's financial board. It was after midnight, and she wanted to go home.

"Very striking," he repeated, extending a hand toward her hip, palm open. He was toad-shaped, his skin managing to both bulge and sag simultaneously like a balloon half full of water, sloshing from side to side.

"Mr. Webster," she said, eyeing the liver-spotted hand he was sliding toward her, "I don't think that would be wise."

And, she thought, *I'd probably throw up if you touched me.*

His hand hovered; then, as if he had decided to read her rebuttal merely as coyness, it started toward her again. She flinched away.

"Mr. Webster," she said, her smile a little weary now. "Please."

He changed tack, his leer opening into a smile, his hand retreating upward in a gesture of surrender.

"Far be it from me to give offense," he said, the smile spreading wider than the doorway he was still blocking. "I had just hoped you could give me a tour. Now that, you know, everyone's gone home."

The smile stalled for a second, and Deborah glimpsed the calculation behind it. It was uncanny how, for a sixty-five-year-old man, he oozed the smugness of a high school jock. Smugness and, she thought, a touch of menace.

"A *private* tour," he added, smirking so that it was impossible to misread what he meant.

He had been like this all night and, if she was going to be honest, was always like this, particularly after a few drinks. She thought of herself as a fairly tolerant person, but if she had a rope, she was nearing the end of it.

"Another day, Mr. Webster," she said. "When it's light and crowded and I have had the chance to invest in a decent cattle prod."

She grinned to show she was joking, but his smile curdled a little all the same.

"You have a smart mouth, Miss Miller," he said.

"Thank you," she said, embracing the fact that she just couldn't win with him tonight, "though it's not my mouth that's smart."

He sighed and raised his pasty hands in mock surrender.

"OK," he said, smiling again. "I'll be heading home."

"Drive carefully," she said, shrugging slightly aside as he made one last attempt at an embrace.

"I'll be in to see Richard later in the week, so . . . till then."

He stepped back through the glass door, still looking at her as if expecting her to change her mind and invite him back in.

"Good night now, Mr. Webster," she mouthed, adding to herself, *You drunken, lecherous, old slug.*

She felt a ripple of relief as he walked off into the darkness outside, though she guessed that forcing the old man's retreat might cost her something, maybe more than she realized. Webster controlled the museum's purse strings, and he was influential in the local business community, or an elderly, white section of it, at least. The League of Christian Businessmen didn't openly ban black members, but for an organization of its type to have none—particularly in a city like Atlanta—was suggestive. Deborah had tried to balance the League's presence at the museum with comparable organizations which had a more diverse membership, but it didn't stop her from feeling uncomfortable every time they sent a check. She could probably get a Jewish business group involved, she thought, but that made her uncomfortable too, as if that would be exploiting her heritage, a heritage she did her best to disregard in every other aspect of her life. Why risk exposing herself and the museum to anti-Semitism when the vast majority of her Jewishness was ancient history anyway?

Oh please, said a voice in her head. *Webster probably doesn't even know you're Jewish.*

Deborah checked the museum doors and did a quick walkthrough of the lobby under the T. rex skeleton and that ugly galleon prow Richard had unveiled last month like he was announcing Christmas had come early. It was a half-naked woman fused with the neck of a dragon, and looked like it would be more at home airbrushed on the side of a Harley than adorning the front of a Renaissance Spanish treasure ship, but Richard had thought it a wonderfully hilarious blend of history and kitsch. Deborah glowered at the woman's vacant face and excessive curves, then down to where she became scaly and reptilian, the sexy allure turning—not surprisingly—into the serpent of Eden.

She considered the great serpentine thing, its breasts like sixteenth-century headlamps, and grinned a wry, self-deprecating grin.

"Richard," she said aloud, "I love you, but you have a lousy sense of humor."

She shrugged, blew out a sigh, and paused to take in the carnage visited on the museum foyer by the caterers. They had left four trash cans filled with the paper plates they were supposed to have taken with them. In the semicircular alcove where she had done her presentation three hours earlier she found plastic martini glasses and napkins with the remains of the canapés, and a series of sticky spills on the polished floor. She'd be getting on to Richard about *Taste of Elegance,* and not just because their foie gras tasted suspiciously like Spam.

Richard Dixon was the museum's founder, its principal collector, its main source of funding, and its guiding light. He was her employer, her mentor, her friend. On the rare moments she was frank enough with herself to admit it, he was the nearest thing she'd had to a father since her own had died of heart failure when she was thirteen.

Twenty years ago, almost to the day.

Sometimes as she tried to drag the little museum into the twenty-first century, dealing with the likes of Harvey Webster in the process, Richard Dixon was the only thing that kept her going. Suddenly, standing alone in the museum foyer, dwarfed by the T. rex and lit only by the soft lights from the new Creek Indian cases, she wondered how much longer Richard himself would keep going.

And what would you do if he was gone? she thought. *It's been twenty years, and you aren't over the death of your real father yet. Past it perhaps, but not over it. Not really.*

She shook herself.

"You shouldn't drink at these things," she said aloud. "It makes you melodramatic."

She looked around, trying to decide if there was anything else that had to be done tonight. Her passport was still in the office safe where it had been since she had faxed its details to the organizers of the Celtic exhibit (in case, she supposed, she had been planning to leave the country with a few significant pieces stuffed down her blouse), but that could wait till tomorrow. It wasn't like she was going anywhere.

She picked up the mail and leafed through it, separating the bills from the junk, the envelopes for her from those for

Richard. A third of it went straight into the trash. The pieces bearing her name could wait, and those addressed to Richard seemed no more urgent. One had a little triangular mask in the corner: some begging letter from a local theater company, no doubt. Richard got dozens per week. He responded to all but the most generic or crass, often including significant donations. Smiling with a tired and familiar indulgence, Deborah put the letters in her purse and began locking up. She would deal with them in the morning.

She set the alarm, peered quickly out into the parking lot with its surround of heavy Southern magnolias, and braced herself for the heat outside. It was June, far enough into the Atlanta summer that the nights could be sweltering. She caught herself at the door. A homeless man had been hanging around the museum over the last couple of days. He was old, but he had bright, intense eyes and muttered in a language she didn't understand. Yesterday he had been skulking in the parking lot when she locked up, skittering crablike between the cars, draped in a heavy overcoat in spite of the heat. Those eyes of his had followed her with unnerving focus.

But there was no sign of him or of Webster's carefully waxed Jag, so she stepped out into the muggy night, yawning wide, her long, rangy stride bringing her up against her little Toyota in a dozen steps. All tiredness and irritation aside, it had been a good night.

But that sense of Richard's aging stayed with her as she drove south on the interstate through the core of the city, its postmodern towers of office glass still lit up, vibrant, and (like everything in Atlanta that wasn't in her museum) new.

He was, what? Seventy-five, seventy-six? Something like that. And he was slowing. That was why she had been brought in in the first place, to shoulder the burden of putting the museum on the map while he slowly retired to the adjoining residence, staying on only as a generous benefactor. Three years ago, that had seemed a very long way away, but there was no avoiding the speed with which that day was approaching now. They never spoke of it directly, but it hung between them like a shadow. Or maybe it was just that he was fading. Yes, that was it. And then . . . ?

Your museum.

It would be soon. In a sense, it was already. The idea depressed her.

Deborah was startled out of her unwelcome reverie by an irritating salvo of electronic notes. Her cell phone. Richard had thought it amusing to secretly program her phone to ring to the tune of "La Cucaracha." She had yet to reprogram it or to get him back. The idea muted her annoyance and reminded her that he liked to check in on nights like this when he thought the coast would be clear. He had retired a good hour and a half earlier, remarking vaguely to the crowd about an old man's tiredness, followed by a furtive wink to Deborah as he abandoned her to Webster and his cronies. She'd need to get him back for that too.

"Yes?" she said, brisk, poised to unleash her bitterest sarcasm on the old man.

"Deborah?"

Not Richard. Not by a long chalk.

"Hi, Ma," said Deborah, her heart sinking a little. She loved her mother, but there were times . . .

"We were out with the Lowensteins," her mother was saying, as if Deborah had just asked. They hadn't spoken in over two weeks.

"You remember the Lowensteins?" she said, snapping out the words as if Deborah was slightly deaf. "From Cambridge? Anyway they live on Long Island now, but they were in town visiting. We went out to dinner, and I nearly had a heart attack when I got home and there was a message from my eldest girl. The first in—what?—a month?"

"Not that long."

"Close enough."

"Yeah, sorry, Ma," said Deborah, feeling the headache start, powerless to stop it as she was powerless to stop so many things where her mother was concerned. She should never have called. It had been a wild impulse to share the night's triumph with someone—anyone—but now, only an hour later, it seemed like a terrible idea.

Deborah's mom had been a part-time nurse whose great accomplishment in life, she was fond of saying, had been marrying Deborah's dad, a doctor of internal medicine. She had left her job the moment she had become pregnant with Deborah, only returning to it after her husband's death left her with bills to pay. In Deborah's adolescent eyes, her mother had spent almost two years moving to and from the hospital in a kind of affronted daze, like a beauty queen stripped of her crown on a technicality. Deborah, who had idolized her father in spite of—perhaps in part because of—his frequent absence, resented her mother's subsequent attempts to prettify her bookish daughter and her palpable horror when Deborah, always lanky, graceless, and boyish, woke up at the tender age of fifteen to find herself six feet tall and still growing.

"So what's your big news, Debbie? I called as soon as I heard your message. You sounded like you had news."

No one else in the world called her *Debbie*. It was one of the persistent ways in which she willfully misread her daughter's personality.

"Oh, you know," said Deborah, closing her eyes, backpedaling. "Just work stuff. I had a good day."

"That's wonderful, dear," said her mother, barely pausing for breath. "And what else is going on with you? I talked to Rachel this morning, but she hasn't heard from you either."

Rachel, the good daughter, who has the body of a gymnast, and who—as a perpetual gift to her mother—lives with her husband and offspring less than three blocks from the Brookline house in which she was born . . .

"No, I haven't spoken to Rachel lately. Work is going well."

"Work? You work too hard. Just like your father. But him I used to see."

"You're always welcome," said Deborah.

"There?"

"It's not Calcutta," said Deborah. "It's two hours on a plane."

"How do you remember?" she said, arch as ever.

"Funny, Ma."

"So what's new, apart from work? Did you secretly get married or anything?"

There it was, the amiable jibe that killed whole flocks of birds with one highly polished stone. It was her mother's great talent. She could skewer half a dozen sore points with one remark like she was threading hunks of lamb onto a kebab. In this case the remark, so light and quick that it seemed almost casual, said:

1. You work too hard, and your work, let's face it, isn't worth the effort.

2. You have no man in your life. As usual.

3. Keeping things from your family is what you do best.

4. Marrying away from your family would be par for the course. After all, you turned your back on them, your hometown, your cultural heritage, and all we hold dear when you first went down to that gentile Sodom . . .

Before that, actually, Ma, she thought a little wistfully. *Dad's been dead twenty years.*

"No, Ma," she said, managing a thin smile in spite of herself, "nothing new in my life right now."

She was still considering a few half-joking skewers of her own that she should have said when the phone trilled its maniacal song again.

"Ma," she began, "I'm on my way home. Can I call you back when—"

"Is it all still there?"

She had opened her mouth to respond before she realized that the voice was unfamiliar.

"What?" she said. "Who is this?"

"Where are you?"

"I said, *who is this*?" she repeated.

"Did they get it? *Where are you*?"

He was shouting. And the voice . . . There was something about the intonation. An accent? British? Australian? Something like that.

"I'm sorry," said Deborah, with chill politeness. "I think you have the wrong number. Try dialing again, and then begin the conversation by asking for the person you wish to scream at."

"Listen to me, you stupid bloody woman! You have to go back—"

She hung up and switched the phone off.

CHAPTER 2

The interstate was quiet. In less than ten minutes she was off, pulling through the lights on Tenth Street and down toward Piedmont, her mind already getting ready for bed as she drove, shutting down zone by zone like she was tripping circuit breakers. By the time she had parked on the gravel strip of road reserved for residents of the Bay Court condos, she was on autopilot. Out of the car. Lock the car. House keys. Mailbox. Apartment door, and inside.

The light on her answering machine jarred her out of her groove. It blinked red, forcing her awake. She had checked her messages by phone from the fund-raiser, so anything on there had been called in within the last hour. Richard? She frowned, pushed the button, and moved toward the bedroom to get her toothbrush.

"Are you there?" said the machine.

Deborah stopped in the sudden silence, the hair on the back of her neck prickling into life. That voice again. The Brit. Another wrong number.

But that isn't very likely, is it? Last time he called your cell.

True.

"If you are there, pick up."

She stood quite still, hearing the urgency in the voice. There was another long silence, a heavy clunk, and the familiar hum of the dial tone. The machine beeped, whirred, and fell silent. Deborah stayed where she was, looking at it. Something about that voice bothered her, though whether it was the accent, its sense of purpose, or the fact that it didn't announce who it belonged to, she couldn't say.

But Deborah Miller was not easily spooked, or at least that was what she told herself. She shrugged it off as she had shrugged off Harvey Webster's clumsy advances, and got ready for bed. Tomorrow would be a big day, and the one remaining conscious part of her brain turned over her responsibilities as she shut off the bedside lamp and hunkered down under the duvet. Thank God she'd left the AC on.

Richard would want to follow up the new pledges they'd acquired in person. In the meantime she'd talk to the *Atlanta Journal-Constitution* and then start lining up her design plans for the Celtic exhibit. She would call the caterers and angle for a discount since she'd done most of their cleanup herself and would have to deal with the wrath of Tonya, the museum's new janitor, first thing in the morning. Dealing with the incompetent caterers would be peanuts compared to dealing with the overly competent Tonya.

Tonya was unlike any janitor Deborah had ever encountered. She was watchful, even aloof, feisty but not so much defensive as . . . *sardonic*. An odd quality in a middle-aged janitor. Deborah suspected that Tonya's manner, or her own uneasy reaction to it, was tied to the fact that Tonya was also smart, educated, and black, but in what ways she wasn't sure. Anyway, explaining why all these local hotshots *(white folks)* had made such a mess of her nice clean lobby floor would be a bit like defusing a piece of curiously ironic explosive.

Still, there was the Celtic exhibit to work on, and that made her smile: four centuries of Scots-Irish crosses, illuminated manuscripts, and jewelry. Two years ago they would never have landed it. She was still smiling as she settled gently into sleep.

The sudden ringing of the phone woke her like a siren, and she surfaced, gasping and confused. For a second she thought it was the front doorbell and was half out of bed before she could focus. It was dark, and the clock radio by her bed said it was almost three. Had she been awake, she might have let

the machine get it, sure it was a wrong number, but dazed
from sleep, she picked it up without thinking.

"Yes?"

"Why aren't you at the museum? You need to get back."

"What?" For a second she was lost, then it came back. The
same voice. "Who is this?"

"You need to get back!" he said again, the same frustration and urgency as before. "You must not let them take it!"

"Take what?"

"The body!"

"If you call me again—on either number," she said, "I'm
calling the police. Got it?"

She disconnected with a click of her finger and lay there
in the dark, the receiver still clutched in her hand, staring up
at the ceiling, waiting for her unease to slip away.

Body?

What body?

She stayed like that for six minutes, watching the numbers
click over in the clock's illuminated screen, but she was not
sliding back into sleep. In fact, it was like all her circuit
breakers were being snapped back over, and there was power
coursing through her again, flicking on lights, powering up
appliances, so that her head was filled with the steady drone
of electricity. She could smell it in the night air like lightning.

Body?

She got up, pulled on some clothes, and grabbed her car
keys.

CHAPTER 3

The museum was dark, the parking lot deserted, both of which Deborah would expect at three thirty in the morning. She was being stupid. She should be home in bed. She unlocked the front doors and checked the alarm panel. It hadn't gone off. There had been no break-in and everything in the main foyer looked exactly as she had left it.

But the alarm hadn't beeped at her as it did every morning when she arrived, which meant it hadn't been armed. She stared at it. She had been tired after the benefit, but surely she had remembered to set the alarm? She moved quickly to the light switches by the door and flicked them all up with one quick motion.

Nothing. The foyer with its dinosaur skeleton and its information booths and temporary exhibits glowed in the low emergency lights, which never went out. She snapped the switches back and forth. Still nothing. The muffled whisperings of unease which had stopped her from going back to sleep after the phone call spiked suddenly, then settled again, but louder than they had been before. Something was wrong.

Deborah pulled her cell phone from her pocket and switched it on. The foyer was the museum's heart, the building being arranged like half a wagon wheel, each spoke originating here and taking the visitors down exhibit galleries to the perimeter walk, a broad corridor flanked by stuffed animals and birds, connecting the whole in one great semicircular arc. She crossed the lobby quickly, passed the Creek Indian cases, and plunged down one of those "spokes" to the perimeter.

It was darker here, the emergency lights less frequent, the

cases (local fossils, charts of the Jurassic and Cretaceous, a near-perfect velociraptor skeleton along with a series of life-sized models of the beast on its nest) all completely dark, great blank panels of glass like the walls of a vast aquarium. The idea *(unseen shapes swimming behind the panes)* bothered her, and she moved quickly. There was still no sign of damage or disturbance of any kind, but there was a dull, metallic tang in her mouth, as if some primordial gland in her brain stem had activated an ancient alarm. She walked faster, and as she did so, she dialed Richard's home number.

It started ringing. She braced herself for his bewildered voice and then, when it did not come, began to run, the ringing phone still pressed to her ear. At the end of the hallway, she paused.

Ignore the darkness and keep going. Don't look at the exhibits.

The perimeter corridor with its stuffed birds and animals into which the prehistoric gallery eventually emptied itself was her least favorite section of the museum. It was so dead, so Victorian in its sense of what a museum was. It smelled different, like mothballs and formaldehyde, older than the velociraptor by far: musty and bookish, a version of learning constructed by people who blew animals out of the sky with rifles and then mulled issues of Latinate classification over their badly stuffed corpses. Butterfly Collector Logic, she called it. *"Here's something beautiful: let's kill it so we can all see how beautiful it was."* One day, she had told Richard, she would replace it; when they had something to replace it with. He had just smiled and said what he always said: "Just so long as you don't turn my museum into a theme park." The board, of course, wanted to pack people in at all costs.

"Keep pretending you aren't a museum, and eventually you won't be," he would say. "Use your bells and whistles to get them in the door, but then give them something they'll learn from, something they'll take away for the rest of their lives . . ."

His phone was still ringing.

Deborah began to walk again. She never told Richard, but the taxidermy collection didn't just offend her as a museum curator, it scared her. Now, in the dim greenish glow of the overhead lamps, she felt the presence of the long-dead, musty animal corpses like gargoyles in the shadows of a cathedral, dead but somehow watchful. She moved a little faster, suddenly sure that the great curving gallery was getting a hint brighter.

She felt first relief, then doubt and swelling panic. There was only one light source up ahead, and for it to be filtering into the gallery now could not be good news. She began to run, past the stiff and moldering lions with their bared teeth and hard yellow eyes, past the rigid gulls and their frozen chicks, the great blackness of the water buffalo, its head lowered, horns spread, and began to murmur under her breath as the surreal greenish tinge paled with each step.

"No. No. No."

And then there it was, the door between the motionless penguins and the seals thrown wide open, its light bleeding into the corridor, the only door at this end of the building. As she saw it, she became aware that she could hear something too, distant and regular, a ringing. Realizing what it was, she hung up her cell phone. The sound stopped.

Richard lived here, or in the adjoining building, at least, and had since the museum had been founded. Indeed, though everyone assumed the opposite, his house had preexisted the museum, the latter being built at his behest thirty-five years ago as his gift to the city. For almost two decades he ran the museum himself, but his considerable fortune and his equally considerable enthusiasm had not been enough, and in recent years he had handed the reins to a series of trained curators. Deborah was the third, the one he liked, the one he trusted, the one, perhaps, he loved as a daughter.

"The body."

Deborah went through the door, the door that kept his private world from the museum, the door he guarded like an aging pit bull, the door that was never—ever—left open in any circumstances, her heart hammering.

"Richard!" she called.

She went through the living room, the kitchen, the library, the dining room: nothing. She leapt up the great central staircase with its long, slender twists of mahogany for handrails, still shouting. She tried his study: nothing; the spare bedroom, the hall bathroom, the room he talked about turning into a library but which was full of the detritus from his married life. His wife had been dead nine years, but Deborah doubted he'd thrown a single thing of hers away. She checked an upper sitting room she had never been in before, and a kind of pantry linked to the service elevator which Tonya used to bring him food when he was "under the weather" (he had been under the weather a lot lately), stopping only outside his bedroom.

There were large double doors, heavily paneled in oak. She knocked on them, loud, insistent rappings with her knuckles.

"Richard," she called. "It's me. Open the door, or I'm coming in."

She sounded quite calm. Louder than usual, perhaps, but not shrill, not panicked.

Then she tried the door. It opened.

CHAPTER 4

The bedroom was empty, the bed unslept in. There was no sign of Richard. She checked the bathroom, then went back out onto the landing, calling his name. She had just invaded his private sanctuary for the first time since taking the job; skulking around no longer seemed necessary or appropriate.

She paused on the landing, then drifted back into his bedroom at a loss. There was absolutely no sign of him.

Given what you had been afraid of finding, she thought, *you should be comforted by finding nothing.*

She wasn't.

She sat on his hard bed and glanced around the room. It was, thanks to Tonya, immaculate as ever. There was a pad of paper on the bedside table by the phone, and Richard had scribbled something on it in his spidery handwriting, but other than that, everything was neat and orderly, the furniture carefully aligned, the vast bookcase which lined the wall perfectly stacked and dust-free.

Deborah bit her lip and leaned over to peer at the scribbling on the nightstand pad. It was a single word, circled several times and punctuated with a brace of question marks:

Atreus??

Deborah stared at it, feeling the dim stirring of an old memory, a literary memory; then she brushed it away.

Where the hell is he?

She put her head in her hands and saw something on the floor, half concealed by the oversized bedspread, as if accidentally kicked under the bed. She reached down and picked it up. It was a fragment of pottery, tightly concave like part of a very round jug, and it was painted. On a soft turquoise

background was a fragment of a female head in profile, the
eye large and almond-shaped, the hair in dark ringlets. It
looked like a cartoon or a sketch but was full of a casual—
almost flippant—grace and energy. She held it up to the light
and rubbed the surface between her fingers, suddenly sure
that it was not just some broken knickknack: It was old.

Nothing from any period in North America's history
looked like this, she was almost certain. It looked familiar,
but familiar in a way that said she had seen *comparable* pottery before, not identical. Ancient Egyptian? No, it was too
alive, the face too coquettish. It might be that old but . . . She
couldn't be sure. Mesopotamian? Assyrian? No. And anyway, if it really was old, what was it doing there? The museum had no classical antiquities. She looked at it again.
Greek maybe?

The word on the pad, circled and dotted with question
marks, popped back into her head: *Atreus*.

That was Greek too.

Atreus was one the descendents of Tantalus in Greek
mythology, right? His brother . . . There was something to do
with his brother, or his children . . . She couldn't remember.
She moved to the vast bookcase across the south wall of the
bedroom and considered the book spines. Maybe there would
be something in there on Greek mythology.

There was. In fact, as she moved across the face of the
shelves, she let out a half whistle of bewildered amazement.
Every one of what probably numbered four hundred volumes
was somehow about ancient Greece: mythology, history, archaeology, politics, poetry, culture, art, philosophy. She
pulled a heavy volume claiming to be *An Encyclopedia of
Ancient Greece* and flicked to the Atreus entry, reading
dreamily, unsure of exactly what she was doing, what she
was looking for.

Richard. You're looking for Richard.

It was no wonder she had remembered the name. Atreus
was the head of the ruling line of Mycenae, the great citadel
of Bronze Age Greece, from whose lion-carved gate, said

legend, Agamemnon had led the army which laid siege to Troy for ten years. It was his cursed house that had torn apart generation after generation in bloody feuds, dividing brothers, children, spouses, exacting the most terrible of vengeances in acts too appalling to be spoken: fratricide, patricide, matricide, human sacrifice, incest, cannibalism. Deborah closed the book and stared at the fragment of ceramic in her hand as other student memories of Bronze Age history and archaeology surfaced and slotted into place, overwriting the lurid mythology. There was no doubt in her mind. The face on the potsherd was Greek, specifically Mycenaean. But where was the rest of it, and what could it and that ancient mythical name mean?

Richard was missing. This was no time for ancient puzzles and archaeological riddles . . .

Unless they are connected.

She sat on the floor at the foot of the bookcase to read the titles on the bottom shelf more clearly, and it was while she was squatting there that she became aware of a red spot on the carpet. She touched her fingers to it, and they came away tacky. She knew before she had smelled it that it was blood.

CHAPTER 5

Her heart suddenly racing, Deborah got down even lower so that her cheek was against the floor inches from the crimson smear, and she could see that the carpet was flattened into a narrow track as if something had trodden upon it. No, not trodden: *rolled*. Something heavy had rolled over it, and though the drop of blood was not smeared, she thought there was a thin track of something else in the flattened fibers, something brownish and viscous: oil.

She returned to that speck of crimson. Some dark, hollow, hopeless part of her knew that it was Richard's blood.

She tried to focus to keep the implications of what she was seeing at arm's length. She went back to her previous thought. Something had rolled into the bookcase? No, the oil hadn't been tracked into the wall with the bookcase, it had been tracked *out*. In the center of the room it faded to nothing. Back in the other direction it led straight into the wall, or rather into the bookcase which lined the wall. So something had rolled out of the wall, which was impossible, unless . . .

Deborah got up and began running her hands over the bookshelves, her mind stumbling to keep up with her pulse.

She found nothing. She started pulling at the books themselves, but they slid undramatically out. There were hundreds of them.

Stop, she told herself. *Think. If one of these books was . . . Which would it be?*

Atreus. Mycenae.

Something bound to Richard's old obsession with the Trojan War? Richard loved to tell her that the Homeric legends, the stories of gods and heroes, were based on real events. His boyish enthusiasm was infectious, however dubious his archaeological science.

Richard was no archaeologist. He was an enthusiast: less kindly, a dilettante. He didn't want social history out of archaeology; he wanted legend and the confirmation that all those junior high tales of adventure and glory were real. He didn't read archaeology to see what new principles or facts it could reveal. He read archaeology to prove what he hoped was already true. He was like Yigael Yadin wandering around the Negev and Mount Sinai with a spade in one hand and a copy of the Old Testament in the other. He knew what he believed in and wanted to make archaeology confirm it. He was like Schliemann, who had excavated Mycenae and Troy to prove that Homer's tales of Agamemnon and Helen, Achilles and Hector, Ajax and Odysseus were not poetic legend but documentary fact.

Deborah stepped back from the shelves and ran her eyes over the book spines.

In the right-hand corner, four shelves up, was a single heavy black volume bound in gilded leather. *The Iliad,* by Homer. The supreme tale of the Trojan War.

She reached for it, pulled it, felt it catch, tip forward, and stop. The bookcase swung silently toward her.

Deborah stared. The space behind the bookcase was deep, a little over half the size of the bedroom itself, and it took her eyes a moment to scan the interior. It took her mind rather longer to grasp what she was seeing.

The momentary blackness behind the bookcase had flickered into a soft glow from wall displays and a single shaft of light from up in the middle of the vaulted ceiling which cast a long, pale square on the floor. It was here, right beside a recessed power outlet, that the trail of blood began.

She sank slowly to her knees as the dread she had worn like a heavy cloak turned into something else, something which emptied her heart and mind in a crushing wash of despair.

Richard was lying on his back, arms spread wide, a loose

cruciform attitude, one hand open, the other closed. He was bare-chested, his body thin, his limbs spindly, frail. He looked impossibly old, and his pale skin had a bluish translucence that made the thick, clotting wounds in his chest and abdomen all the more dreadful. His eyes, mercifully, were closed.

Deborah took his cold, outstretched hand and raised it to her lips. Eyes shut tight, all breath squeezed out of her chest, she began to sob.

CHAPTER 6

Deborah had no idea how long she had been sitting there: squatting, in fact, half kneeling, like a supplicant at an altar. She had knelt by her bedside like that for seven nights after the services of her father's shiva, replaying the words of the Kaddish that promised life and continuity and a just, loving God she could no longer see, had not seen since. The two deaths were utterly different, but it felt as if the twenty years that separated them had collapsed into nothing, and she was again thirteen, staring from the doctors to her relatives, to the rabbi who had orchestrated the funeral ceremonies and to whom she had never spoken again. She didn't remember the Aramaic of the Kaddish, but the English translation of one of the graveside prayers had stayed with her like a wound that wouldn't fully heal. A piece of it came back to her now.

> O, God, full of compassion, Thou who dwellest on high, grant perfect rest beneath the shelter of Thy divine presence among the holy and pure who shine as the brightness of the firmament to the soul of my beloved who has gone to his eternal home.
>
> Mayest Thou, O God of Mercy, shelter him forever under the wings of Thy presence, may his soul be bound up in the bond of life eternal, and grant that the memories of my life inspire me always to noble and consecrated living. Amen.

It rankled as it always had, bitter not like the Campari of which Richard had been so fond, but bitter as she imagined poison would be, acrid like overbrewed tea.

Full of compassion? Try callous, fickle, or perhaps simply apathetic.

Had the God of her fathers even noticed what had happened tonight? Did He ever?

God, Richard, she thought. *I'm so sorry. I should have been here.*

She had hardly moved at all since finding him, her breath coming in slow, even draughts that barely expanded her chest, as if she was trying to share his stillness, his silence. Her eyes swam, the tears welling up silently and finally breaking free and falling so that they pattered like heavy drops of summer rain onto the carpet.

Yet through her silent anguish came a shrill, insistent voice, an official voice, like a policeman pushing through the crowd that gathered at a road accident, a voice of authority and order, a voice that stifled emotion in favor of reason. It said that Richard had been murdered, that this was not just a place of grief, it was a place of horror, even danger, and she needed to act accordingly.

But she couldn't leave, could barely take her streaming eyes off him, off his wounds.

They had bled heavily, but they weren't cuts so much as flat incisions little more than an inch wide, now edged rusty and crimson but a deep and threatening black in the center. The chest was streaked by trickles of dark blood, but the deep pool in which he lay had come from beneath him. Could he have been stabbed so deeply (*six or seven times,* said that insistent, detail-oriented voice which usually commented on potsherds and burial mounds) that the blade had emerged from his back? What kind of weapon would do that? It had to be as close to a sword as a knife.

And then there were the pair of indentations in the skin on either side of each wound: two small bruises an inch or so to the sides of each flat puncture . . .

She turned hurriedly away, overcome with a sudden desperate nausea that made her retch so that her throat stung, but brought nothing up from her stomach. Her eyes, still bleeding tears, felt perversely dry and prickly. She clenched them shut, suddenly overwhelmed by the idea that she should wash those wounds, rinse the blood away . . .

But you mustn't disturb the body, said the voice, *because the police will need to photograph things exactly as they are. Someone else will wash him later.*

"Oh, Richard. There was so much still to do. To say."

She said it aloud and, as if in answer, her phone rang.

For a long moment she didn't look at it, then her hand moved slowly from Richard's, and she raised the phone to her ear, her movements still small and silent, her breathing calm.

"Yes?" she said.

"Did they take the body?"

The same voice. Deborah said nothing, her eyes still focused on Richard's chest, on what had been Richard.

"Did they take it?"

She felt her breathing stop. He spoke again, more insistent this time. Urgent.

"Did they take the body?"

"No," she said. She didn't know why she answered him.

"Wait there," he said. "I'm coming."

The line went dead.

Deborah stared at the phone buzzing in her hand as his words sank in. Suddenly all her numb stillness left her as the implications of those words worked on her like a surge of electric current. She got hurriedly to her feet, turned from the body, and began to call the police.

CHAPTER 7

He had said he was coming. He hadn't said why, what he wanted, or how long it would take to get there. He hadn't said who he was, how he knew of the events at the museum, why he was so anxious to find out if Richard's body had been taken away, or who might have taken it. Nevertheless, it was obvious that whoever he was, whatever he wanted, he was somehow tied to Richard Dixon's death. She had said as much to the emergency operator, a claim which had worked like adrenaline on a conversation which had, to that point, been sluggish, even dubious. Was she *sure* the man was dead?

"He has multiple knife wounds to the chest and abdomen," she said. "His . . . *body* was in a kind of secret room. He had made a note about Atreus, and it made me think about Troy, so I tried a copy of *The Iliad,* and the bookcase opened—"

"Slow down, honey," said the operator.

She had started off methodically enough *(multiple knife wounds . . .)* but it had all gotten away from her. Her voice had cracked and she had started babbling.

"Sorry," Deborah answered, feeling suddenly stupid and alone. "I'm a bit . . . I'm . . ."

She didn't know what she was, or couldn't find words that began to represent what she was.

"It's OK. Just take a breath."

The dispatcher didn't warn Deborah that wasting police time with hoax calls would get her in a world of trouble, despite that remark about the secret room (which was enough to test anyone's credulity) or her jabbering about Atreus. The woman could hear that it was all real, and that meant that

Deborah had to start getting things together, because she was losing it badly. She cleared her throat.

"I'm sorry," she said again. "Richard was very . . . We were very close."

"That's the man who's hurt?"

"Dead, yes."

She said it quite calmly, her mind blank, the words somehow correct but meaningless.

There was a momentary silence.

"Where exactly are you?" said the dispatcher.

"In the bedroom," said Deborah.

"I mean the address."

"Right," said Deborah, feeling numb and stupid again. "Sorry. It's the Druid Hills Museum, One forty-three Deerborne Street. The house is connected to the museum. You might have to come in that way. Not you, of course. Whoever comes—"

"Uh-huh," said the dispatcher. "You could meet them at the door. Is it close by?"

"Not really," said Deborah.

"OK," said the dispatcher. "And this man who called, you have no idea who he was?"

"No."

"Is there a safe room in the house? Somewhere you can lock yourself in and wait for the police officers?"

"There's a bathroom," she said, feeling again a surge of panic at the seriousness with which the woman was responding to Deborah's mysterious caller.

"And you can lock it? And the door is solid?"

"Yes, but I'll have to hang up. This isn't a cordless phone. I have a cell I could use if—"

"OK, that's good. You OK?"

"I'm OK," she said. "I'm going to hang up."

"You sure you're all right?"

"Yes."

"Just get in the bathroom and lock it up good, OK?"

Deborah nodded, then said yes. Then she hung up and sat

on the edge of the bed for a moment looking at the bathroom door. Then she looked away, stood up, took two steps, and peered into the dimly lit chamber behind the bookcase, keeping her eyes from the floor and the body upon it, taking in for the first time the remarkable—no, the *impossible*—collection that lined its walls.

CHAPTER 8

Even without stepping inside Deborah knew that the glass-fronted displays contained artifacts that matched the fragment of pottery she had held in her hands moments before. One of the cases on the walls was open, and there was a conspicuous vacancy on the glass shelf inside. Deborah looked down. In the corner shadows, three feet from that central square of light, was a random clutter of ceramic fragments, the remains of a pot, some of whose shards were of the same turquoise as the fragment she had found under the bed.

Deborah stayed where she was, staring hard over the body at her feet (*Don't look at him again, whatever you do.*), her gaze moving slowly around the room's perimeter in a kind of daze which increased as she absorbed the contents of those display cases: a gold, two handled cup she thought was called a kantharos, four decorative plates with stylized lions, and a pair of seal rings, also gold. There was a stone slab carved with the figure of a chariot and driver, possibly a gravestone, a silver bowl overlaid with bulls' heads, strings of glass and polished stone beads, and then more gold: necklaces, pendants, diadems, rings, and pins, all remarkably delicate and rich. There were three cases loaded with ceramics, from finely painted jugs decorated with geometric patterns to elegant kylikes and jars inscribed with warriors and hunting scenes. The last case held spear points, swords, and daggers, inlaid with gold and precious stones, slim and elegantly purposeful, their bronze green with age but remarkably undamaged . . .

If it is all real . . . ?

There was no reason to suggest it wasn't, except the obvious. There were forty or fifty pieces here. If they were what they appeared to be, this had to be the largest, richest collection of Mycenaean or Minoan artifacts outside the National Archaeological Museum in Athens. Its value was impossible to estimate.

So it has to be fake.

A collection of this size and quality just couldn't exist. Most of the Greek sites had been excavated or plundered centuries before. Everything from Mycenae, Tiryns, the Minoan sites in Crete was catalogued, documented, the pictures reproduced in a hundred books devoted to art and history. A collection like this, unknown to modern archaeological science, was unthinkable.

But Deborah, rooted to the spot, her eyes still streaming with tears, knew at a glance that what she was looking at were not copies or reproductions of known pieces. True, she wasn't an expert on Grecian antiquities and couldn't identify every pot ever found in Mycenae, but she had seen enough of the famous ones to know that this little room contained objects as large, as richly ornate, as complex as any anywhere else. She also knew that these were *different,* similar enough to mark them out as Mycenaean, but new finds nonetheless. She stared at a bronze dagger held in place on a delicate Perspex stand, leaning into the room to get a closer look. It was adorned with inlaid gold and silver lions chasing deer. It was exquisite. It was three and a half thousand years old, and she was as sure as she could be that no serious archaeologist or historian alive had ever lain eyes on it.

No serious archaeologist.

What did that mean? She forced herself to admit the dull dread that had gathered like ground glass in the base of her stomach. Serious meant *ethical.* If this stuff was real, it had been stolen, kept secret, traded outside the purview of the archaeological community, squirreled away, its lessons and delights hoarded for private consumption only. She felt dread and a disappointment that left her drained and hollow, even stopping her tears with a sudden and emptying weariness.

"Richard." She sighed. "What did you do?"

And, whispered a hurt and resentful part of herself she didn't want to listen to right now, *why didn't you tell me?*

She remembered Richard's old Indiana Jones–esque righteous indignation: *"This belongs in a museum."* Quite. It should have made her smile, but the hollowness in her bowels was turning into something small and sad. She looked at him again, lying there, pale and unfamiliar, striped and splashed with the garish red of his blood.

You were my friend, my mentor, my . . .

She couldn't bring herself to add *father.* This hiding from her was a betrayal, of her, of her values, of what they had tried to do at the museum.

Unless . . .

Could he have bought this extraordinary collection through black market channels with a view to displaying it in the museum? She caught her breath. He had been distracted of late, secretive. But it had been a wait-and-see kind of secretive. Was this room merely a holding pen for use until the legal paperwork was all in order, and the collection could then be displayed in their humble museum? What a coup that would have been!

But the room didn't look temporary. Her rush of hope and idealism floundered. Richard had been dealing with the worst kind of illegal artifact traffickers, and they had turned on him. What other way was there to read the evidence?

But they had been inside. So why hadn't they taken it all with them? If this had been a botched deal, why leave all these extraordinary treasures behind? Why wouldn't Richard's killers just take the lot? If . . . ?

Deborah spun around. Very slowly, almost noiselessly, the handles of the bedroom door were turning.

CHAPTER 9

Deborah had no more than a second or two to decide, and all options felt like gambles. Then, with the bedroom doors starting to swing slowly inward, she ducked and rolled into the only hiding place in the room: the space under Richard's bed.

For a moment there was silence. Deborah was on her stomach, her legs pointed at the bed head, her face at the foot, only a couple of yards from the door. She held her breath and listened. There was no brash entry, no heavy regulation boots. Whoever was coming in had no business being there. She should have locked herself in the bathroom.

Deborah hugged the floor, palms spread. There was an oversized bedspread hanging over the mattress so that it touched the ground along most of the length of the bed. It afforded her childish hiding place a degree of secrecy, but it also made it almost impossible to see anything in the room beyond. Except in one spot. Right at Deborah's waist on the left side, the bedspread was puckered up into a shallow V, created when she had slid under. Slowly she turned her head till she could see through the gap.

Carpet, the leg of an end table, the dim space behind the bookcase. Richard's outstretched hand.

This is crazy. Get out now.

No. She didn't like the stealth with which those doors had opened, the care with which those feet had entered.

It was a long moment before Deborah heard anything at all, so long that she had begun to think that the intruder had gone back out, but then it came, clear and distinctive: a long, expelled breath, perhaps a sigh. Deborah shifted fractionally, straining for a wider field of vision through the notch of fabric. It made no difference, but then whoever was in the room, only feet from where she lay, took two quick steps, and a pair of shoes came into view: white gym shoes marked with a Nike swoosh on the heel. Women's shoes. They were turned to face the body and the secret room which housed it. As Deborah stared, they rocked forward on the toe, as if craning to see something, but then everything stopped.

The feet turned, pivoting sharply back toward the door, and then were gone. Deborah heard the door open and close again, a good deal less stealthily this time, and then dimly, farther away, she heard something else, male voices coming through the lobby downstairs: the police.

Now.

She rolled out in one quick movement, passed her hands over her clothes, and opened the bedroom door. Still on the landing, preparing herself for the officers coming up the stairs, was Tonya, the middle-aged maid, in the spotless Nike gym shoes purchased for her, no doubt, by a daughter or niece. Hearing the bedroom door, she spun around, her mouth open, and stared at Deborah with undisguised hostility.

CHAPTER 10

The two women considered each other in silence, momentarily oblivious to the sound of the uniformed policemen cautiously announcing their presence as they came up the stairs, one bald and fat but probably no more than thirty, the other lean and black.

"Miss Miller?" said the bald guy, looking from one woman to the other.

"Yes," said Deborah, turning from the black woman with an effort. "In there."

The two cops exchanged looks, and the bald guy moved toward the bedroom doors. He was gone no more than thirty seconds or so, but it felt like an age and a silent one at that. The other policeman hovered, looking embarrassed, as if he had interrupted a church service, though whether that was because he was dealing with two women or with one corpse, Deborah wasn't sure. He said something, but Deborah wasn't paying attention, was straining to hear the chatter of the bald cop's radio as he emerged from the room. She thought he looked a little green but was putting a brave face on it. It was strange, she thought. She had been too consumed by her own grief at who the corpse was to have been horrified or revolted by it.

"I thought I'd get a jump on the day's work," Tonya was saying. "I knew there'd be a lot of cleaning up to do. We had a party in the museum last night."

"And you, Miss Miller?"

"I'm sorry?" said Deborah, turning to the black cop. He had taken out a notebook and was watching her anxiously. He was probably terrified of getting the procedure wrong, she thought, feeling something oddly like compassion for him.

"I got a phone call telling me I needed to get back here," she said. "It was a little before three, I think."

It was now almost four. This was what Tonya called getting a jump on the day's work?

"Did you know the caller?"

She said that she didn't, and then went over her movements and the manner in which she had come to find the body. Tonya tried not to look like she was hanging on her every word.

"And you had never seen the room behind the bookcase before?" said the bald cop who had now rejoined them and taken over.

"I had no idea it was there."

"Neither did I," Tonya volunteered. She didn't meet Deborah's gaze.

"It's going to be a little while before the crime scene team gets here," said the bald cop. "Is there somewhere you can wait?"

They left the black cop to guard the bedroom, and Deborah led the way downstairs to the sitting room where she and Tonya perched on Queen Anne chairs, staring silently at the walls, while the bald cop paced, studying pictures and knick-knacks at random. Occasionally he made notes, as if proving himself to be a detective rather than a beat cop. It was twenty minutes before they heard a door slam at the front of the house. Then came the swelling babble of voices as an army of investigators and specialists moved in, lugging their equipment with them.

"Why don't we move back upstairs," said the cop. "In case anyone wants to talk to you."

He seemed uncertain, but they followed his slightly faltering lead and took new seats on the landing in a pair of wing chairs, while the cop vanished to consult with whoever was in charge.

"I'm sorry about Richard," said Tonya. It was abrupt, almost brusque: a concession of sorts, but one which stuck in her craw.

Deborah nodded but didn't know what to say. Tonya was a good maid, almost too good in fact, and took the kind of pride in her work which suggested that the work of the museum itself was a colossal inconvenience. She was tough and forthright and—despite doing a job which surely meant she was used to being given instructions—resented any show of authority over her.

Any authority from you, at least, Deborah reminded herself. She seemed respectful to the point of docility where Richard was concerned. It was just Deborah she didn't like. Deborah had put that down to the fact that she was Tonya's boss while also being young and white and female, but she always felt that there was something else, something personal, a resentment she couldn't quite put her finger on. Now Richard was dead, and Tonya was creeping around his bedroom in the middle of the night . . .

Don't think about it. Leave the detection to the detectives. Let it go.

Deborah sighed and continued to watch as the house filled up with people, several armed with cameras and evidence bags and rolls of yellow tape. Occasionally people—men, they were all men—muttered to each other and gave her and Tonya sidelong glances, but for what seemed like a long time no one spoke to either of them, so that she began to feel like the audience of a strangely intimate and surreal performance. For a half hour, people came and went, talking and scribbling notes, lit by the occasional brilliant flashes of cameras from inside, and still no one spoke to her. A female police officer arrived after another twenty-five minutes, a heavyset, kindly woman who offered her water and tried to occupy Deborah's eyes as the body—Richard's body—was wheeled out of the bedroom on a covered gurney. A man she took to be the pathologist was talking to the detective who seemed to be in charge. He gestured with his hands, indicating something about fourteen inches long, then again with his finger and thumb showing a space about the width of the incisions.

The weapon.

"Miss Miller?" said the detective, as the medical examiner bustled away. "We're ready for you now."

He nodded to Tonya. "If you wouldn't mind waiting here for a few minutes," he said, "we'll be out to ask you some questions shortly."

He was tall, about her height, square-shouldered and athletic, dark-haired and tanned. Most women would find him handsome, she thought vaguely, not bothering to wonder why she didn't.

"I'm Detective Chris Cerniga," he said. "Do you think you could step back in here?"

He said it delicately, as if the trauma of returning to the bedroom might be too much for her, though his earnest look faltered when she rose to her full height and strode in. He straightened up, throwing his shoulders back a little more than was strictly necessary, and followed her in past the black uniformed cop. There was another detective inside, a balding man in a stained synthetic suit. He was studying the bookcase as they came in and didn't turn round.

"Dave," said Cerniga. He turned to acknowledge the witness, and his gaze lingered on her. She was unexpected, it seemed, though why—beyond the obvious—was uncertain. "This is Miss Miller," said Cerniga. "She found the body."

"Detective Keene," said the balding man, not offering either a hand or a badge. In fact, now that she had been brought to his attention, he acted as if she didn't deserve it, turning back to the bookcase and considering the titles.

"I realize this must be very difficult for you," said Cerniga, "but I was hoping you could answer a few questions."

She nodded, mute. The bedroom was as she had left it, the hidden alcove behind the bookcase still open, its walls glowing with their strange treasures. Only the corpse was gone. The space on the floor where Richard's body had been was stained a dark and telling crimson in the curiously focused lights that shone down, forming a rectangle around that very spot. The entire alcove had been marked off with crime scene tape. Deborah felt like she was seeing it all through someone else's eyes, or that she was experiencing some strange waking dream where the world seemed skewed and unreal.

"Would you happen to know if the museum contains any ceremonial weapons?"

Cerniga's voice brought her back to the moment. She blinked.

"Ceremonial?" she said, momentarily baffled. "There's a tomahawk in one of the cases downstairs . . ."

"No," he said. "I mean a weapon with a slim blade, like a dagger or a sword."

She stood there for a second, her mouth slightly open, as she realized what he was talking about, then flushed.

"Right," she said. "Of course. No. There's nothing like that here. Sorry."

She didn't know why she said *sorry*. She could tell her hand was shaking slightly. Cerniga was checking his notes.

"Rough night for old guys in the ATL," said the cop who had called himself Keene. He flashed a hard grin at Cerniga.

"I'm sorry?" said Deborah.

"Second homicide tonight," said Keene, shrugging. "The other was, like, a block away. Another old guy."

He said it like he was commenting on a sandwich.

"Are they connected?" said Deborah, still bemused as much by his glibness as by what he was saying.

"Nah," he said. "Totally different MO."

"You told the officer outside that you had never seen this room behind the bookcase before, is that right?" said Cerniga, looking up from his book.

"Yes," said Deborah.

"You just stumbled on it tonight," said Keene, "by chance?"

There was something in his eyes she didn't like, something cocky and suspicious.

"Not by chance," she said. "I had been looking for Richard—Mr. Dixon—and came in here. I picked up this piece of pottery, and I saw a trace of oil at the foot of the bookcase . . ."

She held out the fragment of ceramic she had been nursing absently since the whole nightmare had started, and caught herself as the two detectives stared.

"Sorry," she said, feeling yet again like she had done something amazingly idiotic. "I should have given it to the first policeman who arrived. Or left it where it was maybe . . ."

"Ya think?" said Keene with heavy sarcasm.

"Where did you pick that up?" said Cerniga. He looked irritated.

Deborah pointed.

"Great!" Keene snarled. "So the crime scene is contaminated!"

"What is it?" said Cerniga, brushing his colleague's indignation aside.

"I'm sorry?" said Deborah.

"The piece of pottery," he replied. "What is it?"

"A fragment of a vase or pot," she said, turning away from Keene. "It looks old, but it could be fake. Maybe Greek. Mycenaean."

"Greek?" said Cerniga. He sounded . . . what? Impressed? Intrigued? Something.

"Where's the rest of it?" said Keene.

"Over there. I think."

She pointed into the corner of the room where the other fragments lay scattered.

"Is it worth anything?" said Cerniga.

"Depends whether it's real," Deborah answered. "Old, I mean. If it's fake, it's worthless. If it's real . . . different story."

"Even though it would have to be stuck back together?" said Cerniga.

"Everything this old has to be stuck back together. So long as it's done properly, it would still be valuable."

"How much?" said Keene, cutting in like a dance partner in hobnail boots.

"I really don't know."

"Take a shot."

"I'd need to see it assembled. It would depend on the shape and size—"

"I said 'take a shot.' What is this, the freaking *Antiques Roadshow*?"

"Thousands," she said, shrugging. "Tens of thousands. Maybe more."

"For this?" said Keene, looking suddenly baffled and impressed.

"For the whole pot, maybe," said Deborah. "If it's real, it's Mycenaean."

"Mycenaean?"

"From Bronze Age Mycenae in ancient Greece."

"How old is Bronze Age?" said Cerniga.

"Three thousand to about twelve hundred BC," said Deborah. "Or thereabouts."

For a second the two detectives stared at the fragment in Keene's hand with something like reverence, and Deborah, ever the curator, smiled in spite of herself.

"So . . . the rest of this stuff?" said Cerniga, sweeping a hand over the display cases. "It's all Bronze Age? It's all Mycen . . . ?"

"Mycenaean. It looks like it, but . . ."

"But what?" said Keene, as if he thought she was being professionally pedantic, splitting hairs instead of cutting straight to it.

"I don't see how they can be real," said Deborah. "People would know about it. People would have seen it before. You don't just stumble on collections like this."

"But if it is real," said Cerniga, "what would it be worth?"

"Millions. Billions," she said. "I couldn't begin to put a price on a collection this important."

A long silence descended on the room as the two detectives turned from her and considered the gold, bronze, and ceramic artifacts gleaming dully in the soft lights. It was a moment of reverence, like sitting alone in temple between services as she had done once years after her father had died, a moment overwritten with memory and bafflement and sadness.

Could it all just be about money? Is that why Richard died?

"What about this word?" said Cerniga, snapping her back to the present as he held up the pad of paper—now bagged in polyethylene—from Richard's nightstand. "Atreus. Does that mean anything to you? Anything personal or business-related connected to Mr. Dixon?"

Deborah shook her head.

"Only legends," she said.

CHAPTER 11

They sent her home at five forty-five in the morning, telling her they'd need to speak to her again after she had gotten some sleep. She gave them her home number and said she'd be in the museum all afternoon. For the second time that night she went out into the parking lot to get her car. Nothing about the two moments felt remotely similar.

Richard. God, she just didn't know what she would do when the reality of his death really wormed its way into her mind. At the moment there was only a sudden blankness in her heart, like some part of herself had been taken, torn away so fast that she didn't know what to feel. It would come, searing, burning, scarring, but right now there was only a hole, a void, albeit one which would eventually overflow with feeling.

And after that?

How would she deal with the business of life, of running the museum, of carrying on as if everything was normal? That would almost be worse. Right now she never wanted to get to that point, a moment when she could think through her job without thinking of the man who had given it to her. To get past her grief would require some forgetting, and that seemed disloyal, unforgivable.

It was still dark when she pulled into the condo development off Juniper. She parked by the old white dogwood and walked down to her front door, barely aware of the chirping crickets and the heavy, wet air. Her apartment was through a narrow passage with a wrought-iron gate, unroofed except for the twining wisteria. She registered a fragrance in the air as she opened her porch gate but was in the dim, brick-lined

hallway standing at her apartment door with her keys sus-
pended inches away from the lock before she began to process it. Not floral: spice like some exotic liqueur or cologne,
and something else behind it: a dull but sweet tang of pipe to
bacco that reminded her forcefully of her father.

Wait.

Deborah stood quite still. She inhaled again, cautiously, as
if the scent itself might be poisonous, and caught it all again,
sharper and clearer this time. Deborah didn't smoke and
could count on the fingers of one hand the number of times
she had worn perfume of any kind in the last six months. It
was more often than she wore makeup, but not by much. She
had intended to wear both for the fund-raiser tonight, but in
between calming Richard, pacifying Tonya, and goading the
caterers, she had not been able to get home, and had finished
up wearing neither.

There was one other downstairs apartment on this narrow,
vine-hung passage. It belonged to Mrs. Reynolds, a widow
who had, to Deborah's knowledge, never left or entered the
building after dark, and seemed to insist that her visitors keep
the same hours.

She inserted the key into the lock with slow precision, conscious now of a tension in her spine. The thick Atlanta air
seemed denser than ever, and the cricket hum echoed shrill in
the darkened hallway. She turned the key slowly, quietly, waiting for its familiar clunk and the sudden seeming weightless-
ness of the door as it was freed from the lock mechanism. Then
the door was opening onto the darkness of her living room.

Wait.

She did not go in. She stood where she was and breathed
in.

She caught the lingering aromas of last night's dinner, the
pasta she had left spoiling on the stove, smelling of garlic and
basil. What else? The familiar hothouse sweetness of a room
full of plants closed to the outside air for an entire Georgia
summer day. And? A hint of cologne or aftershave, and stale
tobacco smoke.

Run.

She turned on her heel without closing the door, moving quickly back to the green Toyota. She pointed her key ring. The car's side lights blinked once, and the locks popped. She broke into a run.

Someone was in her apartment.

She yanked the door open, slid in, bashing her knee on the doorframe as she did so, and pushed the keys into the ignition. With one quick turn, the locks snapped back into place and the car began to hum with energy.

Thank God.

Deborah flicked on her headlights and swung the car a few feet so that they fell across the path and onto the iron gate to her home. The splash of light brought the night into startling color, as the lush greens of the camellia and the earth red of the bricks leapt out of the blackness. And the white of a man's hand, gripping the wrought iron.

It was there for a second or less, then it released the metal and vanished back into the leaf-shrouded passage. The gate juddered slightly on its hinge and then became quite still.

Deborah reversed the car out, dialing her cell phone at the same time.

CHAPTER 12

Deborah was waved toward the museum doors by a police-man in a squad car, its lights strobing. She went inside, taking deep, steadying breaths, trying to recover her composure before she had to start explaining.

They were waiting for her in the downstairs lobby beside the T. rex and the lady-snake ship prow. She had expected more uniforms, but the two detectives were still there. So was Tonya. Keene looked up at her as she came in, red-faced and irritated.

"You *smelled* someone in your apartment?" he said, un-derlining the word. At least they had everything she had told the dispatcher. She didn't feel like retelling the story.

"I could tell someone was there, yes," she said. She looked at Tonya. It wasn't clear if she was still being questioned or not. The black woman turned sharply away, giving Deborah the back of her braided, graying hair, but not before she had given her a look that said quite plainly, *Precious missy wants her privacy? Fine by me.*

"Any chance of a cup of coffee?" said Keene to Tonya.

The maid stiffened. Deborah braced herself for a tirade, but it didn't come. Instead Tonya merely shrugged.

"Don't guess you'll let me do much else around here to-day," she said. "You want cream and sugar?"

Deborah raised an eyebrow. Cerniga turned to the odious dragon-lady ship prow.

"That's quite a thing," said Cerniga, looking up at it, his voice neutral.

"Isn't it just," said Deborah. Then, relenting a little, she added, "Richard wanted it properly restored. I think it looks like the cover of a Whitesnake album."

"I like it," Cerniga decided, grinning and fishing his note-book from an inside pocket.

"Ten bucks and it's yours," said Deborah, sitting at her desk. "I guess I have to tell you about the person at my apartment?"

"Not really," said Cerniga. "Unless you have something to add to the report you gave over the phone."

"Oh," said Deborah, deflated. "I guess not."

"You didn't see him?"

"Just his hand on the gate."

"White?"

"Yes."

Cerniga drummed a ballpoint on the edge of his notebook.

"Let's talk some more about the museum," he said, "in the office?"

She led him back past the information desk and restrooms to the bookstore (it was really a gift shop, but Richard had in-sisted that most of the "gifts" were books) and the office which adjoined it. There was a pair of desks with computers, a printer, two telephones, and a bookcase. The rest of the room was dominated by an oval conference table in polished mahogany and eight chairs. They sat at one end as Keene came in, muttering inaudibly to one of the uniforms outside. He didn't look at Deborah.

"There's not much to tell," said Deborah, watching Keene's sour consideration of the office walls, his eyes slid-ing off the posters of pre-Columbian art and local photogra-phy exhibits like a minister flicking through *Playboy*. "Richard was a local benefactor of the arts and education—"

Keene snorted. Deborah gave him a look.

"Something stuck in my throat," said Keene, waving it away with a mirthless smile.

"Having always valued the arts, culture, education, and the like," said Deborah carefully, "he decided to open a small museum. Admission was free. The collection was . . . er-ratic."

"Erotic?" said Keene, smirking.

"Erratic," said Deborah.

"Oh," said Keene. "Too bad."

Deborah turned to Cerniga.

"He displayed all kinds of stuff," she said. "Odds and ends from all over the place displayed in old-fashioned cases pretty much at random. Anyway. When he retired he decided to make more of the place. He set up a board of trustees and hired a curator—"

"You," said Cerniga.

"Not the first time," she said. "I am the third. I've only been here three years."

"And you came here from . . . ?"

"I did my graduate work here," said Deborah. "But I'm from Boston originally and went to school in New York."

"Yeah, you sound like you're from someplace like that," said Keene, emphasizing his own Southern drawl in case she might have missed it. "I figured it was just *education*."

Deborah didn't know what to say. Keene resented her, and though she was used to that, she usually had to earn it. The policeman just didn't like her, hadn't liked her since the moment he met her.

"I've been trying to expand and focus the collection ever since," she said, trying to concentrate on the matter at hand. "That was part of what last night was about, actually. A fund-raiser. We are planning to bring in a collection of Celtic antiquities—"

"That's fascinating," said Keene with total disdain. "How about you give us a guest list from last night's little shindig."

"We were wondering," Cerniga explained, slightly apologetic, "if one of the people who was here for the fund-raiser stayed behind, or came back later."

Deborah took a second to process what he was saying: no one cared that Richard was dead. They cared that he was murdered.

She opened a desk drawer and pulled out the RSVP list.

"This has everyone who said they were coming," she said. "I can't be sure that they were all actually here, though I could probably go through it and confirm most of them myself. There were a few I didn't know, and it's possible that Richard invited some others who aren't on the list."

That was Richard all over. Bring her in to get everything organized, then upset her system on a whim . . . It always exasperated her and made her smile.

"What about staff?" said Keene.

"Tonya was here," said Deborah, "and a couple of our volunteers. The caterers had their own people."

"How many?"

"Three food servers, two barmen," said Deborah.

"What time did they leave?"

"Tonya left early," said Deborah. "Nine-ish, I think. She was just staying to see everything got under way properly. The volunteers were here another hour or so. The caterers left around eleven fifteen," she added. "All the guests were gone by midnight."

"And you were the last to leave?" said Keene.

"Yes."

There was a tap at the door, and Tonya poked her head around, smiling sheepishly. She had two mugs of coffee in her hands, which she raised as a request to come in. Cerniga waved her through and cleared spaces on the desk for the cups. She set them down and pushed them toward the cops. She did not meet Deborah's eyes or offer her anything. For a second Deborah considered requesting something, a full English breakfast, perhaps . . . It might be worth it just to see the look on Tonya's face.

Ah yes. Humor. Your usual hidey-hole . . .

When Tonya had gone, Keene turned to Deborah and unfolded a piece of paper that looked like it had been sent by fax.

"You ever seen anything like this?" he said.

As Deborah swiveled to look at it, she caught a look on Cerniga's face, a flash of irritation and a moment of indecision. In the end he just frowned and looked quickly away, but she was sure he was angry with Keene for showing the picture.

It was a knife, she supposed, though it was long and slender like a sword, with a cruciform hilt that arced down slightly from the blade. Thrust deeply into a body, the ends of the hilt, what she thought were called quillons, would dig into the flesh on either side of the stab wound.

. . . leaving little symmetrical bruises . . .

The knife in the picture was sheathed in what looked like black leather, the top and tip of the scabbard were trimmed with bright metal, and hung from a length of chain designed to suspend it at a belt. It was an elegant but lethal-looking weapon, though that wasn't all that made it remarkable. On top of the black handle was a metal disk engraved or stamped with a familiar symbol.

"Is that a swastika?" she said.

"I take it, it doesn't look familiar?" said Cerniga, turning back toward her and reaching for the fax. His face was blank.

"I've never seen anything like it," she said, frowning.

"Nothing like it in the collection?"

"No."

"The swastika isn't relevant," he added after a moment. "It's just the shape of the weapon that we're trying to match."

It was Keene's turn to shoot his colleague a look, though Deborah wasn't sure what it contained. Puzzlement? Doubt?

Deborah opened her mouth to speak, but there was another tap on the door, brisker this time, followed by the appearance of one of the uniformed cops.

"There's a guy here to see Miss Miller," he said. "Says he's Dixon's lawyer."

Deborah stared. She didn't know any lawyer, didn't even know Richard had had one, though she supposed he must have.

"Dixon's dead," said Keene. "He don't need no damn lawyer."

There was something in his tone, something about the way he looked back to her.

"Am I a suspect?" said Deborah.

"Of course not," said Cerniga, cutting in. Keene looked at the floor.

"Also," said the uniform, "I've got word from the patrol-men who checked out her place. Nothing. No sign of forced entry or a search."

Keene regarded Deborah with interest.

"What?" said Deborah. "You think that means I imag-ined it?"

"It has been a very stressful evening for you," he said, too kindly. "But I didn't mean you imagined it, no."

He gave her a sly grin, and she felt her color rise.

"You think I made it up?" she said, baffled. "I thought I wasn't a suspect?"

"Lady," said Keene, "everyone's a suspect till someone's convicted."

"I don't think I understand," said Deborah, feeling that thickness again, that stupid slowness like she was drunk or sedated. "You think I killed Richard?"

"Hey, lady, I'm just saying."

"Please stop *just saying*," she said, some of her old defiance flashing up through her confusion. "I don't understand what you mean by it. And I'd prefer it if you didn't call me *lady*."

"That," he said, looking her up and down with clumsy irony, "will be no problem at all."

Deborah just looked at him. She felt out of her depth. In fact that phrase made sense to her in ways it never had be-fore. She was floating out to sea. The water was dark and cold beneath her, and there were things down there with teeth, watching, circling . . .

"One other thing," said the uniform. "That John Doe: the shooting?"

"What about it?" said Cerniga.

"He had a couple of personal effects in an inside pocket. The writing on them is foreign. Greek, maybe."

"Greek?" said Cerniga.

"Maybe," said the cop. "They weren't sure. They're check-ing it out."

"If he turns out to be a foreign national, won't that just be perfect?" said Keene, his expression sour.

"Maybe we should have you look at him," said Cerniga to Deborah. "See if you've seen him around."

"Because he's Greek and there's a room full of old Greek crap upstairs?" said Keene in a tone of scornful disbelief. "You think that's a connection?"

"Probably not," said Cerniga. His eyes narrowed, and he turned to Deborah. "Did you know that Mr. Dixon made a series of long-distance calls to Greece in the past two weeks?"

"No," said Deborah honestly.

"Do you know why he may have done so?"

"No," said Deborah miserably.

More secrets.

Cerniga sighed and considered the uniformed cop.

"It's probably not connected," he said, "but let's check out the other victim."

"It's not our case," said Keene, petulant now. "We have enough on our plate without making these dumb-ass links from one stiff—wealthy, stab wounds, indoors—to another—homeless, gun shot, outdoors!"

"He was homeless?" asked Deborah, remembering the strange lurker in the parking lot.

"Probably," said Cerniga, "we don't know for sure—"

Without warning, the door kicked open and a tall, young, blond man came in. He was slim and wore a pale, rumpled suit with a stone-colored shirt, open at the throat. He looked like a man unused to being messed about.

"Miss Miller?" he said, ignoring the cops completely, "I'm Calvin Bowers. I was Mr. Dixon's lawyer. Since I'm responsible for his estate—including the museum—I thought I would offer my services."

His eyes were a deep, unsettling blue, almost purple in their intensity.

"Miss Miller has not been charged," said Cerniga, getting to his feet and shooting Keene an irritated look.

"Just as well," said Bowers, his blue eyes flashing dangerously in Cerniga's direction. "But this is Miss Miller's second extended interrogation in a few hours, and on the night she found the body of her mentor. I think that any evidence you gathered in such circumstances would be considered of questionable reliability, wouldn't you? I'm damned sure a jury would."

"Now you just hold it right there," said Keene, rising.

"Are you in charge of this investigation?" Bowers shot back.

The question seemed to give Keene pause, and his righteous certainty flickered. He looked at Cerniga.

"I am," said Cerniga. "Can we get back to the matter of the intruder at Miss Miller's apartment—?"

"An intruder?" said Bowers, his eyes turning to Deborah. "Are you all right?"

She nodded, tense, wondering who he was, why he seemed to be taking her part.

"I got out before I even saw him."

Keene grinned.

Bowers rounded on him. "If I find that you've created a hostile interrogation environment for this witness," he said, "I'll have her entire testimony thrown out. Is that clear?"

Keene's sneer wilted, and though it didn't completely vanish, he shrugged his assent.

"I want to make it clear," said Cerniga, "that Miss Miller is being interviewed, not interrogated."

"Have you determined the motivation for the attack on Mr. Dixon?" said Bowers, still on the offensive.

"Not yet," said Cerniga. He was catching some of his colleague's surliness now. "We think it might be a burglary gone wrong but . . ." He faltered.

"Yes?" said Bowers, reeling him in.

"We don't know if there is anything missing."

"This, no doubt, has been the subject of your questioning of Miss Miller," said Bowers. "Presumably she has been going through the museum properties to determine if anything is unaccounted for."

"We haven't got to that yet, sir," said Cerniga.

Bowers couldn't suppress the hint of a smile. Was it that "sir" or just the ease with which he had pulled the rug out from under Cerniga's feet?

He turned to her, smiling.

"Miss Miller, might you have a complete inventory of the museum's contents?" he said. "It might aid the police in their inquiries and give them something other than you to scrutinize."

The two cops sat quite still as Deborah rose and unlocked a filing cabinet.

CHAPTER 13

Deborah sat with Calvin Bowers in the museum lobby, which now glowed with incongruous morning sunshine. Richard was dead, but the sun still shone. It was the way of things, she supposed, but it felt wrong, and she hated it. There was a uniformed officer standing by the locked front door, but the detectives were still in the office.

Bowers, out of the police presence, was a different person: relaxed, open faced, amiably handsome. He sat with his legs stretched out in front of him, casual in the way a big cat is casual, elegant but poised for action. She didn't feel like making conversation, and his easy good looks made her awkward and unsure of herself, but he had helped her out, and it seemed churlish to just sit there.

"How long have you worked for Richard?" she asked.

"Less than a year. He has done business with our firm for a lot longer than that, of course. Since he bought this place, I think. But I only got involved a few months ago when he sent some paperwork our way. We spoke on the phone a few times and exchanged legal correspondence, but we'd never actually met."

Deborah was impressed. His righteous outrage in the office a few minutes ago had led her—and the police—to assume that Bowers was an old friend of Richard's, that he was personally affronted by the crime and its subsequent handling. But all that had been professional bluster to keep them off balance. His interest in the case was strictly professional.

"I can't believe he's gone," said Deborah. As soon as the words were out there in the sun, she regretted saying them, especially to this stranger. "Sorry," she added hastily. "That was such a cliché. It doesn't begin to . . . God, there's so much work to be done."

Bowers rolled with her change of tack as if he hadn't noticed it.

"There are people who can help shoulder the burden, aren't there?" he said. "The museum board? I would be glad to help out. My relationship with Mr. Dixon was brief, but the firm's goes back a long way and is tied to the value of the property itself, so I'm sure they'll be glad to lend my aid."

Lend my aid. He sounded like a knight offering chivalric services to a damsel in distress.

"I can handle things here," she said with a touch of hauteur. It was a reflex. She didn't even know that she *could* handle things.

"I don't doubt it," he said, smiling so that she relented a little.

"Sorry," she said. "I'm not used to . . ."

. . . being anything other than utterly self-reliant?

". . . being looked after," she said. "Richard gave me free rein . . ."

She caught herself, sensing a tightening in her throat. She smiled and shrugged it off unconvincingly. He just nodded his sympathy, and for a moment she looked out over the lobby she and Richard had assembled piece by painstakingly selected piece . . .

"So you're an archaeologist," he said, peering at the Creek Indian exhibit critically.

"Not really," said Deborah. "I'm a museum director. That's what my graduate degree is in."

"And what does a museum director major in?" he said, smiling easily again so that she felt herself relax a fraction.

"I double majored in English and archaeology," she said, "but a lot of people do business."

"I prefer it your way round," he said.

"So do I," she said, and this time her smile was warmer.

"Still," he said, indicating the case containing a magnificent stone-headed tomahawk. "The company you keep! Look at this nasty little thing. A barbarous weapon if ever there was one. I guess there's something to be said for Manifest Destiny, eh?"

"I don't think the Native Americans were any less civilized than the white settlers because they had less efficient ways of killing people," she said with an ironic smile.

"*Native Americans,*" he said. "Funny isn't it, the way people think they can fix everything with words."

Deborah felt a flicker of irritation but didn't have time to respond.

"Miss Miller?" It was Tonya.

She had emerged from the long gallery to the residence and was hovering, her hands clasped awkwardly in front of her.

"Can I have a word?" she said.

Deborah got up.

"In private, if you don't mind," Tonya said.

Deborah gave an apologetic nod toward Bowers, and the two women walked back to the museum office in silence.

"What's on your mind, Tonya?" said Deborah after they had closed the door behind them. They were both standing, stiff and apprehensive.

"I think you know," said Tonya. "Look," she said. "I was just curious. I have a buddy in the force, and he told me about the murder as soon as the call came through. He said something about a secret room and . . . I kinda wanted to see what was going on, you know? I didn't think it would be Mr. Dixon. I didn't mean nothing by it."

Deborah didn't know Tonya well, but she had spoken to her enough for that last phrase to ring strangely. Tonya didn't talk like a janitor, and she didn't wear her blackness on her sleeve. Her diction was, Deborah had often observed, carefully grammatical, educated, so that she had often wondered from what white-collar profession she had fallen to wind up cleaning out museum toilets. She spoke so that everyone knew that they had no right to look down on her for what she did or what she looked like. The Tonya Deborah knew would never say, "I didn't mean nothing by it," and the phrase somehow threw the entire confession into a strange and uncertain light.

"You probably shouldn't have come in till the police arrived," said Deborah wearily.

"No ma'am," said Tonya, shaking her head, as if amazed by her own audacity. "That's surely right."

No feisty riposte, no carefully worded suggestion as to what the prim white bitch could do with her suspicions. *"No ma'am, that's surely right"?*

From Tonya? No way.

Deborah's eyes narrowed. It was like casting extras in *Gone With the Wind.*

"You want I should get you a coffee?" said Tonya, after a sigh of relief. "I was fixing to make one, but my guts was all knotted up. I think I could drink me something now."

Deborah managed a smile and a nod, and watched her go with a mixture of disbelief and unease. *"My guts was all knotted up"?* Who was she trying to fool, and why?

When she got back into the lobby, Calvin Bowers was talking to a big man in a shiny suit: Harvey Webster. Her heart sank, but she kept her chin up and walked briskly toward them.

Webster looked serious, but his face lit up as he saw her coming. He showed no ill effects from the evening's alcohol or the fact that she had turned him out on his ear.

"Terrible business," he said as she arrived, his voice low and gently musical. "Just terrible. If there's anything I can do, you just holler."

"Thank you, Harvey," said Deborah. "I will."

"The police called me first thing," he said. "Said we should close the museum."

"What?" said Deborah. "For how long?"

"Not long," he said. "Two, maybe three weeks."

"Three weeks!" said Deborah.

"Maybe we can talk them into opening sooner," said Bowers, inserting himself into the conversation in full damsel-protecting mode.

"Seemed pretty firm," said Webster. He gave Deborah a sympathetic smile which did not reach his watery eyes.

So this was to be her punishment. Webster and the board would take over, shut her out for the next few weeks while they regrouped. She looked into Harvey Webster's blandly disingenuous smile, and she thought she could glimpse her future: the steady reduction of her control of the collection until Harvey's League of Christian *(white)* Businessmen could take over, and the museum would become what they had always wanted: a species of theme park, light on content, heavy on profits.

"I'm going to have a word with those detectives," said Webster as he walked away. "See what I can do."

Get the place closed for an extra month, probably, thought Deborah, feeling outmaneuvered.

Deborah turned away, suddenly very tired and frustrated by that feeling of powerlessness which she hated above all things. She could sense Bowers behind her, ready to say something encouraging. She stood with her hands on her hips, staring across the bright, empty foyer. Without Richard, she really was alone, and the building felt no more than a shell, vacant and pointless without him.

Three weeks. All the promotional work for the new exhibits, the glad-handing, the schmoozing and elbow rubbing, the polite smiling through story after story by benefactors, the press coverage pictures of that ghastly ship prow . . . All for nothing. In three weeks Atlanta would have forgotten the museum existed. And what would she do for three weeks? Bounce around in this carefully lit mausoleum while Keene and his cronies made third-hand wisecracks about homo erectus?

God, what a wearying idea.

"We might be able to get the museum open earlier if you can demonstrate that nothing's missing," said Calvin. He was hovering behind her, keeping a respectful distance. She turned and smiled gratefully.

"I'm not entirely sure why I want to keep it open so

badly," she said. "I guess part of me thinks that if I pretend everything is normal, then somehow . . ."

"Yes," said Calvin, sparing her the end of the sentence.

Deborah took a breath and tried to shake the thought off.

"I can do a thorough inventory today," she said, "make sure everything is where it should be. Of course, if there was anything missing from that room behind the bookcase in Richard's room, I wouldn't know."

She shrugged and sighed, finding the memory of the place insist itself on her memory like a familiar and unpleasant odor, the body laid out like that under the lights . . .

Wait.

Something *was* missing.

The pot had come from the open display behind the book-case, and the other cases all looked complete, so she had assumed nothing had been taken. But then there was the curious lighting in that secret room, the square of light shining down from the ceiling, throwing its chill glow on Richard's ravaged body. But what had been there when his poor corpse was not, which needed such special illumination?

There had been a power outlet in the center of the floor, she remembered.

Yes. There had been another display in the center of the room. It had been large, and it had been special, the center-piece of the collection, big enough that it had been wheeled out, tracking oil onto the carpet . . . But what could possibly be so much more extraordinary than the pieces stored in the wall cases, that it was worth taking while the rest of that priceless hoard had not been?

CHAPTER 14

"You feel up to a trip to the morgue?"

This from Detective Cerniga. Deborah sat there mute. She had been en route to the office, but he had flagged her down. She couldn't think of anything to say.

"Honestly," she said, "I know you need formal identification and everything, but I don't think I'm ready to look at him again. I know it was Richard. There's no question. Do I have to look at him again?"

She hated saying it, hated sounding weak and emotional, hated the look of confusion in his eyes.

"No," he said, his face clearing. "I didn't mean Mr. Dixon. Your identification of his body is done. I meant the other body. The John Doe. The Greek guy."

Strange, she thought, as she nodded and followed him to his car, that the idea of looking at a dead body could bring such relief. Strange that someone else, this other man's daughter, perhaps, would have felt for this unknown Greek body the same as she did for Richard's. The thought stayed with her as they drove, parked, and walked through the blank, institutional hallways of the county coroner's office. She avoided people's eyes, hung back as Cerniga muttered explanations, followed in silence as they went into the basement with its bare pipes, painted concrete block walls, and its sterile, echoing passages.

She had never been inside a morgue before but had seen plenty in movies and TV crime shows, so the place felt strangely familiar in spite of its drawers of corpses. It was so exactly as she had expected that it would be, in fact, that she felt a curious thrill of satisfaction, like she was meeting a celebrity whose face she had known for years. The feeling evaporated as soon as the young assistant in his rectangular glasses unveiled the body itself.

He was old, seventy perhaps, heavyset, his body mounding under the synthetic sheet. His eyes were closed and sunken, but she knew that if they were to open, they would be bright and intense and would watch her as she crossed the parking lot.

"Yes," she said. "I've seen him around the last few days. Three days, maybe. He spoke, but I didn't understand him, and he wasn't really talking to me. Just, you know . . . muttering."

"I guess you wouldn't understand him if he was speaking Greek," said Cerniga.

"Not Greek," said the guy in the glasses. "Preliminary translation says his effects were in Russian. It uses some of the same letters as Greek, I guess."

"That probably means he's not connected to the treasure," said Cerniga, frowning.

"Treasure?" said the assistant, perking up.

Cerniga ignored him for a moment, then said, "Can we see his effects?"

"Sure," said the assistant, giving Deborah a searching look. He was still thinking about that preposterous word that Cerniga had dropped so casually: *treasure.*

"You should check into a hotel," said Cerniga, to fill the silence the assistant left in his wake. "Just to be on the safe side." He let the words hang in the air and then added more gently, "Consider it a holiday."

A holiday. Like she'd won it. She couldn't imagine anything she wanted less right now. But maybe it was better for her to be away, rather than sitting on the museum's doorstep loitering . . .

. . . *powerless* . . .

. . . waiting for permission to do her job. Another five seconds of thoughtful silence, and the decision was made.

"OK," she said. "I'll look for somewhere to stay."

"Quietly," he said. She blinked, then nodded, face blank.

The assistant returned with a tray of bagged items and a printed list of their contents. He tipped the bags out. There was no wallet or anything resembling official documents. There was a toothbrush which looked new, a lapel pin shaped like a shield, an envelope addressed in Russian, and a single sheet of torn and stained paper, overwritten in a spidery scrawl in black ink. It looked like part of a letter.

"There was more of that," said the assistant. "But it was . . . *damaged.*"

He gave Deborah a quick, awkward look, then returned his gaze to the tray.

Blood-soaked, she thought. *This was all they could save.*

"Do we have a translation?" said Cerniga.

"Not yet. There's not much that's still legible," said the assistant, checking the printout. He picked up the badge, which was in red, green, and gold enamel with the image of a soldier with a machine gun and Cyrillic lettering around the edge. At the base of the shield was a dagger overlaid by the Soviet hammer and sickle. "This, apparently, says 'Excellent Border Guard,' or something. It's from the fifties."

"What are those letters at the bottom?" said Deborah.

"MVD," said the assistant, checking the sheet of paper. "Stands for Ministry of the Interior. Some minor government department, I guess."

"What's an old Soviet soldier doing in Atlanta?" said Deborah.

"Nothing to do with us," said Cerniga, shrugging. "Come on, let's go."

Richard had been up to something; his recent manner, his contact with the museum's lawyers, his phone calls to Greece, even his uncharacteristic enthusiasm for fund-raising all suggested that whatever had happened to him last night, it had not come completely out of the blue. As soon as she got back to the museum, Deborah went into her office and snapped on the computer. All the house and museum computers were linked via the same network so that, with the right combination of passwords, you could access every file stored on each of the linked machines from any terminal.

The computer came to life slowly. She typed her entry code and pulled up the network but found that most of the other machines—including Richard's—did not appear. She stared at the monitor screen.

The police have taken them.

Then it hit her. The machines were probably still in place, but they were all turned off. The police had done what no one on the museum staff ever did, and shut them all down as they finished copying their contents. She sat there, staring blankly at the useless computer.

Something else had been in that secret room: something large, something Richard had kept secret but which had been the core of some plan. He had been setting something up, a display perhaps, or a sale: something that would have changed the museum forever. It was to be his gift to the people of Atlanta, she felt sure of it. Richard would not hoard his treasures, hugging them to his chest in private. He would lay them out for the world to enjoy. *Surely* that was what he had been planning. But it had all gone horribly wrong, and the core exhibit which had sat under that great central light had been taken . . . or been intercepted before it ever arrived.

Something flared within her, a defiance, perhaps, a sense of purpose, a desire—no—a *need* to do something to help reveal the circumstances of Richard's death, bringing the truth to light as if she was digging up and dusting off some priceless artifact, an act which would bring grace and meaning to this empty and meaningless death. She would tell the police whatever she found as soon as she found it, but she would *do* something. She had to.

The door opened. It was Tonya.

"I'm sorry," she said, starting slightly. "I didn't think you were in here. I would have knocked."

"It's no problem," said Deborah.

"I'll come back later," said the maid, backing out.

"Oh, Tonya," said Deborah quickly, as if she had just
thought of it. "Would you mind switching on Richard's computer upstairs? I have to download some receipts from the
party last night."

It was a feeble lie, she thought, but a harmless one, though
Tonya hesitated a fraction of a second before smiling and
saying, "Sure."

The door closed again, and Deborah sat there, waiting.

The clock in the bottom corner of the computer screen
turned a minute over, then another. Deborah got up, then sat
down again. Tonya would tell Keene, and he would come and
stand over her with that snide look on his face. Deborah
pushed the mouse, pulling up the shut-down menu. But then
something flickered into life: a new monitor icon on the network display. One more password, and she had access.

She didn't know what she was looking for. She scanned a
series of financial statements and spreadsheets, but nothing
looked out of place. She opened his documents file and ran
her eye over the folders inside. One stopped her cold. It was
labeled quite simply: "Atreus."

Hurriedly she double-clicked on it and waited as the infer-
nally slow system flicked the contents up. It contained a single file stored as a JPEG.

A picture?

She clicked on it and waited as the image began to load.

The door opened.

It was Calvin Bowers.

Deborah fumbled for the mouse to minimize the picture,
but her breath caught in her throat as she saw what it was.

The screen was filled with a broad stylized face wrought
in gold: a Mycenaean death mask.

CHAPTER 15

"Getting a little work done?" said Calvin Bowers, glancing over her shoulder at the now-blank computer screen. She had closed the file the moment he walked in, but not fast enough to prevent him from seeing the golden face.

"Don't you knock?" she said, her panic getting the better of her.

"I'm sorry," he said with a genial smile. "What was that you were looking at?"

Deborah faltered.

"It was a Greek death mask," she said. "I had been considering using it on the museum Web site."

The embroidery immediately sounded clumsy and stupid.

"Does the museum have one of those?" he said. It wasn't a real question. He knew they didn't.

"A Web site?" she said.

"A Greek mask," he said.

"No," she admitted. "It's just a kind of archaeological icon. A symbol."

He considered this, watching her.

"You're a bad liar, Miss Miller," he said at last. "It's not your style. That's fine by me, but tell the police these kinds of stories, and you could get yourself into serious trouble."

She frowned and looked away. He was right. She had built her adult life on directness, and such an attitude to the world made for a bad liar. Just how ingrained this bullheaded straightforwardness was to her sense of self was evident in the fact that she took his remark as a compliment. Lies weren't her style.

"The mask may be connected to Richard's death," she
said. "I don't know. OK?"

"OK," he said. "How?"

"I'm not sure," she said. "I'm just beginning to wonder."

"About?"

For a long moment she sat there, not weighing how much
to tell him so much as gathering what she could remember.
Then she started to talk, and he listened, casually at first, then
more seriously, leaning forward, his eyes narrow and alive.

Mycenaean pots, jewelry, and weapons were one thing, Deborah told him, but a death mask was something entirely different. Archaeologists found artifacts in all manner of places,
but death masks were found in one place only: graves. Rich
graves, at that: the tombs of kings.

And it's a face.

Yes, there was that too. Weapons and jars, rings and bowls
all have their special value, but nothing evokes the grandeur
of the past in human terms like the image of the dead man's
face, however stylized. Death masks are regal, but they are
also personal, even intimate; it's like looking down a tunnel
into the past and finding that it ends in a mirror, all the history
and legends stripped down to the face of a human being. It
was no wonder, Deborah said, that they were so prized by
collectors and the hordes of people who filed past museum
displays, their eyes lingering on those of the mask and, by
implication, the man who once wore it in death.

Another reason such masks were especially treasured was
that they often didn't stay in the ground all that long. The
graves were usually well marked, or people just remembered
where those great ceremonial interments took place, and the
kind of finery that had gone in there with the corpse. As a
rule, then, the grave sites got plundered, sometimes right after the burial, sometimes centuries later when the civilization
had died, leaving only folk tales for the grave robbers to follow. By the time legitimate archaeologists got there, the richest

finds were usually long gone. There were exceptions, of course: Carter's discovery of Tutankhamen's gold sarcophagus, for example. And Schliemann in Mycenae.

It wasn't just that that the masks were rare. If one was found today, the chances of it getting out of the country where it was discovered were virtually zero. The great powers of the nineteenth century had filled their national museums with treasures lifted from nations once mighty in art and war, then reduced to the ignominy of the colonized. But those days were long gone, and barely a day went by without some nationalist appeal from Greece or Egypt, Iran or India, Colombia or Peru, that the current owners return to their native land the statues and jewelry, paintings or relics filched from them a century or so ago by the agents of European empire. No, the chances of a treasure trove of Mycenaean grave goods being spirited away to America without raising even a blip on the radar of the cultural community in this day and age were slim to none.

Which took her back to Schliemann.

"Schliemann?" said Calvin. He had been listening intently, leaning forward, and this was the first thing he had said since she had started. She liked talking about this stuff, and she liked him listening.

"I need to do some reading before I can tell you about him," she said honestly. "Richard was the expert, but he didn't like what I said about him, so he tried not to discuss him much in front of me."

She smiled ruefully.

"Why didn't you like him?" said Calvin. "Did you know him personally?"

Deborah laughed.

"Heinrich Schliemann died long before I was born," she said. "He made some amazing finds, but his methods were pretty shady sometimes. And if I remember rightly, things went missing."

"Artifacts?"

"Artifacts."

"Listen," said Calvin after a thoughtful pause. "I have to sort through some correspondence upstairs, but maybe we can talk some more tomorrow? Over lunch, perhaps?"

It was a cautious question. He didn't want it to sound overly interested—not in her, at least—or frivolous. Why had he even asked it? To give her someone to talk to, help her take her mind off Richard's death? Probably. It was kindness, she supposed, though she would have preferred that he just wanted to talk about archaeology. Richard would have liked nothing better.

"Sure," she said, managing a smile, but barely aware of him. Her mind was already focused on the books upstairs and what she might learn from them about Heinrich Schliemann.

CHAPTER 16

Deborah checked into the Holiday Inn round the corner. By the time she was settled in and had ordered a burger through room service, the stack of books she had borrowed from Richard's study (with Cerniga's permission) had begun to look like a wall. She watched television, shuttling from one show to the next, until her tiredness seemed to have seeped into the very marrow of her bones. She shut it off, lay down, and fell asleep in her clothes.

She spent the following morning going through the books, speed-reading, checking references and, from time to time, reading long sections hungrily. When she finished it was lunchtime, but she had no appetite. She had breakfasted on coffee, and the caffeine was still singing in her veins, telling her she didn't need to eat. Or maybe it wasn't the caffeine so much as her reading that left her so pulsing with energy.

At first, the archaeological world had derided Schliemann and his conviction that the Trojan War had really happened, but then he went and discovered Troy in northern Turkey, and suddenly he had everyone's attention. Many were still wary, however, and even his disciples were alarmed by his methods. He was accused of "salting" his finds, of misrepresenting where he had found things, and of collecting them into hoards to prove the ancient poets right and to enlarge his own glory. And then there was the Priam's Treasure episode.

Priam, according to Homer, was the king of Troy during the siege by the Greeks. He was the father of Hector, Troilus, and Paris, who had set the whole war in motion by stealing

Helen from Agamemnon's brother, Menelaus. Homer said that Priam's city was rich in gold, but by the end of his excavation, Schliemann hadn't found it. But then, just as digging was being closed down, he stumbled on it personally, parts of it not completely covered by the earth. Among the hoard was an extraordinary collection of jewelry. This remarkable—and to many, dubious—story grew steadily stranger when, after being photographed (with Schliemann's wife, Sophia, wearing the jewelry) the whole find vanished. The Turkish government was furious, convinced that the archaeologist had sneaked the entire cache of treasure out of the country, out of their reach . . .

If one set of artifacts could go missing, why not another?

After his work in Turkey, Schliemann had begun his Mycenaean excavations with a specific goal in mind. According to legend, when Agamemnon, king of the victorious Greeks, returned to Mycenae, he was lured into a bath by his unfaithful wife, Clytemnestra, where, with the assistance of her lover, she killed him. He was buried with great ceremony; Schliemann believed the grave was there for the finding.

The Greek government, like everyone else, was skeptical, but they eventually granted him permission to dig. Schliemann, who was convinced that the royal grave was within the uppermost walls of the fortress, dug a shaft just inside the main entrance, convinced he was going not through naturally compacted earth but filler. But after digging down over ten feet, he had found nothing, and it was raining heavily. He started another shaft, then another, then three more, and things started getting interesting.

He found a series of graves containing the fragmented remains of multiple bodies. They wore gold diadems piped with copper wire, and with them lay silver vases and obsidian knives. In the fourth shaft grave he found the remains of five bodies all covered with jewels. With them was an astonishing silver bull's head with golden horns, along with bronze swords and golden cups. Most remarkably, three of the bodies wore magnificent golden death masks.

But it wasn't till he returned to the first shaft and took it deeper still that the archaeological world finally ground to a complete halt and all eyes turned in wonder to that ancient Greek hill fortress. In this last grave he made the richest of all his finds: three more bodies, two of them wearing gold masks, and then a third death mask unlike any of the others, larger, more distinctive, more regal.

In a telegram later dismissed as apocryphal, Schliemann reportedly wired an Athenian newspaper and announced with customary hubris that he had "gazed upon the face of Agamemnon."

He hadn't. In fact, the bodies and their accompanying grave goods were three centuries *older* than Agamemnon, if such a person had ever existed. More to the point, some scholars were wary of the spectacular "Agamemnon" mask. It was the wrong shape, they said. The style of the nose didn't match the other pieces. The mustache looked positively nineteenth-century . . . Could Schliemann have graduated from theft and manipulation of the truth to outright forgery?

But as Deborah sat back in her chair, taking it all in, a new possibility was growing in her head. Was it possible that more had been found in the Mycenaean digs than Schliemann had admitted? Was there even a chance that the somewhat unconventional death mask associated (albeit inaccurately) with Agamemnon, which now had pride of place in the National Archaeological Museum in Athens, was a fake, and if so, had there been a real one which Schliemann had replaced? Had the real mask been made to "disappear" as Priam's Treasure had disappeared from Troy? Had that mask been in Richard's bedroom only hours before, and if so, how on earth had it gotten there?

Richard could be a little blinded by his boyish hopes, but he was no fool. If he had believed that the room behind the bookcase contained the greatest single collection of Mycenaean artifacts outside Greece, then he must have had evidence to point to its authenticity. Almost certainly that evidence had to do with provenance: where and when the

mask had been found. In archaeological circles, provenance
was all. Had Richard been able to trace the piece back to the
moment it had first been unearthed? If he did, who else knew?
His killers? Whoever he had been calling in Greece? Was it a
coincidence that an elderly Russian who had appeared only
days before should die on the same night and less than two
blocks away? Could he have known something about these
ancient artifacts?

She took the phone book out of the nightstand and placed
a call, pen in hand.

"Dekalb County police station," said a female voice.

"Yes," said Deborah, "I'm calling with regard to a Russian
who was killed close to the Druid Hills Museum two nights
ago."

"And you are?"

"Deborah Miller," she said, suddenly sure they would tell
her nothing. "I work at the museum. And," she added on impulse, "I helped identify the body."

It was true. To a point.

"That's Detective Robbins's case, but he's out. Can I take
a message?"

"I don't think so," she said. "I was just checking in to see
what the status of the case is."

"It's pretty much closed," said the woman on the other
end.

"Already? They have a suspect?"

"No," said the policewoman, "and unlikely to get one in
the circumstances. I wouldn't expect many leads to develop
unless we can match the bullet to a known weapon."

"In the circumstances," Deborah repeated. "What does
that mean?"

The woman sighed conspicuously, and Deborah thought
she heard the shuffling of papers. When she spoke, she
sounded like she was reading.

"Mr. Sergei Voloshinov was not a U.S. citizen. He was a
foreign national who had overstayed his visa and was, so far
as we can tell, mentally unstable. He was wandering the

streets at night and probably bumped into the wrong people. Simple as that. I don't think there is much for us to do."

"Voloshinov," said Deborah, scribbling on a hotel pad. "How did you find out his name?"

"He was carrying a stamped envelope. Been living rough for at least a couple of weeks. Russian authorities and next of kin have been contacted, but he'll probably be buried here."

"Next of kin?"

"A daughter in Moscow. Alexandra."

"What about the letter? Was the translator able to get anything from that?"

"Wait," she said, searching. "Translator . . . translator. OK." She began to read directly from the file she was apparently consulting, her voice automatic and a trifle bored. "Translator David Barrons reported that the letter was badly damaged, with only a few words surviving definitively. Part of one sentence read, 'I am more sure than ever that the remains never reached Mary,' though that last word is hard to read and may be incomplete. The letter appears to be at least twenty years old."

She paused.

"That's the lot," she said. "You can call back, but Detective Robbins probably won't be able to tell you anything new. Now, if you don't mind . . ."

"I am more sure than ever that the remains never reached Mary . . ."

Deborah found herself turning the phrase over in her mind. Could the *remains* be archaeological? Could they include a Mycenaean death mask? Could this enigmatic Russian have been pursuing them when he fell afoul of whoever took them from the secret room in Richard's bedroom?

CHAPTER 17

Deborah returned to the museum conscious that she still had nothing more than speculations, but they excited her, and she wanted to share them with Cerniga, with Calvin Bowers even, it didn't really matter who. A Mycenaean death mask unknown to the world, smuggled out of Greece by Schliemann a century ago and pursued by a lone Russian to Atlanta, Georgia! It was extraordinary. It was almost enough to keep her mind from Richard's death, and sharing her thoughts with the police would be her contribution: a way to pay homage to Richard and unravel his murder. Who knew, maybe the mask he had died for would be rediscovered. She could think of no more fitting monument to his memory.

But one thing had to be done first. She hadn't eaten all morning and was suddenly ravenous. Remembering that there was food left over from the party, she went downstairs to the kitchen at the back of the building. Tonya, mercifully, was nowhere to be seen.

She uncovered the trays in the fridge and picked over the food, sniffing cautiously. She tried the pâté and found it as unappetizing as she had two nights before. That reminded her. She unhooked the phone from the far wall and dialed the caterers. Rambling her half thoughts to Cerniga (with Keene smirking darkly in the background) would have to wait a moment.

"Taste of Elegance," said a voice, "Can I help you?"

"This is Deborah Miller from the Druid Hills Museum," she said. "Can I speak to Elaine, please?"

There was a pause by way of answer, a crackle as the phone was handed off, and a new voice, slick and prim, came on the line.

"This is Elaine Shotridge."

Deborah began listing her grievances. She had dealt with Shotridge before and knew that polite delicacy would get her nowhere. For a moment it was like nothing had happened. This was just another business call. Richard would be working in his office upstairs, waiting gleefully to hear about Deborah's run-in with Elaine Shotridge, the tyrant queen of Atlanta catering.

"In our defense," said Shotridge, "the fridge space was not what we had expected."

"Fridge space does not account for why your people didn't clean up after themselves or why we ran out of red wine."

"We'll be glad to make a deduction from the bill that takes those things into account," said Shotridge. "Say, ten percent?"

"Let's say fifteen," said Deborah. "I wasn't blown away by the canapé selection."

"Miss Miller," said Shotridge, cooling rapidly, "I have no objection to factoring actual errors into the invoice, but mere matters of taste don't justify an attempt at price gouging. I resent the implication that our canapés are anything but the finest, handmade . . ."

This was the point that she should tell the woman that Richard was dead and that haggling over a few plates of blue cheese tartlets did not rank very highly on her priority list, but she just couldn't. She was functioning adequately for the moment, something she wouldn't be able to do if she started talking about Richard's death. She fell back on the sarcasm she had tried to avoid.

"I resent paying thirty bucks a plate for ham-wrapped melon balls that taste like sheep's eyes in shoe leather," she said, "so let's leave the claims to haute cuisine out of this, shall we?"

"Mr. Dixon's Greek friends praised me personally for the cheese in my feta and spinach pastries," Shotridge huffed.

"Wait a minute," said Deborah, refocusing. "Mr. Dixon's Greek friends? What Greek friends?"

"The two gentlemen he was talking to during your presentation," she said slyly.

"How do you know they were Greek?"

"They looked Greek," said Shotridge. "They sounded Greek and—oh yes—Mr. Dixon said they were Greek."

Shotridge had apparently taken over in the sarcasm department.

"What else did they say?" said Deborah. There were, she was sure, no Greek names on the guest list.

"Nothing," said Shotridge. "They were talking among themselves—in Greek—and I was walking past with a tray, and Mr. Dixon asked if he could take some more for his Greek friends because they liked them so much. Best feta cheese they'd ever had, he said. They nodded and smiled and took three each. Then I left them."

"They said nothing else?"

"No," she said. "Twelve percent. That's my last offer."

"Done," said Deborah, hanging up.

It was time to talk to the police.

CHAPTER 18

Deborah crammed another finger sandwich into her mouth and rinsed it down with a sloppily poured glass of cranberry juice. She was turning to leave when Calvin Bowers came in.

"Calvin," she said, not thinking, just speaking on impulse. "Did you like Richard?"

He frowned as his mind adjusted to the unexpected question and her use of his first name.

"I never actually met him, of course, but yes, I think so," he said. "Why?"

"Would you find it hard to believe that he would put the museum ahead of his own personal fortune, even in front of his reputation?"

"Not for a second," he said.

Deborah nodded. It was the right answer. She felt herself warm to him a fraction.

"Me too," she said.

For the briefest of seconds she saw the entire Greek collection, with the mask as its centerpiece, laid out in gleaming cases for the world, all downstairs in the lobby, or in a purpose-built room at the end of a long dark corridor lined with educational text and images: the finest gathering of Greek antiquities outside Athens. This, surely, was the image Richard had been chasing.

Calvin, who was watching her as if he could see the pictures in her head, nodded once.

"I see," he said. "If there's anything I can do . . ."

She smiled and, exhaling, realized that she had been holding her breath.

"By the way," he added, "I'm missing some of Richard's legal correspondence. Was anything stored down here?"

"In the office," she said. "I keep most of the museum-specific stuff there. Are you looking for something in particular?"

He looked a little sheepish.

"As I said, Mr. Dixon was processing some paperwork that touched on both his personal holdings and his stake in the museum. They may have some bearing on his will. The police are going to want to see how his estate stands legally, in case it has an impact on issues of motive."

Deborah nodded, businesslike, careful to show that this gave her no consternation at all.

"That would be personal then," she said, "and should be in the residence files, not the museum's, unless it came very recently."

"How recently?"

"If it was addressed to the house, no more than a day or two," she said. "If it's personal but comes to the museum, it takes a few days. The residence has a different street number: one forty-three. The museum is one fifty-seven. They're the same building, so don't ask me why. But there are two mailboxes. I deal with the business stuff, sift out the junk and pass along what's left for his consideration. There usually isn't much, and unless I flag something, he gets to it when he gets to it. Is that a problem?"

He was still, and his eyes were narrow, but at her question he shrugged the mood off and grinned.

"I doubt it. I just hate having official papers going through the hands of anyone other than the addressee. It's the lawyer in me."

Detectives Cerniga and Keene were upstairs in the study next door to Richard's bedroom, where they were going over the guest list and the museum inventory. Deborah considered the staircase and then opted for one last precaution before she went up to speak to them.

The ladies' room beside the office was a single boxlike chamber reserved for museum staff. There was a toilet and a washbasin with liquid soap and one of those electronic hand dryers that always left her wiping her hands on her trousers. The light switch was hooked up to an extractor fan which hummed and whirred almost as loudly as the toilet flush. With that and the hand dryer going, it was amazing you could hear anything at all, so the sound of raised voices was a surprise.

It took Deborah a second to realize where it was coming from. There was a vent set in the wall above the toilet, not the extractor fan, the heating and air system. At first she barely paid attention, but then something in her head noted that the voices were male, were, in fact, the voices of the detectives with whom she was about to speak. Even over the hand dryer's automatic blowing she was sure of it.

The pipe must rout directly through the study upstairs.

She had never noticed it before, but then why would she? How often did anyone even speak aloud in that room? It was Richard's private sanctuary.

One of the voices was louder than the other. Cerniga? No, Keene.

You should ignore it, she thought. *You've done enough snooping.*

The hand dryer died with a descending whir, and the voices got clearer.

"That's what *you* say," Keene roared. "How the hell would I know?"

A muttered response from Cerniga, inaudible, and a single bark of laughter from Keene in reply. Then Cerniga was murmuring again, but Deborah couldn't catch the words.

On impulse, she reached out and snapped off the light switch. The room was plunged into total darkness and a new silence as the extractor fan stopped. Cerniga's voice, slightly metallic from the echo of the vent, coiled out softly like smoke.

"I've already told you," he said, cool but irritated. "If you have a problem with it, talk to your captain."

"I already did that," Keene shouted back, "and you know how far it got me."

"Then that's the end of it, isn't it?" said Cerniga.

"No, it damn well isn't," said Keene. "You transferred from Henry County? I called them this morning, and no one there has ever heard of you. No one."

Deborah suddenly felt cold and uncertain in the dark. The hair on her neck was prickling again as it had when she had smelled the cologne and pipe smoke at the door to her apartment.

"Your captain gave you the order to work with me," said Cerniga. His voice was steely now, as if he was restraining a great anger. "If you have a problem with it, you should take it up with him."

"Are you even a cop?" said Keene. "I saw the look on your face when I gave you those forms. You've never filled out anything like them before. I wanna see your badge."

And then someone was pulling on the bathroom door from outside, and Deborah heard no more.

CHAPTER 19

It was Tonya.

"I'm sorry," she said, not sounding so till she registered something in Deborah's ashen face. "I didn't see the light under the door so I assumed . . . Are you OK? You look like you've seen a ghost."

"It's OK," said Deborah. "I was just . . . I'm a little tired. It's been a rough couple of days. I think I'm going to . . ."

But she didn't know what she was going to do. She waved a hand vaguely and tried to smile, but the concern in Tonya's face said she wasn't pulling it off.

"You need something?"

"No, really."

"You want me to get the cops down . . . ?"

"*No*," said Deborah, more urgently than she had meant. "I mean . . . No. It's fine. I'll talk to you later."

And then she was walking away, down the hall, away from the staircase up to Richard's study, and down to the museum. Her pace quickened with her resolve, and by the time she was passing those ghastly specimens of Victorian taxidermy, she was almost running. She ducked into the museum office, opened the safe, and removed her passport. In two minutes she was in the lobby with the T. rex and the dragon-lady ship prow. In four she was in her car and driving away.

Her cell phone was switched off, and she left it like that.

She just needed to go home or at least back to her hotel. Get some sleep. Clear her head.

That won't change what you heard through the vent.

That was true enough, she thought as she pulled through the lights at Buford Highway and moved toward the interstate, but maybe what she had heard would somehow make sense if she could put a little distance between herself and the museum with its strange treasures. She just needed a little time to herself.

As she turned onto I-85 heading south toward midtown, she was startled by a squeal of tires on the road behind her. She checked her mirror in time to see a dark van tear through the signal at the top of the ramp and come pelting down after her.

Atlanta drivers, she thought. *Always ready to risk life and limb to get home five minutes early.*

She stayed in the right lane to give him room, and wondered where to go. She had instinctively begun to head home, moving away from the Holiday Inn, which was too close to the museum. Too close to Cerniga and Keene.

Maybe I'll just drive around for an hour. Or go and walk in Piedmont Park. Yes. Follow the route home, park on Juniper, and take a walk round the lake.

The idea gave her a sense of purpose, and she relaxed a fraction, slipping into her familiar mode as she let the flow of the traffic siphon off her anxiety. Her conscious mind, calmer now, returned to the conversation she had overheard in the bathroom. Could she have misheard? It was possible, she supposed, but she was prepared to bet she hadn't. Could it have been some kind of private joke? Less likely still. So Keene suspected that Cerniga—the man in charge of the investigation into Richard's death—was not actually a cop at all? How was that possible? What did it mean?

Coming around the Grady Curve she was still in the inside lane with a sheer concrete wall to her right, and the less conscious part of her brain which was focused on the driving interrupted her other thoughts with a nod toward a familiar sign: Right Lane Ends, 1500 Feet.

She checked her wing mirror and began to move left, swerving back sharply when she saw a truck, which had been nestling in her blind spot.

Pay attention!

She shrugged all other considerations off and gripped the steering wheel tighter.

The truck to her left was still there, apparently oblivious to the fact she had almost hit him. She sped up to ease past, but the truck (now that she got a look at it, it was actually a van) matched her speed.

Typical.

"Go ahead, then, you macho idiot," she muttered, slowing down to let him go. She didn't have enough road to argue the point, and the Atlanta traffic moved at unforgiving speeds. Without a hard shoulder and with only a concrete wall to her right, there was no room for error.

The van slowed with her, its front end keeping perfect pace with hers. Deborah turned to give the driver a steely glare, but the windows of the van were heavily tinted, and she couldn't see in.

Van?

Two things struck her in rapid succession. This was the same van which had burned rubber trying to stay up with her when she had first come onto the interstate. The driver to her left was not just some road-raging moron playing high-speed chicken.

Lane Ends 1000 Feet, said the sign overhead. Merge Left.

"I'm trying to," she said.

She turned on her signal and blew her horn. He didn't move. She didn't expect him to. He had followed her from the museum and had boxed her in on purpose. She accelerated to fifty, then sixty miles an hour. Ahead she could see the lane turn into a narrow wedge marked by orange cones which lined a dog-legged concrete wall that kicked into her path.

The van beside her accelerated and inched fractionally over the line into her lane. He was squeezing her in. To her right the dark mass of the wall swelled suddenly. She was running out of room. Through her mounting panic, Deborah glimpsed one thing with absolute certainty: if he didn't move and she hit the wall ahead at this speed, the collision would kill her.

Lane Ends 500 Feet.

She braked hard, so hard in fact that the rear of the Toyota slewed slightly, and part of her tail caught the cement apron beside her with a sudden bang, followed by a singing screech of metal. For a split second the van beside her seemed to pull ahead, but then it was braking too, slowing down to hem her in.

She was down to twenty-five miles an hour, but the wall ahead was looming large.

Fine, she thought, *I'll stop completely.*

But then what? What if he stops too? What if he gets out?

For the briefest instant she saw Richard's body lying there on the floor, so pale, so old. Whoever had done that to him had been without mercy.

She fixed her eyes on the concrete wall ahead and slammed the accelerator to the floor.

CHAPTER 20

It was an insane thing to do. It was, she thought as the solid gray mass hurtled toward her, reckless, suicidal.

It was also the last thing the van driver had expected, and by the time he realized what she was doing and gunned his engine to pen her in, she was ten yards ahead of him and sliding left as the wall came to meet her.

She clipped the corner in a juddering cascade of glass, but the car barely slowed, and she fishtailed out into the traffic in a chorus of honking horns and screeching brakes.

That was insane! You could have been killed.

"If I had stopped, I would have been."

That shut the other voice up. For the moment.

She settled into the middle lane, feeling her breathing re-turn to normal. As she began making apologetic waves with one hand and the drivers around her raged at her, she twisted her rearview mirror in time to see the black van hooking off the next exit ramp and out of sight.

She didn't go to the park. She came off the interstate long enough to stop by an ATM, where she drew out as much money as it would let her, then she doubled back and left her scraped and wounded car in the parking lot of The Temple, a reform synagogue she had once considered attending. She walked to the Arts Center MARTA station and concluded the journey on the light rail link which took her right into the terminal of Hartsfield-Jackson Atlanta International Airport.

Someone had broken into her apartment, had—worse—waited there for her. Someone had tried to run her off the road. Someone had killed Richard. Strangest and therefore most distressing of all was the knowledge that the people to whom she most wanted to turn—the police—could not be trusted in this case. She had to get away. Far away. Other than her purse (which was largely stuffed with museum correspondence she hadn't even got round to opening), she had no luggage but, not being especially attached to clothes, that didn't bother her. She would buy what she needed when she arrived.

But arrived *where*?

That, she hadn't decided, and the decision occupied her thoughts as she sat on the sparsely populated train's hard plastic seats which were, for reasons passing understanding, a bilious orange almost guaranteed to induce motion sickness.

She could go home to Brookline, to her mother and her sister, she supposed, knowing immediately that she would not. Her visits back to Massachusetts, as her mother was fond of pointing out, were few and far between and, perhaps as a result, they were stressful, difficult spells of negotiation and awkward circling, which was pretty much how things had been since her father died.

Hi, Mom, it's Debbie. Someone's trying to kill me. Mind if I stop by?

Boy, would that not work.

She got off the train and walked into the airport's south terminal and down through the bustling throngs to the Delta check-in desk. She was glad she hadn't called ahead, and had resolved to try to get her name deliberately misspelled on the ticket, something close enough that it would look like a typo, but wrong enough to delay any police hunt through the airline computers.

No! It's the police! You can trust them. Tell them about the van. You have to be able to trust them or . . .

Chaos is come again? Exactly.

She checked the monitors, then drifted toward a short line,

dominated by a harassed-looking family with vast suitcases spilling out of two carts. The woman at the desk, her hair rigidly coiffed, her eyes tired, was explaining something about electronic tickets. Deborah looked behind her. Only yards away were doors in the plate glass walls, doors to the loading and unloading zone, the road, the normal, everyday world . . .

Where homicidal drivers try to run you into solid concrete, or if you stop, corner you under some deserted underpass with a knife that leaves symmetrical bruises around the entry wound . . .

She turned suddenly and bumped squarely into a middle-aged man in an incongruous three-piece suit. He was sweating and, like almost all air travelers, looked anxious.

"Sorry," said Deborah.

The man, who looked more surprised than affronted, said nothing and, out of embarrassment as much as anything else, she turned back toward the desk.

Look for a policeman.

Who would hand her over to Cerniga? No. The only person who seemed to be on her side was a lawyer she had never even heard of two days ago.

"Can I help you?" said the woman, flashing her practiced smile.

The family trundled away, exchanging anxious words and studying their boarding cards as if they were written in code.

"Are there still seats available?" she said.

"For this flight?" said the woman. "Cutting it fine, aren't you?"

Deborah smiled weakly but said nothing. The woman consulted her screen.

"Yep," she said. "You'll have to get a move on. Security's been a bear. One-way or round-trip?"

"Round-trip," said Deborah, "but can I leave the return date open?"

"Sure," said the woman, tapping her keyboard. "There. How would you like to pay?"

She didn't want to use a credit card, but there seemed no option. Surely they wouldn't be looking just yet? She put her MasterCard on the counter as the woman checked the price.

"Let me see," she said. "One open round-trip to Athens, Greece . . ."

INTERLUDE

France, 1945

Edward Graves removed his white military policeman's helmet, pushed it under his duffel bag on the passenger side of the Opel truck's cab, and strode purposefully into the village post office. He had been a little concerned about this stage of the plan because he spoke no French, but it turned out that he didn't need any. He showed his carefully doctored military ID to the postmaster and waited while some old woman jabbered on—apparently appreciatively—about the liberation. He nodded and smiled, wishing she'd leave him alone.

"One package, monsieur," said the postmaster, holding it up triumphantly as if he had personally swum the damned thing across the Channel himself.

Graves took the package without a word and marched out, noting only its U.K. postmark until he was safely back in the truck. He opened it quickly, tearing the edge with his teeth when the tape wouldn't give. He had long, quick fingers, and they trembled slightly as they pulled out the letter and the wad of British pounds. He counted them quickly and then glanced at the note, which contained nothing more than a shipping address in London and the name of the sender: Randolph Fitz-Stephens. He balled it up and tossed it out of the window, then turned the keys and waited for the engine to catch.

Three hours later he was watching at the quayside as the transport ship *St. Lo* pulled away from Cherbourg harbor, loaded with demobbed soldiers and a cargo hold full of personal effects, French produce (mainly wine), and a few crates, their passage specifically paid by private citizens such as himself. It had taken the dockers no more than ten minutes to unload the box from the back of the Opel and move it into the hold, and he had stood by, trying not to watch too closely, trying not to look anxious in case it prompted the sailors to start nosing for valuables. You couldn't trust sailors any more than blacks.

In two weeks he would be following it back to the States, by which time Randolph Fitz-Stephens would have no way of finding him, even if he knew who he was looking for, which he didn't. Were all Brits this gullible? A few photographs of the goods had left the guy foaming at the mouth. Graves had initially thought he'd ask for ten thousand pounds up front, but when he'd got wind of the Brit's excitement, he had doubled it, and the guy hadn't batted an eyelid. Rich and dumb, thought Graves: just how he liked them. Still, he probably could have gotten more out of him, and that was a pity. It was funny though, to think of the guy sitting by the docks in Southampton or wherever the hell he had been supposed to send the box, waiting week after week for it to arrive, then writing anxious, polite letters to a man who didn't exist in some poky little French crap heap of a town!

It couldn't have gone better. He might still have to deal with questions about that Sherman commander if his buddies talked, but no one would take the likes of those tankers seriously, and there was nothing to link Edward Graves, sergeant in the military police, to the name on that shipping invoice. All things considered, it had turned out to be a pretty good summer. The war—a war he had always been ambivalent about at best—was over, and he had laid the ground for one hell of a future Stateside.

The war in Europe was indeed over, but only by a couple of weeks, and there were scattered pockets of German troops who either didn't know or had chosen to fight on regardless. One hundred twenty miles northwest of Cherbourg, a solitary, crippled U-boat, its conning tower and radio equipment damaged weeks ago by a stray mine, was one of the former.

U 146, a type VII B German submarine out of Saint-Nazaire, had been virtually adrift, with only minimal helm control, for almost two weeks, during which time heavy seas had torn off what remained of her radio antennae, making contact with the Fatherland or its agents impossible. The captain knew the war was going badly and that the forces of the Third Reich were probably in their death throes, but he was career military and loath to abandon his hobbled vessel if there was still work to be done. Unsure of which submarine pens were still in German hands, he had opted to wait one more day before trying to send an SOS. The rescuers, if they made it before the submarine sank utterly, would probably be Americans. He would wait until they were close enough to get the men out of the water before scuppering the ship.

It was the great misfortune of the transport vessel *St. Lo* that it hove into sight of the U-boat with three hours remaining on the clock and two torpedoes still in their tubes and ready to fire.

PART II

OVER THE WINE-DARK SEA . . .

Because the Kaddish voices the spirit of the imperishable in man, because it refuses to acknowledge death as triumphant, because it permits the withered blossom, fallen from the tree of mankind, to flower and develop again in the human heart, it possesses sanctifying power. To know that when you die there will remain those who, wherever they may be on this wide earth, whether they be poor or rich, will send this prayer after you, to know that they will cherish your memory as their dearest inheritance—what more satisfying or sanctifying knowledge can you ever hope for? And such is the knowledge bequeathed to us by the Kaddish.

—A meditation on the Kaddish from *The Sabbath and Festival Prayer Book* by the Rabbinical Assembly of America and the United Synagogue of America

CHAPTER 21

The decision to go to Greece had been automatic. That was where it had all started. That was where the treasure had originated. It was where Richard's mystery guests at the party had come from, where Richard had been telephoning in secret. It was a place for her to begin, since the police at home couldn't be trusted, and it was far away from the museum and whoever had been driving that van. Somehow, she was sure, these things were all connected. With each mile they flew, she got closer to their origins and farther from their murderous ends.

Deborah never slept on planes. They were too cramped for her sprawling, wiry frame, and she disliked the idea of sleeping among strangers. It was bad enough that they were sharing this metal tube in the sky with her; she had no intention of losing consciousness into the bargain. Yet today more than any other, she wished she could snore her way across the Atlantic, down through the Mediterranean, to the sparkling blue waters of the Aegean.

But she couldn't sleep, however much she tried to trick her body into thinking it was night. She was exhausted, and the prospect of flying for ten hours or more only to disembark into the dawn of an Athenian morning suddenly seemed beyond depressing. But her brain undercut all efforts to sleep with its own stream of subtext, the words flicking up on the inside of her eyes like contradictory subtitles to a foreign film. This was no time to relax, they said. She had to plan. She had no currency (*Was Greece still on drachma or had they switched to the euro?*), no hotel, no sense of why she had come on this fool's errand or what she intended to do now that she was committed to it. Sleep was out of the question.

She stared at the movie, ate whatever forgettable stuff was put in front of her, and spent half the "night" (the shades were down, and three-quarters of the cabin were snoozing like babies) walking up and down, knowing that those whose eyes strayed toward her found her gawky and irritating. She saw the man in the three-piece suit who she had bumped into in the check-in line, but he was reading and didn't seem to notice her.

Two hours went by. Then three. For a while she thought she might have actually dropped off, but when she checked her watch the hour had not advanced at all. She sat, and thought, and waited, and wondered what in the hell she was going to do when they touched down. Well, at least it would be safe.

The man in the three-piece suit laid down his book, then twisted at the waist as if stretching out muscles that were stiff from the long flight. As he did so he managed a nonchalant glance backward to where the tall American woman was peering round her companion to see the morning sun through the half-lowered blind. She hadn't recognized him, he was sure, and that was all to the good. He would have to stay close to her once they landed, but not too close. There was, after all, no particular rush, and timing would be everything.

CHAPTER 22

It was hot in Athens, a dry and dusty heat that clung unpleasantly to her skin as she started to sweat. Some of the dust felt gritty, like powdered concrete which, given her first look at the city as she headed in on the shuttle bus from the airport, was more than possible. During the Olympic coverage, Athens and its environs had seemed all ancient ruins and idyllic whitewashed villages on cliffs set against blue water and bluer sky. She hadn't been ready for these miles of faceless gray blocks, many either half finished or half demolished, it was hard to say which.

The man opposite her was at least fifty, slim and well muscled and too carefully groomed. He was gripping the arm of a girl half his age, a curvy beauty with a petulant face, who should have been his daughter except for the proprietary way he nuzzled her neck. Deborah looked away, but there was nowhere to look except out of the window into the smoggy, concrete-faced streets.

What the hell are you doing here?

"Looking for some answers, and keeping my head down," she muttered to herself. "Not necessarily in that order."

She had found a tourist information kiosk and bookshop in the airport and had bought *The Rough Guide to Greece,* discovering belatedly that it had been published in 1995 and its prices were all in drachmas. Greece was, it turned out, on the euro now. How much of the rest of the book was also out of date, she didn't know, and since she found it hard to summon more than a dull irritation, didn't much care. She selected one of the hotels—the Achilleus—which the guidebook listed in central Athens, and called it from the information kiosk, hoping the number was still current. It was. Her reservation completed, she had made her way out to the shuttle bus and the long, disheartening ride into Athens proper.

She got off at Syntagma Square, one of the lushest parts of the city she had yet glimpsed, thanks to the adjoining national gardens and the parliament building, then found her way onto Ermou and headed west. It took her a few moments to pick her way through the side streets, their names lettered in the unfamiliar but ultimately legible Greek script, and to the dim cool recesses of the Achilleus lobby. The girl at the desk was a version of the one on the bus, dark and beautiful, frank and a little bored. Deborah, who always found the effusive helpfulness of the staff in American hotels phony and a little alarming, liked her immediately.

She checked in under her own name. Atlanta, after all, seemed a very long way from this dim Old World building with its marble floors and its lustrous, take-it-or-leave-it desk clerk.

"You have no luggage?" said the girl.

"No," said Deborah, smiling uneasily as if this made her bizarre or suspect.

"OK," said the girl, who didn't care one way or the other. "Here is your key."

The room turned out to be pleasant enough, private, and possessing the same casual elegance she had seen downstairs. The rickety elevator and overly tight staircase had given her pause, but the hotel excelled in the things that mattered, and that was good enough. The bathroom was, again, all marble— real marble that sparkled slightly when you turned your head, not the simulated stuff you got in the States—and the drapes were long and heavy. Deborah closed them and lay in the dark on the firm mattress, listening to the heavy drone of the air-conditioning, until she fell asleep.

She dreamed of driving on I-85 through the heart of Atlanta. The road kept narrowing without warning, and great concrete walls loomed menacingly overhead, but nobody would give her an inch. She was baffled rather than afraid, which is sometimes the way of dreams, until she realized that every other driver was wearing a gold death mask.

When she woke the room was silent and dark enough that for a moment she was quite disoriented. She found her way to the bathroom, but was in it and removing the soap from its blue and white paper wrapper adorned with a stylized Parthenon before she remembered where she was.

Greece.

What had she been thinking? She went back into the bedroom and reached for the phone, but stopped herself.

No. There is no one to call.

She surveyed her meager belongings, showered, peered through the drapes into bright sunlight and the backs of buildings, and went down to the front desk. The dusky beauty with the casual, appraising eyes had been replaced by a man, sixtyish, who regarded her without expression as she asked him if he spoke English.

"Of course," he said, shrugging, and looking slightly put out, as if she had asked him if he could read.

"How can I get to the National Archaeological Museum?" she asked.

He produced a map from behind the counter, conveniently marked with the hotel.

"You are here," he said. "The museum is here. You could walk, but it's hot. A taxi is better."

There was no intonation to suggest a question, but he waited as if he had asked one. Deborah considered the map, looking for a scale that would indicate how far it was, without success.

"Taxi there, walk back," said the concierge. "It will be cooler."

He picked up the phone and waited. Deborah nodded, and he dialed.

* * *

In the back of the cab she watched the nondescript concrete of the city and the dense, honking traffic, and wondered vaguely if the police had started looking for her yet. It wouldn't take them long to track her passport and credit cards, but what they would be prepared to do about it, she had no idea. She might be a suspect in Richard's death, but surely not a strong one, not strong enough to start calling Interpol, if that was who they would have to call.

And if the police are really involved at all.

Keene was police. He didn't like her, but he was legit. Cerniga, who had seemed more reasonable, more balanced . . . Who could say what he was? Part of her wanted to call anyway, to let them know that she wasn't running away exactly . . . But that made no sense. Perhaps she could call Calvin Bowers.

And what would be the excuse for that call? said the wry voice in her head. *You think he'll be missing you? You think he's pining for that awkward, cerebral, and emotionally damaged woman he bumped into while she was being interrogated for a particularly nasty murder . . . ?*

Shut up.

Deborah paid the taxi driver and got out into the heat. The museum was set back from the road at the top of a flight of steps. She passed under the colonnaded portico, paid for her ticket, and wandered in, feeling the open simplicity of the place, its white, sparse, echoing rooms, the windows set just below the high, blank ceilings, the clutter of statuary with their tiny identification cards.

It was the antithesis of most American museums, stripped down, making no concessions to entertainment value or high-culture polish, and only a few to education. It was, somehow, very Greek: a great, compartmentalized box, where nothing was allowed to distract from exhibits which were displayed with a simplicity that verged on the austere. There was no hand-holding, no cheery colors or eye-catching diagrams. "If you want to know more," it seemed to say "—and you ought to—buy a book or, better still, go back to school." She liked it, especially the Cycladic collection with its oddly postmodern statuary recalling Moore and Picasso, artists who postdated them by four thousand years.

She considered the Mycenaean collection carefully, moving from case to case with a studied slowness that left her alone in the room as the tourists sped past. Nothing that she saw was quite the same as what Richard had concealed behind the bookcase in Atlanta. There were other collections elsewhere, of course, but this was the largest, the most complete, and Deborah was struck again by the idea that if Richard's hoard was composed of mere copies, they had been made by artists improvising on a theme, not quoting extant pieces. In other words, they were either real—which would be staggering—or they were forgeries—which would be devastating.

She stood the longest in front of the death masks, the "Agamemnon" mask (she was pleased to see the museum did not call it by that inaccurate title) in particular. She stared at it, trying to recall the image she had seen on the museum computer, increasingly sure that that also had been no copy.

The "Agamemnon" mask was a little larger than life size, gold, a little asymmetrical, though whether that was a design feature or a result of being under tons of earth and stone for three and a half millennia, she couldn't say. It had a slim nose, delicately arched eyebrows, a thin-lipped mouth, a broad mustache, and beard. The ears were party cut away from the hair and beard so that they stuck out like flaps. But it was the eyes that were the most striking. They were almond shaped, and there was no iris or pupil, but they were slit from end to end so that they looked simultaneously open and closed. They gave the slightly uncanny sense that the face was sleeping or was otherwise poised between life and death.

"You have been considering this for some time."

The voice at her elbow was deep and heavily accented. Deborah turned to find a man, late middle-aged, probably Greek, and with serious, bloodhound eyes, watching her with a look of reflective amusement.

"I'm sorry," said Deborah, looking hurriedly around to see if she was holding up a tour. This man was probably a guide. She had been so engrossed in her—*what? Her research? Her sightseeing? Her detective work?*—that she had been completely unaware of his presence. He could have been watching her for ages.

"Apologies are unnecessary," said the man, shrugging them off expressively so that his face aged ten years in the process. His black eyes shone like hard candy. "I am accustomed to people studying the mask, but few are so . . . *exhaustive,*" he said, selecting the word with care, "in their consideration. You are, perhaps, a student of archaeology?"

Deborah smiled.

"I am a museum curator," she said, "from America."

"Forgive me," he said. "I did not mean to suggest a lack of knowledge. My English is . . ."

He waggled his hand: *shaky, unreliable.*

"Not at all," said Deborah, her smile settling in now, becoming genuine. "Insofar as I'm an archaeologist it's only of the Americas. In matters Greek I really am a student."

"Good," he said, nodding. "So you did not come determined to prove our mask here a fake."

"No," she said. "I didn't. Do many people?"

He shrugged his Old World shrug again, aged briefly, and turned his palms up.

"From time to time," he said, and nodded, pleased with the phrase. "Most serious archaeologists do not take them seriously, of course, but there will always be a market for conspiracy, no?"

Deborah nodded, wondering uneasily if she had in fact come to test the mask's authenticity.

He took her silence as an opportunity to offer his hand.

"Dimitri Popadreus," he said.

"Deborah Miller," she said.

It was a reflex action, giving her name, and for a split second she wondered if she should have done so. But the thought—fruitless as it was—was driven away by another.

"Wait," she said, "Popadreus?"

She consulted her guidebook.

"You aren't . . . ?"

"The museum director," he said. "I am, yes."

He bowed fractionally.

"I like to walk among our visitors from time to time," he said, "to see what they give their attention to, which is—generally—not much, and what bores them, which is—generally—everything. Tourists are very strange creatures," he said, turning from her and watching the stray clusters of people. "I am often at a loss to understand what they have come for."

He shrugged again, and she smiled, pleased.

"Your museum displays New World pieces?"

New World, she thought. Europeans had been colonizing the Americas for five hundred years, and they still called it new. Well, she reflected, glancing around the vast, white-washed room with its Bronze Age treasures, time passed more slowly here, perhaps. To the museum director she simply said, "Mainly," and made a sort of deprecating gesture that would have been at home in the Greek's own repertoire. Hers was a small museum, she suggested, with no world-class exhibits.

Except, of course, for the secret Mycenaean hoard upstairs . . .

"So is it real?" she said, going for playful.

"Why would it not be?" he said, looking at it closely. "Stylistically it is different from the others, yes, but that proves nothing. If we had hundreds against which to compare it, that would be something, but we do not. We have six. Variations may be because of the individual maker's tastes or the face of the dead man or . . ."

He gave his patented shrug and blew out a breath of air for emphasis.

"There is no reason to doubt Schliemann's account of where and when he found it," he said. "But to make such a thing in the time he had and given the limited resources he had available? That is far more incredible, no?"

"I guess so," Deborah agreed. "Have you considered having the mask dated just to close the matter?"

"We have considered it," he said, "but it is not possible. Some methods are not suitable. The examination of—what do you call it: the dust from plants?"

"Pollen."

"Right. Pollen dating. To do such a thing when the piece was first unearthed may have been useful, though polished metal holds little pollen. Now, after a hundred years of handling, any finds would be meaningless."

"C-14?" Deborah prompted.

"Radiocarbon dating requires us to break a piece of the mask off," said the museum director. "That is, of course, unacceptable, particularly since there are no good reasons to expose the piece to such destructive testing, and because gold is not well-suited to such a test. If it was smelted with charcoal, and some of the carbon found its way into the metal, then perhaps . . . But the results are unlikely to be convincing. Why damage the piece if no one will be satisfied with what the tests produce?"

"What about helium dating?" said Deborah.

"We may in the future," he said, nodding gravely, "but we need to be surer of the method's accuracy, and that it would not damage the mask itself."

He gave her a shrewd look.

"For someone not interested in proving the mask a fraud you have many questions."

Deborah smiled.

"Professional curiosity," she said. "One curator to another."

"Good," he said, smiling. "Tell me about your museum."

She did, talking about the great stone tomahawk and the rest of the new Creek Indian exhibit and the touring Celtic pieces that would be coming soon, and he nodded and smiled and managed to look enthusiastic, even impressed. She was, of course, self-deprecating. How could she not be, having this particular conversation in front of this particular collection?

After a few minutes, driven by a growing embarrassment about her pride in the Druid Hills Museum, an embarrassment his polite encouragement could not dispel, she returned to the subject of the Mycenaean gold.

"But let me ask one more question," she said.

"Please."

"Assuming this mask is genuine, what chance do you think there is that Schliemann unearthed another mask like this, one that has never been shown to the public?"

Afterward, when she had a chance to think about it, she thought his face had been like a large isolated house facing the street, its windows lit from inside, promising lamp and firelight within. Then she asked her question, and the blinds came down. For a moment he just looked at her, or through her.

"That seems very unlikely," he said flatly. "I do not see how such a thing could happen." He checked his watch and smiled, but the smile was careful and did not reach those dark, hard-candy eyes. "Now, I'm sorry, but you will have to excuse me. I have work to attend to. Please," he said, a version of his former smile flicking back into place, "enjoy your visit. And," he added, turning back to her after he had already taken several steps away, "please come back. Mention your name at the door, and they will not charge you."

Deborah watched him walk away, wondering what she had said that had made him beat what was clearly a hasty and unsettled retreat.

CHAPTER 23

On the way back from the archaeological museum Deborah stopped at a roadside stall and bought a bright yellow backpack: her luggage for the present. She then sought out the least expensive looking boutique she could find, and filled it with clothes, wondering vaguely if this meant she intended to stay more than a day or two. She bought T-shirts, shorts, cotton underwear, a hopeful bathing suit which was probably too small, and a long, flowing white dress made of a soft, breathable fabric that might have been muslin. It was very Greek, or at least what she took in her uninformed way to be very Greek in the classical sense. Today all the women looked generically European, the young ones stylishly flamboyant, suggesting both panache and a curiously sexy naïveté, the old ones wrapped in incongruous shawls over shapeless black frocks that must have been like personal microwaves. She had hoped her purchases would make her blend in, but there seemed little chance of that. She'd seen no one, male or female, as tall as her, and felt interested, unapologetic eyes on her almost all the time.

On Themistokleous Deborah found a large bookstore with a good selection of guides and histories in English. She bought several archaeological and artistic studies, some of them books she had seen on Richard's shelves, and a two-volume paperback edition of Robert Graves's *Greek Myths*. The welter of classical subjects invoked by the museum had left her acutely conscious of how much of Homer, Aeschylus, and Euripides she had forgotten or never known. She had a lot of catching up to do.

By the time she had gotten back to her hotel, it was after

four, and she was tired and hungry. Part of her would have been happy to go straight to bed, but she had to eat something, and she felt the presence of her new books like an unwrapped Christmas present. She read for an hour and a half, then took the briefest of showers, donned some of her new clothes, and went back out into the dry, dusty heat, taking a couple of the books with her.

She walked down Ermou from Syntagma Square and into the Plaka, the newly gentrified Turkish core of the old city. Here Athens's cars and concrete were forgotten, and the cobbled streets were lined with neoclassical houses tiled with terra-cotta, the intersections broken by Orthodox churches, all minarets and domes and rustic brick, many of the buildings looking curiously half scale. From time to time she saw much older remains: the remnants of a Roman arch, a partial colonnade from Greece's classical period. The feel of the place soothed her as the museum (and her slightly cryptic conversation with its director) had not. This was the Athens she had half expected and secretly hoped for: a thriving and elegant city firmly engaged with its storied past.

This thought was passing through her head when she looked up and caught her first glimpse of the Acropolis itself and part of a building lined with columns (Doric or Ionic? At this distance, she couldn't tell), all brushed with golden light. It was breathtaking. She stopped where she was and gazed up at it, feeling the power of the place. She was looking, she gathered from her guidebook, at part of the Propylea, or the Temple of Athena Nike, not at the Parthenon itself, which was considerably larger. The elegant pale marble of the structure seemed to glow, flushing with an inner fire that made it separate, unearthly. From there, said the legends, Theseus's father had awaited news of his son who had gone to fight the minotaur in the labyrinth beneath the palace of Knossos on Crete. Theseus had promised to display his success by dressing his ships with white sails, but in his triumph, he forgot. When his ships sailed into the harbor, their sails still black, his father, assuming his son had been killed, threw himself off the precipice to his death.

Legends. The place positively breathed them. Maybe this was what drove people like Richard, or, for that matter, Schliemann himself. In a place like this, maybe the stories of gods and heroes at war really could be true.

She ate grilled lamb kebabs and a salad of tomatoes, black olives, and feta cheese, in an open-air taverna called The Five Brothers. She read—to deter the romantic interest of the waiters as much as anything else—watched the skinny, ubiquitous cats which snaked through the restaurant's chair legs, and resolved that whatever Greek had told Elaine Shotridge that the cheese in her feta filo pastries tasted as good as anything from his native land was being, at best, polite, at worst, sarcastic. This was the real deal, moist and salty and sharp, perfectly complemented by the slight sweetness of the minted, oil-drizzled tomatoes. She read enough to assure herself of her way up to the Acropolis, paid, and left.

She had less than an hour before the site would close. It wasn't enough time to see the place properly, and she would certainly have to come back for the Acropolis Museum, but it would be good to get a sense of everything in the soft light and cooler temperatures of the evening. Her guidebook suggested that there would be fewer tourists now as well, since most out sightseeing in the evening would be headed for Philopappus Hill, from which vantage they got the best view of the Parthenon as the sun went down.

From the Roman marketplace, Deborah walked briskly, ascending the long, slow ramp which climbed around and up the great rock on which the Parthenon was situated. She was pleased to note that most of the foot traffic was descending, tourists in bright colors and absurd hats, faces, legs, and arms all pink and sweaty. There were some boisterous teenagers with backpacks who seemed (and intended to seem, she thought) ready to climb another mountain, but most looked tired and a little subdued. What caused that? Exhaustion, disappointment, the unavoidable and maddening sense of one's own ignorance, each day's complement of much-vaunted sites blurring together in one great and baffling pile of meaningless stones? Even thinking as a historian and archaeologist, she couldn't blame them. She remembered somebody's remark about being a tourist: "What I see bores me and what I don't see worries me."

But she could not be so blasé. As she neared the summit she looked north to the rocky outcrop known as the Areopagus, or Hill of Mars. This was where Saint Paul had preached, where the Turks had laid siege to the Acropolis 500 years before the birth of Christ, where—in a still more ancient Athens before the world's first (and rudimentary) democracy—the council of nobles had sat. According to legend, Orestes was tried here for killing his mother, Clytemnestra, a son's vengeance for her murder of his father, King Agamemnon of Mycenae, son of Atreus.

The last word Richard wrote, perhaps: *Atreus*. It had led her to his body through the bookcase, but what had it meant to him when he wrote it down and punctuated it with those question marks?

She passed the temple of Athena Nike on her right and moved through the Propylea onto the top of the Acropolis. The Erechtheion with its caryatids —columns shaped like women—was on her left. Directly ahead was the Parthenon itself. She stood and looked at it, glad that she was alone.

It was no wonder this was one of the world's most recognizable structures, its great stepped platform and lines of Doric columns proclaiming a grandeur and mystery almost without parallel anywhere else. Of course, it hadn't always looked like this, and most visitors would be appalled by the gaudily painted and statue-cluttered eyesore which Pericles had ordered built after the battle of Marathon. It lost its roof in the seventeenth century during a siege when the temple—which the occupying Turks had been using as a powder magazine—blew up and burned solidly for two days. Its greatest threats these days, according to her guidebook, were the tourists, who climbed on it every time the security guards

turned their backs, and acid rain. The horrendous Athenian
smog was taking its toll on the ancient marble at an unprece-
dented rate . . .

"The structure maintains a perfect nine-to-four ratio in all
its dimensions," said a voice at her shoulder.

Deborah turned and found herself looking into the face of
a stranger who, though he was gazing raptly on the structure
in front of them, was apparently talking to her.

"Is that right?" she said.

And then she knew who he was, and her smile grew
warmer. He was dressed quite differently now, but he had
been in the airport in Atlanta. She had almost bumped into
him when she had considered not getting on the plane after
all, a plane, she now recalled, that he had also been on.

He nodded and glanced briefly at her, then back toward
the temple.

"I take it you found Richard's little collection," he said.
"Or rather, you found what wasn't there."

And then, like the tumblers of a lock clicking into place,
another part of her memory opened, and she knew another
aspect of him: his voice.

"*Did they take the body?*" he had said in that same
smooth, un-American accent.

Her mouth parted, and frozen, she began to back away,
borne on a wave of slow terror.

CHAPTER 24

He was a big man, broad in chest and shoulder, not trim or athletic, perhaps, but strong and solid. He was, perhaps, forty-five, maybe less. His eyes were fixed on her now.

"You stay away from me," she said. It had come out with a slight catch in her throat and sounded inept, girlish. She took another step backward, cleared her throat, and spat onto the fractured marble blocks at her feet. The gesture seemed to arrest him, but only for a moment. He took a step toward her, and she was dismayed to see how lightly he moved.

"Miss Miller," he said. "We need to talk."

"One more step, and I call the cops," she said, her voice lower this time, firmer.

"Because you have such faith in the police?" he said dryly.

The politeness in the way he said her name and the sardonic bitterness in that last knowing response made his accent more apparent. He was English, she thought, not Australian or South African, though a part of her brain—an old, animal part that saw the world in terms of predators and prey—had taken charge, and it said that such nuances were irrelevant. She had barely felt its presence before, but she trusted it now, and it tightened the muscles of her calves and flicked her eyes for the closest groups of tourists. It watched his careful, balanced movement as it recalled where the last security station had been.

There was no one close by. He had timed his approach perfectly, and the Acropolis, which had seemed pleasantly— even spiritually—quiet, now seemed lethally deserted.

"There's no reason to be afraid," he said, and his tone was more impatient than it was consoling.

"Right," she said. That prehistoric survival instinct had scanned the ground for a hunk of stone she could wield as a weapon, but the Greeks had learned that anything small enough to be picked up by a tourist would be. There was nothing she could shift without a forklift.

"I am on your side," said the man, taking a careful step toward her.

"I don't have a side," she said, defiant. She risked a half glance behind her. A tour group was emerging from the Propylea two hundred yards away, spilling into a semicircle around their guide, cameras at the ready. She inhaled, and another piece of the puzzle slid into place: he smelled of pipe smoke and cologne. Catching the aroma now with her adrenaline starting to pump reminded her she had smelled it on him in the airport but hadn't connected it to the intruder in her apartment.

"You have something I want," he said. "And I am prepared to negotiate to get it, which, considering my family has already paid for the item in question once before, seems more than reasonable."

"I don't know what you are talking about," she said.

"Come now," he said, smiling indulgently. "I'm prepared to pay a good deal more than any museum will offer."

Another lock tumbler clicked into place in Deborah's mind.

"You followed me today," she said.

"Of course." He shrugged. "As you intended."

He's crazy, she thought. *He has to be.*

"If I had anything that had once belonged to Richard, you don't think I would sell it to his killer?" she said, backing toward the tourists who were, it seemed, an almost infinite distance away.

His face clouded.

"So Richard is dead. I feared as much."

She stared at him.

"You know he is."

"I saw the police cars and I wondered . . . But I thought . . . I hoped . . ."

His voice dried up. For a second he looked smaller, but then his features narrowed and hardened.

"I see," he said. "No wonder you left the country." It was an accusation of a sort, but he didn't wait for her to respond. "But if you think that getting your hands bloody will increase the amount I am prepared to pay, you are sadly mistaken. In fact the only thing your murderous brutality means for sure is that you won't be able to sell it to any museum anywhere." He smiled unhappily. "I suggest you consider your terms quickly," he said, "or I shall be obliged to notify the police of your whereabouts."

Deborah felt light-headed at this bizarre change of tack.

He's trying to confuse you.

She felt a bitter, violent hatred for this man rising up in her, a hatred that made her want to pummel his face with her fists. But then perhaps that was what he was trying to do: knock her off balance, upset her.

"You think I don't know what you did?" she said, suppressing a wave of nausea, her voice level and little more than a whisper. "You killed Richard."

Again his eyes narrowed, as if he was trying to gauge something about her.

"You know I had no hand in that," he said. It wasn't a passionate denial, just a reasoned statement of something he thought she already knew. "Why would I have telephoned you?"

"You knew he was dead right after it happened."

"No," he said, his eyes momentarily dropping. "I did not. I knew there was to be a . . . *transaction* that night. I called and got no reply. So I called you."

"I know about the mask," she said. It was a stupid thing to say, but she wanted to keep him a little off balance till she could get to the tour group. "I'll take it from you and I'll turn you in."

"Take it from me?" he repeated, for a moment seemingly confused. "What are you talking about?"

"You have it," she said. "I know you do."

He shook his head and, in a gesture of parental exasperation, turned away. It was the moment she had been waiting for.

Deborah ran.

CHAPTER 25

She didn't look back. She watched the uneven ground, and she ran, head down, her long legs extended as far as they would go. She didn't stop until she had barreled right into the center of the startled tour group, stumbling to a halt and colliding with a heavyset man who reacted irritably in a language she did not know. She babbled her apologies and, when she had figured out which one was the guide, said, "I'm being chased by a man. Can someone call the police?"

Half a dozen cell phones appeared, and Deborah, framed by the backdrop of one of the world's most famed historical structures, was suddenly very glad to live in the twenty-first century, smog and all.

She told the police officer she eventually met overlooking the staggering remains of the ancient theaters at the foot of the Acropolis that the man had been following her, but that he had apparently fled as soon as she had joined the tourists. No, she didn't know who he was. Yes, she would like a ride back to her hotel. She did not say he had pursued her across the Atlantic.

"Will you stay there?" said the policeman, a young, laconic guy who seemed a little ill at ease with this storklike American female.

"I need to get my things," she said. "But then maybe . . ."

Maybe what? Run again?

"I can wait," he said, "take you to the airport, if you wish."

Run like you ran from Atlanta, like you ran from the Englishman just now? And run where? They're here too. They followed you . . .

"You know what," she said. "Forget it. I'm fine. The guy's gone. I can go back to my hotel by myself. I'm not done in Athens yet."

CHAPTER 26

She half expected him to be waiting for her at her hotel, the mystery man with the British accent. He had been tailing her before she had gotten on the plane, had seen her in the museum, and approached her quite deliberately on the Acropolis. That he didn't know where she was staying was inconceivable.

She kept her wits about her as she made her way through the quiet streets of the Plaka and round to the Achilleus, and she summoned her old defiance. It was the young policeman's knowing smile that had finally triggered it, but it had been lurking much earlier, before the stranger had spoken to her at the Parthenon, before she had left the States even, perhaps as early as when she had fled her own apartment.

Fled.

That was the word, and that was what she hated. Deborah Miller didn't back down. She fought her corner. She stood up for herself armed with a quick mind, a *tough* mind and, as Harvey Webster had pointed out in what now felt like the early fourteenth century, a smart mouth. She was not going to flee anymore.

The hotel lobby was cool and dark when she got back, a little refuge from the outside world. The old man was on duty again. He looked shrunken with fatigue but brightened as she approached, turning automatically to the cubbyholes behind him where the keys were stored. He didn't need to ask her room number.

Deborah thanked him and took the key, which was large and brass, like she thought keys in Athens should be.

"Any messages for me?" she said. "Calls? Inquiries of any kind?"

He frowned, sensing something beneath the question.

"No, miss," he said. "Is there a problem?"

"I don't think so," she said. "I'm going to make an international call from my room."

"You don't need to tell me in advance," he answered.

"I know," she said. "But I think I may be getting another call very soon. My phone will be occupied for a few minutes. You might tell him to call back at, say, ten o'clock."

If he was perplexed by all this extraneous information, he didn't show it.

"Very good, miss," he said with a shallow bow.

Her room was undisturbed and unoccupied. She wasn't surprised, but she was feeling cautious enough to check the place over systematically. All the way home she had been considering who would get that overseas call. The first person on the list was her mother, but the prospect of explaining the situation exhausted her. Unless the police had called them—a horrifying thought—her family didn't even know Richard was dead. She knew she couldn't have that conversation without emerging feeling somehow responsible. The thought saddened her because for the first time in years she really wanted to tell her mother everything—for both their sakes—as she might have done when she was ten.

Sorry Ma, she thought. *I'll tell you later. All of it. I promise.*

She fished in her wallet and dialed a number. It rang for a long time. Then a man grunted on the other end.

"Calvin?" she said.

"Yes, who the hell is this? It's four in the goddamned morning."

"It's Deborah Miller."

There was a pause, and all the sleepiness and irritation fell away from the lawyer's voice.

"Deborah? Where in God's name are you?"

"I'm in Greece, Calvin," she said smoothly, "and I'm staying here, at least for now."

"What is going on?"

"Are the police looking for me?"

"Yes. Not seriously," he said. "I'm not sure. One of them asked me if I knew where you were, but that's all."

"Which one?"

"Which one? What difference does it make?"

"It makes a difference. Which one?"

"Keene," he said. "I don't think he likes you much. He's going to be furious when he finds out you left the country."

"He probably already knows. Listen, Calvin, I know we don't know each other, but I need to trust someone, and you had some dealings with Richard so . . . that will have to do."

"Sure," he said, wide awake now. "What do you need?"

"Anything you can e-mail me on Schliemann, Mycenae, Agamemnon, or Atreus that you can find on Richard's computer."

"What? I can't get access to that."

"Sure you can. You represent his estate. Richard was killed for something in that secret collection upstairs, something they took with them."

"What is missing?"

She hesitated.

"I'm not sure, but I think it included a death mask," she said.

"Like the one you were looking at on the computer," he said.

"Maybe," she said. "Just trust me. I have your e-mail address on your card. I'll write to you, and you can send me anything you find."

She hesitated, then took one last plunge.

"I think there's a chance that the police won't catch whoever killed Richard, that they don't want to."

"What do you mean? You think the police are somehow . . . involved?"

"I don't know yet," she said. "But I'd check up on those detectives before you tell them anything."

He was quiet then, uncertain. She waited for his acceptance.

"OK," he said at last. "I will."

"And Calvin?"

"Yes?"

"If they start saying I killed Richard," she said, "don't believe them."

Suddenly she found there was more on her mind, on the tip of her tongue, but she hung up before he had a chance to respond, before she had a chance to say anything stupid.

Deborah watched the television for ten minutes, then washed quickly in the hard water (she always missed Atlanta water when she was away), and was almost ready for bed when the phone rang.

"Miss Miller," said the now familiar English voice. "I fear I gave you a surprise earlier."

"Never mind," she said. "But we'll need to begin this conversation on more equal footing."

"How do you mean?" he said.

"You know my name, but I don't know yours."

The hesitation was only fractional, and she thought she heard him sigh.

"Very well," he said. "I am Marcus Fitz-Stephens."

He might be lying, of course, but she didn't care. It seemed more important that she force the gesture.

"Let's start from the beginning, shall we?" she said.

CHAPTER 27

In the time she had spent walking back from the Acropolis alone that evening she had gone over the exchange she had had with the Englishman at the Acropolis, and very little of it had made any sense. Either he was a gifted actor and a master psychologist, or his sense of the facts did not square with hers at all. The idea that he might talk his way out of being Richard's murderer by pretending to think that she had done it was absurd, which meant that he was delusional. Unless it meant that he really believed she was the killer. And if he meant to kill her, why seek her out to chat with her in a public place? These questions led to another, which was stranger still: was it possible that he really did believe that she had the mask? It seemed likely. Why else would he believe— as he seemed to— that she had *wanted* him to follow her?

It was questions like these as much as her own bloody-mindedness that had made her come back to the hotel where she knew he would try to contact her, rather than hightailing it for the bus station or airport.

Now she sat very still, a pad of paper with the hotel's name stenciled across the top on the bed beside her, a ball-point poised in her hand, and the phone receiver pinned between cheek and shoulder.

"All right, Marcus," she said. "What's on your mind?"

"Apart from startling you," he said, "I fear I did you an injustice in suggesting that you killed your employer."

The formality of his speech rendered the content of the utterance even more absurd, but she managed to see past it.

"You're right; you did," said Deborah, cautious, waiting to see where this would all go.

"And I fear that you may genuinely believe I might have . . . done the deed."

"Right," she said. "You will now tell me you didn't."

"Indeed," he said.

She could hear nothing on the phone beyond his even, cultured voice, no crackle, no traffic roar or voices. He was probably sitting in a hotel room much like hers . . .

"But when you first called in Atlanta you asked if they had taken the body," she said. "Who was the *they,* and if you didn't know Richard was dead, why ask about his body?"

"The *they* were a pair of Greek businessmen with whom I believe Richard had set up a transaction. One which seems to have gone badly wrong."

"And the *body* reference?"

His silence was a good deal longer this time, so long in fact that she wondered if they had been cut off. When his voice came it seemed to wind out of the darkness like a thin coil of smoke, as if he had turned away from the phone for a moment and had begun speaking before he had the mouthpiece properly in place. She remembered the scent outside her apartment and imagined he was smoking his pipe. It was an odd image, one that made the voice somehow more contemplative, even likable.

That's just because Dad smoked a pipe.

"You never saw Richard's special collection till after he was dead, did you?" he said.

"Is that relevant?"

"It means you don't know what was taken," he said.

"I'm glad to hear that you don't assume I have it," she said.

"I think what we have here is a mutual leap of faith," he said. "A kind of working hypothesis. I assume you are innocent of the murder and the theft, and you assume I am innocent of the murder and the theft. For now."

"For now," she said.

"Then I assume you don't have what was removed from that remarkable little hoard behind the bookcase. And yes, I had seen it before, but not in person and not on the night he died."

"Go on," she said, giving no ground.

"What do you imagine was taken?"

"A death mask," she said. "Like the one in the National Archaeological Museum. The one Schliemann said belonged to Agamemnon."

"*Schliemann said,*" he repeated. "You don't believe that the grave shafts uncovered in Mycenae contained the remains of the man who led the Greeks against Troy?"

"No," she said.

"Richard did," he said.

"Richard was . . ." She caught herself in a smile and banished it. "A dreamer."

"Perhaps this is why he never showed you the treasures he had amassed, treasures which would put the rest of your museum to shame."

Deborah bridled but replied evenly, "You think the mask in Richard's collection came from the grave shafts dug by Schliemann in the 1890s?" she said.

"You know what message Schliemann telegraphed to a newspaper in Athens at the end of his dig in Mycenae? He wrote, 'I have gazed upon the face of Agamemnon.'"

"I read that that story was apocryphal," said Deborah. "He later denied sending it."

"Well, he would have, wouldn't he," said Marcus, unruffled, "since the mask he was referring to never made it to his governmental bosses in Athens."

"You think the mask in the museum is a fake?"

"No, it's real enough," he said. "It just isn't the mask Schliemann was talking about. There was another. It came from the richest tomb of the entire dig, one whose contents he kept secret."

"You think that Richard had the mask which Schliemann believed had covered the face of Agamemnon himself?" she said carefully, clarifying the outlandish claim by putting it into words. It was impossible, even if there really was a historical Agamemnon. But she had not yet heard Marcus's most extraordinary claim.

"Not just the mask," said the voice on the telephone. "You saw enough of the collection to see its richness, yes?"

"Yes," she said. She found that she was getting a little breathless, something like dread or excitement creeping over her as she listened, a thrill which drowned out her considerable doubts about this man and his story with the rush of possibility, however remote.

"And did it not strike you as strange that the killers should leave such things behind and take only a death mask?"

"Yes," she admitted, "though I thought the mask was more . . . distinctive, unique."

"And so it is," said Marcus. "But the mask was not simply removed from a case, was it?"

"No," she said, the breathlessness increasing as she felt some awful truth dancing just out of the reach of sight.

"They took the entire case," he said. "It was a large case which had to be wheeled out."

She remembered the oily tracks on the carpet, the separate electrical outlet in the floor, and that great rectangle of light. Whatever had been displayed in the center of that room had been much larger than a single mask. The hairs on her arms had risen. The room felt impossibly chilly.

"So what was it?" she forced herself to ask.

"I asked if they had taken the body," he said. "I didn't mean Richard's. I meant Agamemnon's."

CHAPTER 28

It was impossible. Of course it was. That the little room in Atlanta had contained the body of Agamemnon himself was absurd. That a nineteenth-century archaeologist could unearth and preserve an intact corpse which had been in the ground for three and a half thousand years was impossible.

She told him so, and then, because she was suddenly irritated that she had listened to such nonsense for so long and that Richard might just have believed it, she was suddenly overcome with a depression she had managed to hold off thus far. She demanded a number where she could call him back (no more would he dictate the terms of their conversations), which he gave her without hesitation.

After she had hung up, she sat there on the bed for over an hour, and a possibility occurred to her. She thought for a long moment, not wanting to pursue Marcus's absurd idea (*Agamemnon?*), and then picked up the phone and started dialing.

The Dekalb County police station took exactly three minutes to find a contact number for David Barrons, the man who had translated the Russian letter on the illegal immigrant called Voloshinov. She hung up and dialed it. Barrons answered on the second ring, sounding awake and alert.

Deborah left her own details vague, trying to sound official without actually claiming to be so, and got straight to it.

"The line in the letter which referred to the remains. Do you have a sense of what those remains could be?"

"The Russian word was *ostaki,* I think," he said, apparently sufficiently enthusiastic to talk about his subject that he didn't much care who she was or why she was interested. "It can mean any number of things. Old things. Leftovers. Things left behind."

"Antiquities?"

"I guess so. Wait a minute. I'll check my notes."

There was a pause, some background noise that might have been a television, and then he was back.

"*Ostaki,* I said, right? Wait, no, that's not it." He sounded less crestfallen than intrigued. "It's *ostanki.* I didn't notice the *n.* Huh."

"What?" said Deborah. There was note of puzzlement in his voice. "What does it mean?"

"Well, it's similar in sense," said the translator, "and it still means *remains,* but now it's a bit more specific."

"Go on," said Deborah, her voice slightly hushed.

"Now it means *human* remains. You know, like a corpse." Deborah closed her eyes.

"Weird," said Barrons.

"And the last word of that fragment," Deborah pressed on, feeling her heart rate increase. "You wrote *Mary.* Do you have any idea what it meant?"

"I'm not even sure those letters were right," he said. "The letter was badly torn and stained, and crudely written to begin with. It looked more like *MAGD,* but I didn't know what it meant, so I put *Mary.*"

"Could it be part of a longer name? A person . . . or a place?"

"I guess. I don't know."

Deborah thanked him for his time, hung up, and lay on her back, staring at the ceiling fan for ten minutes, then she checked that the door was barred and got back into bed. She was asleep in less than five minutes.

Deborah slept soundly for the first few hours but was wide awake before the sun came up. By the time the National Archaeological Museum opened at eight o'clock, she had been sitting on the steps for half an hour. Popadreus, the museum director, was already in his office, she was told, in response to her liberal dropping of his name, and could not be disturbed.

"He is expecting me," she said, which was probably true, if not in precisely the way the remark suggested.

"Wait here," said the faintly military woman who was apparently in charge of admissions. Deborah wasn't sure if her abruptness stemmed from her comfort level with English or from her personality, and she quietly kicked herself for not having mastered a few more Greek phrases. Confined to their own language, she supposed, it was impossible for tourists not to come off looking smug and condescending, content in their assumption that the world would accommodate their cluelessness. Touched with a pang of guilt, she smiled and said, *"Efharisto."* The military woman gave a kind of upward nod which acknowledged the word, but she did not return the smile.

A door opened, and Popadreus walked into the lobby, in conversation with a tall, sallow-skinned man in heavy glasses and a business suit. Some men never look comfortable in suits, she thought, but these men wore them like a second skin. They projected an easy, familiar authority. She turned to face them, and the museum director caught her eye and led the other man across the lobby toward her. Their meeting, it seemed, was at an end. Popadreus gave her a wry look as he approached.

"More examination of the exhibits," he said, "or of me?"

"Both," she said, smiling.

"Naturally." He turned to his formal-looking guest. "Miss Miller is an American museum curator," he said, "with an interest in our Mycenaean collection. This," he said to Deborah, "is Alexander Davos, the minister of culture and antiquities."

"I'm honored," said Deborah, caught a little off guard as she took and shook the proffered hand.

"I trust you are not looking to make any purchases from our friend here," said the minister, smiling his politician's smile. His voice was even, his English impeccable, the words clipped short so that his mouth barely opened. "We prefer to keep our treasures in their native land."

"Of course," said Deborah. "It is unfortunate that that has not always been possible."

There was a flicker of something in his eyes, and he half turned to Popadreus, but then the smile snapped back into place, and whatever he had considered saying was shut down.

"Indeed," he said. "Well, I must be going. Dimitri," he said to Popadreus, "you will . . ." He concluded the sentence in rapid Greek. The museum director nodded in assent and shook his hand.

"Miss Miller," said Davos. "A pleasure."

And then he was walking briskly back to the main doors. The Greek staff recognized him, and they smiled and bobbed their heads, part greeting, part rudimentary bow.

"I hope I didn't offend him," said Deborah.

"Of course not," said Popadreus. "You wanted to talk to me?"

"About Schliemann's excavations."

"Again," he said, tilting his head on one side, his expression laconic. "Naturally. Perhaps you would like to step into my office."

He walked away, and she followed. He walked quickly, and even with her long strides she had to jog a little to keep up.

His office was as spartan as the rest of the museum: bare plaster walls, old—but not antique—furniture, bookcases, a couple of certificates in Greek on yellowing paper, and a framed poster advertising an Egyptian exhibit.

The director took his place behind his desk and gestured her to a chair. The brusqueness which had ended their previous interview was gone. He was genial, even pleased to see her.

"Coffee?" he offered. "It's real. Not Nescafé."

She accepted out of politeness. She suspected that not everyone got coffee in this spare little kingdom. He picked up a phone and spoke quickly into it, then turned his attention back to Deborah.

"So," he said, "you have questions."

"The Mycenaean grave circles," she said, "did they contain bodies?"

"Of course," he said. "They were graves."

"I mean were any of the bodies still there when the shafts were excavated?"

"Ah," he said, shifting. "There were partial remains, yes."

"Really? After all that time?"

"Are you familiar with the peat bog men of northern Europe?"

"Of course," she said.

The bodies of which he spoke (the Lindow Man and the Tollund Man were the most famous) had been found in northern Britain and Scandinavia. They were Iron Age—roughly first century A.D.—and apparently the victims of ritual sacrifice. They had been murdered and dumped into the marshes, only to be rediscovered in the twentieth century in such an astonishing state of preservation that in one case the discovery of the body during construction work in Manchester led the local police to believe they had stumbled on a recent murder victim. Bones, teeth, muscle, skin, hair, stomach contents, the garrote around the neck, were all clearly apparent.

"But the peat bog men were preserved by the chemicals in the marsh, the oil that makes peat burn," she said. "It's a very rare soil composition. There's nothing like that this far south."

"True," he said, smiling, apparently pleased that she knew her stuff. "But such a condition can be created artificially if the body is intact at the point of discovery."

"But it wouldn't be."

"Do you know *Hamlet*, Miss Miller?" he said. "By Shakespeare."

"I've read it," she said, frowning. When she was an undergraduate, her old Shakespeare professor had been fond of saying that all things of consequence led back to Shakespeare.

"You remember what the grave digger says to Hamlet when he asks him how long the bodies stay intact in the ground?"

"I'm afraid not," she said.

"He says that a tanner's body lasts the longest because the skin has been so toughened that it will keep out water for a while, and *'water is a great corrupter of your whoreson dead body.'*"

"You mean that the arid conditions here desiccated the corpse?" she said, catching the idea and running with it.

"The first Egyptian burials placed the corpse directly into the hot sand of the desert," he said. "The dryness sapped the body of moisture, effectively mummifying it. Later Egyptian practices—the removal of the organs, the binding with chemically impregnated bandages and so on—were all attempts to re-create the natural desiccation of the desert sand for corpses which were being interred in tombs."

"But surely a body that was so dried out would crumble on contact with the air when it was unearthed."

"Yes," he said, "and most would be reduced to nothing more than very brittle bones."

Deborah felt some of her certainties about the ridiculousness of Marcus's story shift fractionally, as if the ground they were resting on had trembled or sunk.

"What did Schliemann find in Mycenae?" she said.

"In grave circle A he found the bones of several individuals, including children. The bones were carefully packed and transported off the site."

"To where?"

"Here," he said. "We do not display them, but they are stored in the museum vaults."

Deborah was temporarily stunned.

"Here?" she said.

"Yes," he said, smiling at her reaction. "It is no secret."

"But they were just bone fragments, right?" she said.

"All but one," he said. "One found close to the mask you were so interested in yesterday."

Deborah stared at him.

"There was . . . flesh?" she said.

"Apparently," said the director with his characteristic

shrug. "Schliemann said there was an intact corpse, facial features . . . everything. He summoned local embalmers to try to preserve the remains, attempting to create the kind of conditions which preserved the peat bog men, I assume. Alcohol of some sort, resin, perhaps."

"Was he successful?" said Deborah, still staring.

"Alas, no," said Popadreus. "The body disintegrated."

Deborah stood alone in front of the gold death masks and wondered. If the bodies had indeed been dried out by the arid Greek soil, was it possible that Schliemann, who had clearly tried to save an earlier corpse, had perfected his embalming technique on a body whose existence he never revealed to the Greek government? Was that why his (in)famous telegram about gazing on the face of Agamemnon had later been dismissed as apocrypha, because he had been referring to a corpse he had decided to keep from the authorities? But if so, why? The Schliemann she had read about was a self-promoter as well as a dreamer. Would he not have shouted this discovery from the rooftops?

But in Troy he had not turned over his findings to the Turks. After photographing the hoard he claimed had belonged to Priam, king of Troy, it had vanished. Did it ever reappear? Many of the books in Richard's bedroom had been fairly antiquated, and though some reproduced the image of Schliemann's wife Sophia adorned in the missing jewelry, none had offered any explanation as to what had happened to it. That did not mean there was no explanation to be had. She gazed at the still, gold faces of the masks and wondered: could Richard have acquired the intact body of a Mycenaean king after all?

CHAPTER 29

Deborah had an early dinner and a glass of retsina in another Plaka bar, and then retired to her hotel room to read Leo Deuel's *Memoirs of Heinrich Schliemann* to see if she could discover anything else about the disappearance of Priam's Treasure. She pulled her knees under her and read with a pencil in one hand, underscoring parts which struck her as especially significant. The story as Deuel presented it was roughly as follows.

It was 1873. The Turkish government was threatening to revoke Schliemann's digging permit because they suspected (rightly, as it turned out) that he had already smuggled objects he had discovered in Troy out of the country. He seemed to be digging at random, moving from area to area and level to level apparently unaware that much of what he was turning up came from different periods. He was convinced that the lowest level of the city was the Troy of Homer's *Iliad,* an obsession which blinded him to his workmen's destruction of other levels of the settlement and even to their theft of some of their finds.

Schliemann's strange and controversial triumph came one morning in June, only days before the excavation was to close. He was, he claimed, walking around the excavations when he glimpsed the shine of metal at the base of a wall. He began digging at the piece by himself, quickly revealing a store of gold, vases and drinking vessels, diadems, jewelry, and other treasures. It was, he said, Priam's hoard, a cache the value of whose gold alone totaled over a million French francs. The treasure was, he said, the ultimate proof of the truth of Homer's description of Troy's riches.

Questions were raised about his vague and contradictory account of where the hoard was found, but these quickly became irrelevant. With total disregard for his agreement with the Turks, for whom the hoard was a national treasure headed for the newly established Constantinople Museum, he immediately arranged to have them shipped to Athens, where he then lived. The goods were smuggled out in six baskets and a bag, their contents concealed even from his fellow excavators.

Seventeen years later, his Mycenaean excavations at a glorious end, Schliemann was once more digging in Troy. He found four priceless stone ax heads and repeated his earlier behavior, smuggling the artifacts out of Turkey and back to Greece, declaring them to customs officers to be Egyptian in order to facilitate their subsequent reexportation. He had no intention of leaving these treasures in Greece. They were earmarked for Berlin.

Berlin?

Deborah reread the relevant passage several times. Both caches, Priam's Treasure and the stone axes, were shipped to Germany where, on Schliemann's death in 1890, they were placed in a specially built wing of the Ethnographic Museum in Berlin, the archaeologist's dying gift to the nation of his birth. But that was not the end of their wanderings. Deuel's chapter closed with one last tantalizing piece of history.

At the end of World War Two, the Russian army penetrated Berlin, and in that city's ignominious fall, Schliemann's Trojan hoards vanished, presumably taken by pillaging Russian troops. Whether the treasures were scattered, stolen, or merely destroyed, the book could not say. At the time of printing, their whereabouts were unknown and presumably lost forever.

Russian?

She closed the book, lay back, and stared at the ceiling fan, seeing the dead face of Sergei Voloshinov, a soldier of the Soviet Union . . .

Could Schliemann have done in Mycenae what he did

twice in Troy, secretly exporting a store of undeclared findings more remarkable than those he reported? In Troy he had
shown himself to be convinced of his own proprietary rights
where his discoveries were concerned, and though he seemed
less anxious to keep his discoveries out of Greek hands than
he was out of Turkish hands (his attitudes to the "Oriental"
Turks were ethnocentric if not actually racist), it was surely
possible that he would deem only Germany worthy of his ultimate prize. But if that was so, why was there no record of it
in Berlin? Would he not have proudly displayed it with his
other discoveries for German museumgoers?

But Schliemann had been largely derided by the German
public, and he had felt that derision bitterly. He was, moreover, nothing if not eccentric. This man who had built himself
a classical mansion only a few blocks from where Deborah
now lay, who had named his servants after figures from
mythology, and had insisted that all messages for him were
delivered in classical Greek, this man was surely a law unto
himself. If such a man had discovered and preserved what he
fervently believed to be the body of Agamemnon himself in
all the finery of his burial, what might he not do to keep it to
himself? But if he *had* kept it secret, how had it found its way
into a secret room in a small museum in Atlanta, Georgia,
and what might link that secret trove to the dead Russian
who had been skulking around the museum parking lot only
days before?

The next morning, after a breakfast of cured ham, feta
cheese, and crusty bread with yogurt and honey, Deborah
found the young beauty at the check-in desk downstairs and
asked if there was somewhere she could get online.

"There is a cyber café on the corner of Ermou and Voulis,"
she said, mechanically producing the hotel's trusty map and
circling the intersection with a pen.

Deborah found the spot without difficulty, though it
looked more like a bar, and an empty one at that. She went

inside and looked around at the counter with its chrome stools, mirrored wall with advertisements for Mataxa brandy, and its silent pinball machine. She was considering leaving when a man's voice said, *"Neh?"*

He was twenty-five or so and round-faced, which was the only part of him she could see, since he seemed to be sticking out of the floor. There was a staircase which came up behind the bar.

"Parakalo," she said, *"mipos milateh anglika?"*

Do you speak English? It was pretty much the only Greek phrase she knew. If he answered anything but *yes,* she was screwed.

"Yes," he said, smiling a little uncertainly.

"I was looking for a computer," she said.

His smiled fluctuated.

"Internet?" she ventured, her fingers involuntarily tapping at an imaginary keyboard.

The smile returned, laced this time with a hint of triumph.

"Down there," he said, walking down the stairs, amending the remark to "Down *here*" as he walked.

At the foot of the stairs he gestured proudly to four computer terminals lined up on tables against the wall, each with its own chrome chair, pencil, and neat stack of notepaper.

She beamed her thanks, and he pointed out the Web browser on the screen, then the rates which were posted on a chart by the wall. Two euros for the first half hour, one euro per half hour thereafter. A bargain.

"Coffee, you like?" he asked.

"Yes, please," she said.

"Nescafé," he added, screwing up his face a little apologetically. "OK?"

"OK."

He left, and she navigated to the Hotmail home page. It took her under five minutes to set up a new (and free) e-mail address under the ludicrous name Ancientambassador2@ hotmail.com, at least one of those minutes being taken up largely with her bewilderment that Ancientambassador1@

hotmail.com was already taken. She checked Calvin's address from his card and typed:

Calvin,
    As promised, here is my new account. I don't imagine it can store much, so no pictures or other large files, please. Let me know all your news.
    All is fun and frivolity here. Miss you.
    D

That seemed sufficiently vague.

She wasn't sure why she had added that "Miss you" to the end, or whether it was supposed to make the message cryptically innocuous. But then she had added her initial, which would give the game away to anyone who read it anyway. Did she actually miss him? No, that was absurd. She didn't know him. She missed talking to someone who seemed to believe her, who seemed to be on her side, perhaps, but that was all.

And the fact that he is handsome and amiable and smart means nothing . . . ?

Nothing at all, she decided half seriously. If there were any other whisperings in her brain it was the dull hysteria of her predicament talking, and such voices should be quickly silenced.

She checked her watch and found she still had twenty minutes of her half hour to go, and the coffee had not yet arrived. She pulled up the Google search engine and typed in "Mycenae." The first link to come up took her directly to the Greek archaeological trust's official site. It gave some basic history, a few photographs, seasonal hours, and rates. She tried a different search, this time typing "Priam's Treasure" and pulling up the first hit she found as the moonfaced proprietor returned with her coffee.

"Efharisto," she said. "Thank you."

"Paracalo," he replied, setting the mug down. It looked thin and milky, but appetizing for all that. "You are English?" he said.

"American," she said.

The word could generate a broad range of reactions outside the U.S., and she watched him guardedly, but there was no need.

"Ah," he said, delightedly. "Elvis Presley!"

"Right," she said, smiling as his open smile took another five years off him.

"Blue swathe shoes," he said.

"Right," she said again. "Blue suede shoes."

So long as he doesn't sing, she thought.

But he didn't, indeed his attention was turned to the computer, a frankly interested look on his face. Two euros apparently did not buy privacy.

"Priam," he said, nodding approvingly. He pronounced the first syllable as in "*pre*natal."

"Yes," she said.

"Pusskin," he said.

"I'm sorry?" she said, politely.

"Pusskin," he said again, reaching for a scrap of paper and scribbling the word with the stub of pencil as he said it. "Museo Pusskin."

She frowned quizzically.

He leaned forward toward the keyboard.

"Please?" he said.

"Er . . . OK," she said, leaning out of the way as he tapped on the keyboard, clicked a link, and pulled up the official Web site of the Pushkin Museum in Moscow. She watched dumbfounded as he clicked two more links and pulled up an image of a display case containing what was, quite unmistakably, the collection of artifacts Schliemann had called "Priam's Treasure."

Deborah couldn't believe her eyes. The hoard recovered from Troy, smuggled out, and then vanished away was here in front of her on the screen, apparently sitting in a Moscow museum!

The text below stated in occasionally fractured English that the display contained the finds made by Heinrich Schliemann in Troy at the end of the nineteenth century, that they had been stored in the flak tower of the Berlin zoo until they had been "liberated" by Russian troops. For half a century the treasure was buried once again, this time in the Pushkin's vault, until the museum admitted their existence to the world in 1994 and put them on display, too late, apparently, to be detailed in any of Richard's books. Ownership of the treasure was disputed by Turkey, Greece, Germany, and other excavators. Legal disputes were ongoing . . .

"Very old," said the young man. "Very beautiful."

"Yes," said Deborah.

And if one batch of Schliemann's treasure could resurface after all these years, she thought, why not another? She resolved to call Marcus and arrange a meeting.

CHAPTER 30

Deborah had suggested that they meet in a restaurant, Marcus had picked which one—Kostoyiannis, an upscale place on Zaimi right behind the archaeological museum. He had not needed to consult a map or a guidebook.

Deborah had arrived deliberately early, walked past the place a couple of times, watched it from a department store window across the street, and finally gone in with ten minutes to spare. She was jumpy, and the fact that the restaurant seemed to be patronized almost exclusively by local Greeks made her still more uneasy, as if the overheard snatches of tourist English which she had been accustomed to in the Plaka had provided a kind of safety net, a sense of the familiar.

He arrived precisely on time, elegant in a pale gray suit. He spoke to the headwaiter in easy Greek before taking his seat. Deborah forced a smile.

"I'm glad you called," he said. "We have much to discuss."

On the phone she had told him that she still didn't trust him, still—in fact—suspected him of Richard's murder, but he had waved that aside, recognizing it for the bluster it was. In truth, she didn't know what to believe, but she thought this strange man's stranger tale of long-dead kings made rather more sense than she had wanted to admit. It was the only way she could make sense out of his obvious desire to talk to her.

"The *mezedhes* here are excellent," he said.

She nodded as if she knew what that meant and studied the menu, which was in Greek. She crawled through the list, unpacking the letters as best she could and, coming up with only four items she recognized, felt defeated and a little defensive.

"Would you like me to order for you?" he asked, reading her look.

"No, thank you," she said, wishing he would.

"You should try the rabbit stew," he suggested. "It's a house specialty."

She paused, considering a retort, then gave up.

"OK," she said. "Get that for me, then. And the . . ."

"Mezedhes?"

"Right," she said. "Some of those."

He ordered in Greek, selected a bottle of retsina that was less acrid with the tang of resin than most, then laid his pipe down on the table and looked at her.

"We've already said how little we trust each other, so perhaps we can shelve the posturing and er . . . *get right to it*, as you Americans say?"

"That would be good," she said, setting her glass down and meeting his eyes. "Let's assume we are both looking for the same things: Richard's killer and the treasure which was in his keeping, including"—she swallowed, hating to say it aloud—"the body of an ancient Mycenaean king."

"Agamemnon," said Marcus.

"Whatever," she said.

"Then can I add a 'whatever' to that searching for Richard's killer business?" he replied. "It wasn't me, I trust it wasn't you, and that is as far as I care about the matter. I didn't know Richard, and I assume there are proper authorities who will pursue and prosecute his killer."

"Maybe," said Deborah.

His brow furrowed, but he waited till the waiter had served their food before inquiring further.

"What do you mean?"

It wasn't where she had wanted to start, but it seemed relevant. She wasn't sure how far she could trust him, but this couldn't hurt her and, as a show of good faith on her part, it might get more out of him.

"There are two detectives investigating his murder, an

officer Keene and an officer Cerniga," she said. "Except that Cerniga isn't a policeman at all."

She recounted the overheard conversation, and Marcus's face clouded.

"Your turn," she said, sampling her stew. It was, as he had said, excellent.

"Very well," he said. "Then let me offer this. The *Atlanta Journal-Constitution* revealed that Richard's body was stabbed, but they said no more about the wounds. I believe that those wounds were made by a curiously long blade with a hilt that curved down on either side. Am I right?"

She remembered the blood-streaked body, the wounds that cut right through Richard's pale corpse so that the blood pooled beneath him. She remembered the strange weapon in the picture with the swastika on the handle, and felt an impulse to shudder.

"If you didn't kill him," she said, "how did you know?"

"Richard was not the first man to die like that," he said. "Ten years ago in a French village on the Brittany coast, another elderly gentleman perished of the same wounds."

"Ten years ago?" she said. "In France? Are you sure there's a connection?"

"Oh yes, I'm sure there's a connection. In fact, I know what the connection is."

She waited as he took a bite of his meal, then a sip of wine.

"The gentleman in question was a potential buyer of the ancient royal corpse which found its way to America and into Mr. Dixon's collection. He had been pursuing it for many years."

"You think Richard had something to do with it?" she asked, incredulous.

"No," he said. "In fact, I think the people who killed the first man also killed Mr. Dixon. They too had been pursuing Agamemnon's body and were prepared to stop at nothing to get hold of it. In France it slipped through their fingers, and it took them years to track it down again. I think that whoever was doing the selling went underground after the murder in France, but the killers were still waiting when the piece went back on the market earlier this year. They intercepted the transaction, and the rest, you know."

"Richard was selling it?" Deborah asked. That meant he had indeed kept it from her, that he wasn't looking to display it at their museum. Her heart sank.

Marcus nodded, first slowly, then faster. He put the end of his unlit pipe into his mouth and chewed on it.

"Yes," he said. "He had had it in his possession perhaps since it left France a decade ago. He decided to sell it. When he began to put out feelers for a buyer, the killers were finally able to track it down."

"Years later?" said Deborah. "Who would be prepared to kill—at least twice—and wait decades for a corpse? Why does it mean so much to them?"

"It is the most remarkable historical find ever made," he said simply and with something like vehemence.

"I think there are people who would dispute that," she said.

"Collectors are an odd breed," said Marcus. "Their desires border on obsession. And for a piece like this which is so rich in history as well as sheer market value, something so steeped in legend and power . . . Some men will do anything to get their hands on such a piece."

She believed him, and the look in his eyes troubled her.

"How did you know about it?" she said.

"I had been keeping my ear to the ground for some time," he said with a bleak smile. "The body, its grave goods, and the other Mycenaean pieces which were left behind had been known to me for many years. I also knew that when they went missing they were being transported with other less interesting or valuable artifacts. I knew that if I ever found one of them, I would be close to finding Agamemnon's body as well. One of those artifacts is quite distinctive, perhaps even unique. A couple of months ago that piece resurfaced and in the most unlikely of places. Do you know where it was?"

He smiled again, but it was that thin, dry smile that contained no real humor.

"How would I know where it is?" Deborah answered, irritated by his knowing manner. "I don't know *what* it is."

He set down his pipe, leaned across the table, and took both her hands. His fingers were strong and cold; she started to flinch away, but he held her tight and leaned across the table toward her, his face suddenly wolfish as the lips drew back from his teeth.

"It is," he said, "an early Renaissance Spanish ship prow, half woman, half snake. Does that sound familiar, Miss Miller?"

CHAPTER 31

Deborah tried to remember Richard's gleeful unveiling of the grotesque dragon-woman. It had been two or three months ago, no more. She had come in one morning and it had been there in all its hideous glory. It had been there for the first of the recent fund-raisers. Its picture had appeared in the paper . . .

"Yes," said Marcus, watching the realization dawning. "I don't know how long he had had it, or why he chose to reveal it then, but as soon as I saw it I knew what it was and what had been traveling with it. And if I knew, I'm pretty sure other people did too."

"Maybe that was the idea," said Deborah. "If he was hoping to sell the body and its treasures, maybe making that thing public was a way of announcing that he really had what he claimed to have."

Deborah considered her food, her appetite suddenly gone.

"What's the matter?" said Marcus.

"Nothing," she lied.

"You're wondering why he never told you about it," he said, "why he never bequeathed it to the museum."

"Yes," she said.

"I don't know," he said, gently now. "And I suppose we'll never know."

"Odd, isn't it," she said. "You work with someone for years, and you think you have a clear sense of who they are, what they want out of life, and then . . ."

She shrugged out of the confession and the mood.

"If only we knew more about who else might have linked the ship prow to Agamemnon," said Marcus.

"There is something," said Deborah, focusing. "You said you thought Richard met two Greek businessmen. There were two Greeks at the party the night he was killed. They weren't on the guest list, and I never saw them. They spent some time with him, apparently but . . ."

An idea dawned. It was probably a kind of desperate hope, but it made a sort of sense, a sense that reinforced the image of Richard as she had known him.

"Richard was obsessed with Greek legend," she said, "with the Trojan War. But he was also a man of principle. What if he bought the entire collection some time ago. He spent years researching it quietly, trying to discover whether or not it was genuine, intending to make it part of the museum collection. But," she went on, speaking quickly, barely seeing anything but the idea unfolding in her head, "part of him thinks that Agamemnon—because he really believes that the body he has is Agamemnon himself—shouldn't really be in the States at all. It belongs in Greece. Richard was like Schliemann in his passion to prove Homer right, but he wasn't like him when it came to the ethics of ownership. Either he was approached by—or he initiated contact with—some Greek antiquities organization, maybe even the Greek government. He told them what he had and revealed that ship prow to the world so that they would know he was telling the truth. Maybe he cut a deal: they get to take Agamemnon's body back to Greece, he gets to keep the rest of the collection and put it in the museum. At last, representatives of the Greek organization come to view the piece. Something goes wrong. Or they aren't the people he took them to be, or . . ."

She ran out of words and sat, suddenly deflated. It was all speculation, and it got them nowhere.

Marcus didn't think so. The light that had been in her eyes had transferred to his.

"If you're right," he said, "they'll try to bring it back to Greece. They won't dare risk flying it back, so they'll put it on a ship."

"Like Schliemann did," she said.

"We need to get to Corinth," said Marcus, putting down his knife and fork as if he intended to leave right away.

"Corinth? Why?"

"Do you have a guidebook or something?" he said. "A map?"

Deborah produced her *Rough Guide* and flicked to its map of Greece and the surrounding region.

"Look," he said, pointing to the map. "Athens is here. Any shipping from the United States will eventually dock in Piraeus here, but Piraeus is too major a port for convenient smuggling, and it requires ships to sail through the Mediterranean past Italy and then all the way round the Peloponnese and through the Cyclades. But they can save a good deal of time and inconvenience coming straight down the Gulf of Corinth and through the canal. They can off-load any dubious cargo as they go through Corinth, then proceed to Piraeus. If nothing else, using the canal saves them two, three hundred miles in open water.

"If we go to Corinth," he continued, "we can find out if there are vessels scheduled to arrive from the Unites States. Passage through the canal is no picnic, and it has to be scheduled in advance. We could track the cargo as it arrived. Intercept it, even."

"Surely that won't be for weeks," said Deborah.

"Then we'll be ready."

"I suppose we could alert the authorities before it arrived," she said.

"For all we know, it's *the authorities* who are bringing it in."

Deborah shook her head.

"I don't think the Greek government would stoop to theft and murder to recover a national treasure."

"Don't you?" he said. "The Greeks feel very strongly about their heritage. It's not surprising, given the way every colonial power in the region has filched from them over the centuries."

"Including the British," Deborah reminded him. "The

frieze on the Parthenon was the jewel of the Acropolis till Lord Elgin levered it off and packed it off to London."

It was now in the British Museum collection and showed no signs of being returned to Athens despite continual requests from the Greeks. Lord Elgin had claimed that had he left the frieze where it was, it would have been destroyed by the Turks, and he may have been right. Now, however, the British hold on the marbles—though it was occasionally buttressed by complaints about the inadequacy of Greek museums—was more about possession being nine-tenths of the law.

"Thank you for that lesson in cultural mores," snapped Marcus. "Can we get back to the subject, please."

Deborah smiled, surprised to find herself warming to him.

"You know," she said, "you've still not said how you got involved in this business. Yes, you're an art collector and historian; yes, you seem as obsessed with Mycenae and its legends as Richard was, but how did you know about the body or—for that matter—that it was traveling with that sixteenth-century Spanish gargoyle?"

She was still smiling, and her tone had been light, so she was surprised to see that his face looked distant.

"The old gentleman who was murdered in France told me everything," he said. "He had been in contact with an unscrupulous dealer decades earlier but had never laid eyes on the body itself."

"How did he come to tell you all about it?"

Marcus frowned.

"He was my father," he said.

CHAPTER 32

Deborah was at the little subterranean cyber café as soon as it opened. The moonfaced young man seemed pleased to see her, flattered perhaps. She was careful not to engage him in conversation, and she politely refused coffee; there was a look in his eyes she didn't want to encourage or exploit. He seemed a little disappointed but did not begrudge her her privacy.

There were two messages in her Hotmail box. One was an automated welcome from the e-mail service itself; the other was from Calvin. It was agonizingly brief.

"Computers impounded," it said. "They know where you are. Miss you too."

There was no attachment.

Deborah blew out a long sigh and wondered whether to respond. She didn't know what she wanted to tell him or why. She barely knew the man, after all. But Richard had trusted him, and that had to count for something. More to the point, perhaps, it was prudent to let someone know that she was planning to go to Corinth with a man who twenty-four hours ago she had believed to have been Richard's killer. Her eyes came back to the last sentence fragment: Miss you too. She felt a ripple of nonsensical pleasure, then shook it off.

Don't be so damned adolescent.

She took a breath and typed before she had chance to change her mind.

"Going to Corinth with Marcus. Weather's lovely. Wish you were here."

That was supposed to be a joke, she told herself, an attempt to lighten the strangeness of the situation. As soon as she had sent it she kicked herself, hating the tonal vacuity of e-mail.

Well, she thought. *It's too late now.* If Calvin thought she had the hots for him, there was nothing she could do about it from here, and it wouldn't do her any harm. Maybe he would be less likely to turn her exact whereabouts over to the police. That was a depressingly callous thought. And a disingenuous one. She wasn't merely flirting with him (albeit in a pathetically ambiguous and adolescent fashion) to keep him in her corner. She was doing it because a part of her wanted to, because she liked the way he smiled and the way he stretched out his legs in front of him when he sat down . . .

Let's not get carried away.

Deborah, after all, didn't do romance. She didn't do relationships (whatever the hell that odious word was supposed to mean), and she sure as hell didn't do love.

And you don't trust men, she reminded herself.

Even the cute ones?

Especially the cute ones.

He would probably run a mile the second he picked up any whiff of interest on her part anyway. Calvin Bowers probably had the pick of a lot of upwardly mobile and generally nubile lawyers and businesswomen all over Atlanta. A long-distance relationship *(odious word)* with a fugitive with legs like stilts probably wasn't high on his to-do list.

As she sat staring at the screen, a new message winked into existence. For a second she thought he was responding to her last mailing, and her heart seemed to catch in her throat as she sensed a sudden and crushing humiliation coming her way. But it was from an address she had never seen before, all numbers and random characters. Frowning, she opened it.

It contained seven words, none of which suggested who had sent it.

"Come home now. Your life in danger."

CHAPTER 33

How could she be in any more danger now than she had been in Atlanta? It made no sense. Come to think of it, it probably wasn't even intended for her. No one had her new address except Calvin, and he was unlikely to have shared it with anyone else.

Come home now. Your life in danger.

It was probably some hacker joke sent out to her and a million other random addresses—not a very funny joke, admittedly, even by hacker standards, but still . . . That was why it was so unspecific in its wording: it was trying to be relevant to everyone who got it. There were probably panicked office workers rushing for the door to get back to their houses even now. More likely, those office workers were probably sharing a good belly laugh at it like they did over the spurious requests for bank account numbers that were supposedly going to lead to millions of dollars being transferred from Africa. It just seemed more real to her because she was far away and knew nobody and had left home *(fled)* because of a murder . . . If there was any danger for her, it was back in Atlanta, not here.

Unless, of course, the killer has tracked you from Atlanta to Greece . . .

Nonsense.

Back at her hotel there was a phone message from Marcus. The timing was unfortunate. She had gotten used to the idea that Marcus was an ally, even a friend. The cryptic message on her computer, however rationally she could blame some faceless teenager with a talent for writing code, had upset that conviction a little or nudged it so that it wobbled precariously. In time it would settle again, but for now she didn't feel like talking much to Marcus.

"Deborah," he said, his voice brittle with urgency, "where the hell are you? I spoke to the shipping operator in Piraeus. There is only one American container ship due to pass through the Corinth Canal in the next month. It was due in three weeks but has apparently been delayed in New Orleans. I'm going to Corinth to see if I can find out why. Call me back."

Corinth was only a stone's throw from Mycenae. At some point, she knew, she would finish up there.

She made a reservation at a midprice place in Corinth through the Achilleus concierge, packed, and called Marcus, privately hoping he would be out. He was, but there was no automated messaging system, only an operator who asked if she wanted to leave a message. She didn't want to wait around for Marcus to get back. She was impatient to be doing something.

"Yes," she said into the phone. "Tell him it's Deborah and that I'm staying at the Ephira in Corinth. We can meet there."

There was one other thing to do before she left. She went down to the concierge with the grave eyes and asked if he could help.

"I want to make an international call, but I don't know the number I'm trying to reach," she told him, "only the name."

"We can try," he said. "Though it may be expensive."

"That's OK."

"What country?"

"Russia," she said. "Moscow. The woman's name is Alexandra Voloshinov."

If her answer surprised him, he didn't show it.

He made three calls, scribbling numbers between each and speaking in Greek. On the last call he switched to English and then handed her the phone. The voice on the other end was female and had an accent which Deborah took to be Russian.

"There are three Alexandra Voloshinovs living in Moscow. Would you like all three numbers?"

Deborah took them down, hung up, and dialed the first on the list.

The man who answered spoke no English and became irritated as she continued to repeat her inquiry. When he hung up on her, the concierge smiled sardonically and underlined the second number.

"Da," said a woman's voice.

"I'm sorry," said Deborah speaking painstakingly slowly, hating the fact that she could speak no Russian, feeling a sudden sense of futility and idiocy, "I'm trying to reach Alexandra Voloshinov, but I do not speak Russian. I am an American. I am calling about—"

"My father," she said, the tone blank. "I already know."

"I'm so sorry for your loss," said Deborah, meaning it and knowing how flat it sounded.

"Is there some news?" said the woman. She didn't sound hopeful or even curious.

"Not really," said Deborah, feeling traitorous. "I wanted to ask you a couple of questions."

The woman said nothing, so Deborah pressed on.

"Do you know of a person or place connected to your father beginning with the letters *MAGD*?"

The woman didn't hesitate.

"Magdeburg," she said. "In Germany. He lived there for a while."

"Right," said Deborah, encouraged.

Germany again?

"Your father worked for the Ministry of the Interior," she said, playing for time. She wasn't sure what else she wanted to know. "The MVD?"

There was a pause this time, and when the woman spoke, she sounded brusque.

"Yes. Many years ago."

"What did he do?"

"What did he do?" she repeated, quizzically.

"His job," said Deborah.

"I don't know," she said.

Deborah frowned, suddenly sure she was being dodged.

"I'm sorry, I don't understand," she said, trying to sound polite.

"The MVD," said the woman doggedly. "He worked there."

Deborah shifted tack.

"What is the MVD?"

"It does not exist anymore," said Alexandra Voloshinov. There was another long pause, then she added, apparently with great reluctance, "It was originally called the NKVD."

"The NKVD?" Deborah repeated.

The concierge, who had been listening with mild amusement, straightened up. His eyes looked suddenly wide and a little hunted. For a second Deborah thought he was going to take a step backward. She mouthed a *what?* at him, but he just stared. His usual laconic ease was gone. He looked unsettled, almost scared

"I'm sorry," said Deborah into the phone. "I don't know what that was."

"I do not wish to discuss these things, not on the tele phone," said the woman.

"Please," said Deborah. "What were they, the MVD, the NKVD?"

"Kind of police," said the woman, and Deborah could tell that even this inadequate answer was a great effort for her. "But secret. They watch, in foreign places and at home."

"Like *spies*?" said Deborah, still watching the frozen concierge with a swelling sense of unease that bordered on panic.

How could a few capital letters create such terror?

"NKVD became MVD," said the woman, enunciating carefully, a touch of dread clearly audible in her voice. "MVD became KGB."

And those letters, Deborah knew.

CHAPTER 34

The bus which idled at the Kiffisou 100 terminal, its windows heavily tinted, was, mercifully, air-conditioned, and was not the rickety affair stuffed half-full of goats and chickens that she had—rather condescendingly—feared. That said, it was still primarily a mode of transport used by locals, and she detected no other foreigners on board.

It took a good forty minutes to get out of the city, but then the landscape changed utterly, morphing into open, sandy hills liberally dotted with olive trees, the clear blue of the sea flashing along their left-hand side as they moved from Attica to the Peloponnese, home to the greatest density of ancient sites in Greece: Corinth, Mycenae, Bronze Age Tiryns, Epidaurus with its unparalleled theater, and Argos, after which the region—the Argolid—was named.

The bus stopped briefly at Elefsina, giving the passengers time to buy overpriced snacks and drinks, and Deborah took the opportunity to stretch her legs and breathe the clear, un-Athenian air. They proceeded on and eventually over the canal itself, crossing the great slice through the isthmus on a girder bridge which afforded the briefest dizzying view of the cliffs down to the channel carved in the rock where massive ferries moved like toy boats hundreds of yards below. The journey ended on another Ermou Street, walking distance from her hotel.

The Ephira was located on busy Ethnikis Andistasis, a few blocks from the seafront. It was small and clean and bright, more a center for business travelers than for tourists, the ancient city of Corinth having nothing like the appeal of Delphi, Epidaurus, or Mycenae for most foreigners already sated with the spectacular remnants of ancient Athens. Deborah entered through glass sliding doors and waited while the man she assumed to be the proprietor tore himself away from a game of backgammon and what looked like preternaturally strong black coffee in a glass. His rival, a younger man in shirtsleeves, monitored her directly from behind a potted palm.

The elder issued Deborah an electronic key card and then fished a slip of paper out of a numbered cubbyhole.

"Miss Miller?" he said, double-checking. "This came for you."

It was written in long, loopy pencil scrawl, probably his. It read, "Meet me at the Acrocorinth at five this afternoon. Marcus."

Deborah frowned. She didn't like being told what to do. Still, it saved her the bother of sitting around waiting for his call.

She napped for an hour, went out into the street, ate a spinach pie hot from a bakery oven, and walked down to the pebbly seashore. Everyone on the crowded beach was Greek. She gazed out over the blue water and watched the constant parade of oil tankers and container ships, funneled, she supposed, through the canal. At a little before four o'clock she hailed a cab and directed it to the Acrocorinth. She would be early, but that would give her time to browse around the remains before Marcus arrived.

Ancient Corinth (the modern city is properly named Kórinthos) was an extremely wealthy site in the days of classical Greece and, after a brief hiatus, became so again under Roman rule. It was perfectly situated to control trade between the Ionian and Aegean Seas, effectively serving as the gateway between the eastern and western Mediterranean. It had been home to an important temple to Apollo under the Greeks, and under Roman rule its religious importance was coupled with fabulous wealth, so that the city became synonymous with luxury, excess, and the "sins of the flesh." Corinth was home to a Roman shrine to Venus (whom the Greeks called Aphrodite) which was served by a thousand sacred prostitutes. Saint Paul had stayed there for over a year, and the city housed an important early Christian community, but the new Church struggled to keep its head above such hedonistic waters. Paul wouldn't stem the pagan culture of the city, leaving that task to a pair of powerful sixth-century earthquakes *(the wrath of God, no doubt)* which led Corinth to be abandoned.

Deborah was excited to see the city not despite its lack of great monuments but because of it. Apart from some of the temple to Apollo and the large expanse of the Roman forum, most of the city was under-excavated and overgrown, something which made the place sound oddly domestic and real in ways the marvels of Athens couldn't be. In America she was a cultural anthropologist as much as an archaeologist, a scholar of ancient peoples, not their architectural marvels. All this business about Schliemann and his gold had distracted her from what had always driven her interest in the past: the opportunity to glimpse something of the lives of the ordinary people who had populated it. In the books about Troy and Mycenae she was stuck in legends, in tales of epic deeds and treasure. Such things, however much they dazzled the eyes of the general public—and it was a sign of their dilettante status that the likes of Richard and Marcus were similarly dazzled—were ultimately fairly incidental to serious archaeologists. Even in Athens the sheer elegance of the remains had been overwhelming, and had made the past remote, heroic, and aestheticized in ways that actual human lives never really were. In the humbler remains of Corinth's bustling and prosperous city, she might catch the echo of long-absent feet about the business of everyday life.

The taxi made good time along the Skoutela road and was soon slowing into a side street suddenly lined with cafés and tourist shops, their windows stuffed with reproduction ceramics and plaster statuettes. Along the sidewalks, crammed with rickety postcard racks, coaches with heavily shaded windows were parked, their engines running. Gates in the wall beyond them gave glimpses into the white expanse of the forum, dotted with elaborately carved column capitals: Corinthian columns, Deborah remembered. The old Doric simplicity and Ionic elegance were supplanted under the Romans by more ornate "Corinthian" columns, their capitals carved with patterns derived from acanthus leaves. She craned her neck to see more, but then the cab was moving again, and she lost it all.

For a moment she thought he was just looking for a better parking space, but as the entrance to the site proper went by and they negotiated another narrow street without stopping, she tapped him on the shoulder.

"We're going to the old city, right?"

"Acrocorinth," he said.

She had assumed that the Acrocorinth was the highest part of the ancient city, a rock escarpment on which the temple of Apollo stood, perhaps.

"Is it not inside?" she said, peering back through the window to the ruined town whose perimeter wall was fast receding as the taxi left the tourist traffic behind and had the road to itself.

"No," said the driver, leaning out of the window and pointing. "Up there."

Distantly poised on an almost vertical mountain crag hundreds of yards above them, looking down on the ancient city and the surrounding country, and barely visible at this distance in the glare of the sun, were jagged walls and towers. He turned and gave her a grin as the car began to labor.

Deborah did not grin back. It was a long way up, and she sincerely doubted that the tourist coaches would go up there, even if they could make the climb. The road zigzagged its way up in a series of hairpin bends, and even so, the gradient seemed almost impossibly steep. She doubted there would be anyone else up there, especially under the hot afternoon sun. The taxi gears groaned and clanked, and for a second the engine seemed to have stalled altogether, but the driver revved it hard, and the car lurched forward, climbing slowly, inexorably toward the summit.

It took them almost fifteen minutes to make the climb, and in that time they passed no other vehicles. Below them there had been farmland and the ubiquitous olive groves, but as they got higher, the orderly fields fell quickly away and were replaced by rough, sandy ground and occasional low and twisted trees, some pines, some ancient olives. It was bitterly harsh country, arid, exposed, and difficult to reach even with twenty-first-century technology. Clearly, she was not going to a city like that below, but to a fortress.

As the first remnants of ramps and walls came into view, her guess was confirmed, but she was surprised to notice that these were not ancient Greek or Roman fortifications. They were brick and tile, Byzantine, perhaps, medieval. Some of them looked later still, remnants of Turkish occupation and war. It was the first such sign of those long hostilities which she had seen, and she wondered if the nationalistic fervor of the Greeks had effaced the rest. The taxi driver, unlike most of his compatriots which Deborah had encountered so far who were quick to volunteer insight and commentary on their nation's culture and history, said nothing.

At the top, the car pulled into a large, dusty, and completely deserted parking lot and stopped, though the driver did not shut off the engine. She paid him, dismissing the expensive and cowardly impulse to ask him to wait. She was still well in advance of her appointment and could be here a while. The thought was not encouraging, but she got out, managing a smile and an *"Efharisto."* The driver grinned widely, looked around the barren, heat-blasted mountaintop, and shrugged expressively: *It's your funeral, tourist.* As he drove away, he put one hand out of the window in a kind of wave and watched her in the rearview mirror until she was out of sight.

Deborah turned to the moldering gatehouse with its high arch and walked slowly, warily up the long ramp into the fortress, pausing in the deep shade before proceeding into the blistering heat of the lower ramparts. She had only one bottle of water with her, and her cell phone didn't work outside the U.S. Suddenly she wondered how she was going to get down and hoped to God that Marcus would bring a car with him.

She could already tell that the Acrocorinth wasn't just a fortress. Some of the partially ruined buildings looked like chapels, some like mosques, presumably built on top of each other over the centuries as this impressive vantage was taken and retaken in a continual struggle to control the region. There was no doubting the strategic importance of the place. Climbing up onto one of the great fortified walls, with its casements for cannon and musket positions, Deborah could see right out, not just to the ancient city she had glimpsed before nestled at the mountain's foot, but out over the Corinthian gulf. From higher up the tier of walls and towers, she would be able to see east across the Saronic Gulf toward Athens. She stared up at the rising lines of battlements, shielding her eyes from the sun as she began to climb the path which meandered up through the ruined buildings and fortifications. There was no one around, and the air was thick with the shrill hum of crickets and grasshoppers, the drone winding up and down in pitch like an electric current coursing the air on waves of heat.

The citadel, if that was what it was, was roughly concentric, with lines of inner defenses zigzagging crazily around the contours of the mountain. The top wasn't so much a peak as a ridgeline with a clearly defined square tower, almost a keep, looming over the parapeted stone walls and acres of unkempt, sun-scorched grass. She walked heavily, conscious of the sweat on her shoulders and face, feeling the weight of her shoes as she climbed. It was way too hot a day for this . . .

She paused midway up, where the path spread out into an open area with a flagged floor, and gazed back over the way she had come and the distant blue of the sea. And it was at that moment, as she put her hands on her hips and took a deep, steadying breath, that there was a sharp crack and a shower of stone fragments as the first bullet slammed into the masonry beside her.

CHAPTER 35

Deborah moved instinctively, but her first impulse was not so much to take cover as it was to wave and scream in fury. Unused to being shot at, she assumed this was some stupid mistake, that some idiot example of whatever the Greeks had in place of rednecks had decided to start blasting squirrels. She happened to be in the vicinity. The second shot thrummed past her ear and a piece of Byzantine tile on the wall at her back exploded.

What in the name of God . . . ?

Even as she dived low onto the stony ground, even as she rolled toward an irregular pile of rock which might once have been the corner of a building, even as she heard the third shot thud into the earth where she had been standing, part of her thought it was a mistake.

Disbelief and outrage coursed through her racing heart:

Nobody shoots at me!

Then there was a pause, a silent hole in the afternoon.

Keep still. Listen. Breathe.

She waited, feeling the ache in her wrist and the scrape on her forearm. She had landed badly when she had thrown herself to the ground. Her hair was in her eyes, and the sweat was pricking out all over her so that the dust clung. This was insane. Even if she was being targeted deliberately, it had to be some lunatic, right? Some nutcase taking potshots at tourists. The alternative—that they were targeting her, Deborah Miller, specifically—was too unsettling to consider right now. She pushed the thought aside and flexed her wrist. Sprained, probably.

Where is he?

It was the first useful thought she'd had. She glanced back to where she had walked in through the arch and up onto the rampart, seeing if she could find the bullet holes and deduce something of the shooter's trajectory. That was how to handle the situation, she thought, forcing some sort of rationality to battle the swelling tide of panic. Yes: logic, deduction, reason. These were the things she was good at. These were the things that would keep her alive . . .

God: will it come to that?

He must be up high, she thought. It was the obvious vantage point that would give him the most effective field of fire. She peered up, trying to figure out what kind of arc he might be able to cover from the tower on the ridge.

The fourth shot slammed into one of the rocks inches from her head, splitting it into three fragments, one of which caught her squarely in the temple. She hugged the earth, feeling the shock of impact and pain, wondering for a moment if the bullet had actually hit her. She put her hand up to the side of her head and felt the thick wetness of her own blood.

Not pumping out. Just superficial.

But it didn't feel superficial. For a second the world swam.

Concussion?

Perfect.

She forced herself to look around, moving only fractionally, trying not to draw his fire. She needed better cover.

His fire. She assumed it was a man. Marcus? Who else knew she was here? Unless it was a random act aimed at whomever showed up . . .

She wished she could believe that, but no, those bullets, she thought, had her name on them. The clichéd absurdity of the phrase was almost funny, a line from a film which she had strayed into by accident, one of those Hitchcock adventures like *North by Northwest* or *The 39 Steps.* She lay in the dust, feeling the sun on her skin and thinking these nonsense thoughts, and it was as if she was watching herself through a telescope or, more accurately, watching someone else, and hearing their thoughts like movie voice-over.

Got to get out of here.

If she lay here all day, the shooter could come down and find her. In fact, he probably wouldn't have to. She had little cover, and if he moved a few yards from where he was, he would probably be able to see her clearly. She wouldn't know he had shifted till he got her in his sights and opened fire. But he wouldn't expect *her* to move. He would—surely expect her to play the rabbit which freezes so the predator's fix on its movement will be lost: it was half strategy, half terror, that motionlessness. That was what he would expect of her. So she had to run.

God, no . . .

Yes. It was the only way. She rolled into a crouch, trying to keep any weight off her wrist, straight up and into a dash, like a sprinter out of the blocks. She had taken four long strides before the first shot rang out. She didn't see where it fell, so she guessed it was behind her. Two more strides and she came to a wall, waist high, ragged with age. She vaulted it as the next bullet roared past, gouging her thigh on a shard of stone so badly that she fell into the coarse grass on the other side, crying out and clutching at it. Two more bullets slammed into the stone in rapid succession, then silence fell once more.

How many shots had he fired? It didn't matter. She knew nothing about guns. Still, those last shots had seemed more like frustration. Maybe he had emptied the weapon deliberately and was now reloading while she was temporarily safe. Maybe this was the time to make another dash . . .

No! Stay here behind the wall. You're safe here.

But she knew her first thought was better. It was a gamble, but one that could get some crucial distance between herself and the gunman. She forced herself to stand up quickly and run another few yards down the path.

She had guessed right. She had covered twenty feet or more before the first shot came. It fell yards to her right, and she couldn't help grinning fiercely as she ran: rushed that one, didn't you? She kept going, cutting from side to side, leaping over the uneven ground without breaking stride, gazellelike. Her legs, her great long stilts, her stork pins, her gangly, flamingo, armpit-reaching, all-the-way-to-Canada legs paid in ten seconds for every insult and snide remark they had ever drawn in her direction. By the time the last shot came, she had got back down to the inner gatehouse. Unless her would-be assassin was moving very fast down the mountain, she was now invisible to him.

But there was only one road down to the town. If he was to drive down after her, he could make up for his poor marksmanship. There had been no cars in the parking lot when she had arrived, she was almost sure of it. So either he had walked up, or been dropped off as she had, or there was a vehicle concealed somewhere out there. She weighed her options as she moved through the cool arch of the gatehouse and down the stone ramp to the parking lot.

Wait. Get your breath back. Maybe help will come if you hide . . .

She saw no cars, nor anywhere one could be concealed. She thought furiously, made the decision, and began to run across the dusty lot and along the slow half spiral down the mountain. She would hug the mountainside so that he couldn't get a shot at her from above, and she would keep moving. It would take her a half hour to get to the town, maybe less if she could keep going, jittery, dehydrated, and exhausted as she already was. Her thigh was throbbing, but she hadn't developed a limp yet and could probably get halfway down before it started to really bother her. Maybe someone would pass, and she could hitch a ride . . .

Just so long as—whether on foot or in some hidden car— he wasn't faster than her. She picked up speed, letting the steady downward slope carry her forward till she was almost out of control, hurtling down the road with heavy, stumbling strides. Two minutes, and she was barely aware of the heat or the pain in her leg. Five minutes. Seven. Then she heard it: the distant mosquito whine of a small engine. There was a motorcycle coming down from the mountaintop.

CHAPTER 36

There was a good chance he hadn't been able to see her since she left the Acrocorinth, and that he could only guess how far down she had gotten. She looked around for a place to hide as the dentist-drill drone of the motorbike went up in pitch.

It's getting faster. Closer.

On the mountainside there was only a concrete drainage gully and then a steep retaining wall. On the other, lower side was the edge of an olive orchard, the trees gnarled and squat.

She dashed across the road, ran twenty yards into the orchard, and flung herself facedown like she was stealing second base. Before the dust had settled she could hear the bike rounding the curve. He may have seen her run for cover. He only had to look carefully into the thin shade provided by the trees, and he would see her still.

Safe, or out?

She kept very still. The pitch of the engine had dropped a tone. It was slowing down.

She wanted to run, but then he would see her for sure. She forced herself to lie motionless *(the rabbit tactics after all)*, not even turning her head to see him until he pulled within her field of vision.

The bike was little more than a moped: a couple of hundred cc's at most. It was an indeterminate dark color, patched with rust. The man on it looked slight, clad in boots, a stained T-shirt, and what might have been army fatigues. He wore a full helmet of a fluorescent green that seemed better suited to a bigger, faster bike. It completely covered his face.

Marcus?

She couldn't be sure, but she didn't think so. There was a

long, thin object wrapped into a ragged bundle slung across his back: a rifle.

Suddenly he turned, and the dark visor of the helmet looked right at her, so that she could almost feel the eyes behind it. She remembered the bright yellow of her backpack and wished she had lain on top of it. But then the bike revved a little more, and he moved on, picking up speed as he headed down.

Safe. For now.

Deborah lay where she was for a minute or more, listening to the slowing of her heart and breathing.

He would come back. He would go another quarter of a mile or so, realize he had missed her, and would start back up the mountain, hoping to catch her in the open. She considered her position. The olive grove would cover her for another thousand yards or more if she headed straight down toward the town instead of zigzagging with the road. It would take her longer, and she didn't know what kind of cover she would get thereafter, and she would have to cross the road as it cut back across the orchard, but for a while she would be safer.

She considered jettisoning her backpack altogether but opted instead for draping it with a suitably drab overshirt she had brought along for the cool of the evening, but not until after she had slipped a stone the size of a cantaloupe inside it. It wouldn't be much help if they continued playing big game hunter and distant prey, but if he got close to her, she would be glad of something she could use as a weapon. She felt its heft and the way it swung on the shoulder strap, and she thought she could probably kill him with a well-directed swipe. The thought sickened her a little. She swallowed a long draught of water and started moving swiftly, quietly down through the scented and dusty trees, listening all the time.

The olive trees were small and widely spaced, so they never offered anything like a canopy or the kind of dense shadow and limited sight lines of a real forest, so she kept moving, ready to throw herself back to the hard earth at the sound of the motorbike. If, on the other hand, he had decided to park it by the road and come after her on foot, he would almost certainly see her before she saw him.

Well, no point thinking about that.

After a few minutes of brisk descent, she saw a ridge of concrete running along the orchard floor twenty yards ahead and knew that this was where the road cut back across her path. If she started clambering down the retaining wall, she would be visible from any number of points, so she got down on her belly and crawled the last ten yards to the lip, till she could see beyond the trees, over the road ten feet below, and down into another grove of olive trees on the other side. She looked all around, all senses reaching out for signs of the bike or its rider.

Nothing.

She pulled herself forward, feeling the sudden leap of pain in both wrist and thigh, ignoring them both as she dropped first one leg, then the other, over the sharp edge of the retaining wall till she was hanging awkwardly from her fingertips. She dropped into the ditch, scraping her elbow and face against the stone as she tried to absorb the shock of the last few feet with her knees. It was an ungainly landing, but she hauled herself out of the gully and onto the road, head snapping from side to side in search of her pursuer.

Still nothing.

She loped across the hot asphalt, into the trees on the other side, and, stooping a little now as the throbbing in her thigh grew more insistent, began stumbling down to the next crossing.

It seemed he had gone. She was getting much lower now, closer to the outlying farm buildings behind the old town and the huddle of tourist shops and cafés that lined the road fronting the Roman ruins. Surely he wouldn't risk shooting at her down here? He had missed his chance and ridden off, to report back, perhaps to . . . whomever.

Again the trees thinned into a vista of sky. In the distance

she could see rooftops and the five monolithic columns of
the ancient temple to Apollo. She crawled the last yards as
before to the upper lip of the retaining wall, looked up and
down the road, and across to the final huddled ranks of ancient trees and freedom. She was about to throw one leg over
the rim when it occurred to her to make sure the drop was no
worse this time, and she peered over the edge.

Below her, nestled in the drainage ditch by the road, was a
motorcycle. Beside it, lying flat in the grass, his rifle trained
on the bend in the road which arced sharply back up the
mountain to the Acrocorinth, was a slight figure in a lime
green helmet.

CHAPTER 37

He was no more than ten feet away, and Deborah would have laid a good deal of money that it was only the helmet that had stopped him from hearing her approach. She drew back sharply—too sharply, in fact—and then lay in the dust and dry grass wondering if the movement had given her away.

Now what?

He seemed to have dug in, prepared a little quasi-military foxhole—as he probably had done on top of the Acrocorinth—waiting for her to come waltzing down the road blithe and stupid as only a tourist could be. The idea irritated her like something small and hard lodged in her gut.

If she dropped on him, she thought, she would have a momentary advantage. She could swing her rock-weighted backpack and . . . But the helmet rendered such an approach risky at best and, with something like relief, she discarded the option.

She could wait him out, though God alone knew how long that might take. The sun was on its way down, and though it wouldn't be properly dark for hours, she didn't like the idea of being caught out here after sunset, particularly if he was out here with her.

She could try to distract him, flicking stones into the underbrush like they did in the movies, so that she could slip past as he went to investigate. She frowned, rolling carefully onto her back and looking up through the tree limbs to the sky. That seemed a pretty surefire way of getting herself killed.

No. Ruling out the naïve impulse to just introduce herself and somehow talk her way out of this whole morbid farce, that left waiting. She didn't like it, because she wanted to be doing something constructive, but it seemed the safest plan: assuming she could keep quiet until he decided to abandon his watch.

Immediately she ran through more movie clichés, all of them better suited to comedy than tragedy, though all of them would probably leave her with a bullet in her head: an irresistible impulse to sneeze, the ringing of a cell phone, a sudden need to urinate. She forced herself to stop thinking of them and lie still, wondering at the strangeness of the situation, the two of them lying there silently, her head no more than a dozen feet from that of the man who was trying to kill her.

That was unavoidable now. Not only was it clear that she wasn't dealing with some gun-happy idiot who had mistaken her for a rabbit, it was clear that he was after her, specifically her, and—really for the first time—the question of *who* was gradually eclipsed by the question of *why*.

She had fled to Greece to avoid what had looked like danger at home. Lying here less than five yards from the motorcyclist, it was tough not to see the irony—as well as the stupidity—of that decision.

"Come home now. Your life in danger."

Those words didn't seem quite so arbitrary now . . .

She had been afraid that one of the policemen investigating Richard's death was not a cop at all, and she had been sure that someone was following her and with no official purpose in mind. That someone had turned out to be Marcus, with whom she had formed a kind of investigative pact, though that was also starting to look like a questionable decision. All idiocy aside, however, she couldn't see why anyone would want her dead. It wasn't (God knew) like she'd learned anything significant about Richard's death. Surely his killers would want her alive so that she could eventually incriminate herself completely with her absurd activities.

But what if it wasn't so much about what she knew as it was about what they *thought* she knew?

She had had momentary access to Richard's—now partial—secret collection, as she had to his computer files. Perhaps she had actually seen something significant but hadn't realized what it was, something that joined the dots from Agamemnon, to Schliemann, to Richard, to his killers. She stared at the extraordinary blue of the sky, listened to the buzz and thrum of the crickets, and wondered what she could have missed.

Then she heard movement below. The motorcyclist was stirring.

Oh God. This is it.

For a wild moment she thought that he had decided to climb the retaining wall to get a better view of the road. She shut her eyes and strained to hear but could make nothing of the sounds below. In a single movement she pulled herself into a crouch and pivoted as noiselessly as possible, unconsciously raising the heavy backpack to strike if a hand and then that helmet appeared over the concrete rim.

The sound of the motorbike being kicked into life was so loud in the anxious stillness that she almost cried out. A second later she had the presence of mind to throw herself back onto the ground so that he wouldn't see her as he pulled away.

She lay for twenty or thirty seconds, following the sound. He was going back up the mountain, hoping to catch her on her way down. She waited another ten seconds, peered over the road to check he was out of sight, and threw herself down. Her twisted ankle gave a shout of protest, but she went straight into a stumbling run, across the road and into what promised to be the last olive grove before she reached the farms below. She could still make out the thin whirring of the motorbike climbing the mountain. From above, she realized, he could turn and see her running through the trees. But maybe he wouldn't look back, and trying to run down the road itself would take too long and leave her even more exposed. Her great loping strides had become short and uneven, a stuttering limp that would get worse the longer she went. No: return to the road, and he would catch her for sure.

It took her no more than a minute to stumble through the next grove of trees. When she came to the steep drop down to the road she barely paused. The sound of the bike had receded to nothing, and she was sure she would have heard it had he returned. She glanced, dropped, and ran not across the road, but along it. Fifty yards ahead it turned sharply toward the north, down toward the ancient ruins and the bay. She put her head down and tried to block out the pain as she ran. Her shirt was drenched with sweat, and her face was streaming so that her eyes stung from the salt. She had made it round the corner when her ankle gave way, and she sprawled into the rain ditch.

This time she did cry out, but it was more frustration than fear or pain, as if that long-dormant reptilian instinct had decided that that was the more useful emotion. She was dragging herself to her feet when she heard—or imagined she heard—the high-pitched whine of a small engine. She paused for the briefest of moments to be sure. Yes. It was him. He was coming back down and, judging by the new shrillness in the sound, he was moving very fast. He had seen her.

Now it's a race.

She looked straight ahead. The road stretched forward, a long straight ribbon of hot, shimmering asphalt. In a hundred yards or so, there were buildings to the side, but they were set back in coarse meadows and looked like little more than garden sheds. Then there was the high fencing around the back edge of the ruins, some of whose columns were just visible through the trees which lined the site. Another two hundred yards beyond there, the road joined what passed for the main drag. Take the right fork, and she would be at the tourist shops and cafés in no more than a minute or two.

If she had minutes, which she doubted. She forced her legs to work as hard and fast as she could manage. The blood from her thigh had now trickled down to stain her sock, leaving what looked like a savage gash that ran almost the length of her leg. She shrugged the sight off. It wasn't as bad as it looked. Her sprained wrist was irrelevant. What counted now was dehydration, exhaustion, and the slight twist to her ankle which had halved her road speed.

Just a few more yards . . .

She passed the sheds, watched by a solitary goat, and did not pause. The motorbike sound had receded a little as the road had carried him over to the eastern side of the mountain, but now it was getting louder again. One more zag, and he'd be racing flat-out, straight down on top of her. She ran.

The ancient columns of Apollo's temple flickered into view, but the ruins seemed deserted, and with the thick wire fence between her and them, it probably wouldn't much matter if there was a busload of off-duty marines on the other side. The bike engine had faded again. Maybe he would reconsider, think she had gone back to hiding, and would double back. Deborah grimaced through the pain in her ankle, gritting her teeth like some ancient Roman biting down on a leather strap during surgery. She ran on, light-headed, starting to weave involuntarily across the blazing pavement.

The difference in sound when the bike rounded the corner behind her was like another gunshot. One moment it was a distant whirr, a cicada, perhaps, or a neighbor's lawnmower, then all barriers to the sound were gone, and he was roaring down the road behind her. She didn't turn. If he was poised to shoot her now, she could only hope he missed. She didn't have the energy to dodge.

She ran on, ten yards, fifteen yards, twenty-five yards, then she was at the junction and rounding the corner to the right in a sprawling, staggering trot. The ancient site's perimeter was walled here with high, regular stone blocks which cut the motorbike's engine noise in half. Ahead she could see tables and chairs spilling out onto the sidewalk, the sudden flare of color from a stand of postcards, a shop front, a bus . . . people.

She blundered into the first café she found, overturning a metal table as she fought her way through to the back where the kitchens were. The place was empty of customers, but a waiter was smoking by the bar. He turned as the table clattered to the ground, startled and irritated, then a middle-aged woman in black, hair pulled back in a bun, face lined and severe, was coming toward her looking focused and lethal.

Deborah's will to keep going finally left her, or she finally allowed herself to let it go. She lost her balance and crashed to the floor, scattering chairs and overturning another table. Bruised, bleeding, and tired beyond anything she had ever experienced, she felt completely unable to move.

"Sorry," she muttered, as the Greek woman's face loomed into view.

The woman barked something at the waiter, then turned back to Deborah, her hard face breaking into a look of concern.

"Ees OK," she said, as the waiter thrust a bottle of water into her hands.

The woman raised Deborah's head and pressed the lip of the bottle to her mouth.

She took a long swallow, feeling the delicious cold course through her like life.

Deborah still felt that she might pass out but lifted herself onto her elbows and forced herself to look back through the chaos of chairs and tables to the road. The motorcyclist was there, the green helmet's blank visor turned impassively toward her. Then the bike revved, a great nasal bellow, grating and metallic, and it surged down the street and out of sight.

CHAPTER 38

The Greek woman, who said her name was Sophia (like Schliemann's wife), gave Deborah food (grilled lamb and sliced cucumbers) and water, then swabbed her grazed and sliced skin, daubing her thigh with iodine from an ancient-looking brown bottle with a glass stopper. She spoke only a few words of English, mostly connected to her menu, but chatted continually in an amiable fashion that put Deborah strangely at ease.

Deborah told her she had been chased from the Acrocorinth by a man on a motorbike. She did not say she had been shot at and waved away Sophia's suggestion that they call the police. She wasn't sure why, though she sensed the Greek woman was slightly relieved, probably because she knew with what skepticism her story would be met. When Deborah stood up and said she was well enough to find a bus or taxi back to her hotel, Sophia said simply, "No," and started shouting at the waiter, till he left looking hard done by, returning in the driver's seat of an old Fiat.

Before gratefully, if a little apprehensively, clambering into the tiny, rusted vehicle, Deborah accepted first a bottle of water and a loaf of bread, then—and most surprisingly—an ungainly embrace. Sophia, who spoke a steady stream of unintelligible Greek, patted her cheek and gave a last smile of encouragement, and Deborah, squeezing her long, stiff, and wounded legs into the car, felt inexplicably close to tears for the first time since she had arrived in Greece.

Sophia made sure that the waiter knew how to get to the hotel, which was as well, since his English seemed to be confined to the names of British soccer players ("Beckham, Scholes,

Owen," he said, grinning and making enthusiastic but unspecific noises), and they drove off back to the modern city and the Ephira.

For reasons she couldn't see clearly, Deborah expected there to be some form of news waiting for her at the hotel: a note from Marcus, or the man himself sitting smoking his pipe in the lobby, word from Calvin in Atlanta, perhaps. That there was nothing at all, and no one to express interest or concern for her hellish afternoon, depressed her deeply. It would have been nice to hear from Calvin today.

Ah, a little self-pity to add to your adolescence. Great.

It wasn't just a sense of anticlimax though, she thought, as she thanked the waiter, who seemed happier to have been of assistance outside Sophia's rather overwhelming presence, and returned to her room. It was more than that.

She had fled Atlanta because she had felt in danger, but she was no safer here, and she had made no real progress toward discovering why Richard had died. She had found out nothing of real significance, and she was left, as she sat in the café and sipped her rapidly cooling coffee, with the sense that she had failed Richard as well as herself. It was also quite clear now that no discovery would make sense of Richard's death if by that she really meant that it would make it somehow comprehensible, acceptable.

She rubbed her swollen ankle and accepted the words that had suddenly appeared in her head: *It's time to go home.*

She checked the lock on the door, lay down naked under a single sheet, and slept till morning, waking only once with the shrill whine of a motorcycle arcing through her dreams.

The depression with which she had gone to bed stayed with her into the following morning, returning as she awoke, like a hangover or the memory of some terrible loss. She checked in with the concierge before breakfast, but there had been no messages for her. Marcus had, apparently, abandoned her. She went down to the cyber café and checked her e-mail, but there was nothing there either.

She changed the dressing on her thigh, wiping it clean to

see if it had become infected. So far it looked OK, but the cut was deep, and the area around it was pink and swollen. Maybe she could get some antiseptic lotion from the concierge. For some reason the thought sapped her of energy, and she sat back on the bed, staring out of the window over the tiled rooftops to the domed basilica and beyond to the sea.

It was indeed time to go home, to face the music, hand over the investigation to the people who knew how to do it, and concentrate on not finishing up in jail for hindering the investigation of the murder of her friend and mentor. There was only one thing to do before she went back to Athens and the airport: the one thing she had always known she would have to do before she left.

CHAPTER 39

"Mikines," barked the woman who had taken her ticket. She wore heavily tinted glasses and a curious wrap about her head, in multiple colors tending to mustard. "Mikines," she said again, pointing to the door of the bus as if Deborah was costing them valuable seconds.

Deborah disembarked and considered the dusty road junction with its ancient gas station, as the bus bellowed and surged off in a cloud of brown and bitter smoke. As it moved away, the driver leaned out and stabbed his finger in the direction of a long, straight side road.

Mikines (three syllables) was the modern village which had grown up on the ancient site of Mycenae, though the ancient citadel was another mile or two up the hill. Deborah hoisted the backpack and set off in the direction the driver had pointed, testing her ankle and her bandaged thigh before she got into stride. She winced, then decided that it was just stiff and that the discomfort could be walked off. It wouldn't go completely, and it might start getting worse if she walked on it too much, but this was her last day, and she was going to see the citadel that had started it all, even if she had to spend a week in convalescence back in Georgia. She would, after all, have nothing better to do.

The village fell quickly away, leaving only a handful of small hotels and restaurants with large, empty patios under dusty umbrellas. The tourist coaches would be along later, she thought, and these places would quickly fill with Brits, Germans, and Americans sheltering from the fierce afternoon sun, especially since the excavated sites were notoriously short of shade. After the cafés there was only pale farmland with twisted, dwarfish olive trees, dust gray in the strong light, and the tall, fragrant eucalyptuses which lined the road. Deborah had seen enough olive trees the day before to last her a good long while.

At the first sight of the citadel walls, red and gold and imposing, rising out of the dry mountains to the northeast, she paused to drink from her water bottle and just look at it for a moment. There were no columns or decoration that she could see from here. It was rugged and grand, a place of might and legend.

She paid the nominal entrance fee and climbed the paved ramp up to the celebrated lion gate. The walls of the fortress were made of immense, irregular stones, boulders really. Cyclopean, the poets had called them, alluding to the tradition that the citadel had been built by the great one-eyed giants. It was difficult not to be impressed, even awed, by the capacity of the city's ancient inhabitants to maneuver these vast hunks of rock, levering them into position, stacking and mortaring them without access to the most basic of modern construction equipment. Here, as with Stonehenge or the great pyramids, Deborah felt the extraordinary smugness of her twenty-first century self take a significant hit. People were so used to a sense of cultural evolution that they assumed their ancient forebears were their inferiors, but presented with achievements like this, it was hard to imagine what she would be able to contribute to the civilization that had once thrived here if she could step back in time into their midst. Without motor vehicles, computers, or access to electricity, what wonders of the modern world would she be able to demonstrate to these long-dead and forgotten people? Nothing. She could tell them a few principles of science or astronomy, perhaps, but nothing she could prove. They'd probably execute her for being a witch or, more likely and infinitely worse, ignore her, like she ignored the homeless man on Roswell Road who had told her the world was ending.

She passed under the relief of the two stone lions and wondered again if Richard had been right. Had a great army

bound for Troy once marched through this very portal, the
sun gleaming on their spear tips and their boar's tusk hel-
mets? Had Agamemnon himself ridden in a war chariot at the
head of the column, his horses pawing the ground she now
trod? Here, looking up at those massive walls and their
guardian lions, walking into the city and finally being presented with the circle of shaft graves which Schliemann had
sunk into the dry, red earth, it all seemed both perfectly possible and of no real consequence.

"What's Hecuba to him or he to Hecuba that he should
weep for her?" said Hamlet, after an actor had performed the
Trojan queen's grief at the murder of her husband, Priam.
The memory from some undergraduate literature class suddenly struck home, became clear. What did any of those ancient stories matter? What did it matter whether or not
Agamemnon had marched forth through the lion gate? What
did it matter if his body had been found and saved by Schliemann? None of it would bring Richard back. Suddenly, she
wanted to be gone, to be back in Atlanta, rebuilding her
life or—she hadn't thought of it before, but it suddenly
seemed a better scheme—starting over somewhere else.

But she had made it this far and would dutifully tour the
site like the thousands of others who wandered about here
every year, wondering exactly why they had come. The shaft
graves were now, of course, quite empty, and nothing in their
stony depths attested to the remarkable finds Schliemann had
uncovered there a little over a century earlier. Deborah
leaned over the side and peered down, wondering vaguely
what she had expected to see, some clue overlooked by a
hundred years of visitors?

She walked the ramparts, looking out over the dry hills,
watching the goats, and smelling the wild thyme that grew
there. She paced the floors of the palace at the highest point
of the acropolis and considered the small bath in which, said
the legends, Agamemnon had been murdered by his wife and
her lover, Aegisthus. She considered the domelike tombs at-
tributed to the two killers by Schliemann, and the remains of

the once impressive "house of columns" at the citadel's southwestern edge. It was all indistinct, even to her archaeologist's eye, a baffling jumble of low walls and thresholds and the dust of ages. Her guidebook said that you could walk the ramparts to the postern gate and that somewhere back there, there was a treacherous, lightless stairway down to a subterranean water cistern built in the twelfth century B.C. The passage ended, said the book, in a sudden and unannounced drop through seventy meters of space down to water whose depth was unknown. Though the idea of walking under the cool, dark earth was vaguely appealing, she was tired, and the passage sounded positively lethal. Suddenly the exhaustion, the fruitless searching, the stress of the previous few days seemed to descend upon her like the wings of a great, dark bird, and all she wanted was to be on her way home. She left the site and began walking back along the road toward the village feeling deflated and a little lost, uncertain what she had come for, certain she had not found it.

Back along the street which curved slowly around the mountain, lined for a while with the remains of Bronze Age merchants' houses, Deborah left the steadily filling parking lot and was heading back to the bus stop, feeling a little sorry for herself, when she noticed a cluster of people on the other side of the street. There was something else there, a site of some sort. She had only glanced at her guidebook and had replaced it in her backpack after a quick consideration of what it had to say about the citadel itself. She was hot and not looking forward to the walk back, so a part of her brain rebelled at the idea of going out of her way to do more vague and uninformed sightseeing, but then the little crowd cleared and she saw clean through to a steep-sided passage which tightened formally at a vast doorway into the mountainside, flanked with vast slabs of stone. Above it was a triangular blank, a dark *V* pointing skyward. This was familiar, this image of the high door with the imposing approach and the triangular blackness above. She had seen it before, long ago, in some undergraduate lecture perhaps.

And there was something else, something which had been nagging at her, a dim half memory which suddenly flickered into the light of her searching mind. She tore her eyes from the image of the door and wrestled out of her backpack, unzipping it and dragging out the guidebook so that her water bottle fell to the ground and rolled away.

She found the page she had been looking at. It was stained with sweat and sunblock, but her eye skipped over it in little more then a second. The lion gate. The walls. The tomb of Clytemnestra. The house with the pillars. She turned the page. More. Schliemann. Ancient history. She turned another page, one she hadn't looked at before, and there it was, the doorway into the mountain, and under it the phrase her memory had been tugging at for days: *"The Treasury of Atreus."*

CHAPTER 40

It was another of those fanciful names, no doubt, she thought as she crossed the street, and had more to do with nerds raised on ancient myths than it did with archaeology. More to the point, it could have nothing to do with Richard, nothing she would be able to glean from examining the place now, at any rate. But her pace increased as she walked down the great stone-sided passageway to the dark and empty doorway, forcing herself to return to the guidebook as she walked in case it said something—anything—that might be useful.

It was a tomb, said the guide, but a tholos or chamber tomb, unlike the shaft graves inside the city walls. It was sometimes called (and she couldn't help swallowing hard at the reappearance of the name) the tomb of Agamemnon.

More nerd myth stuff, she told herself. *It's strictly for the tourists. Nothing more. Assuming every find in the area has something to do with Agamemnon is like the way people who claim to have had past lives are always attached to someone famous: Cleopatra's waiting woman or Marie Antoinette's gardener . . . Tourist stuff*.

Yes, but still . . . The place had a kind of power, whatever you called it. She glanced up at the doorway which now loomed black and cool ahead. It was forty or fifty feet high. A king's final resting place, perhaps. She went back to her book. The tholos was roughly contemporaneous with that called the tomb of Clytemnestra, Agamemnon's murderous wife, and, since it dated from about thirteen centuries before Christ, matched approximately the date ascribed by archaeologists to the destruction of Troy.

So maybe Agamemnon had been buried here after all.

It was called the Treasury of Atreus because of folk tradition which linked the tomb to the ancient royal house of Mycenae, combined with Schliemann's frankly bizarre fixation that that royal house had stored its gold and precious artifacts outside the city walls. Recent scholarship dismissed the idea that the structure Schliemann had excavated was anything but a tomb and said that it was this and not the older grave shafts inside the city that squared with the sacking of Troy. If Atreus and his son Agamemnon had ever really lived, this—and not the grave shafts in which Schliemann had found the death masks and grave goods—might have been their last resting place.

Almost breathless, Deborah entered the darkness of the tomb.

It was vast, perhaps a couple of hundred feet across, and circular. The roof, which was only dimly visible, was domed, giving rise to another name for the style of tomb: a beehive. There was a hollow in one side, but the chamber was otherwise empty. Deborah sat on the floor in the center and waited for her eyes to get accustomed to the dark as the last of a tourist party wandered out, shielding their eyes.

There was, she had to admit, little to see, and she felt the disappointment settling on her skin again like the cool tomb air. From inside there was only the roof, that dark alcove in the side where the bodies had probably been interred, and the main entrance now bright with sunlight. The lintel above the massive doorway must weigh tons, she thought, but the weight of the masonry above was incalculable. No wonder they left that triangular space over it. Originally it would have been filled with a thin stone panel, carved on the outside, designed to look solid while sparing the lintel any further weight. It was all very impressive but told her nothing relevant to her life and Richard's death.

Another dead end.

She smiled mirthlessly at her bleak and all-too-accurate pun and then closed her eyes and put her chin in her hands. She had been sitting in the cool, dark silence of the place for almost a minute before she realized that she was not alone. She turned toward the sound of movement and saw someone coming toward her.

"I knew you'd come here eventually," said a voice.

She knew that voice, but for a moment, even after she thought she had given it a name, she stood staring mute into the darkness.

It can't be.

But then she saw the pistol pointing toward her and everything else went out of her mind.

CHAPTER 41

"Tonya?" said Deborah. "What are you doing here?" Then, as the gun raised a fraction and aimed at her throat, she added, "Get that thing away from me."

"Don't talk to me like I'm the maid," said Tonya in a hushed voice.

But you are the maid, Deborah wanted to say. *You are!* Instead she said simply, "I don't understand. Why are you here? I don't—"

"Then shut up and listen," she said. "In a minute or so the next busload of tourists will arrive, and I want to be quite sure you aren't going to do anything dumb, OK?"

"OK," said Deborah, all thought of Atreus and Agamemnon forgotten, her focus on the black eye of the automatic.

"Let's begin with some ground rules," said Tonya. "Take one step closer, and I'll shoot you where you stand."

Deborah, who had been absently moving toward the other woman, became quite still.

"Second," said Tonya, "try to talk to anyone else around here and I'll—"

"Shoot me where I stand?" said Deborah. She was being arch, even amused, though it was taking a tremendous effort. She forced her eyes away from the gun and onto Tonya's. "No you won't. Have you noticed the size of the black population of Greece, Tonya? They'd pick you up in minutes."

It was the wrong thing to say.

"Probably so," said Tonya, even colder now. "I really don't care."

She said it with no dramatic flourish but with such finality that Deborah took a step back, immediately convinced that she was telling the truth. Deborah also felt that drawing attention to her blackness had somehow made the other woman even more determined and for reasons that went beyond the usual unarticulated wariness they felt toward each other. Dimly and with no sense of how it could possibly be true, Deborah felt that Tonya's presence here and the reason for the gun in her hand had something to do with race.

Race?

"I came here to take back what was never yours," said Tonya. "Or, failing that, to kill you. I really don't mind which, and I expect to do both. If I die or get thrown into some Greek prison as a result, that's fine by me."

She spoke with a resignation that came from a long and bitter anger. It was chilling to hear, and Deborah, who knew that there was no point protesting the absurdity of it and that Tonya had no love of weakness, just asked, "Why?"

The black woman smirked slightly, one of those *as-if-you-don't-know* smirks that wasn't even slightly amused, was—in fact—wounded, embarrassed, even sad.

"Why?" she repeated.

"Yes," said Deborah. "If I'm going to get shot, I think I should know why. It's only fair."

"For the father I never knew," she said.

Deborah stared at her.

"Sound fair to you now?" said Tonya, raising the pistol a fraction.

CHAPTER 42

"Richard was your father?" Deborah said. "How is that possible?"

"It isn't, you stupid bitch," said Tonya. "Don't play dumb with me, or I swear to God—"

"You'll shoot me where I stand," said Deborah. It was neither a question nor a joke. She could see the barely suppressed fury in the other woman's eyes, and she knew she would do it.

"That's right," said Tonya.

"Are you working with Marcus?"

"Who the hell is Marcus?"

"Cerniga, then."

"Cerniga?" Tonya repeated. "The cop?"

"He's not a cop," said Deborah. "Not according to Keene." There was a long silence, but it was too dark to read Tonya's face properly. When she spoke, she sounded uncertain.

"I'm not working for anybody."

"You're not a maid, that's for damned sure," said Deborah.

She should be afraid, she thought vaguely. She had no reason to believe that this woman wouldn't kill her. In fact she thought Tonya was more than capable of killing her, that the other woman was actually looking for an excuse to do so. She didn't know why, and the reference to Tonya's father made no sense at all, but there was no question that the woman she had considered a maid hated her, and that the wrong choice of words would make her tighten her finger on the trigger and blow a hole in her heart, regardless of how many bystanders there were to see it.

That said, Deborah was tired of being scared. *"If it be now,"* said Hamlet in her head, *"it is not to come. The readiness is all."* She wasn't sure she was ready to die, but she sure as hell wasn't ready to beg for life.

"You got that right," said Tonya. "I'm no maid."

Deborah was sure she had heard the hint of a smile in her voice.

"Then what?"

"It doesn't matter," she said. "As far as you are concerned, I'm just someone here to dig up the truth. You should be able to relate, right, *archaeologist*?"

She said it like it was a mild slur.

"The truth about what?"

"Richard's secret stash behind the bookcase."

Deborah went quiet. She didn't feel like going over all this again.

"Other than the issue of your shooting me," she said, "why should I?"

"The shooting-you thing isn't enough?" said Tonya. She sounded unsure, taken aback.

"I got shot at yesterday," said Deborah with a grim smile, as if a repetition of the event would merely bore her. "Why don't we go outside? I can't talk to you in the dark."

Tonya turned to the entrance. There were people coming, and a guide's voice could be heard proclaiming half-truths over their heads.

"OK," she said. "But stay close till we get to the car."

"You hired a car?" said Deborah. "How resourceful of you. I've been relying on buses and cabs. And you got a gun through customs. That must have taken some cleverness as well."

"You wanna shut up and walk?" said Tonya.

Deborah shrugged and made for the great rectangle of light slowly.

She didn't feel the nonchalance she was performing: not all of it, anyway. But her earlier depression had not wholly left her, and what she felt had more to do with curiosity than it did with fear. Her earlier apathy had somehow freed her of everything but a distant interest in how things would turn out, and how they came to involve Tonya in the first place. No more than that.

She walked out into the sunshine, squeezing past the throng of tourists who were channeling into the tomb itself. Tonya took a couple of quick steps to catch up and gestured significantly with the small purse in which her right hand was concealed, to show that she still had the gun trained on her. Deborah smiled with careless understanding, and Tonya's determined frown flickered with discomfort.

I don't care, said the voice in her head. *You wanna shoot me? Knock yourself out.*

They walked to the parking lot without speaking, and Tonya shepherded her to a small red Renault, telling her to get into the passenger side. Deborah did so, convinced that the middle-aged black woman was improvising, that she had never done anything like this before, and that she was far from clear about what was going to happen next. But the steady rage in her eyes hadn't gone away, and Deborah knew she was a long way from being out of danger.

It was an inferno inside the car, and it smelled of melting plastic. Tonya turned on the engine and wound the windows down.

"No AC," she said, almost apologetically.

"OK," said Deborah. If this was an abduction, it was a very strange one.

"I'm going to drive us into the village," said Tonya, "and we're going to talk."

"OK," said Deborah. "Can we get a drink? I'm pretty thirsty."

Tonya gave her a quick look, and for a second Deborah was sure she was going to sputter, *"I ask the questions,"* or something equally absurd, but then she just nodded and turned her gaze back to the road.

"When did you first see Richard's collection?" said Deborah.

"The night he died, while you were hiding in the bathroom or whatever."

"But you knew it was there," said Deborah, remembering the sight of Tonya's sneakers from under the bed.

"Kind of," said Tonya. "I knew something was there, and I knew it was what I was looking for."

"What does that mean?"

"It means I didn't know *what* I was looking for, but I knew I was looking for *something,*" said Tonya, snapping back, "OK?"

Deborah said nothing. They had left the ancient citadel behind them and were now passing the obligatory restaurants and gift shops that lined the road up to the remains. The car kept moving all the way to the end. At the junction where the bus stop was, it turned left, into the village proper, and stopped at a less ostentatious café.

"Get out," said Tonya.

Deborah did so and, following Tonya's lead, took a seat at one of only three tables outside. The place looked deserted. Deborah peered up and down the street. There was only one tourist-oriented store, a vast shop front boasting The Finest Antique Reproductions in Greece! which probably got most of its business from coaches whose guides worked on commission from the store. Few other tourists would ever stray into the village itself.

For a long moment, the two women looked at each other in silence, both trying to gauge which way the conversation would go. Then the waiter was there. Deborah ordered water and ouzo, swilling it around the ice cubes when it arrived till it turned milky.

"What the hell is that?" said Tonya.

Deborah pushed it across the table to her. Tonya, who had taken her hand off the gun in her purse, regarded it suspiciously, sniffed it, and sipped.

"Licorice?" she said, startled. "Like absinthe."

"But rougher," said Deborah.

"Does it make you crazy like absinthe?" said Tonya, fighting her corner. "Or blind?"

"I don't think so."

"Chalk one up for New Orleans," said Tonya, a tinge of pleasure putting a little swagger into the remark.

"You're from Louisiana?" said Deborah.

Tonya nodded, unable to keep the pride out of her eyes.

Deborah nodded and raised her glass in salute. New Orleans? That made sense of Tonya's oddly non-Southern accent. She'd known New Orleans people taken for New Yorkers in Georgia: a port thing, perhaps.

A port thing . . .

According to Marcus, the delayed Greek container ship was at port in New Orleans. A coincidence?

"So what is it?" said Tonya.

"What's what?"

"The thing that's missing from the collection?"

"You really don't know?" said Deborah.

"You're gonna tell me," said Tonya, steely again.

"Depends who you believe," said Deborah. "Richard, and this British guy called Marcus, think it's the body of Agamemnon."

Tonya didn't react, but not, Deborah felt sure, because the name meant nothing to her.

"There's a death mask," Deborah said. "Other grave goods too. Weapons. Jewelry. Pottery, maybe. But the mask is the big thing, and the body."

"Valuable?"

"If it's real," said Deborah, sipping the ouzo. "Priceless."

"Do you have it?"

"I've never even seen it," said Deborah. Tonya gave her a hard look, and Deborah put her glass down on the table so that it banged. "Listen, Tonya, I've been run ragged over the last few days. Richard was my . . . friend. He was, if you want to know the truth, like a father to me. I came here because I felt in danger and because I thought I could . . . I don't know, help somehow. Yesterday someone tried to kill me. Seriously. Not a random push in the back at the bus stop: a sustained effort over a couple of hours."

"Who?" said Tonya. She looked both curious and surprised.

"I have no idea, but I'll tell you what: I'm not in the mood to mess about. I don't have what you're looking for. I don't know who does. I don't know much of anything, apparently, and unless you blow my brains out with that little peashooter of yours, I intend to take a bus back to Athens first thing in the morning and get on a plane to Atlanta."

Tonya considered this, her eyes fastened on Deborah's face as if scouring for a hint of duplicity. After a long moment she looked away, breathed out, and settled back in her chair.

"The police will be waiting for you," she said.

"I know," said Deborah. "Time to face the music, I guess. In the end they probably can't convict me of anything except stupidity and paranoia."

"You said Cerniga wasn't a cop," said Tonya. "Are you sure?"

Deborah told the story, and Tonya's frown deepened.

"I trust Keene," said Deborah. "I don't like him, but I trust him. He may try to throw the book at me, but I'll deal with him, and if there's any chance of trouble, I'll go to the next county and turn myself in to the first beat cop I see. It's probably what I should have done in the first place."

She shrugged at the admission of her own bad judgment, and Tonya nodded fractionally, even sympathetically. The look announced a shift in the mood, and both women seemed to relax a little more. Tonya's purse—and therefore her pistol—was still right beside her, but her hand had moved away from it.

"OK," said Deborah. "So you came here to find something you've never seen, presumably because you thought I had it. You were going to hold me up and then sell it?"

Tonya shook her head and frowned. "No," she said, as if slightly revolted by the idea. "I'm not all that interested in the thing itself beyond what it means for my family."

"Your father?" said Deborah.

"Right."

"I don't get it," said Deborah.

Tonya smiled, ruefully this time, then gestured to the waiter who had been hovering in the shade inside.

"Get us two more of these damned licorice things," she said, holding up Deborah's glass. "OK," she said, turning her attention back to Deborah with a last appraising look and a shrug of decision. "Here's what I know."

CHAPTER 43

Tonya took a drink of the ouzo and considered the glass, as if still unsure whether she liked it or not. Deborah waited, wondering if Tonya was having second thoughts about telling her story.

"OK," said Tonya, leaning forward and putting her hands on the table in a businesslike fashion. "My father was killed in World War Two. He was in the 761st Tank Battalion, commanding a Sherman M4A3E8 tank: what the tankers called an 'easy Eight' because of the smooth ride."

"He was a tank commander?" said Deborah, unable to contain her surprise. She hadn't known that black soldiers had served in that capacity.

"That's right," said Tonya. She wasn't indignant, just proud. "The 761st was an all-black battalion. They were shipped from England to Normandy in October 1944 as part of Patton's Third Army. They fought their way through the Battle of the Bulge and into southern Germany. They even liberated some of the death camps."

Deborah blinked. *The death camps.*

Deborah's family had moved to the States from Germany in the twenties, in the brief moment of doomed stability between the ruinous conditions of the Treaty of Versailles that ended the First World War and the Depression which brought the end of the Weimar Republic, rushing the dubiously titled National Socialists to the forefront of German politics. Her grandfather had been a young, single man looking for opportunity, and he chose it in the States though, by accounts, reluctantly and with little sense of what National Socialism—soon more commonly known as Nazism—would bring under Hitler.

Her grandmother had moved to Boston from Poland three years later, by which time a considerably darker future was visible on the European skyline, though many stayed. Deborah had Jewish relatives in both Germany and Poland who had felt the full brunt of the Nazi "philosophy," and many of them had not survived till the end of the war. She knew them only as young, unsuspecting faces in very old photographs and not, she was suddenly ashamed to say, by name. Her parents had been successful people with an unusually un-Jewish lack of concern for the past.

"Leave the dead to bury the dead," her father had always said. *"Tradition is built by the people who keep going forward. Too many people blame their present on the past. Get over it. Get past it. Move on."*

Deborah's parents didn't talk about the family who had stayed in Europe, and though her father nodded seriously when a TV show touched on the Holocaust, he never spoke of it, never—now that she thought about it—ever said the word aloud.

"It's not good to look backward," he had said. *"It stops you seeing the kind of future you can make for yourself."*

Deborah had always believed this a useful and healthy attitude to the world, despite her choice of profession. Archaeology was about discovering a dead past, she had told herself, about learning of those who had gone before, to find out who they were, not to define the present or the future. It had never really occurred to her that this might be some attempt to compensate for her own oddly *past-less* family.

She frowned. The reference to the death camps had unsettled her, made her feel a little unsteady, as if stone flags she had paced a thousand times had shifted unexpectedly beneath her. She looked at Tonya, who was watching her thoughtfully.

"I'm sorry," she said. "Go on."

"My father died at the end of the first week of May 1945," said Tonya with a grim little smile. "The war was officially over, but some fighting went on afterward, I guess. That's the way war is, right?"

She paused and settled back, and Deborah dragged her mind from her own concerns to see Tonya afresh. The black woman didn't look old enough to have had a father in the war, but she supposed it was possible. The hair was graying now, though that was clearer at the roots, so maybe it had been dyed black before, and the eyes were certainly old enough. Deborah was surprised—and a little ashamed—that she had never really noticed before.

Strange, she thought, *to think that people born then are only in their sixties now, that some who actually fought in that most myth-making of wars are still alive, still remember what it was like.*

"I never saw him," Tonya said. "My mother was pregnant when he went into basic training. I was born while he was in England awaiting deployment. I grew up with the story my family was given: he was killed in fighting in southern Germany on the last day of the war. There was no reason to doubt the official account, so . . . I grew up, went to school, got jobs as a journalist and freelance writer in Louisiana, and finally joined the *AJC* eight years ago. I moved to Atlanta and started getting interested in telling my father's story. I pulled military records and tried to track down any surviving members of the unit in which my father had served. I found this guy called Thomas Morris who was still alive and living in College Park. He had served in the same platoon as my father, though it wasn't till I got in touch with him that I found out that he had been the driver of the tank my father had commanded for a while.

"I had assumed that if a tank commander was killed in action that meant that his tank had been destroyed, so I was kind of surprised to find a member of the crew still alive. Turns out it doesn't work like that. When a tank gets hit, the shell can blow right through it, or bounce around inside, killing some, maiming others, leaving one or two untouched. Unless it caught fire, of course, which Shermans were prone to do.

"Anyway," said Tonya, picking up her drink but not tasting

it. "I phoned this guy Morris and managed to convince him to meet with me, but right from the start he was cagey: friendly and all, but . . . careful, like he was holding something back. He told stories about my dad, when they had met, what he was like, the way he used to write to my mom . . . and it was clear he had liked him, been his friend. But when I asked about the day he died, his memory seemed to get vague. Suddenly he couldn't really remember much of anything beyond what the army had already told me. They were north of Munich, their platoon was separated from the rest of the company, and they ran into a German convoy which had fought its way south from Berlin, apparently trying to escape into Switzerland. There was fighting, and they stopped the convoy, but my father was killed in the process."

She shrugged resignedly.

"I kept doing my research," she said. "I figured it might make a good feature for the *AJC* if not being the basis of a book, and I found out a lot, but nothing more about the circumstances of his death. After a while I got used to the idea that Morris's memory had been uneven because he had screened out something that was painful and traumatic, and then Kareem Abdul-Jabbar's book on the 761st came out, and I kind of let the whole project go. I didn't think I had much that was new to add, so I got on with my job."

"Which section do you write for?" asked Deborah.

"Food," she said, smiling a little wistfully, "but it's *did* write, not *do*. I quit to become a maid at the Druid Hills Museum."

"Why?"

"I'm getting to it," she said. "Three months ago I got a call out of the blue. Thomas Morris, my dad's driver. He said he had something to tell me and that he didn't have much time. I went to see him, and he was in a bad way. He was over eighty, I guess, and had lung cancer. He said he had to get something off his chest—other than sixty years of tobacco smoke, I mean. He said my father didn't die in the tank. They had hit this German convoy just like the military reports had said, but the convoy itself was weird: the wrong kind of equipment for the mission, he said. I didn't really know what he meant, but the gist of it was that it seemed that everything in the convoy was there to protect a single truck. The Germans went down to the last man to defend it."

"Anyway. My father's platoon took some heavy damage, but they destroyed the enemy tanks and captured the truck without putting so much as a shell anywhere near it. My father was the first man to get to it, though Morris and a couple of others were with him when they opened it up. There was a single crate, marked with a shipping number. They radioed back to HQ and let them know the situation, and for a while, they just hung out, dressed their wounds, and paid their respects to the dead. They pretty much forgot about the crate. A few hours went by, though, and my father got curious about what the Nazis had been so anxious to defend. He said he was going to open it up, just to get a look inside, you know? Some of the others said they should wait for the MPs to get there, but he figured he'd lost buddies over this wooden box, and he had a right to know what they had died for.

"He used a pickax off the side of the tank to crow it open, with Morris and the rest of the crew standing behind him. He was opening it up when the MPs arrived. Morris didn't see much, except for this big carved figure, sort of green, part woman, part—"

"Snake," said Deborah, "or dragon. Yes."

"Yes, I thought you'd know that," said Tonya. "Two days before he called me, Morris had seen that same carving in the Living section of the paper I worked for, a feature article on new exhibits at your museum."

"So you got a job there to find out what else your father had seen," said Deborah.

"In part," said Tonya. "But there's more. Whatever my father saw in that box fairly blew his mind. When the MPs arrived, they immediately cleared all the soldiers back to their vehicles. There was this one young officer, white—of course—who was running the show. Now, you have to remember what it

was like back then between blacks and whites. The white soldiers resented the kind of equality that had been given to the
black troops, even if it was actually nothing like real equality. When the black units were being trained in the U.S., it
was said that there was at least one black soldier killed by
white mobs every weekend when the troops were allowed to
visit the neighboring towns. The military police were fre-
quently involved, and if they didn't actually do the killing
themselves—which sometimes they did—they sure as hell
made no effort to prosecute those who did, military or civil-
ian.

"Many of the blacks thought they'd never see actual service, and it was only the massive loss of tank crews after
D-day that got them to France in anything other than a supply
and service capacity. Still, they were treated as cowards, unfit
to serve," she said, a new bitterness coming into her voice,
"by a lot of the white commanders, even though the 761st
was continually applauded by those whites who worked close
to them for their valor and determination under fire. Even as
they died to protect their country, that country didn't want to
know them."

She settled back and took a calming breath.

Deborah said nothing but watched and listened, afraid of
breaking the fragile truce.

"So anyway," said Tonya, "while everything was being
taken off, the truck and the crate inside it were being guarded
by this one MP. Morris never got his name, but he said he was
this good old Southern boy who made his feelings about the
platoon quite clear, called them 'nigger troops' to their faces,
suggested that they would steal anything of value in the
truck. When they asked what was inside, he drew his sidearm
and said he'd blow a hole in the next one to come near it."

"The tankers withdrew to their vehicles, but my father
went back. About two minutes later, Morris heard a shot, then
two more. The MP came back and told them that one of the
Germans had still been alive, that he had shot my father before the MP could finish him.

"They all knew it was a lie, but they also knew that any kind of protest on their part would get them arrested or worse. Morris's gunner became the tank's new commander, and they assigned a new trainee to take his place.

"Morris was the last surviving member of the crew. The gunner who had been made commander was killed by a mine three days after the convoy incident, and the rest died off gradually over the years. Morris succumbed to the cancer four weeks ago."

Sensing something else was coming, Deborah waited.

"But," said Tonya, leaning forward, "he said that my father had seen something 'wild' in that crate, something he didn't want to discuss till he'd gotten a better look at it, and Morris was convinced that it wasn't just the usual black-white stuff that got him killed that day: it was something about what was in that box. That's why I threw my job in to get close to it. That's why I'm here now with you."

For a while Deborah said nothing; then she nodded. "You remember there was a homeless man killed near the museum the night Richard died?" she said.

Tonya nodded. "They said it wasn't connected," she said.

"It might not be," said Deborah. "But here's the thing. I spoke to his daughter. He was Russian and—get this—a member of the KGB, or the organization which became the KGB."

"What was he doing in Atlanta?"

"I'm not sure," said Deborah, "but I'm beginning to think he was chasing the same box that your father saw on the back of that German truck."

Tonya's eyes widened, then narrowed almost as dramatically.

"He was carrying a letter," said Deborah. "Most of it was too badly damaged to read, but there's a reference to some 'remains' which the letter writer believed never made it to their destination, a town in Germany called Magdeburg. I haven't checked yet, but I wouldn't be surprised to find it sitting right on the Swiss border. Whatever those 'remains' were—and they could be human remains, could therefore be the body of Agamemnon himself—your father helped stop them from leaving the country, I'm sure of it.

"The Russians," she added, "grabbed a lot of ancient antiquities from Berlin. They still have them. This batch, however, the biggest, richest, most legendary trove of the lot, slipped through their fingers. Fifty years later, they are still looking for them."

There was a long silence between them. Beyond the table a car horn blew and someone shouted to a friend in Greek and someone else laughed loudly in response, but the two women barely heard any of it, sitting instead quite still, their eyes locked on each other.

CHAPTER 44

The two women ordered lunch, something that should— Deborah thought— have felt surreal, given the nature of their relationship in the States and the fact that Tonya had held her at gunpoint only an hour earlier. But it didn't. Instead there seemed to be a tacit and unexpected unity forged between them that went well beyond their both being Americans (and uncommon ones at that) in a strange land. They were both fairly tough-minded women trying to make sense of loss and tragedy, trying—it had to be said—without much success.

Deborah told Tonya everything: Richard, Marcus, her e-mails to Calvin (though not their tentative flirtation, if that was what it was), and the cryptic warning she had received before the attempt on her life at the Acrocorinth. She told her everything she knew about Agamemnon's body, about Schliemann's checkered reputation as an archaeologist, about the MVD, even about that damned ship prow whose sudden reappearance had set so much of what had happened in motion.

"And this guy Marcus has disappeared?" said Tonya.

"So far as I can tell," said Deborah. "I haven't been able to reach him in Corinth or Athens. He may have left the country, for all I know."

"You think he was the one trying to kill you yesterday?"

"It wasn't him personally, I'm pretty sure of that," said Deborah, eyes narrowed. "But whether he set it up . . . I don't know. I don't think so, and I don't see what he would gain by it, but I don't really see what *anyone* would gain by it, so that doesn't get me very far."

There was another thoughtful pause, and then Tonya asked

the question that had been hanging over them since they had started to pool information.

"So," she said. "Now what?"

Deborah just shook her head. She had absolutely no idea. "I'm ready to go home," she said. "I don't see what else there is to do. You?"

"Well, I was going to shoot you," she said, grinning. "It's still kind of tempting actually. I don't know who would take over at the museum, but they couldn't be as big a control freak as you."

"Thanks," said Deborah, returning her grin.

"How about a little shopping?" said Tonya, snapping on that sudden grin that shook ten years from her face, and squinting down to the tourist store across the street. "Cheers me up second only to church. How are you fixed for souvenirs?"

"Haven't bought a thing," said Deborah, smiling a little grudgingly. "Sure. What the hell."

They settled up and wandered over to the shop with its windows full of "Greece's finest antique reproductions" and went inside, looking a little ruefully at each other. However much they were putting a brave face on it, it was a woefully anticlimactic way to end their respective investigations.

Both stopped awestruck just inside the doors. The place was vast, the size of an aircraft hangar, and every inch of it was filled with shelves, display cases, and wall hangings. Deborah gaped and took it all in: statues of all sizes in marble and plaster, miniature vases, bowls, and amphora, Geometric pieces and Cycladic sculpture like those which had invoked Moore and Picasso in the National Archaeological Museum, red and black classical urns adorned with scenes from mythology, bronze sphinxes and charioteers modeled on originals from Delphi, bulls' heads and axes based on those in Crete, Bronze Age, classical, and Roman pieces of every kind in every medium, some of them tacky bits of cheap tourist rubbish, some museum-quality replicas. Tonya picked up a little bronze Priapus and smirked.

"These Greeks think pretty highly of themselves," she said.

Deborah barely heard her. Her brain was starting to run ahead, and her eyes were struggling to keep pace. Her legs followed and, for a moment, she forgot the throbbing in her ankle.

She ignored the cheap stuff. Even the midrange pieces, though well-executed, and perfect for the souvenirs she'd come in to buy, barely caught her eye. Her eyes were on the top shelves, where sat artifacts that would have looked at home in the National Archaeological Museum, pieces she could tell weren't real only because of the price tags. Because it wasn't their mere accuracy that made them special. They looked old, like they had just been taken from the ground. Pots, plates, even bronzes: they all looked like they were thousands of years old, and if that wasn't enough, Deborah was convinced that some of them weren't reproductions at all so much as new pieces inspired loosely by ancient artifacts. She hadn't seen anything like these pieces in Athens's many tourist shops or in Corinth. In fact, the only place she had seen anything like them was behind the bookcase in Richard's bedroom.

"Excuse me," she said, grabbing the hand of a salesgirl who seemed taken aback by her urgency. "Where do you get these?"

"All around," said the girl. "Some of them are made overseas."

Deborah could tell the girl wasn't really paying attention.

"No," she said, "not the whole store. Just these pieces. The expensive ones."

The girl, perhaps scenting a substantial commission, gave her all her attention now, and her mood became politely ingratiating.

"These are local," she said. "Very special works made by a single family who have been in the business of making the highest quality pieces for several generations. These are not reproductions. These are art."

Deborah forced herself to calm down.

"I'm very interested in buying some," she said, gesturing vaguely toward a shelf of bronzes she couldn't possibly carry without a massive increase in her luggage space. "But I would really like to meet the artist."

Tonya had wandered over and was listening to this earnest exchange with bemused interest.

"I am sorry, madam," said the girl, "but the artists are very private. Sometimes they bring things to the shop, but usually they stay at home, where they have their own . . . what is the word? Where metal things are made."

"Forge?" suggested Tonya.

"Right," said the girl. "Forge."

"Where is that?" said Deborah.

"I'm sorry, madam, but I cannot tell you that. It is their home."

"Yes," said Deborah, "but—"

"I'm sorry. I cannot."

Deborah thought fast.

"Listen," she said. "I'm looking for something very specific, something that has to be commissioned. I've been looking at pieces all over country, and I've decided I want whoever made these pieces to make one specially for me."

"These are all unique," said the girl.

"Yes, but the piece I want has to be made to my specifications. If you connect me to the artist, I'd be happy to make sure that you get a commission as if we bought the piece here."

The girl hesitated, then shook her head. "I'm sorry," she said. "We can't do that."

"You still want it made of gold?" Tonya said to Deborah.

The girl looked quickly at Deborah, who recovered her poise and said, "If they can do something that large."

The girl blinked. "Come with me, please," she said.

CHAPTER 45

The house, an unremarkable white plastered structure, was on the other side of the village. The three women walked quickly, saying little, as if all feared that uttering a word would cost them the opportunity of a lifetime. The girl had alerted the family to the fact that they would be having visitors in a hushed phone call, and a boy of about ten was waiting barefoot at the door when they arrived, stroking a white, rail-thin cat.

He showed them through a plain, narrow hallway, past a kitchen which smelled of oregano, and into a living room where an elderly man and his wife were waiting, both dressed in dark, heavy fabrics. The room was surprisingly bare, a few framed black-and-white pictures the only decoration.

The girl from the store spoke to the elderly couple in Greek, nodding toward Deborah. The man, who wore a heavy salt-and-pepper mustache, murmured but showed no readable signs. Eventually he muttered something to his wife, and she nodded once before turning her gaze onto Tonya appraisingly.

"What is it that you were looking for?" the old man said simply.

Deborah was surprised. She had assumed he would not speak English.

"Well," she said, "I don't know really . . ."

She looked at Tonya to buy herself a moment and then said suddenly, "A death mask. A gold death mask like the ones found in Mycenae."

She had said the magic words. The old man's face lit up in

a smile. He spoke quickly to his wife, and she too began to beam broadly, babbling in Greek to the two Americans, her hands joined in front of her as if she was caught in the action of applauding. Then the old man was up on his feet and hobbling out of the room, waving for them to follow.

"Like the masks Herr Schliemann found, yes?"

"Yes."

He led them through the kitchen and out into a yard lined with sheds, several of which had metal chimneys.

"Kiln," he said, pointing to one. "Forge," he said, leading them to another.

"Herr Schliemann slept in the village," he said. "Three houses down the street. Not just Schliemann. Many famous people. Himmler and Goebbels slept here too."

Deborah shot him a glance, half expecting him to say he was only joking.

"The Nazis?" she said.

"Certainly," he said, shrugging. "Mycenae was very important to them. Schliemann himself was . . . how they called it . . . a *Teutonic superman*."

He laughed croakily at the phrase, or his recollection of it. Deborah and Tonya exchanged a wry look.

He threw open a heavy door and flicked on the light. The room had a concrete floor with a series of large metal braziers at one end. There were several different anvils, and a wall full of long-handled tools, fire-blackened forceps, bluish pliers, and hammers with heads burnished from use till they shone like chrome. Along one wall was a workbench covered with wax statues in various states of completion.

"We use only the ancient techniques," he said. "Even with the bronze castings. Each wax figure makes only one mold, each mold makes only one statue. Very slow process, very expensive. No one but us does it like this anymore."

"What about the masks?" said Deborah. "Can you make them?"

"Certainly."

"Have you made them before?"

"One or two," he said, shrugging. "Many years ago. Small like this."

He cupped his hands to indicate an area about six inches across.

"Can you do them bigger?" said Deborah. "Life-size."

"Of course," he said, repeating the shrug, reminding Deborah of the museum director in Athens. "But the gold is expensive. Very hard to find in Greece today. In the old days, in Agamemnon's day, the gold had many impurities. Tin. Zinc."

"Can you make them like that, with the same mixture?"

He frowned.

"Almost," he said. "The original masks are all different. Each one is probably made of metal from different places, so there is no single correct . . . er . . . *composition*. Which one do you want copied, the Agamemnon?"

"No," said Deborah. "I want a mask which is like them, but different. Could you do that?"

He nodded and held up a solitary finger as if telling them to wait. Then he left the room and was gone for several minutes, in which time the women merely smiled and looked around, studying the work that was already in progress. When he returned he was holding what Deborah thought were two of the black-and-white photographs from the living room.

"Look," he said, showing the first picture.

Deborah's heart seemed to hammer and then stop. The monochrome picture showed a man bent over an anvil. He was holding a large death mask. It was different from any in the National Archaeological Museum. It was the mask she had seen on Richard's computer.

"My grandfather," the smith said proudly. "See."

He pushed the other picture toward Deborah. It showed two men smiling into the camera, one brawny, with a heavy mustache and a jovial expression, the other also mustached but thinner and professorial in wire, rimless glasses. Both were dressed in antiquated dark suits with curiously small collars.

"Again, my grandfather," the old man said.

"Who is the other man?" said Tonya.

"That," said the smith, tapping the glass of the photograph like a conductor bringing in the violins with his baton, "that is Heinrich Schliemann."

CHAPTER 46

Deborah had known the moment she had seen the photograph. She had recognized Schliemann's habitual pose, half addled academic, half pompous showman, and her heart had sunk. It had taken the two women ten minutes to talk their way out of the house, and they had bought two pieces from the elderly couple and several from the showroom sight unseen to make the escape a little more palatable, and in that time Deborah had been almost incapable of thought. It was as if news of a family emergency had been interrupted by a telemarketer, and she had lost the capacity to be either reasonable or civil. She had to get out of the forge, the village, the country. It was over.

Because the photographs could mean only one thing as far as Deborah was concerned. The mask and everything with it, all the pieces for which Richard had died, were fakes made by a gifted Greek craftsman at the end of the nineteenth century. The fact that Richard and Marcus—and perhaps people in both the Greek and Russian governments—had also been duped into thinking those pieces were real was no consolation whatsoever. Everything she had been doing, the probing and digging, risking her life, risking her freedom and reputation as a scholar and businessperson back in the States, was all based on a lie.

It didn't matter how the mask and the other pieces had found their way to America. It didn't matter if there was a body. It didn't matter if the Soviets had been chasing it for fifty years. It didn't matter who had it all now. It was all so much trash, worth no more than any other better-than-average tourist souvenir. This was what Tonya's father had been killed for, what Richard had been killed for. It was all a bitter, humorless joke, a joke in the worst possible taste that got drier with each new corpse it created. Back out in the sun-baked street of the village, Deborah felt the sudden urge to throw up.

Tonya didn't need to ask what Deborah thought or felt. It had taken her a moment longer, but it was clear from the humiliated tears that she wiped from the corners of her eyes before they even got out of the forge that she knew all too well the implications of those proudly displayed photographs. Had Schliemann known or been involved, a little caper to raise the funds for his Athenian mansion? Probably not. It didn't make any difference either way. Tonya's father had died for nothing. It might have been better, she thought, if it really had just been complete and undiluted racism. At least then her rage would be righteous and morally indignant. As it was, it made her father somehow the unwitting victim of some stupid accident. Yes, it was all no more than a bad joke.

They left addresses with the shopgirl to have their purchases shipped to them, handing over their euros without concern. They wouldn't need them now anyway. They would be going home. As they walked back to the little red Renault, Deborah tried to recall what she had bought and couldn't remember a single item.

"You want a ride back to Athens?" asked Tonya.

"I'll go back to the hotel in Corinth," said Deborah. "Get my stuff. See if Marcus or Calvin called. I'll go back tomorrow first thing."

"You sure?"

"Yes."

Tonya nodded. She took the car keys from her purse and then, as if on an impulse she had been trying to fight back, took Deborah's arm and pressed it. Once more their eyes met, and both women nodded and smiled, squeezing back the unshed tears, saying nothing. Tonya got in the car and drove away. Deborah did not wave good-bye.

* * *

She began to walk back to the bus stop. A car blew its horn, and she veered toward the wall of a house to get out of its way. It honked again. She turned, irritated, and found it was a taxi. The driver thought she wanted a ride.

What else would a gawky American be doing around here?

"You want to see old city?"

She didn't, not again, but a part of her knew that she was now ready to say good-bye to Richard. He had probably been buried by now. She would say good-bye here, in the fortress with which he had been so fascinated, however misguidedly. She opened the back door and got in without speaking.

Everything that had happened in the last few days seemed remote and irrelevant, wiped out by her half discovery in the village. One last act of closure, and she could go home.

She still had her ticket from the morning, so they let her in for nothing. Mycenae was the same as before, except that now it seemed smaller, less grand, like a theater after you've been in the dusty ordinariness backstage. She made the same climb up through the lion gate, saw the same circle of the grave shafts where it had all begun, and went up onto the acropolis itself. It was late now, and most of the tourists had gone home or, more likely, moved on to restaurants and souvenir shops. Some would be en route to Athens, some to Delphi, their sense of the grandeur of myth and history still enviably intact.

From the highest point of the citadel Deborah turned to look back down to the walls with their Cyclopean masonry, the grave circles and tholos tombs, then the merchants' houses and the road and the dusty scrub of the hills.

"I came for you, Richard," she whispered. "I came to try to help. I kind of wish I hadn't, but I guess I had to." She stooped and picked up a handful of coarse dust and gravel. "Good-bye Richard. You were a good man. A bad historian and curator, but a good man. I loved you very much."

And she threw the dust and gravel down in a broad arc into the empty air, where some of it might drift down into the grave shafts themselves.

She stood there in silence for a moment and then looked about her. The sun was beginning its slow descent behind the hills, and the last of the tour guides were filing out of the citadel for a brief look at the Treasury of Atreus. There was only one person still with her in the ruins, a skinny boy, eighteen or twenty perhaps, sitting smoking on the steps she had come up, looking blankly at her with small, hard eyes. When he felt her gaze on him, he stood up slowly, a sideways smirk creasing his pale lips. He had been sitting not on the steps, but on a lime green motorcycle helmet.

CHAPTER 47

Deborah became very still. The boy was only thirty yards away, close enough for her to watch every detail of his casual drag on his cigarette and then the way that, watching her with thin amusement, he flicked away the smoking butt. She was still standing there, staring at him, as he rose slowly to his feet, still smirking and looking off to the side, cocky, amused by some private joke. He was sinewy thin and chalk pale, except for the bluish prickle of hair on his shaved scalp. His eyes were small and close together, and they seemed to peer sightlessly into the middle distance, studiously ignoring her but feeling and enjoying her panic. When he chose to look back at her it was with the smug confidence of a showman, as if there were ranks of people there waiting to watch his inevitable triumph.

He's come to kill you: up close and personal this time.

Deborah looked quickly around, tearing her eyes from him to break his cobra spell. The acropolis was not especially high, but if she was to launch herself over the edge she'd probably break something as she tumbled down among the ruins of the next concentric circle of the site, and he would still be on her in seconds. The citadel had been designed to resist attackers, and there was only one way down: the staircase where he was now getting languidly to his feet. There was nowhere to go but up and back, hoping that he would follow and she might find a way to get past him.

He waited for her eyes to stray back to him before casually unbuttoning his shirt. The action bothered her unreasonably, doubly so for what the open shirt revealed. There was a knife in his waistband, not the knife which had killed Richard—she

was sure—but a large Bowie-style hunting knife with a long
blade whose cutting edge swept up to a cruel point. Yet the
knife was somehow less alarming than the tattoos. Even from
here she could see them: an ornate death mask that went from
nipple to nipple, from throat to pubis, and something overlaid
on top of it, a stylized bird, perhaps an eagle, its angles square
and imperial. Yes, a Roman eagle, she thought. There was a
word written across the mask in Greek script, and though he
was giving her plenty of time to find her fear, she couldn't
read it from where she was, though she had a pretty good idea
what it said.

It seemed an eternity before he moved, and when he did it
was a kind of joke, a mock lunge designed to scare, the fingers of one hand spread and reaching, the other switching the
grip on his knife so that it pointed down from his fist. Deborah started, and he laughed, a gurgling, boyish laugh, almost a
giggle. To Deborah it was scarier than either the knife or the
tattoos. She didn't wait to see what would happen next but
turned and began to run, back across the top of the acropolis
mount, trying frantically to remember the map in her guidebook.

He didn't come after her, not right away, and when she
glanced back over her shoulder, she saw him gathering up his
helmet and walking slowly after her, still smiling as if glad
that there would be a chase. He looked studied, in his element, like he was reliving some movie fantasy. He was the
Terminator, perhaps, slow, inexorable, coolly brutish. Deborah kept going, heading for the northernmost wall.

Mycenae, like most castles, had what was called a postern
gate, a secret exit in times of siege through which supplies or
troops could be smuggled. It was located away from the
main approach to the fortress, and compared to the massive
spectacle of the lion gate would be little more than a gap in
the wall. She had seen it this morning. It was on the north
side, she was fairly sure, but where, she couldn't say, and little of the walls was visible to her now. She crossed behind

the royal palace, striding quickly, clambering up and making a rapid survey of the walls. They arced a good deal farther east than she had remembered.

The postern gate must be that way.

She moved to the right and broke into a full run. If she could get through the gate and down, he might still be able to catch her by coming down from the front, but down there would be the last straggling tourists and the site's security guards. She checked back and saw him, tracking her, still a good thirty yards behind her, his mouth slightly open and head lowered, like a hunting dog.

No, she thought, *a hyena.*

She kept well left of the house with the columns and reached the broad walkway on top of the walls. She turned right again, and moved east along the battlements toward the rear of the citadel. She was moving quickly now, conscious that he had picked up speed, probably sensing what she was trying to do. She felt the steady throb of her ankle but kept going. Behind her she heard him clamber onto the top of the wall and begin to follow.

She picked up her pace. She had thought he was scary in the bike helmet, as if not being able to see his eyes made him less human and therefore more dangerous. But now she had seen his eyes, and they gave her no comfort at all. They seemed full of a blind and stupid malice that was far worse than the automaton he had been before. And the tattoos . . .

Something about the tattoos seemed familiar. Something about the mask, she thought, but that made no sense. She knew what the image of the mask was and had been staring at various representations of it constantly for several days. Of course it was familiar. Still, there was something else . . .

Deborah took another half-dozen strides and then allowed herself to admit the nagging doubt which had started to nose into her consciousness. None of this stretch of the walls looked familiar. She had seen the postern this morning from above, but she hadn't been this far back in the ruins.

"No," she muttered, aloud. "No. Please God, no."

But the truth was getting less avoidable with each step. She had misjudged her position. The postern gate was closer to the western end of the acropolis than she had thought, closer to him. She could keep running along the walls, but there was no way out, and she was just taking herself farther and farther away from whatever people might still be down at the entrance. She counted five more strides and decided to go no farther.

She glanced back. The wall had a slight curve, and he was temporarily out of sight.

As good a time as any.

She reached up the stone of the acropolis mount and clawed her way up back onto the top platform. This might be just what she needed. If he didn't her climb out, he might go right by her, and she could double back, run across the top of the citadel and down through the lion gate to safety. Desperately she scrambled, tearing her fingertips against the rock, till she could throw her shoulder over the top and heave herself up onto the platform. She looked down onto the ramparts and breathed. He wasn't there yet. She had made it.

It was only as she started to get up that she saw him standing on the platform, closer now, watching her. He had done the same thing moments earlier, perhaps intending to drop on her from the platform. In any case, she had lost crucial yards, he was now between her and both gates, and there was nowhere to go.

CHAPTER 48

Nowhere to go but down. In the far western corner of the remains she saw a triangular portal in the rock, its top arching to a point like the quasi-Gothic windows of the Ohabei Shalom Temple back in Brookline where she had attended Sabbath and festival services until she was thirteen: it was the passageway to the secret water cistern she had read about, the one with the plunging drop. She hesitated for only a second.

Nowhere else to go . . .

She ran toward it and down into the hollow The entrance was perhaps a meter across, three or four meters high. The stones of the floor looked burnished with centuries of use. The passage seemed dark and cool, but ominous, and to go inside committed her to . . . *something*. She wasn't sure what, but an idea was forming in her head: a dim, dreadful idea.

She ducked inside, pausing to peer back. If he had missed her coming this way, she might get past him yet. But there was no real chance of that. He had been too close. Now she saw him coming toward her, closer than ever, close enough for her to read the word tattooed across the mask and the eagle: Atreus.

For a moment she just stood and looked at him, her mouth open, though the word itself was no great surprise. It was just the sheer unavoidable and terrible reality of the thing that gave her pause. He kept coming, grinning unpleasantly, and she had no choice but to turn back into the subterranean depths and improvise.

The first few steps didn't seem so bad, but with one sharp turn virtually all light was gone. The walls were surprisingly smooth, as if plastered, but there was no rail or rope to guide her hand, and she was soon slowing down, feeling with her feet for the edges of the uneven steps. Another turn, and she was in complete darkness. She took two more steps and stumbled, her unsteady ankle giving way as she missed her place with the other foot. She crumpled but was able to stop herself falling down more than a couple of stairs, stopping her momentum with her hands so that her injured wrist flashed pain into her head like migraine, then dulled to a slow smolder. She righted herself and took two more ragged steps. She needed light.

She could hear him coming behind her, his footfalls echoing in the tunnel. He had slowed too, but then there was no great reason for him to rush. He had her, she supposed, exactly where he wanted her. There was nowhere to hide, no alcove into which she could flatten herself as he passed. There was only the sudden end of the passage and, as the guidebook had said, a seventy-meter plunge through blackness to the cold, fathomless water below.

She unhitched her backpack and tugged at one of its side pouches. Inside was the cell phone she hadn't used since arriving in Greece. She knew she could get no service outside the States, and she wouldn't get a signal down here anyway, but it might have enough power to give her . . .

Light!

As soon as she flipped it open, the phone's tiny digital display glowed firefly green. It wasn't much, but in the lightless cavern, it was immeasurably better than nothing. She held it out in front of her, keeping it low to the ground, and she saw the stairway swim into soft, phosphorescent focus, as if the floor was lined with those microscopic plants which make the waves of tropical oceans glow in the dark. Cautiously, she picked up the pace.

She had quickly lost track of how many stairs she had come down, but she guessed it was at least fifty, and the passage had curved sharply several times, corkscrewing through the stony ground like some hellish rabbit hole.

And I'm Alice, she thought. *But the White Rabbit is chasing me, not the other way round, and he has a knife instead of a pocket watch.*

She moved farther forward, farther down, one arm spread out to feel the chill wall, the other stretched forward holding the phone and its soft life-giving glow, and she tried to remember what she had read in the *Rough Guide*. The passage was long and difficult, it had said, and it twisted as it went, but if it had said how far it went, she couldn't remember. How many steps had she taken now? Sixty? Eighty? Something like that, perhaps, but neither number helped her recall anything from the book except the way that it ended: in a sudden, sheer drop through nothingness to deep water and death.

In the book that had sounded inconvenient and tricky, but down here in the tomb cold and coffin dark, it was terrifying. Even with the phone's dim light, she might not spot the edge in time, and there would be no rescue party on hand to get her out.

The fall would kill you anyway, said a voice in her head. *Even if you hit nothing but water. Seventy meters? That's— what?—a hundred and twenty feet. It would be like landing on concrete.*

"Shut up," she said aloud. "Just, shut up."

She counted her next ten steps, just to distract herself, and a new thought started to shape itself.

Surely there would be a rope across the passage where it emptied into the cistern? There must be. If she was fast— especially since she was moving faster with her limited light than he was doing with none—she could unhook the rope from one side, get a grip on it, and lower herself over the edge into the darkness of the cistern. He wouldn't see the edge, he would take one last step and find there was nothing beneath him, and he would fall past her, down, screaming, into the black waters so far below.

God, she thought, as the horror of the idea insisted itself into her mind, the feel of his fingers scrabbling for purchase against the rock, even against the fabric of her clothes as he tumbled over her and into the black void . . . *God*.

Could she do it, even if there was such a convenient length of rope securely fastened into the wall? Could she get it unfastened in time? Could she hang there in the blackness, waiting for the sound of his approach, the emptiness of the vast, deadly cistern all around her, hoping that he would make the mistake she hadn't? And what if he realized what she had done and just sat chuckling to himself as she hung there (*seventy meters* . . .), her arms burning with the effort of holding on till exhaustion—with his help—turned her off, kicked her free, and she fell . . .

We'll burn that bridge when we come to it, she thought. One of Richard's favorite hybrid phrases.

"Deborah," called a voice from back up the tunnel. It was lilting, singsong, a kind of taunt, *"Deb-rah."*

Him.

Deborah hesitated, then started off again, her heart beating faster than ever and something like nausea growing in her stomach.

Don't say anything. Just keep going.

"Gonna get you, Deborah," he sang.

Not Greek, that was for sure. American. Southern? Maybe.

"How does it feel?" he called. *"About to die and no idea why."*

He giggled to himself at his rhyme, but Deborah was not listening. Refusing to.

The passage turned sharply again, and then once more, and then it stopped.

For a moment she moved the phone's glow over the rock on all sides, but there was no getting away from the awful truth.

There was no rope across the drop. There was no drop at all. They hadn't roped off the cistern. They had filled it in. The guidebook was out of date, and she was trapped.

CHAPTER 49

Her last burst of speed had put some distance between herself and her pursuer, and it was several seconds before she could hear him, seconds in which she clung to the hope that he had changed his mind and decided to go back. Having him wait for her outside would be better than being caught here, cornered in the dark like a rat.

The image revived her defiance.

I'm not the rat, she thought. *He is. Smug, murderous little weasel . . .*

He was getting close now, and through the scrape of his feet she could hear something else, something barely louder than his heavy breathing.

He's whistling.

It was a flat, tuneless sound, the notes shrill and undifferentiated, like he was blowing the air through his teeth, his lips pulled back like a jackal or—the image came back—a hyena. The casualness with which he was going to kill her, the sheer mindless flippancy of the thing, made her suddenly furious. She set the glowing phone down on the step at the last turn in the passage and stepped back into the end of the tunnel.

He was almost on her now. Without the greenish light to guide her senses, she would have sworn he was close enough to touch. She braced herself against the walls of the dammed-up cistern where so many idiot tourists had doubtless fallen to their deaths over the years, and her muscles flexed from calf to shoulder like a spider in one of those funnel-shaped webs, tense and ready to spring. She would have only the briefest moment of advantage. No time for half measures.

Her eyes didn't catch the outline of his shape till the whistling stopped, but he loomed into view as he stooped to the glow of the cell phone, his face suddenly clear and ghoulish in its green light.

The White Rabbit . . .

She saw his eyes tighten, briefly overloaded by the glow after so much blackness, and she flung herself forward, kicking hard at his face with her good foot. She connected, and he rocked backward.

"Surprise," she said, and struck him hard on the cheek with the heel of her palm.

He rolled backward, sprawling and jarring his back against the steps so that he gasped as if winded, but the action took him out of the phone's glow, and she lost him. She kicked out again, but made no contact and almost lost her footing in the process. She took a step closer, realizing too late that she was probably silhouetted in the green glow which came from a foot or two behind her. His knife caught her across the shoulder and the side of her neck.

Wincing, she fell back, clutching at the wound, first instinctively, then feeling for spurting. How she knew to do this, she didn't know, but she did it, probing with her fingers, testing for severe arterial damage. There was none that she could feel, and she didn't waste any more time in the examination. She kicked the phone away, flung herself to her right side—away from his weapon hand—and came at him again, head lowered like a charging bull.

Someone of her size might have had an advantage fighting from the steps where he was, but he was shorter than her by several inches, and he seemed completely unprepared for her fury. Her shoulder made contact with something (his arm? his face?) and flung him hard against the wall. There was a dull thud—his head against the rock—and the clear, metallic ping of the knife hitting the floor. She didn't look for it, or wait to see if he was conscious. She elbowed past his slumping body and began running back up the stairs.

She slipped twice on the treacherous steps (the only thing the guidebook had gotten right), but she could feel the air warming as she climbed. It was still utterly dark, but ahead was light and warmth and life. She ran on, leaping blindly, bashing heavily into the wall where the passage twisted, but never stopping. Then the blackness was brown, and some of the rock floor had contours and depth. Around the next turn the pallor was clearer, and she sucked in the light like oxygen. Five more steps and another wrenching twist of the tunnel, and she was out, half blinded by the glare, and suddenly feeling a rush of sweat and nerves and pain from the stinging gash across her shoulder, none of which stopped her from running back to the palace ruins and down past the grave circle to the lion gate and out. Remembering the myth of Orpheus trying to save his wife from the underworld, she did not look back.

CHAPTER 50

This time, she told the guards who, in turn called the police. Was he dead? they asked. She didn't know. She didn't think so, though he might be unconscious. It took over twenty minutes for a police car to arrive, and by the time they had secured flashlights and got to the mouth of the cistern tunnel, another ten or twelve had passed. The two policemen ventured inside, one with a drawn pistol, but the sound of a small motorcycle leaving the parking lot told her they would find no one inside. He had emerged, no doubt, from his rabbit hole while she was making her report, and had slipped quietly out through the postern gate, making his way round to his bike at the foot of the fortress walls.

She sat wearily in the late afternoon sun while one of them hunted through an ancient first aid kit for something to dress her wound. It was shallow on her neck, thank God, but deeper across her shoulder blade, and it had taken longer to stanch the blood. The policeman muttered encouragement, but she barely heard him and had to be prompted several times to answer their questions.

The police returned her cell phone and took her name and that of the hotel where she was staying but, when she said that she intended to be on the next plane back to America, they put their notebooks away and checked their watches. They did, however, drive her back to Corinth and the Ephira, sparing her another bus journey and a walk she wasn't sure she could make.

There were no messages for her at the hotel, and though she was tempted to return to the cyber café so she could check her e-mail, she was taking no chances. She instructed the woman on duty at the desk that she would be checking out first thing in the morning and locked herself into her bedroom with a sandwich bought at the bar in the lobby. She ate it quickly, drank some water, showered, and booked her return flight over the phone, requesting the kosher meal on impulse, something she had never done before.

Trusting to God in the face of murderous little white rabbits?

Hardly.

She hadn't really planned it, not consciously anyway, but she called Calvin Bowers, dialing quickly so that she wouldn't have to consider what she was doing or what she was going to say.

"Hello?" he said. He sounded groggy and a little irritable. She ought to think about the time difference before making these calls. For a moment she just sat there, holding the phone, saying nothing, panicking like she was fourteen again and had phoned the starting quarterback out of the blue, cutting across all the spiderweb threads which gave high school culture its structure, its hierarchy. She was quite still, remembering making that very call, blissfully unaware of how stupid she was being until said quarterback (Tim Andrews, his name was: her brain kept it locked in a lightless little dungeon in her head) had begun to laugh.

"Deborah?" said Calvin Bowers. "Is that you?"

The voice, suddenly careful, nurturing, even hopeful, as far from Tim Andrews's gleeful contempt as could be imagined, brought her back to herself, or to something like herself.

"Yes," she said. "I'm sorry to bother you. I'm really terrible at figuring out—"

"It's fine," he said. "Where are you?"

"I'm coming home tomorrow," she said. "Someone tried to kill me today. Again. But I'm OK."

It had almost been a joke, that "again." She listened to her own deadpan composure as she made light of his concerned inquiries, and wondered where it had come from. The panic, the stress, the brutal, crushing disappointment, the sense of utter failure, the terror and exhaustion had all just evaporated like morning fog burned off by a strong noon sun, and she felt inexplicably content.

"What time do you get in?" he said. "I'll meet you at the airport."

She checked her schedule and parroted back the relevant numbers, wondering vaguely why he cared, and why it pleased her so much that he did.

"Good," he said. "It will be good to see you."

She smiled and just thought about that for a moment and answered simply, "Yes."

The next day she took the earliest bus to Athens, called the airport to confirm her flight was on schedule, then took a taxi from the bus station to the archaeological museum. Popadreus was in his office, wearing the same—or a very similar— immaculate dark suit, but his hair was rumpled and he looked harried, and when he realized who it was, his good-humored and laconic smile took a moment to take hold.

"Miss Miller," he said. "How nice to see you. I am, unfortunately, rather busy today."

"I just came to say good-bye," said Deborah. "My plane leaves in"—she checked her watch—"three hours."

He relaxed visibly, and his smile grew warmer.

"I'm sorry to hear that," he said, apparently meaning it. "Please, sit down. Will you have a cup of coffee? It's—"

"Not Nescafé," she finished for him, smiling. "Yes, please. That would be nice."

He made the request over the phone, keeping his eyes on her. When he hung up, she leaned forward and decided to get right to it.

"I won't take much of your time," she said. "I just wanted to tell you why I first came here."

He seemed to sense something purposeful in her manner,

and he straightened in his chair, as if preparing to receive bad news.

"I didn't come here merely as a tourist," she said. "The man I work for, the man who established and funded the museum which I run, was killed a few nights ago. I found his body in a small but apparently rich collection of Greek antiquities which I believe he had intended to bequeath to the museum. There was, however, something missing. I never saw it, but I believe it to be a body wearing the death mask and other grave regalia of a Bronze Age king of Mycenae. I think that Richard—the man who was killed—believed it to have been discovered by Schliemann and smuggled to a private collection in Germany. At the end of the war the Germans tried to smuggle the remains to a town called Magdeburg and into Switzerland, but they were intercepted by an American tank unit. The collection found its way onto the black market, slipping through the fingers of at least one interested collector and the Russian government, who wanted to take them back to Moscow as they had already taken the collection known as Priam's Treasure. I also think that Richard believed the corpse to be the human remains of Agamemnon himself."

There was a pause.

"And what do you think?" the museum director asked. His voice was low and level, measured even. He had shown no sign of shock or disbelief so far. But Deborah had not really expected any.

"If there is an actual corpse, or parts of one," said Deborah, "I'm fairly sure that it is neither Agamemnon nor especially old. I'm also fairly sure that the death mask and other grave goods were manufactured by a local Greek craftsman at the end of the nineteenth century. How they found their way to Germany and under whose auspices, I cannot say, but I know now what happened to them at the end of the war and that they wound up in a secret room connected to a small museum in Atlanta, Georgia."

The coffee arrived. They both fell silent as it was presented to them, still watching each other, cautious.

"This is all very interesting," said Popadreus. "I'm curious as to why you wanted to tell me about it before you left, however."

It was his first bad move. He avoided her eyes and concentrated on putting sugar in his coffee.

"I think you know why," she said.

"Really?" It wasn't so much defiance as a real question. "Why is that?"

"I think that the Greek government got word, perhaps through this institution, that a body had, perhaps, been smuggled out of Schliemann's dig, that it had been lost in Germany for almost fifty years, and then elsewhere for another fifty. It turned up in Atlanta, but the man who owned it might be persuaded to return it to its native land. He may have even made the offer of the body and its regalia in return for the rest of the collection staying in the United States. The minister for culture and antiquities (who I happened to meet in this very building) may have suggested the matter be pursued, perhaps authorizing a substantial payment in order to recover the missing items in the interest of Greek national and cultural identity."

Popadreus said nothing for a long moment, then he sighed and smiled.

"Interesting," he said. "Based on nothing but speculation, of course, but interesting all the same."

"Thank you," said Deborah, sipping her coffee.

"So interesting, in fact, that I am curious to hear how the story ends."

Deborah put her cup down and looked at him. He wasn't teasing or dismissing what she was saying. It was something else, something that showed in his eyes, something knowing and a little sad. It was a real inquiry, an invitation, almost a supplication, and it was intended to reveal as much as it asked.

"OK," she said. "Well, I would say that a pair of experts on Mycenaean artifacts, probably employed by this museum or somehow serving under it, were dispatched to Atlanta to meet with the owner of the corpse and to negotiate its return to Greece, pending tentative proof of its authenticity. At about the same time, a Russian man also went to Atlanta to try to secure the goods, though whether he was operating on his own behalf or was similarly serving his country, I don't know."

This much she was fairly sure of. There were a couple of alternate endings to the story, however, and she wasn't sure which to float first.

"When the Greeks saw the artifacts, they were satisfied enough to want to remove them immediately, but the owner made certain objections, and some sort of disagreement resulted, a disagreement which turned violent—"

Popadreus raised his hand to stop her. For a second he just sat there, one palm raised, a slightly pained look on his face. When he spoke, Deborah guessed he had read something in her manner, something which suggested she wasn't convinced of her own version of the story.

"Let us try ending B," he said.

"The two agents—cultural attachés or whatever you want to call them—are impressed by what they see," said Deborah, "impressed enough to want to take the body with them for further examination. Richard agrees and lets them remove the display case containing the corpse and its treasures, glad to be returning the body to Greece, but still intending to hand the rest of the collection over to the museum. But after the Greek agents leave with the corpse, someone else comes, finds he has missed the transaction he had hoped to prevent, and kills both Richard and the Russian who was posing as a homeless person in order to monitor events at the museum. Meanwhile, the Greek agents scrutinize what they have recovered and decide that it is *not,* in fact, genuine. They opt not to try shipping the objects to Greece and go underground, afraid of being implicated in Richard's murder."

"And," the museum director inserted heavily, "of embarrassing their government. It would, after all, be extremely

awkward for a country to go to such lengths to retrieve something which turned out to be historically and culturally without value."

It was, Deborah knew, as close to an admission that she
was right as she was going to get.

"So someone else killed Richard?" she said.

"The Greek people are very proud of their past," said
Popadreus. "They have good reason to be so, particularly of
their ancient past. They need it. It helps them to keep a sense
of who they are. That said, I do not believe that any Greek
would sanction the killing of a living man in order to bring a
dead one home."

He paused, suddenly small and defeated.

"Richard Dixon was," he said, "a man of principle and a
friend to the people of Greece. That what he had to offer was
not what he believed is—while not, perhaps, the stuff of ancient tragedy—a bitter and costly pill for him and for us. You
have my heartfelt condolences."

Deborah looked at the floor. She wasn't sure who he
meant by "us," but it seemed to include her, and she was unexpectedly touched by it, and could think of nothing to say in
return.

"You will miss your plane," he said, rising.

She blinked twice and forced a smile as she got up.

"Thank you for the coffee," she said. "It was very good."

"You are more than welcome, always," he said.

INTERLUDE

France, 1997

Randolph Fitz-Stephens had turned eighty-seven two days before. His doctors said that the trip was inadvisable, possibly even dangerous, but he had waved them away. He had been waiting half his life for this, and he wasn't about to let his health stand in the way. Over half a century he had waited, searching files and registers, sponsoring dives, urging international inquiries: half a century with nothing to show for his labors except the derision of all those he confided in. All but his son. Marcus would want to be here when he saw it, but Marcus would have tried to prevent his making the journey in his current state, so Marcus would have to wait in ignorance to applaud his judgment.

In a matter of days they would bring Agamemnon, king of Mycenae, to England! Then, and only then, would they begin talks with the British Museum. If Randolph didn't live to see the hero of the Trojan War lying in state under the Parthenon frieze salvaged by Lord Elgin, he could at least trust Marcus to ensure it was done.

He had always known there had been some foul-up with the paperwork. The chaos of the war's last days and those which had immediately followed had been an administrative nightmare. It was not surprising that unscrupulous Americans had been able to slip away with cargo they were supposed to deliver elsewhere, nor was it entirely surprising that no adequate records could lead to where said cargo really had been moved. What had never occurred to him was that some nameless ship might have taken his precious treasure to the bottom of the sea, or that fifty years later a shifting sandbar would send the wreckage of that ship rolling and drifting onto rocks along the Brittany shore.

A boy, twelve years old, apparently, had been the first to raise interest in a particular box, now rotted to pieces by the seawater, a box from which he had recovered a few trinkets to sell in the local antique stores. Only when Marcus had stumbled on discussion of a particular amphora's antiquity did he realize that he was reading the salvage reports of priceless heirlooms his family had already paid for. Would the body of the man himself have survived the journey and—worse—the years underwater? It would depend on how the corpse had been preserved. But if only a fragment of bone had survived, it would be worth all the money, all the years.

The dealer claimed that the contents of the crate were all intact, though he had nothing to base that on beyond the sense that it seemed full. He had been coy about whether other bidders were involved, but Randolph was sure he was prepared to pay more than anyone else. He still carried the pictures, now badly faded and creased, which his first duplicitous contact had sent him all those decades ago. He had to be the one to claim possession. Morally, it was already his.

He sat, ramrod straight at a metal table in the appointed café, waiting. The dealer was an hour late. Randolph sipped his tea (or whatever you called the result of a tea bag in a cup of tepid water) and tried not to think of a return journey without even glimpsing the dealer, let alone the body itself.

A man came striding across the village square, his eyes on the café patio.

This must be the dealer.

Randolph's irritation at being kept waiting evaporated like mist.

"Mr. Fitz-Stephens?" said the man, sitting down opposite him. "I'm afraid Monsieur Thibodaux has been detained, but I think I can help."

"He won't be joining me?" said Randolph the mist returning, thicker than ever, so that for a second he felt quite stifled.

"More a question of you joining him," said the other. "Do you mind a short walk? I have a car parked on the other side of the square."

"Where are we going?" said Randolph, getting slowly, creakily to his feet.

"The beach," said the other breezily. He had no French accent at all.

They walked, and then they drove, and then they walked again, pacing out the firm dark sand of the deserted spot only a few hundred yards inland from where the wreck of the *St. Lo* had come to rest, her hull torn and flooded. It was cloudy and getting darker by the minute, promising rain, and heavy rain at that. Randolph had left his umbrella at the café. His legs ached, and he had already walked farther today than he usually did in a week.

"I'm curious," said the younger man. "What exactly do you believe is in the remains of that crate?"

"The body of Agamemnon, king of Greece, preserved by Heinrich Schliemann, with all that was interred with him in death," said Randolph. He intoned it, like it was a litany: reverential, a familiar statement of awe and of faith. "And the prow of the galleon," he added, "though I'm not interested in that."

"Anything else?" said the man. He was smiling in a dry sort of way, and though Randolph had seen versions of this smile before when he talked about what he believed had been aboard the *St. Lo,* there was something different about its manifestation here, something colder. He found himself looking for signs of life on the beach and feeling a pang of anxiety that there was no one else around.

"What else would there be?" he said, mustering a little bitter amusement to mask his discomfort. "What more could anyone ask for?"

The man laughed once, a voiceless snort of contemptuous amusement.

They had rounded a long, irregular outcrop of rock which jutted abruptly from the glistening, sea-washed sand, and ran out into the surf. At its height it was perhaps ten feet tall, tapering as the shore fell away into the gray water.

"That amuses you?" said Randolph. He didn't think he liked this man very much.

"Fifty-three years," said the other with unabashed disdain, "and you still have no idea what you are dealing with! I swear to God, killing you is a mercy. This, by the way, is Monsieur Thibodaux."

The body was facedown behind the rock, half submerged in the encroaching tide so that the hair on his head floated briefly with each wave.

"Who are you?" said Randolph, barely able to take his eyes from the corpse before him.

"Just another bitterly disappointed client of a dealer," he said, half smiling as he considered the corpse, "who did not adequately consider the claims of all interested parties."

To Randolph's amazement, he found himself smiling back.

"You don't have it either," he said.

"I will," said the other. "And you will not be in a position to tell anyone else that it is even out there."

"My son will find you," said Randolph. "And he will find Agamemnon."

"You know," said the other, "I hate to see you die so full of confidence. How about I tell you what you don't know about that crate, *then* I kill you? It will wipe that supercilious grin off your face, trust me. What do you think? You want to die in ignorance, or you want to know what it is you've been so cluelessly searching for all these years?"

Randolph faltered, uncertain, and taking his silence for assent, the younger man drew his curious knife with its overlong, straight blade, then told him.

The old man fell very slowly, his eyes wide and staring, stricken not so much by the blade in his chest as by the idea which had been driven into his mind, an idea which bore him on a wave of terror as the waters of the Atlantic would soon bear him up onto the pale sands at the foot of the dunes.

PART III

RETURN TO ITHACA

While the Kaddish is recited in memory of the departed, it contains no reference to death. Rather it is an avowal made in the midst of our sorrow, that God is just, though we do not always comprehend His ways. When death seems to overwhelm us, negating life, the Kaddish renews our faith in the worthwhileness of life. Through the Kaddish, we publicly manifest our desire and intention to assume the relation to the Jewish community which our parents had in their life-time. Continuing the chain of tradition that binds generation to generation, we express our undying faith in God's love and justice, and pray that He will speed the day when His kingdom shall finally be established and peace pervade the world.

> —A meditation on the Kaddish
> from *The Sabbath and Festival Prayer Book*
> by the Rabbinical Assembly of America and
> the United Synagogue of America

CHAPTER 51

Delta flight 133 left Athens on schedule shortly after noon bound for JFK, then Atlanta. All told it would be a fourteen-hour trip. Deborah stared out of the window at the blue sky and the heat haze on the runway and tested the legroom with a familiar and self-deprecating hopelessness.

Face it, she thought. *The world is designed for smaller women, and in oh so many ways.*

As they became airborne she tried to get a last glimpse of the Acropolis from the air but could see nothing but the pale rectangles of faded concrete that made up such a depressingly large amount of that intermittently graceful city. Her sojourn in Greece was at an end, and she was going home. Hopefully, she thought, she would fare better than did the Greeks after the Trojan War. Most of them never got back, and those who did found only murder and chaos awaiting them. Odysseus did better than most, but it took him ten years to make it back to Ithaca and the pandemonium that his return unleashed. For the next hour Deborah scrutinized the flight plan in the in-flight magazine, gazing at all the places she had never been, wondering how many she would see before she died.

If this last week is anything to go by, she thought, *you'd better go on safari or something soon, or you can forget it.*

Funny. In fact, the familiar, sterile environment of the plane, its muffling drone and the dulling pressure in her ears, made the idea that she had fought for her life twice in the last few days almost impossible to believe, impossible even to imagine. For the first time since she had heard the motorcycle whining up and down the road to the Acrocorinth, perhaps since the first rifle shots had rung out in the ruins, she wondered if it could all have just been some colossal accident or coincidence.

He called you by name, there in the tunnel to the cistern; he called you "Deborah."

The memory sent a cold shudder through her body.

"About to die and no idea why."

It had been the same assassin both times, and he had been tattooed with the word which Richard had scribbled perplexedly the night he died. It was no accident, no coincidence. Someone wanted her dead.

But why her? To kill Richard for treasures that had no real value was one thing, but to pursue her across another continent days after the event made no sense. If she could figure out that the gold and grave goods had been made by some local village craftsman as a souvenir for overreaching tourists, why hadn't whoever was hunting her? It hadn't been hard to figure out. Surely the people who had been chasing after the stuff knew what it was, and what it *wasn't* worth. And if her would-be killer *did* know, then why pursue her further?

It makes no sense.

(. . . *no idea why*)

Could the treasure trove be real after all? She had no hard evidence to the contrary, just a hunch and some pretty compelling—albeit circumstantial—information. Could Popadreus have misled her into thinking the collection was fraudulent, trying to throw her off the scent while he still awaited its transfer to Greece? It was possible, she supposed, but it seemed unlikely. If they ever got the masked corpse to Athens and put it on display, she would immediately know where it had come from and would plunge the Greek government into a complex and expensive lawsuit about who owned the hoard and how they had gotten hold of it.

Unless you're dead by then, said the voice in her head that loved to say such things. *You talk to Popadreus about your interest in the death mask, and suddenly you're being stalked by a killer. Coincidence?*

No way. She just didn't believe the museum director was capable of such bloodthirsty calculation. It wasn't much of an argument, she knew, but it was all she had.

She settled back into her seat, closed her eyes, and turned her mind deliberately to Calvin, who had promised to be waiting for her when she got off the plane. She smiled secretly, the pleasure of anticipation briefly drowning out the attendant terror she reserved for *relationships*, and all the dire cautionary warnings (several of them based on examples from her own fairly tragic past) in which that voice of hers so delighted.

But underneath it all, the assassin's taunt *(about to die . . .)* echoed in her head with the ring of truth. She had no idea what was going on. In fact, the more she learned, the more it all felt wrong, like she was trying to complete a jigsaw, but the pieces had been mixed up with another puzzle. The more of the picture she thought she could see, the more she sensed another picture behind it, an utterly different picture which she had missed completely.

Miraculously, she slept for about three hours, waking to find the crew clearing up the remains of dinner and beginning the preparations for landing in New York. Once they were on the ground, Deborah bought a *New York Times* and read it hungrily, cover to cover, while she waited to reboard.

Forty-five minutes before they were due to touch down in Atlanta, the stewardess or flight attendant or whatever the hell they were called these days, appeared beside her, bending low, her conciliatory smile not quite masking a note of wariness.

"Miss Miller?" she said, her smile expanding to show her perfect teeth. "Deborah Miller?"

"Yes," said Deborah. "Is there a problem?"

"No, no problem," the woman lied happily. "We're going to be coming in for landing in Atlanta soon, and I just wanted to confirm that you were in the correct seat."

"OK," said Deborah, cautious now.

"When we touch down," she said, "one of the stewards will come and get you."

"Why? I don't think I understand."

"We just have to have you deplane first."

"First?"

"Before the other passengers," said the flight attendant, her smile now strained like a rubber band.

"What?" said Deborah. "Why me? What's going on?"

CHAPTER 52

Deborah's unease blossomed, but the more she demanded details from the flight crew, the more they protested ignorance and told her to settle down, always stooping and smiling like they were dealing with a tantruming three-year-old or someone who wanted the beef which had run out three rows earlier. At least there was nobody sitting next to her whose curious glances or questions would have to be endured for the last twenty minutes of the flight.

Why did they want her off first, and who were *they*?

Was this a special treat arranged—somehow—by Calvin, to spare her the tiresome pushing and standing around which ended all flights? That seemed a little hopeful. Perhaps it was intended to protect her, maybe from someone on the plane. She looked round quickly, rising and flashing her eyes over the blank, staring faces behind her. No one looked familiar, and the only attention she received was from some kid who remarked loudly to his mother that "that tall woman" was blocking the video screen. She sat down again and buckled herself in, before she had to sit through any more polite reprimands from the flight attendants.

Or maybe Calvin wasn't the only one waiting for her in the airport. The idea unsettled her. But even if someone on the ground meant her harm, how would they get the flight crew to comply?

The same way "Detective" Cerniga took over a case without actually being a cop, she thought.

She felt the plane descend, and her stomach seemed to float up in her body, like a boat caught and lifted by an unexpected wave. She began to drum her fingers on the armrest.

The PA system rattled off the usual requests: tray tables stowed, seat backs in their upright and locked position . . .

Come on. If we're going down, let's just go.

Deborah stared through the window. The plane dipped through a wisp of cloud, and then there was the city, spread out and waiting. She tried to orient herself so she could figure out which suburb she was looking at, a way to keep her mind occupied, but she had no idea. Nothing looked familiar. It was all industrial complexes of warehouses and vast parking lots, then white houses barely visible through a mantle of trees, and large, heavily trafficked roads lined with gas stations. It could be anywhere.

The stewardess who had warned her that she would be escorted off first sat in a folding seat by the cabin door and buckled herself in. For a brief moment, their eyes met, and then the woman looked quickly away. Caught without her professional smile, she looked tired and a little anxious. Deborah wondered if that last had something to do with her.

The plane emitted a low whirr and clunk as its landing gear locked into position, a basic, mechanical sound that reminded everyone of the sheer unlikely physicality of this great metal tube actually flying.

She could see cars now, a MARTA bus, even a few of Atlanta's rare pedestrians, then treetops, power lines, and suddenly, almost life-size, a busy highway and an overpass. They crossed the road, three lanes in each direction, and a high wire fence, and then there were runways with painted symbols and letters striping acres of scrubby turf. There was another bump down of a few feet, a moment of stillness when the aircraft seemed to be gliding without engines or gravity, and then the soft push of wheels on asphalt and the tightening of brakes, so that Deborah felt herself falling forward into inertia.

They were still taxiing toward the terminal when one of the male stewards, a young, athletic guy she imagined was gay, appeared beside her.

"Where are your things, Miss Miller?"

She looked at him stupidly, then nodded to the overhead bin. He reached up and lifted the backpack and a shopping bag down.

"Anything else?"

"No."

"As soon as we stop," he said, as if they were about to set off on a roller coaster ride, "we'll head out."

She nodded and said nothing. Her mouth was dry, and she was glancing around, though what she was looking for, she didn't know. She remembered giving a piano recital when she was ten, peering around the curtain of the Brookline civics center hall to find her father in the audience, her hands sweating and unsteady. It felt a bit like that, like stage fright.

The plane slowed, turned, reversed, adjusted, and pulled forward to a stop. Before the seat belt light pinged off, the steward beside her was helping her to her feet and leading her to the exit door. The woman who had been sitting there scuttled off, looking busy, eyes averted.

Deborah's escort threw the lever on the latch mechanism and heaved the panel out of place, and the world came into view. In the mobile tunnel beyond the door, maintenance men and women in rainproof uniforms and fluorescent pink trimmed jackets moved aside to reveal a uniformed policeman. Standing beside him were Keene and Cerniga.

"Thanks," said Keene to the steward. "We'll take it from here."

The uniformed cop took her bags, and the steward disappeared back into the plane without a word.

"Will you come with us, please, Miss Miller," said Cerniga. "We have some questions about—"

"I'm not going with you," she said.

"One way or another, you are," said Keene, taking a step closer.

There was a commotion farther down the tunnel, and a man, tousle-haired and harried-looking, came running into view, a security guard at his heels. It was Calvin Bowers.

"Deborah," he called.

"Get him out of here!" yelled Keene.

"They're trying to take me away!" Deborah shouted back to where Calvin, now half screened by the security guard, was straining to see what was going on.

"I'm her lawyer!" he shouted back. "You can't arrest her without taking me along."

"We're not making an arrest," said Cerniga, still watching Deborah, "though we can and will if this nonsense persists."

Calvin broke free and plunged the last few yards to join them. The security guard followed like a beaten cornerback.

"Can we get some other cops involved?" said Deborah to Calvin.

"You are perfectly safe," said Cerniga.

"With you?" she shot back. "Really? Let's see your badge."

Cerniga's face clouded.

"We really don't have time for this," he began.

"I said, let's see your badge!" said Deborah, her voice louder than she had meant it to be and a trifle shrill.

Cerniga shot Keene a sideways glance. The other detective shrugged fractionally and looked away. Cerniga pulled a sour face, reached into his jacket, and plucked out a black leather item the size and shape of a wallet. He flipped it open and held it up.

Deborah stared. The wallet contained a card with a picture of Cerniga on it, not unlike a driver's license, and three large letters: FBI.

CHAPTER 53

"FBI?" said Deborah. She glanced instinctively at Keene, who shrugged and nodded his assent. "Why didn't you say so before?"

"It wasn't considered necessary," said Cerniga.

"Wait a moment," said Calvin. "Why is this a federal case? Who has jurisdiction here?"

"I do," said Cerniga. Keene had taken a step back to watch. Deborah could sense his amusement.

"This is crazy," said Calvin, his indignation shaking off his professional restraint. "You can't pass yourself off as a cop and then—"

"Yes sir," said Cerniga, digging his heels in. "In this case I can do exactly that."

"I'm sorry," said the steward, reappearing at Deborah's elbow and looking shamefaced. "We have a planeload of people waiting to get off. Can you move this into the terminal building, please?"

Cerniga turned on his heel and led the way out.

They passed through customs and passport control in a flurry of badges and explanations, still arguing among themselves. Ironically, considering she was the one being marched about in this degrading fashion, Deborah seemed the calmest of the group. After all, she told herself, it could have been much worse, and while she was baffled by Cerniga's duplicity, she felt a lot safer now than she had on the plane or, for that matter, at almost any moment since she had first overheard the policemen talking through the vents.

Calvin was not so easily pacified.

"I still want to know why the Feds are even *involved* in this case!" he blustered.

"I told you already," said Keene. His enjoyment of the proceedings had quickly paled, and he had become his usual dour and irritable self again. "The stolen items have been moved across state borders, and there are international smuggling charges as well. Too big for us poor flatfeet, apparently."

The uniformed cop left them in a black-and-white at the curb. Deborah and the three men drove in Keene's elderly Oldsmobile (parked illegally right outside baggage claim) out of the circular airport system and onto Interstate 85, the cops in front, Deborah and Calvin in the overly hot and intimate back. No one spoke for several minutes.

Deborah shot Calvin a glance. He was staring out of the window, frowning, but he turned toward her, apparently sensing her look, and smiled.

"Not the way I had wanted to welcome you back," he said.

Deborah just nodded.

"Where do you want it?" said Keene from the front.

"What is that supposed to mean?" asked Calvin sharply.

"I'm just asking where the lady would like to be taken," said Keene. He grinned at Cerniga, who, so far as Deborah could see, did not react.

"I have a choice?" she said.

"You wanna go to your place, shower and such," said Keene, "or you wanna go to the museum?"

She didn't like the idea of Keene loitering while she was in the shower.

"The museum," she said. When she went home tonight, it would be alone to decompress, not to break out the best china and be politely interrogated.

And if Calvin wants to come with you? she wondered.

Shut up.

She looked out of the window and bit her lip till the smile went away.

* * *

"Let's go back to why you left the country," said Cerniga

He had become terse, even confrontational since the meeting at the airport, though whether this was because he had been forced to declare his status as an "agent" rather than simply a "detective," Deborah wasn't sure. It probably originated rather earlier. She got the distinct impression that he was not happy about her little overseas excursion, though no one, as she had been quick to point out, had actually forbidden her from leaving the country.

"I told you already," she said. They had been talking for an hour in the silent museum's tiny office, and she was beginning to lose patience.

"Miss Miller," he said, "I don't think I would have difficulty justifying charges for obstruction of justice based on your activities to date. If you continue to be uncooperative, I will have no choice but to press such charges."

He wasn't bluffing. He was angry, possibly even a little humiliated by the way she had slipped away and how little progress the case had apparently made in her absence. She had to be less adversarial. After all, however deceptive he might have been initially, as a federal agent he was, surely, an ally in getting to the heart of Richard's death. If she didn't treat him as such, she might yet find herself being considered as a serious suspect.

"OK," she said. "I left because my friend had been killed, because someone had been waiting for me in my apartment, and because I thought you weren't a real cop. I went to Greece because what little I knew about the circumstances of Richard's death pointed there, and I wanted to see if I could . . . I don't know."

"Play Nancy Drew," said Keene, not looking up from his notebook.

Deborah shrugged.

"I didn't know who I could trust," she said. "It made a kind of sense."

"That must be the kind of sense you learn about in museum school," sneered Keene. "Out in the real world, it doesn't mean dick."

"There's no such thing as *museum school*," said Deborah, "but if you mean academia or some other aspect of the world I work in, it's just as real as what you do."

"Is that right?" said Keene, cocking his head as if he was daring her to throw a punch.

"Yes, that's right," she said, staring him down.

"And let's go over what you did in Greece one more time," said Cerniga, speaking loudly and levelly, shutting down the petulant spat that had flared up between Deborah and Keene for the third time in the last hour.

So far, Deborah had told them the truth about her trip to Greece in all but two respects. First, she had not revealed the idea that the missing death mask was actually being worn by a partially preserved corpse. The police still thought they were looking for an artifact of strictly monetary value. The idea that she had actually been pursuing the body of Agamemnon himself now seemed too preposterous to speak aloud. If she could keep it to herself, she might salvage the dignity of those who had been conned into looking for it in earnest: Richard, the antiquities and culture department of the Greek government, Sergei Voloshinov, maybe even Marcus, though she was in no mood to cut him any amount of slack.

She had tried to interest Cerniga in the dead Russian, but he was having none of it, and Keene had rolled his eyes at her use of the letter's reference to "remains" as evidence.

"Not even a coincidence," he scoffed. "There were two drug dealers killed in Fulton County the same night; you think they were out to buy themselves a Greek death mask too? Something nice to hang on the gun rack in their Mercedes, maybe?"

"The Russian isn't involved," said Cerniga, closing down his colleague's sarcasm in the only way he would accept. "That case is closed."

"I don't see where this conversation is getting us," said Calvin Bowers. He looked tired and a little gaunt, as if he had slept poorly the night before. "Why don't we resume this in the morning, if you have questions my client has not already answered several times."

There was a tap at the office door. Cerniga opened it, and Tonya, dressed in overalls of battleship gray and armed with a broom, put her head round the door.

"I'm going to lock up," she said. "Is there anything you need before I go?"

She didn't look at Deborah.

"Thanks," said Cerniga, shaking his head. "We're all set."

Tonya bobbed her head respectfully and began to back out. She stopped, apparently gripped by an afterthought, and turned to Deborah.

"Miss Miller," she said formally, "I'd like to give my two weeks' notice. I liked Mr. Dixon a lot, but with him gone, I don't think I'd fit in round here."

Deborah thought fast. The black woman's manner was snooty, defiant, and Keene's grin seemed to confirm that she was snubbing the new boss-missy. But there was something a little cautious in her eyes, something that said, *Play along* . . .

The other thing that Deborah had not yet reported to the police about her trip was that she had met Tonya in Greece, that she too had a personal stake in the missing antiquities, however fake they appeared to be.

"Fine," she said, "but I'll dock your pay if this place isn't up to scratch when you finish. I've only been gone a few days, and it looks like you barely moved a mop in my absence. Were you even here?"

"I took the opportunity to visit family in Louisiana," Tonya said, her defiance ratcheting up a notch. "It's not like the museum was open, and the police were underfoot all the time. No offense," she added, nodding to Keene.

"None taken," he replied, enjoying himself.

Clever, thought Deborah, suppressing the impulse to smile. By turning things back to him, she took attention off

Deborah's response to this little fairy story. It was a good thing she had opted to keep Tonya's name out of her tales from Greece.

"Miss Miller?" said Tonya, her tone haughty, as if she was the curator and the Deborah the maid, "could I see you before you leave tonight with regard to my tax documents?"

"Sure," said Deborah, guarded.

As the maid—or rather the reporter—left, Deborah wondered why she was still here at all, and why she was trying to stay under the FBI's radar, especially since the two women had privately decided that the treasures they had been searching for were all copies anyway. Well, Tonya's last remark had set up a rendezvous of sorts, so she'd know before the night was out.

"I've got a question," said Keene, as the door closed behind Tonya. "If you had stolen this mask, what would you do with it?"

Deborah thought about it. Keene was probably making what passed in his less than subtle mind for a veiled accusation, but the question was valid nonetheless.

"I guess I'd try to get it on the black market, if I wasn't working on behalf of a specific buyer," she said. "Or I would lie low, bury it until things had died down a little, till everyone but the hard-core collectors had stopped looking for it."

Keene raised an eyebrow, but unironically. He may not have expected a real answer, but he thought the one he had gotten was helpful.

"And if they were working specifically for an interested party," said Cerniga, "say, the Greek government, and had come not to steal the mask but to inspect it?"

Deborah had tried to be vague about her conversations with Popadreus, but Cerniga had seen through her pretense.

"I guess I would do what I could to get it authenticated," she said.

"And how would they do that?"

Deborah sighed.

"Ideally, they would get the mask examined by an expert,"

she said, "though I suppose the men in question could have been experts themselves. Then I would get it to a lab where real tests could be performed."

"Surely," said Cerniga, "if Richard was selling or giving the piece away, he would have proved its authenticity to the buyer beforehand."

"Not if it was not easily moved around," said Deborah, "and not if he was keeping it secret. If he thought the mask might make him a target for less scrupulous dealers, he'd keep it hidden, give out only enough to get the buyer interested. In any case, he couldn't simply ship lab results to the buyer and expect them to accept his word for their authenticity. The buyer would want to oversee the tests themselves."

"I don't get it," said Keene. "If it's a big gold thing, then it's valuable. Why does it matter how old it is or where it came from?"

"Because," said Calvin, "this is not a matter of intrinsic value. It's a matter of cultural value, the mask's aesthetics, its historical associations, its links to myth and legend. That's what makes it priceless."

"I don't get it," Keene repeated, proud of the fact, as if thinking that this was all so much bullshit made him a bigger man and a straighter shooter.

"There's really no difference between intrinsic value and cultural value," said Deborah. "Gold is only valuable because people have decided they like it and it is comparatively rare. Diamonds, likewise. There's nothing essentially more valuable about diamonds than any other rare compound or element, except that people have decided they like them. This is just the same. But while gold and diamonds are continually being dug up from many places, a Mycenaean death mask is one of a kind. There won't be any more made, but since their value is impossible to separate from their age, who they may have belonged to and so on, the process of authentication is crucial."

"And how would they go about doing that?" said Cerniga. "You said they'd do lab tests. Like what? Carbon dating?"

"You can't carbon date gold," she said. "Radiocarbon dating measures the half-life of material that was once organic. It doesn't work for gold, not reliably."

"What other lab tests are there?"

"None that are scientifically reliable without hard evidence on provenance."

"So what the hell are we talking about this for?" said Cerniga.

"Other materials in the collection could be carbon dated," said Deborah. "Ceramics, for example. We don't know what else was in the case with the mask. If there are other items which purportedly came from the same site, dating them would give a better sense of the mask's authenticity."

What Deborah didn't say was that one thing that could certainly be carbon dated was any fragment of a human body that might have been in with the mask. If Agamemnon himself had really been laid out in that little room behind the bookcase, a radiocarbon examination would probably be able to pinpoint the age of the tissue to within a hundred years or so. In the old days, a considerable amount of the tissue would have had to be destroyed in the course of the test—something archaeologists were understandably loath to try. As someone once said, "He who destroys a thing to discover what it is has left the path of wisdom." Anyway, accelerated mass spectrometry had changed all that. Now the better-funded labs (AMS machines ran in the millions of dollars) had the ability to get the same results from the tiniest fragment of testable material.

Such labs were, of course, few and far between, and if the Greeks had wanted to avail themselves of such a test, they would have a limited number of options in the United States. Fortunately for them and, Deborah thought, for her, she happened to know where there was one such lab not two hours' drive away.

CHAPTER 54

"You need a ride home?" said Cerniga.

It was an awkward question. Calvin was standing at his elbow, and Deborah caught the way he looked quickly away. Cerniga had beaten him to the offer, and with her own car still parked in the parking lot of The Temple (unless they had had it towed), Deborah could think of no reason to say no.

"I have to deal with Tonya's employment papers before I leave," she said. "It might take a few minutes."

She didn't dare look at Calvin.

"I can wait," said Cerniga.

Deborah forced a smile and a "Thanks" before looking back to her desk and pushing papers around meaningfully.

"I guess I'll head out then," said Calvin.

Deborah looked up. For a second their eyes met and groaned their silent frustration.

"OK," she said. "I guess I'll see you tomorrow."

She didn't know what he was thinking, what he had been hoping might happen tonight—wasn't even certain what she had been thinking or hoping for herself—but he was clearly disappointed by Cerniga's professional chivalry.

"Right," he said. He hesitated for a second as if about to say something else, but he was just stalling, and when Cerniga turned to look at him, he began backing out. The sound of the door closing behind him had a finality that made her want to scream.

"You wanted to see the maid?"

"Right," said Deborah, coming back to herself. "I'll be back as soon as I can."

And with this excuse, she left the room as quickly as she could manage without actually running. Calvin was almost out of the lobby door. She called him by name, and he stopped mid-stride and spun around. She remembered the first conversation they had had, and how he had irritated her by remarking that the tomahawk in the case not twenty feet from where he was standing now was the weapon of a barbaric culture. She smiled at the thought.

"What's up?" he said.

"Hey," said Deborah. "I'm sorry I have to . . ."

She gestured vaguely back toward the office.

"Right," he said, "no problem. I'll see you tomorrow."

"Yes," she said, suddenly feeling stupid and girlish. "OK."

He lingered for a second, his upper body swaying slightly as if caught between contradictory impulses, and then he was smiling apologetically and pulling away.

"Tomorrow," he said.

"Yes."

"Looking forward to it."

She watched him walk away, unsure what more she really wanted right now.

Tonya was in the kitchen wringing out a mop in the sink. When she saw Deborah come in, she crossed hurriedly to her, checked over her shoulder, and pushed the door shut.

"Hey," she said, leaning into a brief embrace. "How you doing? OK?"

"Yeah," said Deborah. "Tired is all."

"I'll bet," said Tonya. The expression on her face was that of a concerned friend, and Deborah found herself wondering at how their relationship—which had always seemed so strained—had been altered by their encounter in Mycenae. "Listen," she continued, her voice hushed, "I'm sorry about that before. Tell me you didn't say that you saw me out there."

"I didn't."

"Thank God," said Tonya, her whole body registering the relief.

"Why?" said Deborah. "You know Cerniga is FBI, right?"

"Yeah," said Tonya. "He told me as soon as I got back, like that would make me spill all my secrets or something. I didn't believe it, but I called to check up. I'm pretty sure he's legit. But here's the thing. Why would the Feds be involved in this? It doesn't make sense."

"The body—and, for the record, I've only mentioned the mask, not the body itself—has been moved across state lines, probably been smuggled through international waters. That makes it a federal crime, doesn't it?"

"Sure," said Tonya, "but when did they know about that?"

Deborah saw her point, and it stilled her, like the echo of her panic when she first overheard Keene and Cerniga arguing through the vents in the bathroom.

"They came to investigate a murder, right?" said Tonya. "They both came together. At that stage no one knew anything about smuggling or stolen goods, or at least they didn't say so. So why is the FBI involved? I called my buddy who works over at the Clayton County department and asked him what the most common reasons are that the Feds get involved in murder cases, and you know what he said?"

"What?"

"Hate crimes," she said.

"Hate crimes?"

"He didn't hesitate. First thing out of his mouth. Hate crimes."

And there it was again, that sense that she was completely off track, searching for all the wrong clues, putting together the wrong puzzle . . .

"But how could Richard's death be a hate crime?" said Deborah, shrugging off the familiar uncertainty. "He was white, male, and, so far as I know, straight. His wife had been dead a long time, but . . . No. He was straight."

"But what if the hate crime they are looking into doesn't involve Richard at all?" said Tonya. "What if it happened years ago?"

Oh God, Deborah thought, *here it comes.*

"Your father?" she said. "You think they are investigating the death of your father?"

"I'm just saying," said Tonya, backing off a fraction. "I asked a lot of questions. I contacted the military authorities and even talked about getting him exhumed. I'm just wondering if someone decided to pursue it."

"Then why keep the investigation secret? Especially from you?"

"You've got me," she said. "But I'd rather play my cards kind of close to my chest right now. You see what I'm saying?"

Deborah nodded slowly, thoughtfully, but she had nothing else to say. Hate crimes? She didn't buy it, but she knew that to say so to Tonya would put their new friendship on very shaky grounds. For the reporter-turned-maid, the story of her father's death was too vital, too tied to other deeply emotive issues, for her to take skepticism about it lightly, and Deborah knew Tonya just enough to guess how she would react. She would be hardheaded, defensive, secretly hurt, and angry in ways that would shut her out.

Sound familiar?

Deborah stood there in silence, looking grave.

"Speaking of keeping things close to your chest," said Tonya, her manner abruptly becoming intimate and amused, "I notice you've started wearing a little makeup and perfume, huh? I wondered when you'd figure out that your graduate school wouldn't actually strip you of your credentials if you came in a little girly once in a while."

Deborah waved the remark off, blushing. She had begun the day with the thinnest smear of lipstick and a couple of dots of Chanel No. 19, products she had been hoarding unused for almost as long as Schliemann's gold had been buried in Mycenae.

"There was a time," said Deborah with mock hauteur, "that maids knew their place."

"And weren't they just the good old days," said Tonya. She punctuated her remark with a whoop of derisive laughter and left the room, mop and bucket at the ready.

Deborah grinned, and then found herself coming back to their previous conversation, and the way it promised trouble for the future.

Hate crimes?

"By the way," said Tonya, sticking her head back round the door. "That town you said was near the Swiss border: what did you say it was called?"

"Magdeburg."

"Yeah, that's what I thought," said Tonya. "It isn't. At least, not that I could find. There's a Magdeburg close to Berlin, but there wouldn't be a lot of point in trying to smuggle stuff to another town a few miles over if the Allies were breathing down their necks, would there?"

"I guess not," said Deborah, frowning. "Maybe there's more than one."

"Maybe," said Tonya as she left.

Deborah logged on to the office computer, went online, and Googled "Magdeburg." The first page of results were all in German. One looked like it was about a theater, another was a tourist site, but none had maps locating the city in Germany as a whole, and the search engine's knowing prompt that she might want to try "Magdenburg" didn't help. The next page, however, produced something like a chamber of commerce site which was, impressively, in English. A link for directions took her to a map.

Tonya was right. Magdeburg was indeed slap in the middle of the country, only a hundred miles or so southwest of Berlin, in what was called the Saxony-Anhalt province. Surely to send the body in that direction would have been to send it to the Western allies? And if the German intention was just to get it away from the Russians who were approaching from the east, that still didn't explain how it wound up two hundred and fifty miles farther south.

Deborah returned to her search and tried one more page. A single article in English stood out from the rest. She clicked on it, and her puzzlement deepened. It read:

Blood and Blossom:
New Evidence in Magdeburg Atrocity

During construction of a new building in 1994, laborers stumbled upon the skeletons of 32 bodies, all apparently young men, all murdered at the same time. Since the grave seemed to date from a moment between 1945 and 1960 it was initially assumed that evidence of another Nazi atrocity had been discovered, though it would be unusual for the Gestapo to create such a mass grave in the centre of a town. New evidence, however, suggests that the atrocity took place not at the end of the World War II but seven years later, and that the perpetrators were the Soviet secret police.

While it has become commonplace to use pollen in forensic examinations of bodies to discover where they died, biologist Reinard Szibor, of Magdeburg's Otto von Guericke University, has used pollen in this case to demonstrate that the victims perished in the early summer. Szibor discovered that the skulls of seven of the victims all contained pollen from plantains, lime trees, and rye, plants whose pollen is released in June and July, significantly after the fall of the Nazis in 1945.

This lays the responsibility for the crime squarely at the feet of Soviet intelligence.

That was all there was. Deborah's puzzlement deepened. Why did the blame automatically fall on the Soviets, and what were the story's implications for Voloshinov, the supposed homeless man who had died so close to the museum? Was the massacre itself relevant to her search for Richard's killers and the trail of faux antiquities which apparently led them to him? There was no reason to think so, but all these old corpses seemed linked somehow, as if each bone she uncovered so blindly was part of a larger, stranger creature whose true nature would only be clear when she could step back from the complete skeleton.

It made about as much sense as Tonya's new idea about hate crimes, though she was trying not to think about that. As she walked back to Cerniga and her ride home, she told herself that it wasn't based on any hard evidence, just a chance observation by Tonya's cop friend about why the Feds got involved in murder cases. It didn't add up to anything real. But she found herself recalling the skinny white boy who had twice tried to kill her in Greece: the mean, smug look, the skinhead do, the tattoos . . . *Hate crimes?*

Cerniga drove her home in stiff, professional silence. He waited behind her while she opened the apartment door and then hovered in the doorway as she satisfied herself that she was otherwise alone in there and that everything was as it should be. She didn't realize that it wasn't until after he had left.

Everything looked fine at a glance, but after she had been back for an hour or so, she had started to notice the tiny incongruous details: clothes hung up that she had thrown into the laundry hamper, a desk drawer left locked, books out of place on the shelves. Marcus had said he had not disturbed anything in her apartment, and she had believed him. If he had been telling the truth, then someone else had been in there since she left, and they had apparently been searching for something. They had taken their time over it, as if they had known she wouldn't be back in the immediate future, and they had done a pretty good job of concealing the search. If she didn't have such a perversely controlling nature, she thought wryly, she probably wouldn't have spotted anything out of place. What they could have been looking for, however, she had no idea.

She called Cerniga and told him, but said that she didn't want anyone coming round. She checked the place over again and then used the hammer from the kitchen drawer to ram home the long painted-over bolts on the door.

"Probably take me ten minutes to get out in the morning," she muttered, laying the hammer on the table where she couldn't miss it.

In the silence of the apartment, with the brooding humidity of an Atlanta summer night all around her, she began to wonder if she had even the beginnings of an idea about why Richard Dixon had died. In Greece everything had seemed clearer, though that already seemed long ago and far away, a distance in time and space that made her experiences there as foreign and exotic as the ruins themselves. There her problems and confusion had seemed appropriate, but she had expected to find clarity with her return home that was somehow tied to the familiarity of her environment. Now that she was here, however, with the strangeness of the police presence at the museum still in effect, with Tonya's stranger theories hemming her in, and with the space which Richard's death had left in all which had once made up her sense of home, she felt completely at sea.

On impulse, she picked up the phone and dialed.

"Hello?"

"Hi Calvin," she said. "It's Deborah. I'm sorry it's so late."

"I thought that one of the upsides of getting you back into the country was that I'd get a decent night's sleep," he said.

She smiled, all the discomfort slipping off her like fine sand as she heard the pleasure in his voice.

"Don't tell me you need your beauty sleep," she said. *You, of all people,* the tone had implied. She bit her lip as he chuckled.

"Since you are clearly awake at all hours regardless of what continent you're on," he said, "the whole beauty sleep thing is clearly a myth."

She flushed and shifted the conversation before she could screw it up by being sarcastic about how easily he flirted.

"Did you think it odd that the Feds showed up to investigate Richard's death before anyone said anything about smuggling or the kinds of crimes that might involve different states or nations?"

"I hadn't really," he said, focusing quickly. "But now that you mention it . . . What's on your mind?"

"Can you think of any reason that Richard's death could have somehow been connected to a hate crime?"

He was silent for a second, as if the air had been pulled right out of him.

"A hate crime?" he said. "Against Richard? How?"

"I don't know," she said lamely. "I was just wondering."

"An odd thought to come into your head in the middle of the night," he said.

She could hear the smile again. At least he hadn't said "pretty little head."

"I know," she said, brushing it off now. "I'm sorry. I shouldn't have bothered you."

"It's no trouble," he said. "I'm glad to talk to you. Before . . . with the cops, I mean . . ." He faltered. "This is better."

"Yes," she said.

"Are you OK? Would you like me to come over?"

She hesitated a fraction too long before breezily saying that it was fine, that *she* was fine, and there was no need. That she was all bolted in tight . . .

"If you're sure," he said.

"You feel like taking a drive tomorrow?" she asked. "I have to make sure Cerniga doesn't need me around, but I was thinking of taking a trip."

"Yeah?" he said. "Sure. Where to?"

"Athens," she said.

"You're going back to Greece?" he said, and he was more than shocked; he was concerned, panicked even.

"Athens, Georgia," she said, laughing. "Home of the Georgia Bulldogs and, among other things, the Center for Applied Isotope Studies."

"What in the name of God is that?" he asked, already sounding relieved.

"That is the home of a very large, very expensive machine which may well have been the first stop for what someone believed to be the body of Agamemnon when it left Richard's bedroom."

"The body of what now?" he said.

And she told him.

CHAPTER 55

Deborah spoke to Agent Cerniga first thing in the morning by phone. No, he said, he didn't need to talk to her today. Yes, she could get on with some work in "the area" but she should keep her cell phone on and she should not leave the state. Deborah agreed and managed to evade further problems with vagaries rather than outright lies.

Why, she asked herself, *don't you just tell him about the lab, that it might be worth looking into as a place the Greeks—if indeed it was the Greeks who took the masked corpse—may have visited?*

Because it was probably a blind alley. Because the stolen goods weren't worth looking after. Because she suspected Cerniga was still keeping his real investigation secret from her. Those things were all true but weren't the real reason. The real reason was because Richard's reputation would be wounded if it came out that he'd put so much energy into a collection that wasn't worth shelf space.

It's not because you like playing Nancy Drew?

No, she thought, defiantly. *It's not.*

She called Calvin, and he asked that she pick him up outside his office. He had some paperwork to take care of before he slipped away for the day. He managed to make their excursion sound like it should be accompanied by champagne and a basket of strawberries, and Deborah found herself dressing to meet him with an attention to detail that was unlike her. She wore earrings and perfume, and did so with a sense of girlish glee that was as uncharacteristic as it was unironic. She tried a stronger shade of lipstick, but that was too big a step, and she wiped it off again, embarrassed both by the impulse to put it on and the feelings that made her get rid of it.

God, she thought, *I hate courtship. Or whatever the twenty-first century has in place of courtship. All the careful playing back and forth, and simpering smiles, and word-association conversations, the minor deceptions, studied nonchalance, and gamesmanship. Yes, that's it. Courtship is like playing tennis to lose—to get a respectable score, so that it doesn't look like the match has been thrown, but to lose all the same. It's playing tennis in heels and a veil.*

Or, said another voice in one of her mind's darker corners, was she just scared of what it all pointed to: romance and relationships *(dreadful word)* and that most absurd of sacred cows, sex?

Who cares? she said to herself, flinching away from the thought like it might electrocute her. *Let's just say I hate courtship and leave it at that, OK?*

OK.

She dressed determinedly in a summer dress that was just professional enough to legitimate her visit to the lab while suggesting a certain casualness, as if she had grabbed it off the rail without really looking at it.

Probably should have done just that . . .

She went out to the car pointedly without checking her reflection in the mirror.

Calvin's office was in a glass tower which was the iridescent blue of a hot blade. It looked across Centennial Park toward the Coca-Cola Center and the Omni from some of the most expensive real estate in a city where land prices were steadily beginning to challenge their counterparts in Boston and New York. Deborah, who was usually unimpressed by such places and felt their professional opulence to be a challenge to what she did and valued, was unsettled by the tang of pleasure she got from seeing Calvin come strolling out of the building's smoked glass doors, smiling: one of those who belonged within its sheer and graceful lines.

"Quite a place," she said, as she pulled away.

He shrugged.

"It's dark inside," he said, "and there aren't enough elevators. But I live right around the corner."

She smiled and powered through the lights and round to the northbound freeway, wondering if that was the prelude to an invitation.

They drove for forty-five minutes up I-85, then across on Route 316 toward Athens, chatting about books and movies and food, never referring to Richard or their day's ostensible mission. The town surprised them, appearing whole and bustling out of miles of pine forest, like the goddess who was its namesake, born fully grown from Zeus's head. Deborah had been to the university for a symposium six months before and still had a campus map with her, though she only had to check it once before finding her way to Riverbend Road and the CAIS.

It being summer, the building lacked the buzz of students who populated it during term time, but the Center for Applied Isotope Studies had a commercial dimension as well as being geared to university work, and testing was continuous. They spoke to a receptionist, and Deborah confirmed that she had indeed called ahead to set up their appointment and that they had the sample with them, though they would need it to be prepped. Yes, Deborah said, they were prepared to pay extra for the lab to prep the sample themselves, and no, they were not interested in liquid scintillation counting, just the radiocarbon dating. Throughout this exchange, Calvin hovered, looking serious and a little out of his depth. Deborah flashed him a smile as the receptionist conveyed their details to the lab, and he smiled back, a little nervously.

"I don't understand," he said. "You have a sample?"

"Nothing relevant," she said. "Just play along."

The technician who eventually came out to meet them was a sallow-skinned young man with a trim beard. He might have been Middle Eastern, possibly even north African, but he spoke without any trace of an accent.

"I am Dr. Kerem," he said. "Please step this way. You have the sample with you?"

Deborah produced a stoppered test tube containing what looked like a fragment of wood little larger than a splinter.

"Is that enough?" said Calvin. Deborah gave him a look.

"Plenty," said the technician. "And it needs prepping?"

"Please," said Deborah. "We're pretty sure it's a fragment of a sixteenth-century Spanish galleon, but we need to be sure."

"Very well," he said, showing them into a large, rectangular room lit from above with fluorescents and humming with the steady pulse of electricity.

"This is where the tests will be performed?" said Deborah.

The equipment in the room was a series of consoles, metal cylinders, bafflingly complex instruments, and miles of colored cable, much of it encased in wire cages and framed in blue-painted metal. Kerem smiled suddenly, a wide, proud smile, as if he had been complimented on his son's Little League performance.

"She's a National Electrostatics 1.5SDH-1 Pelletron Accelerator Mass Spectrometer," he said. "You thought it would be bigger, right?"

"Right," said Deborah, judging this to be the desired response.

"Five hundred kV," said Kerem, still beaming. "Can measure isotopic concentrations on a parts per quadrillion basis. This little beauty will give the Goliaths a run for their money, and I mean detection in the half percent range, detection limits down to four times ten to the minus eighteen moles of C-14."

Deborah and Calvin looked suitably impressed.

"That's right," said Kerem, as if somebody had suggested otherwise. He pointed at the various components and intoned their name and function, apparently assuming Deborah had some idea what he was talking about.

"One thirty-four sample ion source," he said, indicating the contents of one of the caged areas. "That," he said, pointing in turn to each section of the apparatus, "is the injection magnet, then there's the Pelletron accelerator itself, the analyzing magnet, off-axis Faraday cups, electrostatic analyzer, and the C-14 particle detector. If it's less than sixty thousand years old, we'll nail it."

"Right," said Deborah again. "Excellent."

Kerem put out his hand for the test tube containing the fragment of wood.

"You can leave that with me," he said. "Process the paperwork at reception, and we'll be in touch when the tests are completed. It will be four hundred dollars."

"How long will it take to get the results?"

"Approximately two to three months," he said. "Is it urgent?"

Deborah's face had fallen. "Kind of," she said.

"We can do a two-week turnaround for six hundred dollars," he said. "Maybe a little faster."

Two weeks?

She thought quickly.

"When will the other results be ready?" she said.

"Other results?"

"Yes," she said, not looking at Calvin. "Our museum sent some other samples by a week or so ago. Human remains and some ceramic shards. A couple of Greek guys brought them. Maybe we could pick up both sets of results at the same time."

She held her breath. The technician frowned and flipped the pages on his clipboard.

"I don't see any other samples pending for your institution," he said.

"It might be under Dixon," she tried. "Richard Dixon. He's the museum's principal trustee and handles the larger expenses."

Another pause. Deborah bit her lip.

"Dixon," he said. "Yes, here it is. There was an extra fee paid to speed up the process, and they should be ready tomorrow afternoon. The contact information is different, however. We'll have to put them in the mail."

"That's fine," said Deborah, her heart thumping. "Maybe we can swing by tomorrow before you send them out. Mr. Dixon is anxious to hear as soon as you know something. We have a rather pressing decision to make about a display."

"That should be fine," said Kerem. "You are staying in town?"

"About to check into a hotel," said Deborah, still not looking at Calvin.

CHAPTER 56

They booked two rooms, though Deborah thought the chances of them using only one of them were better than average. The thought made her nervous and clumsy. She wasn't sure what he was thinking, and though she thought they were on the same page, her doubts—always the loudest voice in situations like this—made her nervousness increase.

Situations like this.

That was a joke, like they happened on a weekly basis. In fact it had been ... too long to give numbers to. She shrugged the thought off and watched him eat.

She would have been happy with a sandwich and a beer, which Athens—college town that it was—could supply in spades. Perhaps, she had thought, they could catch an up-and-coming local act, hot on the heels of REM and the B-52s. Calvin had had other ideas, however, though she wasn't entirely sure what they were, except that they involved raising the tone of their evening somewhat.

He had found and booked a table at what had to be the city's most exclusive and expensive bistro, where they could be sure of seeing no summer school kids, and ordered lamb with what he pronounced a fine Bordeaux, with the air of a man showing that he knew how to do these things. Deborah resisted the urge to order a beer to make a point, partly because she wasn't entirely sure what the point was, partly because it amused her to see him turning up the class like this. Nevertheless, the bistro did rather starch the evening, and she found it hard to settle. The place was almost unnaturally quiet, more like a temple than a restaurant, and it loaded every utterance with significance until, unable to think of anything

especially worthy of significance, she opted, for once, to let
him talk.

He told her about his job, emphasizing its general te-
diousness rather than its details, for which she was relieved,
and about his passion for fly-fishing, sparing her the details
of that too.

"It's all about strategy," he said. "Selecting the right fly for
the fish and the conditions—better still, tying your own, making new ones: learning to outthink the fish."

She grinned.

"I know that sounds like it should be easy for someone
who is paid what I am," he said, "but trust me: outwitting a
brown trout up there in a fast-moving stream . . . More fulfill-
ing than any deal or contract that comes out my way, no matter the price tag."

She liked that.

"So you're a schemer," she said.

"I like a little gamesmanship," he said, nodding and smiling
so that the precise subject of the conversation became entic-
ingly murky. "I like a pursuit you have to think about, plan for."

"A pursuit of fish," she said.

"What else is there?" he said, grinning.

She laughed and then took a moment to consider him.

"You remind me of Richard a little," she said.

His brow clouded, unsure of whether this was a compliment or not.

"How do you mean?"

"Just a feeling, I guess," she said, flushing slightly, wishing she hadn't said it.

"Go on."

"Well, you both have a kind of playful wit," she said, feeling for the words as she spoke. "I mean, there's a cleverness
there that can be a little off-putting."

"For you?" He laughed. "Surely not."

"I don't mean intimidating exactly," she said. "I mean
there's a thoughtfulness, a calculation almost, that keeps people at a distance, like you are sizing them up all the time: like

they're little fish and you are carefully zipping your flies or whatever you do."

"Tying." He laughed.

"Whatever."

"I don't know about me," he said, "but I know what you mean about Richard. Sometimes when he looked at you, it was like he knew all your secrets."

"Do you have many secrets?"

"None," he said, shaking off a pensive moment with a grin. "I'll tell you anything."

"I'll bet," she said.

"Anyway," he said, reverting to their previous discussion. "I'm not sure I like the sound of this version of me as calculating and conniving, however clever it makes me sound. It doesn't sound wholly positive."

"Oh, I don't know." She shrugged, looking away as if it didn't matter. "It has a kind of allure."

She reached for her wineglass and took a long drink, her eyes down.

When they got back to the hotel it was clear that they still didn't know how the evening would end. They had flirted back and forth, always withdrawing to cover as soon as anything deeper or more physical was visible on the horizon. Deborah told herself that she was happy with this, that it was good for her to move slowly since she was so unused to moving at all, that she didn't really know this man that well, but when he moved to kiss her in the hallway outside his room, she gave herself utterly to the moment.

Inside, they kissed some more, gently, cautiously at first, then deep and hungry and urgent. Still, when his hands moved to the buttons of her shirt, she felt herself stiffen, almost against her will, so that he stopped and looked at her. She blushed, unsure of what to say or feel, wishing that his eyes were not exactly on a level with hers. His silent gaze made her less comfortable still, and she turned away, maddened by the feeling of his eyes upon her, until he reached over and shut the bedroom light off.

The heavy, generic drapes blocked out every trace of light, and the darkness made her heart skip, as if she was back in the Mycenaean passage delving down to the ancient cistern. As he renewed his kisses, however, and his hands, cautiously, slowly, seeking permission, began to move over her, she embraced the freedom of the darkness, as if she had shed some part of herself. It was like being drunk or on holiday, nameless and absolved of all responsibility. She drew him to her, holding back a strange, unexpected, and alarming impulse to weep.

CHAPTER 57

Calvin was up and off looking for somewhere for them to have breakfast when Deborah awoke, so that for a few minutes she just lay there by herself, worrying in an unspecific sort of way about what the day would bring. She showered, dressed, and was staring blankly at a newspaper when he got back.

They breakfasted at a diner on omelets and waffles, the former excellent, the latter almost certainly prepackaged and suspiciously cold in the center. They ate hurriedly, speaking little, as if they were in a rush. In fact, they probably had several hours before the results were ready, but they couldn't sit around in the hotel or in this or any other diner. Deborah checked her watch three times in five minutes, and they resolved to wait at the lab itself, so that they would know the moment the staff were ready to tell them something.

It reminded Deborah vaguely of being a teenager, waiting for the doctors who had been working on her father to emerge from surgery. She had sat with a sleeping neighbor for six hours, unable to close her eyes, watching the minute hand on the clock so closely that she had been able to see it move. Several times the doors through which they had taken him had kicked open, only for some intern to march out on her way home, not giving Deborah a glance. When the doctor finally did emerge, there was a fraction of a second before the door swung shut behind him when her heart had leapt, galvanized into hope by all the waiting, and she had gotten to her feet. By the time she was fully upright she had read her father's death in the doctor's face, and she had just hung there, effectively alone in the unnaturally white room, while the doctor fumbled for the right words, and the sleeping neighbor grunted back into consciousness. When she woke properly, the neighbor, who was more religiously conservative than her family had ever been, told Deborah to tear the clothing over her heart as a sign of her grief. Deborah obeyed, baffled. It was the last remotely Orthodox Jewish act she had committed. The following week, she had eaten two shrimp from a salad she had bought on purpose at a Brookline deli. Her family had never been especially careful about keeping kosher, so they may not have recognized Deborah's act for what it was, even if they had known about it. She had not kept kosher since until ordering that meal on her way back from Greece, and she had never returned to Judaism.

In truth, she regretted that day and the furtive shrimp, her thirteen-year-old self's version of contempt for the God who had taken her father. It had been a cheap gesture, and one her father would have found offensive, not for its violation of Orthodox religious practice so much as for its spiteful pettiness.

Well, she thought. *That's all in the past.*

Except, of course, that it wasn't. Not really. She had been reminded of it by waiting for the test results, but surely this would be different? The death of her father had been both an end and the beginning of a new, difficult phase.

Surely, she thought, *the test results will be an end, not a beginning, not a restart. The body was old, or it wasn't. Period.*

They waited in the reception for an hour and a half before Dr. Kerem appeared.

"Eager beavers," he said, flourishing an addressed envelope from which he produced a sheaf of folded, computer-printed pages. "I'm ready to put those results in the mail. I take it you still want to see them?"

"Sure," said Deborah, affecting a ludicrous casualness that made the doctor peer at her over the top of his glasses. They had been waiting for hours. Of course she wanted to see the results.

Kerem produced a sheaf of papers for each test. Each consisted of a graphic readout accompanied by pages of numbers and technical schematics which amounted, Deborah assumed, to a kind of narrative.

"What am I seeing here?" said Calvin, brandishing the first packet

"These are the ceramics," said Kerem. "They are consistently showing to be eighteenth or nineteenth century. We can't be too precise because this is the period when the widespread use of fossil fuels tends to fudge the results."

"You're sure," said Deborah. "They can't be ancient?"

"What do you mean by ancient?"

"Bronze Age," she said. "Say, twelve hundred B.C."

"Absolutely not," he said.

Deborah felt her body sag as if the air had suddenly been released from a balloon in her gut. It wasn't a surprise, but it was still depressing. Richard had died for those worthless copies, had—and this was somehow worse—lived for them.

"What about the human remains?" said Calvin.

"Different," said Kerem.

It took a second for Deborah to realize what he had said.

"Different how so?" said Calvin. He looked focused, his eyes bright and unblinkingly hard.

"The body doesn't come from the same period as the potsherds," said Kerem.

"How much older is it?" said Deborah, a trifle breathless. This, she had not expected.

"Oh," said Kerem, "it's not older. It's more recent."

"What?" said Deborah, staring.

"Not by much," said Kerem, "but pre-1950s."

"Are you sure?" said Calvin.

Kerem looked a little put out.

"The AMS machine detects radiocarbon decay," he said. "It measures age based on the known decay rate of radioactive isotopes naturally present in organic material, and is accurate up to ages of fifty or sixty thousand years. Anything older than that no longer contains radiocarbon. At the other end of the spectrum is the fact that extensive nuclear testing in the 1950s significantly increased radiation levels in

organic material. The difference between material which pre-
cedes those tests and that which comes during or after them
is quite marked. The human remains clearly come before the
atomic tests, but after the eighteenth/nineteenth century window. The body is early twentieth century, death occurring,
probably, in the mid-1940s."

Deborah felt her jaw go slack. The 1940s? That made no
sense at all.

"Can I see that?" said Calvin.

Kerem handed him the envelope, and he went through the
pages of data quizzically.

Deborah wanted to ask Kerem if he was sure but knew that
such a question was pointless and disrespectful.

"OK," she said, vaguely. "Right. Well, I guess we'll be
going."

"The other results will be ready for you in a couple of
weeks, probably," said Kerem. "Should I just mail them to
the museum?"

"Other results?" said Deborah, still feeling slow and stupid as if she was slightly drunk.

"Your Spanish galleon," he said.

"Right," she said. "Yes. Send them to the museum."

He thanked them for their business, took the envelope
from Calvin, and left them standing in the spare, pale lobby
which now felt even more like a hospital waiting room.

"You OK?" said Calvin.

"Yeah," she lied. "I'm going to call Cerniga."

There was no choice. The time to play detective was long
past.

"OK," said Calvin, giving her a searching look. "Probably
smart. Let me swing by the bathroom while you call him.
Then I guess we'll get our stuff and hit the road."

It was almost a question, as if this new sense of conclu-
sion might make her suggest that they spend a few days in the
mountains with him or something. She barely heard it,
merely nodding her agreement and fumbling for her phone.

So it wasn't Agamemnon. She hadn't really believed otherwise, not lately, but this was a new and alarming strangeness. It wasn't an ancient corpse unearthed after centuries underground, nor was it just a few bones taken from a convenient cemetery at the end of the nineteenth century. This was more recent and less connected to Schliemann, to the dig, to Mycenae, even to archaeology itself. Indeed, it was recent enough for a new and pressing question to dominate Deborah's thoughts as she unsteadily pushed the numbers on her phone. She had been thinking of her search for the items missing from Richard's bedroom in terms of *how* and *what* and *why*. Now all those questions were eclipsed by another: *who?*

Who was the body that had lain in state behind Richard's bookcase?

And who killed him?

CHAPTER 58

"Agent Cerniga," said the voice on the line.

"Yes, this is Deborah Miller," she said. "I'm in Athens."

"You're *where*?"

"Athens, Georgia," she said. "I've just learned something you need to hear about."

"Go on."

She talked. She suggested that she'd come to test the galleon's age and had stumbled onto the test results from the Agamemnon crate by accident. Cerniga said nothing, so she barreled through, moving from point to point, making no attempt to consciously conceal anything. Even so, she did not mention that Calvin was with her, did not in fact even allude to him, and when he emerged from the building looking solemn and smiled at her, she turned away to focus on her phone call.

"What's the phone number of the CAIS lab?" said Cerniga, after listening in silence to her description of the test results.

Deborah checked her receipt for the ship prow test and read it back to him.

"They probably won't tell you more than I've already said," she added.

"I don't want more details," he said. "I want the contact address of whoever took the samples to be tested. Right now, finding the men who ordered the test is more important than the test results. Come back to Atlanta and keep your phone on."

Of course it was, she thought as she hung up. How could she have thought otherwise? This wasn't about some ancient archaeological mystery, it was about the murder of her closest friend. They were looking for a killer, not a corpse, and the fact that she had somehow forgotten left her feeling wounded, humiliated, and guilty.

Deborah drove fast, her mind trying to make sense of what she had learned so far. The new development had made her private, and though she regretted nothing of the previous night with Calvin, part of her wished he had brought his own car. She didn't want to talk. She didn't want to be playful or tender. She wanted to think, and she wasn't used to talking until she knew what she wanted to say. Usually the gap between the two could be measured in milliseconds, but right now she felt confused, uncertain, and a little afraid. She didn't want to discuss such feelings or even give them voice.

"What's wrong?" said Calvin.

She shook her head and then forced herself to say, "Nothing. Just concentrating."

"On driving, or on the test results?"

It had begun to rain. She snapped on the wipers and hunkered down in the seat.

"Both," she said. She didn't smile, and she didn't take her eyes off the road. The monosyllable was supposed to close the conversation.

"What do you think about this body?" said Calvin.

She sensed that he didn't care about that so much as he did about reestablishing contact between them, but she couldn't bring herself to play along. She shrugged.

"No ideas?" he said.

"Not really."

He turned and looked out of his rain-streaked window.

"You sure you're OK?" he said. "With me, I mean."

"I'm fine, Calvin," she said, the irritation in her voice showing. *Just shut up and leave me alone.* "I'm just concentrating."

* * *

In fact her thoughts had fastened on three things: the age of the body, the fact that the FBI had jurisdiction over hate crimes, and the death of a black World War Two tank commander who had never known his daughter. But if the person—or people—who had killed Richard and had tried to kill her in Greece knew that the crate contained not the body of Agamemnon but that of Tonya's father, a forgotten Sherman commander executed for his curiosity by a racist military policeman fifty years ago, why were they so anxious—so murderously desperate—to get hold of it?

She was startled out of her musing by the ringing of her phone: "La Cucaracha" still. Richard's joke. They had been driving in silence for over an hour and were now heading south toward the city, coming down from the wooded slopes around Red Top Mountain where the waters of Lake Allatoona flashed darkly through the rain-swept trees.

"Pass me that, will you," said Deborah, reaching across Calvin as her phone skittered out of her hand and onto the floor between his legs.

"So you *can* talk?" he remarked. It was a joke, but a brittle one.

"Just . . . thank you," she said, taking it brusquely from him and flipping it open. "Hello?"

"It's Cerniga," said the FBI agent. "Where are you?"

"Half an hour north of the perimeter. Maybe less. Why?"

"I'm going to give you directions to an address," he said. "I want you to get down here right away. Don't go anywhere else first."

"OK. Shoot."

"You need to pull over to write this down?"

"I'll remember it," she said, pinning the phone against her shoulder with her head and using the free hand to make an impatient scribbling gesture to Calvin.

"What?" he said.

"A pen," she mouthed, turning her face from the mouthpiece.

"OK," said Cerniga. "It's 136 Greencove Street. It's about twenty minutes south of the airport. Come off I-85 at the Palmetto exit, go left off the ramp, and go four miles to Haysbridge Road. Go left, then right onto Greencove. The house you want is the first building on the left. It's set pretty far back from the road, but you should be able to see it. It looks abandoned."

Deborah repeated each stage of the directions to Calvin, who wrote quickly and with a look of sour disapproval at being reduced to stenographer.

"What is this place?" she said. "And why do you want me there?"

"It's where the Greeks have been holed up," said Cerniga, his voice flat. "Where they have been storing the crate."

"How did you find them?" said Deborah, suddenly exuberant.

"We called the CAIS lab. They had the contact information."

"Right," said Deborah. "Of course. That's great."

"Not really," said Cerniga. "Someone beat us to it."

"Is it . . ." Deborah couldn't find the words. "Is everything OK?"

"Just get here," he said, and hung up.

CHAPTER 59

"I'm going to drop you off," she said to Calvin, still staring into the rain ahead. "Where's good?"

She felt him turn to look at her, but for a while he didn't say anything.

"Calvin?" she said, prompting.

"Did I do something wrong?" he said. "You regret last night?"

"No," she said, not sure if it was true. "I just don't think we should show up together."

"Why not?"

"Well, for one thing, you weren't asked to go."

"Nice," he snapped. "You know what, Deborah? That's fine. I have to go back to the museum later, but just drop me back at my office."

She almost protested, almost apologized, almost tried to explain that it wasn't really about him at all so much as about being seen and treated as a couple by other people in ways that made things real and therefore scary, that it was about a sense of dread about what she was about to find out at the end of this drive, but in the end she just nodded and said, "OK."

After she had dropped him off and he had stalked back to the great glass tower with only the tersest of good-byes, the city fell quickly away behind her. Once past Turner Field, the only major exit was onto I-20 and then the perimeter loop, then only signs to the airport and small towns like Fairburn, Jonesboro, and Union City whose names were unfamiliar to her. As the traffic thinned to almost nothing, and the exits spread themselves along miles of heavily wooded highway which gave no sense of place beyond the strip of asphalt and concrete itself, she began to wonder if she had missed her exit.

She considered Calvin's uneven scrawl and looked up just in time to catch the Palmetto exit sign looming overhead. She slowed, took the ramp, and followed the directions carefully as the freeway gave way to single-lane highways and open horse pasture punctuated by russet-colored barns with white timber frames. The city could have been hours away, another world entirely. Almost another time.

The house seemed to have been numbered 136 at random, there being no other visible properties on the street. As Cerniga had suggested, the building itself was set some way back from the road and was only dimly visible through the steady rain. Even so, it looked ramshackle and close to derelict. It was an old house, possibly Victorian, large and ornate with gingerbread trim and a square turret off to one side. If it was still salvageable it would probably be a spectacular home, graceful despite its immensity, elegant without being fussy. Right now it was surrounded by cars and strobed by the lights of emergency vehicles so that the house looked like the heart of the storm, its walls intermittently slashed by red and blue lightning.

All thoughts of Calvin vanished as Deborah parked the car, composed herself like a diver taking a steadying breath, and got out into the rain. Putting her head down, she ran along the uneven gravel driveway up to the house. A uniformed officer stopped her at the stoop but was clearly expecting her and stepped aside as soon as she gave her name.

It seemed unlikely that anyone had lived in the house for some time. It was sparsely furnished, and what pieces there were seemed to have been abandoned, as if they hadn't made the cut when the last owner had died and the better items had been sold off. Somewhere in the house was the steady patter of running water. A ruptured pipe or a leaking roof? Probably the latter.

"Up here."

It was Keene, leaning over the banister of a dusty staircase. Deborah pushed her wet hair back from her face and climbed the stairs, as Keene descended.

"Ah," he said, grimly satisfied, "if it isn't Her Eminence the lady museum curator."

"What is it?" she said, too apprehensive to bother sparring.

"Brace yourself," he said. "It ain't pretty."

The first body was on the landing, sprawled on his back. His shirt had been torn open and a now-familiar word etched into his chest in large, savage slashes resembling Greek letters: Atreus. Apart from the letters themselves, the flesh was pale and unmarked, but there was a large and irregular puddle of thickening blood beneath the body. Deborah put a hand against the wall to steady herself.

"They were done postmortem," said Cerniga, appearing from one of what were, presumably, bedrooms. "He was shot twice in the back with a shotgun at close range. Then the carving. The blood is from the shotgun hits. Trust me when I tell you he looks better this way up."

He spoke quickly, his words clipped with what she took to be anger or frustration.

"Does he look familiar to you?"

Deborah considered him. He was slim, perhaps fifty, dark skinned. His hair and mustache were both a little longer than the fashion and flecked with gray. She shook her head.

"I don't think so," she said. "Is he Greek?"

"According to his passport," said Cerniga. She wasn't certain if that was supposed to be a joke. "There are other papers with him, but nobody can read them. I'm sending them in for translation, but yeah, they're Greek."

"The documents?"

"The victims," he said. "There's another in the bedroom. Take a look at him and see if he looks familiar. A good long look, please, Miss Miller. Then come downstairs and tell me whatever you haven't already told me, and we'll try to figure out just how much trouble you are in."

He stormed past her and stomped his way downstairs, but paused halfway down to add, "If you had told me about that lab, we could have gotten this address days ago, and these two men would still be alive. You might want to give that some thought."

She stopped in her tracks as if he had slapped her hard in the face. Keene was looking at her from the other end of the hall, his eyes hard and unforgiving. Deborah looked quickly away, her face hot, her mouth open as if trying to find words to respond, as if anything she could say would be useful, true, or remotely adequate.

CHAPTER 60

The rain had stopped by the time she got home, and the roads steamed as the chorus of crickets and tree frogs began anew. Deborah got heavily out of the car and into the thick, hot, night air, the oppressive humidity dense as a Turkish bath, sapping her of what little emotional energy she had taken away from the meeting with Cerniga in Palmetto.

In truth, it hadn't really been a meeting so much as a verbal beating, a torrent of invective about her meddling amateurism, her irrational need to keep secrets from the only people who were likely to bring Richard's killers to justice, and her culpability for the deaths of the two Greeks. Keene had joined them late and, for once, he was content to listen and watch. Deborah hadn't cried, and wouldn't, but after a few lame protestations of innocence and indignation, she had sat there in silence and taken the weight of it all, knowing that there was no point in arguing, knowing—and this was far worse—that the FBI man was right.

It was true that she had had good reason to be suspicious of the police and of Cerniga in particular at first, and it was also true that her suspicion of Cerniga had survived the announcement of his FBI status because he continued to withhold information from her, but these were thin justifications for her tactics. As the investigating officer he had, after all, every right to tell her as much or as little as he thought was necessary. She, on the other hand, had no such rights, had, in fact, probably done enough to get her charged with obstructing justice if they chose to prosecute her. That might well be determined by how much heat the FBI took from the Greek government for failing to protect its citizens. Privately, Deborah was fairly sure the Greek government would say little or nothing, but the fact that she would probably evade prosecution did nothing to alleviate her guilt.

"All you had to do was pick up the phone," Cerniga had roared into her face. "All you had to do was say, 'You know what, Agent Cerniga? I'll bet they took that crate to the University of Georgia to have it carbon dated.' That's all you had to do. You would have been the hero of the hour. But that wouldn't have been enough for you, would it?"

She had not been able to think of anything to say. She couldn't even come up with an explanation that would have satisfied herself. Why had she driven up to Athens without telling them? Was she doing it for Richard, unraveling the truth behind his death out of quasi-filial obligation? Maybe. A rather less dignified possibility, one that insisted itself into her head only as she was driving home, pushing into her brain like the point of a nail slowly tapped home, was that she had done it to impress Calvin. The thought left her feeling shrunken and hollow, eviscerated by shame and self-loathing.

"Who do you think you are?" Cerniga had said. "Some kind of amateur detective sleuthing her way right past the professionals on sheer genius? Not only have your inquiries set us back and cost two men their lives, they haven't even revealed anything relevant. You think this is about archaeology?" he concluded, aghast at the absurdity of the idea. "You know, Miss Miller, for a well-educated woman you can be remarkably stupid."

His tirade still rang in her head as night fell on her silent apartment. She tried music and television to drive it out, but both seemed irreverent, disrespectful to the men who had died and to the mood she had no right to escape. Resigning herself to the silence and her own guilt, she lay for a while on her bed, staring up at the fan, feeling its breeze on her sweating skin. Then she got up, turned on the computer, and checked her e-mail. Nothing. She had half expected something

from Calvin, but it was probably as well that she didn't have
to deal with his remonstrations right now. He had, no doubt,
every right to be baffled and hurt by the way she had closed
him out on the drive back from Athens, but she had sensed
what she was about to find, and it had taken priority over her
budding romance. Surely he would see that?

But that wasn't strictly true either. There had been something else that had turned her back inside herself before she
spoke to Cerniga and Keene: a sense that she had let Calvin
too close and needed now to beat him back a little so that he
couldn't stifle her with his attentions. She frowned as she
thought this. Perhaps her patented self-reliance and proud
isolationism, which had stood her so well from those earliest
school days when she had felt herself different from the other
girls, had suddenly turned on her like a trusted dog whose tail
had been stood on. Twice, perhaps. Because sitting here
alone in front of her computer's ambient glow, staring at her
empty e-mail box, it occurred to her that the impulse to with-
draw from Calvin and the impulse to keep her findings from
the FBI might actually be one and the same.

*And you're just figuring this out now? You know, Debs,
Cerniga was right. For an intelligent woman you can be pretty
damn stupid.*

She was still thinking this when she noticed the light on
her answering machine blinking slowly. She pushed the Play
button and heard an unexpected but familiar voice, polished
and a little stiff.

"Hello, Deborah," it said.

The voice took her back to the night this had all started,
the night Richard died.

"Hello Marcus," she said, as if he was standing in front of
her, pipe in hand.

"I'm sorry I missed you in Greece," said Marcus. "I was
following another lead which brought me back here. Listen,
Deborah, we need to talk. This thing . . ." He struggled to find
the words, his voice was suddenly a little higher than before

and charged with urgency. "This business we have been looking into. It's not what we thought it was at all. It's . . . I'm not sure, but . . ." He paused, and Deborah thought she heard movement in the background. "I'll call you back," he said.

There was no second message.

CHAPTER 61

Deborah returned to the computer. Marcus would call back, she thought. And even if he didn't, she had probably learned as much as he had. He had decided the corpse and everything with it was fake, that their little crusade had all been for naught, and that was why he sounded so . . .

Distraught?

. . . impatient. Disappointed. She knew the feeling.

The rationalization made a kind of sense, but it left her uneasy, unconvinced. She pulled up the Google home page and stared at the blinking cursor in the search field for a long moment. Then her fingers slowly tapped out six letters: "Atreus."

The screen flickered to a blank and then began slotting up the first of several thousand hits one page at a time: student projects on Greek myth, cheat sheets on ancient drama, a version of Dungeons and Dragons set in ancient Greece, even some holiday images of Mycenae. In her present mood, the sunlight and smiling faces seemed grotesque.

She went back to the previous page and added other words to that already in the search field: "Agamemnon," "Tholos," "gold," "Schliemann" . . .

Nothing. A suggestion that she check her spelling.

She tried Atreus with "ceramics," with "grave," "tomb," and "body," and got versions of the pages she had already seen arranged in slightly different order. She tried "Atreus" with "1940," with "World War II," with "Sherman tank." The last two produced a different group of hits, but none of them seemed to feature the word *Atreus* at all, focusing instead on the war references. She sighed, fighting a swelling tide of apathy, and typed "Atreus, hate crime." She was waiting for the dial-up modem to pull up the results when she heard a knock at the door.

She checked her watch. Ten thirty. Let it not be Cerniga or, worse, Keene.

Calvin, she thought, relief struggling with shame and anxiety as his name came to mind.

She pressed her eye to the peephole and took a step back, frowning. It was Tonya.

CHAPTER 62

It was strange to see Tonya in her apartment, Deborah thought, as the two women sat at the kitchen table and shared a glass of the wine Tonya had brought with her. They had really only talked properly once before, and that had been thousands of miles away in a small Greek village. It barely seemed possible.

"Agent Cerniga came back to the museum this afternoon," she said. "Told me what happened. From the look on Keene's face I figured you could use a drink."

Deborah smiled her thanks, but it was a wan smile. "That man really doesn't like me," she said. "Keene, I mean."

"If it's any consolation," said Tonya, "I don't think he's too fond of me either."

"What were you doing at the museum?" said Deborah. "I thought you quit."

"Gotta work out my contract," she said, grinning. "Anyway, I haven't lined up another job yet. I really only quit to show the Feds we weren't friends, but I may have to ask you to give me a second chance. If the police charge me with interfering with their inquiries, I'll have to declare it when I apply for another job. If the *AJC* wants me as an investigator, that might actually help, but since they're more likely to want me to go back to being a food critic—and a junior one at that—I doubt they'll want any felonies on my record. Shit," she said, "I never thought I'd finish up cleaning toilets for real."

"It's not for real," said Deborah. "It's just—"

"Till I get something better, yeah," she said. "That's what

my mom used to say." She shrugged, then developed a roguish grin. "But I want to hear about your little overnight with Mr. Calvin Bowers, attorney at law."

Deborah gaped.

"Cerniga told you about that?" she said, not wanting to discuss it.

"Hell, no," said Tonya. "No one did, till now. I was just guessing."

"Never trust a reporter," Deborah said.

"How about a maid? Come on, girl, I want details."

"We had a nice evening," said Deborah.

"I'll bet you did. Still wearing lipstick, I see."

"Did you come here to give me grooming tips or to hear my news?"

"What news?" Tonya said with mock suspicion, as if she was being distracted from the hunt.

"The test results on the corpse," said Deborah. Her voice sounded slow and sad in her own ears. Tonya was trying to blow off any idea that Deborah was responsible for the deaths of the two Greeks, but it wasn't helping. The truth floated unseen between them, making Deborah feel distant and separate as if she was at the end of a long, dank tunnel.

"You found it?" said Tonya.

"No, but I got to see the results of the carbon dating."

"Is it what we thought?"

"Kind of. The ceramics and probably the gold, are nineteenth century. The body is later. Mid-forties."

Tonya set down her drink very carefully. "You think it's my father?"

"I don't know."

"But what do you think?"

"I guess it's possible," said Deborah, too tired and depressed to argue. "It doesn't make a lot of sense to me—"

"That would explain why the Feds are involved," said Tonya, getting to her feet, a flush of excitement breaking out through her eyes. "It was a hate crime."

"I don't know," said Deborah, shaking her head. "I don't see why people would be so anxious to get hold of the body, even if there was evidence of how he died. I know the military don't like to have such things exposed, but it's pretty old news now. I doubt it would be considered that big a deal."

Tonya gave her a swift, affronted look.

"I'm sorry," said Deborah. "I just think—"

"What if the guy who killed him," Tonya cut in, "the military policeman—if that was who it was—became a big shot in later life, or was the *father* of a big shot. That might make it a big deal. Somebody is trying to protect the killer or his family."

"Maybe," said Deborah. She had never felt so weary and humiliated, but Tonya, caught up in her own story, didn't seem to see it.

"You don't think so?" said Tonya.

It was a challenge and one Deborah didn't feel like facing.

"I guess it's possible," she said.

"But you don't think so."

Tonya wouldn't let it go. She wanted nothing less than wholehearted encouragement and wasn't getting it.

"You don't think my father was worth the attention?" she said, a hint of that swagger Deborah had seen before coming back into her attitude. "You don't think anyone's nose would be put out of joint by the murder of a black man in 1945?"

Deborah backpedaled, suspecting that it was already too late.

"I'm not saying that," she said. "I just don't think it fits. Why would your father's killer go to the trouble of putting his body in with the fake grave goods, putting the death mask on him?"

"To conceal the fact that he was an American," she snapped back, "that he'd killed one of his own."

"But you said your father's body was buried," said Deborah. "No one tried to cover up the fact that he was dead. They didn't have to. They knew that the word of a white MP was enough to silence a division of black soldiers in 1945."

A spasm of rage crossed Tonya's face, but it wasn't just anger. There was hurt and humiliation in her eyes too, as if Deborah had hit her.

"Well then everything's just fine," she said, turning and marching toward the door.

"I'm not saying that," said Deborah, rising and going after her. "I'm not saying they were *right*."

"I know what you are saying," said Tonya, still walking.

"Tonya," said Deborah, pleading a little now. "I'm sorry. Today has been . . . I didn't mean . . ."

"It's fine," said the other woman over her shoulder, yanking the door open. "I'll see you in the museum."

And then she was gone, the slam of the door reverberating throughout the apartment for a moment. Deborah listened to Tonya's heels clacking through the tunnel outside, but she felt weighed down with weariness and a penetrating, numbing sadness, and she did not give chase.

The perfect end to the day, she thought, *the alienation of your last ally.*

She shut the main light off and then crossed to the computer to turn it off. She had guided the mouse to the Shut Down menu before she realized what was displayed on the screen. It was the results page for her last search: *Atreus, hate crime.*

The first hit was one she had not seen before. She clicked on it and waited.

The page that came up was headed "Southern Poverty Law Center: hate groups by region."

In the middle of the page was a red map of Georgia, dotted with colored symbols: confederate flags, swastikas, a white hood, a black jackboot, a crucifix. Underneath them was a list of clickable organizations keyed to the symbols above: Black Separatist, Ku Klux Klan, Christian Identity, Racist Skinhead, Neo-Confederate, Neo-Nazi, all subdivided into specific groups from the Nation of Islam and the New Black Panther Party, through the North Georgia White Knights and Aryan Nations, to a group called White Revolution in Brooks,

Georgia, and a National Socialist group in Morrow. Deborah's heart was in her throat. At the bottom of the list was a cluster of groups listed simply as "Other."

One of them was labeled simply "Atreus."

The symbol representing it, the only one of its kind on the map, was situated right where Atlanta should be. The tiny image looked like a yellow triangle, but as she leant closer, Deborah saw with a sudden chill that the triangle had jack-o'-lantern eyes. It was a gold death mask.

CHAPTER 63

Her first impulse was to read everything the Web site had to say, her second, to call Cerniga.

He already knows, she told herself. *This is why he's here. This is what it was always about. Not Schliemann. Not Agamemnon. This. Whatever this is.*

She went back to the Web site and began clicking her way through all the information she could find.

The entry on Atreus was a good deal shorter than those on the other hate groups. It read:

Small, possibly defunct organization with racist skinhead leanings. Atreus was apparently founded in the fifties, but was so shrouded in secrecy that some analysts deny it ever really existed, and for several decades the organization either disappeared or became dormant. Its name reappeared in skinhead tattoos in the early nineties, and occasional Web postings have suggested that it has a small and secretive membership. Their agenda is not clear, though it seems—like other skinhead groups—strongly linked to violence, as well as to hatred of gays and nonwhites, particularly Jews and blacks. The image of the gold mask which has been observed on banners and tattoos linked to the group seems to date back to the organization's founding, though its meaning is obscure.

The mask again.

She stared at it. Her mind wanted to shy away, but something caught in it, like a trailing fishhook snagging hair or fabric. The mask looked different from the real thing somehow, as if making it small had taken all the primitive craftsmanship out of the thing, made it neat and precise, a logo like a theater mask or . . .

A logo.

She had seen it before. She was sure of it. She knew the mask inside out by now. But there was something different about this stylized computerized miniature that was familiar but which was not about the mask itself, either the countless photographs she had seen or the thing itself in its case in the archeological museum in Athens.

Now that she thought about it, she had had the same impulse when she had first seen the tattoo on the chest of that murderous kid in Mycenae: a vague sense that she had seen the image before, not the mask itself, but this miniature impression of it . . .

She gazed at the image on the computer and then got up and began to pace back and forth around the room, trying to remember when she had first seen it. And then she became quite still. The image had suddenly clarified in her head, not gold or the yellow of little electronic pixels on the computer screen, and not the blue-black scoring of tattoos on pale skin, but black ink stenciled onto thick white paper.

She came back to life, moving quickly into the bedroom and to the purse she had carried halfway round the world and back. It was heavy with unopened correspondence from two weeks ago, letters and bills she had collected the night of the fund-raiser and never passed on because Richard was dead by the time she next saw him. She leafed hurriedly through them and saw it: a white business envelope, heavier than usual with a rich texture like linen. It had been addressed on a manual typewriter to Richard at the museum—which was why she had gotten it. Had it been sent to his residence, she never would have seen it. In the upper left corner where a return address might be, there was only a small, stylized mask.

It looked quite innocuous, and Deborah felt sure that when she had first seen it she had thought it a request for donations to a local theater company. But in the context of everything that had happened, in the context of that little yellow icon on the computer screen over there on the desk, it was anything but innocuous.

She opened it cautiously and with difficulty, using a knife to slice through the heavy paper, tipping the contents at arm's length into a bowl on the table, one hand over her mouth. If she saw powder, she had decided, she would not inhale until she was out in the street.

But there was no powder, only a single sheet of the same expensive paper, typed on the same machine. There was no signature and no date. It read simply:

We are aware of the object in your possession and your plans for it. You must change them. Rest assured that if the object does not find its way into the hands of those destined to take up the great man's cause, its terror will be visited on you and the degenerates with whom you associate like the sword of almighty God himself. Do not allow it to leave the country, or expect exquisite retribution when its power is inevitably unleashed.

Deborah put the letter down carefully and backed away from it, as if there might be some contagion beyond anthrax or nerve gas in the words themselves.

"It's not about archaeology," she said aloud, repeating what Cerniga had told her.

Unless these white supremacist crazies thought they were the heirs of Agamemnon himself . . .

That was it.

They had taken the Trojan War—the legendary model of nobility and honorable resolve—and made it into something altogether more brutal and disturbing: a genocide, an attempt by Greece, as the foremost power in Europe, to eradicate its counterpart in the Near East: Occidental against Oriental, Caucasian against Arab, the lands which became the home of the early Christian Church against the infidels of Turkey.

They had taken Achilles, Agamemnon, and the rest and made them Nazi icons, heroes who ground foreign cultures beneath their Aryan heels . . .

However much it was bad history and the willful misreading of literature and culture, Deborah knew it made sense, at least to whoever had written that letter claiming that Agamemnon's Bronze Age war as a racist crusade. But it also seemed that whoever the Atreus group were, they wanted the contents of that crate because it was to be of some dreadful use to them. The crate contained "the sword of almighty God himself," it said, the capacity to unleash "exquisite retribution."

What had Marcus said? *"It's not what we thought."*

Cerniga had been right. This was not about archaeology. It wasn't about history or art or even money. Deborah still didn't know what was in that crate—knew, perhaps, even less than she had before, since all her assumptions seemed to have been wrong—but she knew now why people were prepared to kill for it. They would do anything to get hold of it because they believed it contained a weapon, a weapon of extraordinary destructive power.

CHAPTER 64

"Yes," said Deborah into the phone, "it is urgent."

She repeated her name and then sat there waiting, the room lit only by the computer screen. The voice which came onto the line was brisk and irritated.

"Cerniga," he said. "What do you want?"

"I found a letter that was sent to Richard the day before he died, maybe two days," she said. "He never got it, and I never opened it till now, but I'm fairly sure that that is why someone tried to kill me in Greece. They couldn't find the letter and assumed I had read it."

"What does it say?"

Deborah read the whole thing back to him, holding it up to the light so that she could see it clearly through the Ziploc bag in which she had put it. She was taking no chances this time. When she was done, there was a long pause.

"Agent Cerniga?" she said. "You still there?"

"You're at home?"

"Yes."

"Stay where you are and talk to nobody."

"It's a weapon," she said, as soon as he arrived, "isn't it?"

He was not alone. Keene was skulking, sour-faced, behind him.

"Come on, Cerniga," she said. "Is it a weapon?"

Cerniga sighed and began studying the letter. He didn't speak till he was done.

"You just have to know everything, don't you?" he said. Deborah wanted to smile in a vaguely self-deprecating way, but his eyes were hard, his mouth thin. He looked at Keene, as if too exasperated to do any of the talking himself.

"Tell her," he said.

"All of it?" said Keene, shooting the FBI man a look of doubtful outrage.

"If it will shut her up and get her out of our way for ten minutes, sure."

Deborah looked down, her face hot.

"OK," said Keene, sitting down. "Yeah, we think it's a weapon. There have been references to the Atreus group since the fifties. They come in waves, always full of vague, apocalyptic crap. But they've never claimed responsibility for anything, and though we know they have ties to violent right-wing groups, we don't know what they want. For a time they seem to have been led—and probably founded—by a local entrepreneur called Edward Graves, a multimillionaire. He died in the mid-sixties and we don't know who, if anyone, took up the reins. What we do know is that a lot of his money seems to have gone astray, and it was suggested that a good chunk of it was earmarked for Atreus's future. Anyway, most analysts thought the group dead, even after its name started floating up again a few years ago. Then the name surfaced in connection to the death of a British national in France."

"Marcus's father."

"I guess. The Feds didn't know what the old guy was doing there, except that he was trying to get hold of some archaeo-logical remains on the black market. The British police searched his home and found evidence of some kind of link to Edward Graves at the end of World War Two. They refer-enced a mask—"

"Was Graves in the army during the war?" said Deborah, cutting in.

"Yes," said Cerniga. "He was an MP. Why? Something else you haven't told us?"

Deborah swallowed. Tonya wanted her story kept quiet.

"Well?" said Cerniga, his voice raised. He looked colder, more dangerous than ever, and Deborah saw again in her mind's eye the bodies of the two Greeks, men whose lives she could have saved . . .

"Tonya's father," she said, "was in an all-black tank regiment moving through southern Germany at the end of the war."

She told the whole story, including the possibility that the body under the mask was Andrew Mulligrew, Tonya's father.

Keene scowled and looked down, and Cerniga made her repeat the story twice, taking notes and then double-checking them. This, apparently, was news. It probably changed nothing since it was all ancient history and about as relevant to the current whereabouts of the crate as Schliemann's excavations, but Deborah was pleased to finally offer something he didn't already know, even if it didn't soften the lines about his face when he looked at her.

"I thought the tattoo of the eagle I saw on that kid in Greece was Roman," she said. "But it wasn't, was it? It was German."

"The two are connected," said Cerniga, "The Third Reich fancied itself the descendents of ancient Greece and Rome."

"So," Deborah prompted, "this weapon . . . ?"

"You just can't leave it alone, can you?" said Cerniga.

"I just thought that if I knew what you thought was going on," said Deborah, "I could help."

"Like you helped those two stiffs back in Palmetto?" said Keene.

Deborah looked down again. When Cerniga spoke, it was in a dry, mechanical voice.

"Based on the lighting pattern in the room behind the bookcase," he said, "we figure the display case with the body and grave goods was about seven feet by three, about the size of a funeral casket. We also think it was free-standing, and though the body itself would only be twelve inches or so deep, it almost certainly wasn't at floor level. If we assume it was about three and half feet high, that means we're looking at about seventy cubic feet of concealed space under the body. It's a lot of room in which you could conceal any number of significant weapons."

"And we're not talking about a box of pistols," said Keene with grim relish.

"We think," said Cerniga, his voice still containing no emotion other than a hard, even ruthless frankness, "the weapon is closer to the WMDs we never found in Iraq. It originated in Nazi Germany in the last year of the war and was smuggled out using the fake antiquities as a cover. We know the German nuclear program was fairly advanced, but it seems unlikely that they had material to make some kind of bomb, though that is not to say that they didn't have materials that may have been subsequently turned into a device of some kind, what they call a dirty bomb, maybe."

"If there is radioactive material in the crate," said Deborah quietly, "it is screened so perfectly that the radiation has been absolutely contained. If it had leaked even a tiny amount, the C-14 testing would have detected a massive elevation of radioactive particles."

She was still trying to pretend that this was an exchange of ideas rather than a kind of punishment for her former actions and inactions. *You want to know what's going on?* Cerniga seemed to be saying. *Here it is. And if it scares you to death, you've no one to blame but yourself.*

"We are inclined to think the weapon is chemical or— more likely—biological," Cerniga said. "The Nazis conducted extensive research on the subject."

In the concentration camps, she thought, suddenly feeling that old hollow in her gut.

"Smallpox would do nicely," Keene suggested, smirking at her. "A stockpile of that, or some nasty flu strain, maybe a few vials of bubonic plague . . ."

Deborah lowered her eyes again, but only for a moment.

"Did Richard know?" she said.

"He had absolutely no idea," said Cerniga. "He thought he was about to announce one of the great archaeological discoveries of the century, thought he was going to put your museum on the map and become a national hero to the people of Greece."

This was good news, but in Cerniga's mouth it just made him sound stupidly unrealistic.

"Like you," said Cerniga, as if she might have missed the point, "he had no clue what was going on."

"He thought it was about art and history," said Keene, grinning frankly in her face so that she looked down again. "Can you believe that?"

"What about the Russian?" said Deborah. "The note he was carrying suggests—"

Cerniga cut her off with a shout of fury.

"What the hell do you think this is?" he said, his face suddenly red and throbbing. "You think we want to pick your brains like you're some kind of goddamned expert, some genius who can do our job for us? The Russian, as I have told you about fifty times now, is irrelevant to this inquiry."

"I just thought—" she began, feeling dwarfed by his anger.

"Don't," he said. "Or at least go back to your books and do your thinking there. You aren't a suspect anymore, OK? As far as I'm concerned, you're no more than an obstruction. Get out of our way, and stay out. Take a holiday."

"Hey," said Keene, nastily upbeat, "why not go to Russia?"

"Whatever," said Cerniga. "Just don't let me see you around here until this is all wrapped up. Got it?"

Mute, Deborah nodded.

CHAPTER 65

It was raining in Red Square. Deborah had been in Moscow for two days, and it had rained so unrelentingly that it had become impossible for her to imagine the city without the gray skies, the damp trees, the shining stone pavements, and glistening minarets.

Two days.

It was completely insane, she knew. She should never have come. Having barely been out of the States in the last decade she had launched into two completely unplanned trips to Europe in as many weeks. She couldn't afford it and would be paying the whole ridiculous jaunt off for the rest of the year and well into the next. Greece had been expensive, but newly capitalist Russia had it beat by a mile: by a thousand miles. Why in God's name had she come?

To spite Cerniga? To take his and Keene's sarcastic advice seriously, as if that would wipe from her mind the contempt with which they had called her a fool and an amateur? Or to drive other images from her mind . . .?

The dead Greeks, their eyes open . . .

Or just to hide her head a continent away?

That last was closest.

But there were still questions to be asked. Cerniga said it wasn't about archaeology. He said it wasn't about the Russian, wasn't about Magdeburg. But there was something else; she was sure of it. She couldn't say if he didn't know or just wasn't telling, but there was *something else,* something no one had said yet, something at the heart of this whole tragic farce. She had felt it from the start, that sense that the dog tracks she was following belonged to a wolf or something larger and stranger, something she wouldn't recognize till she rounded the corner and found it watching her.

So she had come to Russia. In spite of pocketbook and common sense, she had come, determined to follow the tracks a little farther, till they faded away completely or showed her the beast.

Yesterday she had done three things after her endless flight. She had booked a hotel room at the Belgrade by the Garden Ring and only one stop on the metro from the Kremlin itself. She had visited the Pushkin Museum and stared, drained and bewildered, at Priam's Treasure, the hoard of ancient artifacts which Schliemann unearthed in Troy and smuggled back to Germany a hundred years ago. What it meant to her present quest she was still unsure, though it suggested that the death of a former Soviet agent a block from the Atlanta museum on the night it was relieved of its own collection of Trojan war memorabilia was no coincidence. That Richard's trove was all fake did not take away from the fact that both collections had been in Berlin in 1945 as the Russians banged on the door with their tanks, and both had been spirited away.

The third thing she had done was to call Alexandra Voloshinov, the dead Russian's daughter. In fact she had called twice. The first time a man had answered, had professed not to understand her, and hung up. The second time the woman herself had answered but had been no more forthcoming, though she had taken Deborah's number at the hotel in case she changed her mind.

This morning, she had called.

"My husband does not like me to talk about my father," she said. "His work, I mean. But I will meet with you."

They were to meet here in Red Square itself, flanked by the elaborately antique GUM department store and, as if in pointed contrast, the tomb of Lenin, behind which were the redbrick walls of the Kremlin. Deborah hugged her inadequate coat to her ribs and stared southeast to where the massive and whimsical onion domes of Saint Basil's gleamed red and gold through the rain. She found a tingle of excitement at being here in this place impossible to suppress.

She was just old enough to remember what the Soviet Union had meant to America in the seventies and eighties, even if much of her sense of the Cold War menace and competition had more to do with hackneyed movies and largely meaningless sports rivalries. Even though it was the middle of summer, a part of her had been surprised to find the square not covered in snow, the same part, perhaps, that had been startled by the familiar icon of McDonald's beside a building whose austere stone façade still wore the emblem of the crossed hammer and sickle. She knew that the Soviet Union was gone, but it lingered so palpably in the wet air that the trappings of Western democratic capitalism seemed like Christmas decorations that would be glumly taken down in a matter of weeks.

Alexandra Voloshinov was heavy, like her father, forty-five or so, and pale, her face blank and a little hard. Her eyes were dark and cautious, and never quite locked with Deborah's, as if she was looking for someone else. She wore a long dark coat and a pale blue head scarf. Deborah who had, for no good reason, expected someone younger, stepped to move out of her way, muttering apologies, before she realized who she was.

"Deborah Miller?" said the woman. Her voice was flat, her face showing no emotion, no politeness or greeting.

"Yes," said Deborah, smiling, "you must be Alexandra."

"Sergei Voloshinov was my father," she said, as if making a fine distinction. "Why have you come?"

Deborah, who had been buoyed by the fact that the woman had agreed to meet her, felt deflated. The Russian still didn't want to talk, didn't want her here at all.

"I'm trying to understand what happened to your father because I think it is relevant to the death of another man."

"But you are not police."

"The other man was a close friend of mine."

The woman considered this, her handbag clasped in front of her broad stomach like a shield.

"Police say he went into bad part of town. He was robbed. That's all."

"I don't think that's true."

"Mrs. Miller," began the Russian.

"Miss," Deborah corrected, smiling.

The Russian paused, and then her face cracked briefly into an echoing smile.

"Not married," she said. "Probably, good idea."

"For now," said Deborah, "definitely a good idea."

The Russian woman nodded and, without warning, took her arm, and began to lead her toward Saint Basil's.

"My father," she said, not looking at her now, "was . . . He did not think well."

"He was . . . mentally unbalanced?"

Alexandra considered this and grinned bleakly.

"Crazy," she said. "My father was crazy."

Deborah could not think of a way to respond, so she let the woman talk.

"My mother died six years ago," she said. "He was very sad for a long time. He did not eat. He did not go out. He had nothing to do except sit in his apartment. After a year or two, he went . . ."

She gestured vaguely with her hand, but the gesture conveyed not so much sadness as exasperation.

"He became interested in his old work. Too interested. Always reading about it. Always talking about it. To everyone! Me, my family, people who worked in stores and restaurants, people in the park. Anyone. Always the same: *he was proud Russian, he worked for his country, he knew its secrets, he did not trust Americans and British, but he did not trust old Soviet government either! They were liars and killers. But what we have now? Hamburgers and street gangs, fancy clothes and mafia while the poor still starve like they did under Stalin and under the tsars . . . Always the same. All the time.*"

The voice hardened as she spoke the litany she had doubtless heard a thousand times.

"He was crazy old man," she said. "Everyone angry with
him. Everyone laugh at him. Now he is dead, and it is good.
For him. For my family. For me."

She said it as if daring Deborah to disagree.

"Why did he go to America if he hated it so much?"

"Because he was crazy." She shrugged. "I don't know."

"Could he have been pursuing some old case, back from
his days in the MVD?"

"Pursuing?"

"Chasing," Deborah said. "Investigating. Trying to learn
more about something from the past."

"Maybe," said the dead man's daughter, without curiosity.
"He fill books with writing about work, but I did not look at
them."

"Do you still have them, these books?"

"At my home," she said. "Boxes and boxes. They cleaned
out his apartment and send me his boxes. What do I do with
them? Why I want them?"

"Could I see them?"

Alexandra looked at her.

"Your friend who died," she said. "A lover?"

The candor of the question made Deborah laugh.

"More like a father," she said.

The Russian frowned and considered for a moment.

"OK," she said, staring directly ahead, "you can see."

They traveled on the metro, Deborah mimicking the woman
and handing her handfuls of coins which she sifted without
comment or amusement. From time to time Deborah found
herself gazing rapt at the relief carving and mosaics that decorated the older stations: Ukrainian farmers, their arms laden
with wheat sheaves, embracing Russian tractor manufactur-
ers who carried wrenches, images of Lenin in high oratorical
mode, elegant carvings of triumphal Soviet infantry and

tanks. It was, as she had felt in Greece, another world altogether.

"You said your father lived in Magdeburg," Deborah prompted as soon as they were out in the open again. Alexandra showed no willingness to speak in the crowded confines of the train.

"MVD headquarters in East Germany," she said. "My father was . . . positioned there as a young man."

"In the fifties?"

"Yes."

Deborah frowned. It made no sense to her. Why would the Germans have tried to send the body to a town which would fall to the Russians and become part of the Soviet empire? Magdeburg was southwest of Berlin, but not far enough from the Polish border to be considered in any way safe, and certainly nowhere near the considerably safer haven of Switzerland. Anyway, if Tonya's story was true, the Americans had hit the German convoy a long way south of Magdeburg. Which left one disconcerting alternative high on the list of possibilities: Cerniga was right. There was no connection. Whatever the Russian letter had referred to, it wasn't the convoy which Andrew Mulligrew had attacked.

The remains never reached Magdeburg . . .

Still she felt the link, like something just out sight, like a picture that had to be held in just the right way for its lines to make sense.

"You said your father was always talking about the same things," she said. "That he was obsessed with old ideas and issues."

"Obsessed," Alexandra said, liking the word. "Yes."

"Were there particular cases, events that he was obsessed with?"

Alexandra hesitated.

"Just general," she said. "Not particular."

She looked away and, for the first time, Deborah felt sure she was not being told the truth.

* * *

Alexandra and her husband lived in a gray and decrepit
Brezhnev-era tower block a good half hour outside the city
center, the final approach to which was made down a path
through a small wood of silver birches, their bark white and
shining. They ascended to the fourteenth floor in a rickety elevator which was painted a virulent acid green and smelled of
stale urine. The inside of the apartment was as sparse and
small as the outside was moldering, but it was clean, and
Alexandra showed no great embarrassment for it. Indeed, she
showed Deborah in with an almost imperial grace, proud of
what she had and how she kept it. From the window Deborah
counted four other identical buildings and countless similar
ones stretching back the way they had come.

Alexandra's husband, Vasily, a burly man in shirtsleeves
who looked to be in his early fifties, spoke—or professed to
speak—no English. He gave her a long, appraising look, taking in her gawky stature as she entered the living room like
some lost, flightless bird. Alexandra babbled to him in Russian, her expression stern, her voice matter-of-fact, and he
grunted agreement several times. Finally, he greeted Deborah
more warmly than she had thought likely, and went out
whistling.

"Shopping for dinner," said Alexandra. "You eat here."

It was an invitation, of a sort, and Deborah thanked her,
thinking also that Alexandra's banishment of her husband
had at least as much to do with what Deborah wanted to discuss as it did shopping for dinner.

There were five large cardboard boxes, labeled only with
what Deborah took to be the apartment address.

"There," said Alexandra, gesturing dismissively to where
they nestled in the corner. "Open them."

She went into the kitchen to make coffee, leaving Deborah
alone with the boxes and with a distinct impression that the
dead man's daughter would just as happily burn them all. She
opened them and found them full of old manila files and

papers, some punctiliously typed and methodically organized, others just packets of paper covered in seemingly
random scribblings. Deborah blew out a long breath. Everything, not surprisingly, was in Russian, and she couldn't
make sense of a single word.

"Could you help me read some of this?" she said to
Alexandra as the woman returned, balancing a tray of coffee
and small cakes.

"It is not important," she said, scowling.

"If you could just tell me what the words on the files
mean . . ."

Alexandra's frown deepened, then she grunted like a large
animal and eased herself into a squat beside the closest box.

Deborah wasn't sure what to expect. It was, after all, unlikely that Sergei Voloshinov would have kept official files in
his own home, less likely still that whoever had found them
after his death would have sent them to his surviving family
if they were in any way sensitive. As Alexandra thumbed
through the first file, her face, always masklike and restrained, seemed to tighten, close down.

"Nothing," she said. "All nonsense."

From what Deborah could see, a large amount of the file
seemed to contain letters, many of them on official-looking
stationery marked by the state emblems of the Soviet Union.

"What are they about?" she said.

"His . . ." She searched for the word. *"Obsessions."*

"Is this all classified?" Deborah asked. "I mean, is it secret? Is it dangerous for you to tell me about them?"

Unexpectedly, Alexandra's face split into a dark smile.

"No," she said. "My father worked for Border Guards Di-
rectorate. He was a soldier and small official, a bureaucrat.
He worked with men who did secret and dangerous work.
Men with power. But he? No."

"Then, I don't understand. What is in here that you don't
want to tell me?"

Alexandra got to her feet so quickly that Deborah winced,
sure the big woman was going to throw a punch. Instead, the

woman kicked at the first box, twice, overturning and spilling
its contents, crying out some fractured Russian phrases. Her
normally still face was suddenly flushed with anger.

Deborah got hurriedly to her feet, babbling apologies.

"No," said Alexandra, still furious. "It is not you who
should be sorry. It is him."

She kicked again at the box, tearing it.

"Your father? Why?"

"For this. This foolish . . . shameful nonsense."

"I don't understand," Deborah said again, taking Alexandra's hands as if to steady her. "Please tell me. What are all
those letters about?"

Alexandra calmed slowly, but her face was still hot with
rage.

"My father was a fool," she said, and the bitterness had
turned to hurt and shame. "For years he was a good soldier for
his country, working for the old Communists in East Germany."

"In Magdeburg," Deborah prompted.

"In Magdeburg, yes. They gave him medals, awards. But
then he was moved back to Russia and his . . . *status*?"

"Rank?"

"Rank. His rank was lowered. They did not trust him then.
For fifteen years he kept working for KGB, but he was never
the same. When he finished . . . When he *retired,* he was still
of lower status—*rank*—than when he was in DDR, in East
Germany."

"What did he do?" Deborah asked, cautious now, sure she
was on the edge of something important.

"He wrote these," she said, grabbing a handful of the letters in her fist and holding them up.

"What are they about?"

Alexandra became very still, and her head tipped forward
a little, her eyes half closing as if she was in prayer. Her
hands moved by themselves, sensing apparently by touch
alone, and drew a single sheet out of the stack.

It was different from the others, glossy, and clustered with images: a black-and-white photograph which had been marked by red lines, arrows, and scribbled Cyrillic letters in felt pen. She placed it on the thin carpet carefully, delicately, as if it might be very fragile or somehow explosive, her eyes still half shut and sightless, and pushed it across the floor to Deborah.

"What is this?" said Deborah, picking it up and flashing a look at the Russian woman, who squatted there still in silence. When she did not answer, Deborah considered the photograph.

It was actually four pictures, the same subject shot from four slightly different positions. The subject was a man lying on his back, his eyes closed, his mouth slightly open. Two of the pictures were gray and fuzzy images from head to waist, the others were close-ups of his face, sharper and with higher contrast. Both showed a dot on the man's forehead, very slightly off center. It looked like a bullet hole.

"I don't get it," said Deborah, a hint of impatience creeping into her voice. The Russian woman was being overly dramatic. "Who is it?"

Alexandra still said nothing, and Deborah had the strange sense that the Russian woman was waiting for something. Deborah frowned and looked back at the picture.

"What?" she said. "Who is . . . ?"

But even as she started to ask, the details of the face began to slot into place in her head: the thin black hair brushed clean of the face and ears, the pallor of the skin, the eyebrows, the chin, the shape of the mouth, the thick wedge of the tightly cropped toothbrush mustache . . .

"No," she said. "It can't be."

She stared at the picture and the red lines and pointers that had been overlaid onto it.

"It can't be," she repeated. "It looks like . . ."

"Hitler," Alexandra said, not looking at Deborah. "It looks like Hitler."

"Adolf Hitler," said Deborah. "Yes. But . . ."

"At the end of the war," said Alexandra, her voice whispering now, "Hitler killed himself in his concrete . . . *bunker,* yes?"

"Yes," said Deborah. She wasn't thinking clearly. It was like she was in a fog or, and this was somehow worse, was emerging from a fog. What awaited her on the other side, she could not imagine.

"The Russians got there and found his body, with others," said Alexandra. "They were taken for examination and burial, but they were badly damaged and it was very hot. So they were not taken to Moscow. They were taken to SMERSH— that is Military Intelligence—headquarters as ordered by NKVD . . ."

"In Magdeburg," Deborah added. She spoke slowly. The fog was melting away, but now she was falling, turning head over heels, plummeting as she had imagined she might plummet through the darkness of the Mycenaean cistern, dropping through impossible distance in agonizing slowness.

"Yes, Magdeburg," said Alexandra. "It was all straightforward. True. Everyone knows this. Except my father. My crazy father went to work there, and he became obsessed with the idea . . ."

"That his body never reached Magdeburg," said Deborah, her own voice sounding like a distant bell in her head. She rephrased it, inserting the word from the letter Sergei Voloshinov had been carrying the night he died. "Adolf Hitler's *remains* never reached Magdeburg."

But that would mean that the body you had carbon dated . . . ?

No. Richard had Hitler's body in a secret room in Atlanta? It was impossible. How could he have? How could it have gotten there?

The same way Priam's Treasure finished up in the Pushkin, said a voice in her head.

CHAPTER 66

It was three hours later. Vasily was back and unpacking their dinner supplies in the kitchen as Alexandra cooked. Deborah sat in a chintz armchair and stared at the boxes they had sorted through, as the new possibilities settled in her brain.

If Sergei Voloshinov had been right, she and—for that matter—Richard, Marcus, and his father—had been off track all along. Deborah had assumed the note he had been carrying when he died had referred to the body in the box, the body which had been moved by German convoy and had wound up in a secret room behind Richard's bookcase, and in that she now believed she was right. She had been wrong, however, to assume that it was the Germans who had intended the body to reach Magdeburg. They had meant it to reach Switzerland and safety. It was the Russians who had sent it to Magdeburg, though that was later, and by then, if Voloshinov was right, they were dealing with an altogether different corpse.

Voloshinov believed—and he was not alone in so doing—that the body taken for Hitler which the Russians found in Berlin had belonged to one of several men who were employed as the führer's body doubles. It was this body which was taken to Magdeburg for investigation, verification, and eventual burial, while the real one was spirited away. It took Voloshinov a decade of research to happen on the story of an American unit hitting a German convoy only miles from the Swiss border, longer even than that to determine what happened to the contents of that convoy thereafter. When he believed he had isolated its final resting place, he got a visa and flew to Atlanta.

But it was all, surely, mere insanity?

That was how his superiors had treated his theories, so much so that his refusal to drop them had resulted in a stripping of his medals and reassignment to a desk job in Moscow. But Deborah—thanks to Alexandra's grudging help as a translator—had gone through the gist of his argument, and she was not so sure that it was all just conspiracy-theory craziness.

There was, to begin with, considerable evidence that Voloshinov had been alone only in pursuing his theories long after he had been told to drop them. Plenty of other people had had their doubts about the remains buried in Magdeburg. Stalin himself had accused the British and Americans of allowing Hitler to escape, even of setting him up in some foreign—probably South American—country. This was probably just misinformation designed to paint the Western allies as soft—even friendly—toward the man every Russian had good reason to despise. But it was also clear that Stalin was far from sure that the Russians had found the right body.

The story, as Deborah was able to unravel it, was derived from a combination of official records, eyewitness accounts, and hearsay, the final picture being inconsistent and sometimes even contradictory. Voloshinov apparently had no problem with such inconsistency, actually drawing attention to the holes and problems with the account as if these pointed to flaws in the official version of the events themselves. One particular strand of the argument came from an MVD colonel called Menshikov, and whose handwritten testimony was addressed in letters directly to Voloshinov, letters very like the one he had been carrying the night he died. Menshikov, it seemed, before his meeting with Alexandra's father, then a young recruit just learning the ropes of his East German posting, had been an infantryman with the seventy-ninth SMERSH unit on the front lines during the fall of Berlin. He had, he claimed, been present when the bunker was searched. He had heard the testimony of the survivors and had watched as—based on that testimony—the charred bodies of Hitler and Eva Braun were dug out of a shallow grave in the chancellery garden.

Hitler had died on the thirtieth of April, 1945, the victim, according to that same testimony, of a self-administered gunshot wound to the head fired from his own Mauser pistol. His new bride took cyanide. The two corpses were then taken outside, doused with gasoline bought for the purpose several days earlier, and burned, under the supervision of Hitler adjutant, SS Major Otto Gunsche. The cremation was witnessed by Gunsche, Martin Bormann, Joseph Goebbels, Heinz Linge (Hitler's valet), and Erich Kempka (his chauffeur), but owing to heavy Soviet bombardment, the pyre had to be abandoned before the cremation was complete. Guards in the building—including Ewald Lindloff and Hans Reisser, who buried them—testified that the bodies were burned beyond recognition. Other members of the German high command also committed suicide, including the entire Goebbels family, Joseph, Magda, and their six children.

It was several days after Hitler's death that the Russians found what they took to be his remains, days in which, according to Voloshinov, the real corpse was packed into a crate, given an armored escort, and sent south to the Swiss border. The body which the Soviets dug up, he said, was one of Hitler's doubles, though which one, he seemed unsure. Some evidence pointed to Gustav Weber, other to an actor called Andreas Kronstaedt, still other evidence pointed to Julius Schreck, a Nazi Party member since the twenties and Hitler's favorite driver. It was one of these men, said Voloshinov, who had been so conveniently photographed by the Germans before the pyre had rendered the body unrecognizable. It was this body—not Hitler's—which was placed in a wooden shell crate and transported to the Russian pathology lab in Berlin-Buch. On May 8, 1945, as Europe celebrated V-E day, Russian forensic pathologist Dr. Faust Sherovsky and an anatomical pathologist called Major Anna Marantz performed an autopsy on the remains.

The corpse was eventually buried in a piece of waste ground at 30–32 Klausenerstrasse in Magdeburg and remained there until 1970, when the KGB, apparently in an attempt to prevent Hitler from attaining the status of martyr to right-wing sympathizers and German nationalists, dug up the body and destroyed it, scattering the remains over the River Ehle, near the village of Biederitz.

Apart from the window between Hitler's death and the discovery of the corpse by the Soviets, a window which certainly allowed for the real body to be spirited away, Deborah initially thought that there was little to give credence to Voloshinov's story. The more she learned, however, pressing Alexandra's plodding and broken translation from file to file, the more she began to wonder.

The accounts given by those captured Germans who had found Hitler's body after he had killed himself and then participated in its burning didn't tally in small but significant ways. The gunshot wounds were identified as being in different places: some said in the mouth, others said in the temple, or the corner of one eye. One said the body was on a couch with the body of Braun, another said it was in a chair by itself. The bloodstains on the couch were reportedly of the wrong type.

But the first thing which really struck her was a bizarre detail about the journey which the body made from Berlin to Magdeburg. According to official records, the Russians buried the corpse on the road itself and then dug it up again. This curious pattern was repeated as many as nine or ten times between Berlin and Magdeburg. No clear reason was offered by the state for why this occurred, and Voloshinov had drawn his own conclusions, namely that the Soviets were torn between wanting to learn more about the body and wanting to make it disappear. Both impulses came from a deep uncertainty about the nature of the corpse itself, a nagging anxiety that they had gotten the wrong one.

Even when the formal autopsy was performed, the results raised as many questions as they answered. The Germans who had survived the bunker were adamant that Hitler had shot himself—as was suggested by the baffling photographs whose veracity was impossible to verify—but the body showed traces of cyanide and shards of glass in the mouth, and no bullet could be found. Of course, the Nazi leader could have bitten down on an ampule of poison as he shot himself, and the bullet could have been lost, but the discrepancy clearly caused some unease. Later reexamination of the bunker site produced a piece of the body's skullcap, apparently blown out by the bullet's exit wound. This piece was kept separate and, so far as Deborah could see, was still in the possession of the Russian government, though it remained pointedly untested for DNA evidence of its origins. Voloshinov believed that the very recovery of this bone fragment was suspicious, an attempt by the authorities to close up the holes in the autopsy report. It could not, moreover, prove the identity of the corpse, or even prove categorically that it came from the same corpse.

Dental examinations were performed on a piece of bridgework found in the chancellery garden and, again, seemed to confirm that the body was Hitler's, but the records used to verify those examinations were based on the dubious memories of dental assistant Kaethe Hausermann and dental technician Fritz Echtmann. These two had worked for Hitler's dentist, Dr. Fritz Blaschke, and were committed Nazis who—Voloshinov argued—could have colluded on false testimony well in advance of its use. The crucial bridgework itself could, he argued, have been reconstructed and placed where it would be found to mislead the Russians. It was further evidence, he claimed, that the Nazis had planned an exit strategy for Hitler's remains which would leave just enough evidence to convince the Soviets, while not actually proving anything. This was why the corpse was so conveniently burned beyond recognition but not destroyed, so the Russians would not keep searching for the real body. This was why the similarly convenient photographs had been allowed to fall into Russian hands. Why, he said, would any loyal and respectful Nazi shoot pictures of his leader's body before it was incinerated? It made no sense, except as a strategy of misinformation.

When the remains were finally dug up and destroyed in 1970 by the KGB, Voloshinov argued, the Soviets were not trying to rid the world of a potential Nazi shrine so much as they were trying to end the constant disputes about a body they knew had not belonged to Hitler. This one act alone suggested that the Russians believed it impossible—even with new forensic technologies—to prove that the corpse had really been Hitler.

It wasn't him. They knew it wasn't. The Soviets had brought a body to Magdeburg, and they didn't want to admit to the world that they had got it wrong, but they had *got it wrong, and they knew it.*

The final pieces of evidence, and the one which led to Voloshinov's obsessive pursuit of this personal crusade, concerned his friend and mentor, Menshikov. It was Menshikov's original testimony shared privately with Alexandra's father about what he had seen and not seen in Berlin in May 1945 that had set Voloshinov thinking. The piece of information passed on to Voloshinov seemed to Deborah more astonishing and compelling than all the rest combined. She read the account three times, barely breathing.

In the corner of a roomlike portion of the bunker's central corridor, a corridor which led to the stairs up to the garden where the bodies were burned, Menshikov, moving cautiously, his submachine gun gripped firmly in his hands, had found a dagger. It was not a Nazi dagger but something far more beautiful and strange with a slender blade made of bronze and inlaid with golden images of lions and a charioteer: a ceremonial weapon from Bronze Age Greece.

At last. The link.

But it wasn't the Mycenaean dagger which had driven Voloshinov to pursue that crate across fifty years and half the globe, nor was it the inconsistencies in the official story which had kept him searching and writing to the government as his rank and status was gradually stripped away from him.

It was a hatred for what the Nazis had been and a deep and paradoxical relationship with his own country and its problematic authorities. The last, most crucial event which had driven him was the death of his friend Menshikov, who had been executed secretly with thirty other Russians by his own government for refusing to put down an East German rebellion in Magdeburg in 1953. It was this fact more than any other which had driven Sergei Voloshinov to champion his cause.

Deborah sat in her chair and held up the knife Menshikov had found, the dagger he had passed on to his disciple in his quest for truth, the only object from the boxes that wasn't paper. She barely had to look at it. It had been, she was sure, part of the collection which now sat in a hidden room in a small Atlanta museum.

That's it, she thought. *That's the missing piece of the puzzle.*

CHAPTER 67

Deborah stared out of the window as Moscow fell away behind them and thought about Alexandra and her husband, who had served her dinner which had included caviar and vodka as if she were an ambassador and they had a duty to demonstrate their Russianness and hospitality. Vasily had watched her cautiously through dinner, but after a while his attention had gone to his wife, whose habitual silence seemed preserved only with a great effort. As dinner progressed, Deborah thought that Alexandra's face resembled a dam at flood stage, and as the vodka began to go round the table for a third time, the dam cracked.

"You think . . ." she began, her face pink, "you think my father, perhaps, was not crazy?"

She could hardly breathe, had hardly been able to get the words out, and Deborah felt a heavy silence and watchfulness descend on the room as she tried to decide. Had Alexandra always carried a candle of hope that her father had not been the clown he was painted, carried it in shame and embarrassment, never able to snuff it out completely? It would explain, perhaps, why she had allowed Deborah to see the files she would not read by herself.

Deborah looked at the woman as she wrestled with her feelings and was glad that she could be honest.

"No," she had said at last, "I do not think he was crazy. I think . . ." She paused, half amazed by the idea still. "I think he was right."

The dam broke then, and Alexandra wept for herself and for her dead father.

So now she knew. From time to time she had had the impression that she was on the wrong track, that the story she was discovering was somehow the wrong story, and now she knew why. It had never been about archaeology, except insofar as the Nazis had seen themselves as the new Greeks. Hitler saw himself as a new Agamemnon waging his xenophobic war against inferior peoples, and when that war ended and he killed himself, he wanted to lie in state like the Greek kings of old.

She remembered talking to the Mycenaean craftsman about the list of famous Nazis who had come to tour the sites, butchers and lunatics like Himmler and Goebbels who had thought Schliemann a Teutonic superman, in part because he had unearthed other supermen: the heroes of Agamemnon's army. It all made a kind of warped sense. This was why Hitler had wanted the 1936 Olympics in Berlin, she thought; he believed it was Germany's right as the inheritors of the ancient Greek physical and cultural supremacy. She had flicked through a book on Nazi aesthetics in a Moscow bookstore before making the trip to the airport, and had done so with a sort of dread, fearing it would contain images of savagery and degeneration; the opposite was the case. Nazi art was restrained, classical, eschewing the abstract and the expressionist in favor of the conservative. Above all, they loved the art and architecture of ancient Greece. The book was full of building plans—many drawn up by Hitler himself—that looked like the Parthenon in Athens, and of statues clearly modeled or copied from classical originals. Even the Aryan political "philosophy" was grounded in a Greco-Roman aesthetic, or in a nationalistically, ethnocentrically, and racist version of it which said that the decline of the classical world into the degeneration of the modern was the direct consequence of racial mixing. In purging themselves of "inferior" people, the Nazis believed they were reconstructing a golden age exemplified by the art and culture of ancient Greece.

At the last, then, they had dressed their general in the grave goods of Agamemnon in tribute to his classicist dignity and imperial ambitions, but the artifacts—whether they knew them to be fake or not—had been mere trappings: grave goods. It was the body that had counted.

Deborah had been struck by the fact that in all of Voloshinov's papers, there had been no whisper of the possibility that Hitler himself had not died in the bunker. It had all been about the real corpse escaping the Russians, not about Stalin's old notion that the living man himself might have walked free. There was, she supposed, too much information out there to make that particular conspiracy stick, though it had been peddled for a while quite extensively. But it raised another question. Why, with the country burning around them, had the Nazis bothered to try to preserve the body of their leader, a leader whose plans had failed and who was already dead?

For next time, said the voice in her head, darkly.

This was no mere corpse. It was an icon, a monument like Lenin's body lying beside the Kremlin wall years after the social system he had striven to create had finally broken down, a symbol. Whatever other motive the Russians had had in destroying the remains buried in Magdeburg, they had known that a martyr to a dead cause was only fractionally less dangerous than the living man himself. His very bones could be a rallying point for Nazi sympathizers . . .

OK, thought Deborah, *so what had happened next?*

Some body double had been left for the Russians to identify, but en route to Switzerland Hitler's actual body—decked out in all its Mycenaean finery—had been intercepted by one of the units most clearly opposed to all Hitler had represented: an all-black tank battalion.

Ironic, huh?

She supposed that if it had remained with them, that would have been the end of the matter, but Nazi Germany did not hold the monopoly on racism.

"Pretty wild stuff," said Deborah aloud.

That's what Tonya's father had told his driver, Thomas Morris, about what he had seen in the crate. "Pretty wild stuff."

I guess Hitler laid out like Agamemnon would qualify, she thought.

An MP had stolen the crate, killing one black tank commander in the process, a crime he believed—correctly—would not be considered serious enough to warrant full investigation. At first he probably didn't know what the Greek pieces were, except that they could be valuable. He put out some feelers and contacted a British collector to find out what he could about the gold mask and other artifacts carried in there with the corpse, presumably promising a sale, a way to raise money to move Hitler's body. That done, he sent the crate to the United States, but for some reason it never arrived, and the MP lost track of it. He set up a secret right-wing society to track it down.

For years the crate's whereabouts were unknown, till it surfaced on a French beach. Richard got word of it through black market channels and brought it to Atlanta, but decided that the body—which he took to be Agamemnon—should be returned to Greece.

But it wasn't, and she had no idea where it was now or who had it. And could it still be what those long-dead Nazis hoped: a way of uniting all those white supremacist lunatics under a single banner, rallying them, making them multiply, sending them forth to storm Troy from within: the housing estates and subdivisions, the office towers and small businesses all falling to an enemy who had always been slumbering inside them like the Greeks in the wooden horse? Surely, it was impossible. Or was she being naïve? She remembered the mapping of the hate groups on the Southern Poverty Law Center's Web site, the way the screen had filled with icons, the KKK, Aryan Nations, skinheads, New Confederacy . . . Maybe it wasn't so impossible after all.

The moment they landed she would call Cerniga, tell him everything. Tell him about Hitler and Voloshinov, tell him about Magdeburg and the fall of Berlin, tell him . . .

. . . he was wrong?

That too. It would not be an easy conversation.

She thought about Calvin and wondered what he would make of all this. Last night, in bed, she had finally let her mind go back to the night before they had gotten the results from the CAIS lab, the night they had spent together, but she found she could remember almost nothing. What recollections she did have were in her fingertips, not in her mind's eye because he had turned the lights off and the heavy hotel drapes had shut out the streetlamp glow utterly. In the morning he had been up before her, and she found herself regretting she had never seen him out of his professional clothes, if only because such a memory would feel more real, more concrete than that vague fumbling in the dark which was all her brain could summon now. It would have been nice to see his face then, nice now to remember it.

Well, she thought, *it needn't be the only time it happens. Next time you'll see and remember.*

Perhaps. But to get back to that moment would require a more difficult conversation than any she would have with the police.

CHAPTER 68

"This is conspiracy-theory garbage," said Keene.

Cerniga had agreed to meet with her reluctantly and had shown up at her apartment with Keene in tow.

"Listen," said Deborah. "We have a dead Russian obsessed with Hitler tracking him down to the Druid Hills Museum . . ."

"Just because some crazy old Soviet believed that—"

"Listen," said Deborah again. "You think this is all convoluted what-if-the-moon-landings-were-really-shot-in-a-film-studio rubbish, but it's actually the simplest solution that fits the facts. We have a neo-Nazi group chasing what you take to be a weapon. We have an art collector chasing what he believes to be an ancient artifact. We have a body from the mid 1940s laid out like an ancient military hero. What if they are all the same? What if you aren't looking for a nuclear device or a store of smallpox? What if the body *is* both the artifact *and* the weapon?"

Keene opened his mouth to protest, but Cerniga was listening. The anger with which he had dismissed her at their last meeting had been replaced by a sort of resignation, but the more she talked, the more uncomfortable he had seemed, and Deborah knew in her gut that he thought that—preposterous though it sounded—she might be right.

"What do you mean?" he said.

"Maybe the weapon isn't biological or chemical," said Deborah. "Maybe it's *ideological*. Political. To these Nazi lunatics Hitler is God and father. His body is overwritten with a significance that borders on the magical."

"Magical?"

"It seems so to them. It's more than just a banner, it's a tal-
isman, an icon, the supreme human symbol of what they are
and believe."

"OK," said Cerniga, "but how does that make it a weapon?"

"Because people flock to that kind of symbol. The body
was supposed to have been obliterated decades ago, destroyed by the enemies of all Hitler stood for. For the body to
reappear now in glory is as close to a resurrection as they can
get. It's a triumph, a war standard and, whether they are right
or wrong, the Atreus group thinks it can help lead them to exactly that: war."

"Against who?"

"Jews, Arabs, blacks, gays, the handicapped, the Left, inter-
racial couples," said Deborah, ticking them off on her fingers,
"and anyone who helps them or believes in their right to exist."

They were both looking at her now, silent, uneasy.

"The rediscovery of Hitler's body—in the hands of his
friends—could be just what is needed to get the ball rolling,"
she said.

"It couldn't happen here," said Keene, quietly now.

"I hope you're right," said Deborah.

"Even if it did, they couldn't win."

"They didn't win last time," Deborah said to Keene, "but
look what happened along the way. Anyway, it won't be like
that: not tanks and uniforms and invasions. It will be terrorist
attacks: blow up a bridge, shoot up a McDonald's, bomb a
power station. It doesn't need to be open war to have unacceptable consequences. One casualty in a war like that is one
too many."

There was a long silence, and then Cerniga got up. He
looked unsettled, as if he too had been doing a jigsaw puzzle and Deborah had turned the whole thing upside down.
The picture looked different now, stranger than before, disturbing, but it made a kind of sense.

"I don't know," he said. "It seems . . . I don't know. But we
have to pursue it. I'm not saying you're right, but there might
be something to it. Thanks."

Deborah just nodded. Keene studied his shoes.

"Listen," Cerniga said, shifting gears as he moved toward the door. "I was too hard on you before. It wasn't your fault those Greek men died. You didn't do the shooting . . ."

"I know, but if I had told you . . ."

"It's still not your fault."

He waited, and she nodded small, her mouth set in a tight line.

"Is there somebody you can stay with?" he said, getting to his feet. "Friends, family?"

Deborah looked away.

"There's someone," she said, wondering if it was still true.

CHAPTER 69

After they had gone, Deborah sat on the edge of her bed looking out of the window into the night and the rain. A steady drizzle had come and gone and then returned with a greater sense of purpose. There were thunderheads rolling in now from the west. They'd get lightning—probably a lot of it—before the night was out.

She checked her address book and found a home number for Tonya. She didn't know if it was still current and couldn't remember ever having used it before, but it was all she had. It rang eight times before the machine picked up. Deborah stammered an apology and then, even more awkwardly, a kind of plan, an absurd contingency strategy involving all those products Tonya called "girlie": makeup and perfume . . . Whatever. She trimmed her nails and slipped the file into her back pocket.

She called Calvin at home and got his machine too. Unable to think of anything brief and witty that would be in any way adequate—particularly if he was sitting there listening to it as she spoke—she hung up. It was insanely late, but she tried his office anyway, just in case, and got more voice mail. She was getting ready for bed when she remembered his penchant for working late at the museum. She could swing by as if by accident, to work, and they could hash it out there.

Ready to explain why you didn't even speak to him after the CAIS lab visit? Why you fled the country again without a word . . . ?

She got back into her street clothes and dialed the museum on her cell as she locked the apartment door behind her.

It rang for a long time and then was snatched up. It was Calvin, and he sounded impatient.

"Yes, Deborah, what is it?"

"How did you know it was me?"

"Who else would call at this time?"

"I'm coming over," she said. She wouldn't do her apologies over the phone.

"Just like that?" he said. He was angry, and she couldn't blame him. "You leave the country without so much as a call, then just show up on my doorstep—"

"Actually it's my doorstep," she said, opting for cute in an attempt to defuse the situation. "You're at the museum."

"That makes no difference."

"Can we talk about this face-to-face?" she said.

He seemed to consider this.

"OK," he said.

"Should I bring something?" she said. "Chinese?"

"Why don't you come over and we'll see how it goes before doing anything as rash as eating together."

"Fair enough," she said.

"I printed a menu off the Web," he said, as she walked into the museum office. "It's from the Hong Kong Garden."

"I thought we were going to see how things went before we did anything rash," she said.

"I played a hunch," he said.

They still hadn't smiled at each other.

"And what was that hunch based on?" she said.

"I figured you were coming to apologize and that you had a lot on your mind—judging from what I heard about that house in Palmetto—and I would therefore be more sympathetic than you deserved and—"

"Shut up and give me the menu," she said.

Now he smiled, and she returned a slightly more self-mocking version of the same thing.

"What do you fancy?" he said.

"Kung Pao chicken," she said.

"What else?"

"Pot stickers," she said.

"Anything else?"

He was standing beside her now, and his tone was amused, playful.

"Oh," she said, looking up and grinning at him as he slipped his arms around her waist, "you mean what would I like other than food?"

"Right."

"Hmm," she said thoughtfully. "I think that's all. Maybe a spring roll."

He pushed her away, laughing.

"Tease," he said.

"A girl has to eat," she said. "We'll discuss dessert later."

"OK," he conceded. "Wanna walk round to pick it up? I've been in here for hours, and you have a lot of explaining to do."

The museum was nestled in a wooded hollow a couple of hundred yards from the main road, and as they walked along under the oaks and sweet gums, the freshness of the rain-washed night was intoxicating.

Calvin listened to her heavily edited history of the last few days and took her hand when she said how responsible she had felt for the Greeks who had died.

"You're not," he said. "The only person responsible is the one who shot them."

She squeezed his hand and looked at him. He was wearing a thin white T-shirt under a khaki shirt, with chinos and dock-siders: *"Southern lawyer casual"* he called it. In the high, amber light of the sodium lamps, his face was perfectly balanced, angular: handsome. She smiled properly, a reward for his compassion, and then they were at the restaurant, which was large and red and Disneyfied: China as imagined by snow globe makers.

Their food was ready and packaged to go as soon as they reached the counter, but that didn't save them from the rain, which had begun again in earnest by the time they got outside. For a moment they sheltered under the vast crimson portico of the restaurant, before deciding that it was going to get heavier before it got lighter. They made a run for it.

The thunder started properly before they had gone two blocks: a great bark of it chasing a flare of lightning downtown. They laughed and kept going. Calvin sang a little Fred Astaire, and Deborah danced sportingly through a puddle deep enough to come over her shoes. The water poured down the drainage ditches, rushed into the sewers with an exuberant roar. Even the twinge of Deborah's ankle couldn't take the fun out of the thing, running with this beautiful man through the rain, feeling her clothes sticking to her, her hair dripping. They would have to get undressed as soon as they got indoors. It was the only smart thing to do . . .

By the time they reached the museum doors, and Deborah was fighting to get the key into the lock, she was laughing almost too hard to stand. She was soaked from head to foot as if she had been sitting in a bath fully clothed. Calvin plucked his arms out of his top shirt, and his T-shirt looked painted to his skin.

They almost fell through the door when it opened, into the cool stillness of the museum lobby, so that their laughter echoed recklessly. It was like being taken with the giggles in temple as a kid, she thought, all this unstoppable good humor shattering the moldy, reverential silence. Calvin closed the door behind him and turned to her, grinning from ear to ear.

"I think I'm wet," he said.

Deborah just looked.

No. No. No. Not this. Anything but this.

The khaki shirt was dripping in his hands. The lights above the entrance picked him out and made him glow against the dark, storm-battered glass behind him, like a saint. The white T-shirt plastered to his chiseled chest and stomach, the fabric thin and transparent with its weight of rain, was like the merest skin, as if something reptilian had been sloughed off, so that she could see the faint lines underneath the shirt, dark and bluish, the tattoo etching of a death mask overlaid with a German eagle, and the single word: *Atreus.*

CHAPTER 70

So, she thought, *it's true.*

She had wondered, feared, fought not to believe it, but there it was.

If I just turn away and behave normally, she thought, *maybe he won't notice. He'll dry off, or he'll put his shirt back on, and he'll think I never saw it. He'll think he got away with it like he did when he turned out the lights in the hotel room. He'll think I won't know what he is.*

But faking her feelings wasn't Deborah's strong suit; never had been. She could walk away, keep to herself, and kill a minute or two, but he was expecting them to eat together and, probably, rather more than that. She wouldn't be able to look him in the face. She wouldn't be able to endure that smile without asking if he had used it on Richard before he had stabbed his Nazi dagger through his chest. She wouldn't be able to listen to his voice without hearing him whispering the address of the house where the two Greek men were waiting into the phone from the CAIS lab restroom.

She didn't need to ask him what he had done or how. It was all quite clear. It had fallen into place in the hollow of her chest where her heart and lungs had been a moment earlier, filling her with certainty, as if she had seen him do it all firsthand.

And you knew. You convinced yourself you didn't, but you knew.

She could turn back to him now, chat, laugh like nothing had happened, and then later, after dinner and their tentative lovemaking, she could call the Feds and end this once and for all. She just had to get through a few hours: less if she could find a way to make a phone call without seeming awkward.

You could use the bathroom, she thought. *That's what he did when he gave the order to kill the Greeks.*

"You OK?" said Calvin, smiling his easy, feline smile.

"Yeah," she said, turning and smiling. "Just wet. I think I'll change."

"Eat first," he said. "I've always wanted to have dinner off some thousand-year-old relic. What do you say we dine on the Indian display over there?"

She forced her mouth to stretch wide.

"Sure," she said. "Set things out while I wash up."

"You sure you're OK?" he said. "You seem, I don't know . . . nervous."

"Let's call it anticipation," she said.

"For the Chinese food?" he said, smiling a lewd and oily smile.

You found him attractive.

"Not just the Chinese food," she managed.

He grinned and took a step toward her, reaching for her.

"Not till I'm all washed up," she said, backing away, grimacing.

"Maybe I'll come with you," he said, leering.

"You can use the little boy's room over there."

"Are big boys allowed to use it?" he asked.

He was being playful. She wanted to scream.

"Just this once," she said, taking another step away.

"Hurry up," he said. "I won't wait long before I come looking."

Deborah sat on the toilet inside the locked stall and fumbled with her cell phone. Her hands were unsteady.

Please, God, let it be working.

Come on . . .

Eternal God, who sendest consolation unto all sorrowing hearts, we turn to Thee for solace in this, our trying hour.

The words had come unbidden from some long-sleeping half memory, and she shook them off as if forcing herself awake. She stared at the phone. The lightning storm could play havoc with signal strength, especially down in the creek basin where the museum was located.

She fished Cerniga's card out of her purse and punched the numbers in.

"Yes," she said, as a female voice answered, "can I speak to Agent Cerniga, please."

"Agent Cerniga has gone home for the night. Can I take a message?"

"I need to reach him right away. It's an emergency connected to the case he's currently working."

Come on. Come on.

"Which case would that be?"

"Richard Dixon and the two Greek men," she sputtered. "Please, I don't have time for this."

"And who can I say is calling?" said the woman, unflappable.

"It's Deborah Miller," she said. "Please, I need to reach him *right now*."

The force of the stall door being kicked in knocked her backward and sprawling onto the tiles. She landed badly, and the phone skittered across the floor.

Calvin Bowers picked it up and dropped it neatly into the toilet bowl.

"You really ought to do something about the way sound carries in these vents," he said, his voice level and calm, his face impassive. He was a man she had had never met before. "You just can't get any privacy in this building."

CHAPTER 71

She didn't cry. She didn't beg. She would not try to explain or appeal to his sense of justice or friendship or romance because she knew instinctively and beyond any doubt that none of those things had been real. She would have expected to be stricken with panic, but the strangeness of the thing robbed her of the terror which she knew was appropriate, leaving her oddly composed and separate and full of righteous defiance. She would not cry. She would not beg.

But she was not quite on her feet when he struck her hard across the side of her head with the back of his hand. It didn't hurt so much as it surprised her with its casual brutality, and she crumpled down the side of the commode. With Bowers still standing in the doorway, there was nowhere else for her to go.

It occurred to her then that he might be planning to kill her where she was. What else was he to do? She pulled herself into a crouch and looked up. For a moment their eyes met, and he snapped on a clownish grin, deliberate and malevolent.

"You know," he said, unrecognizable now, "I think it's better this way. I really don't think I could endure having you touch me again, you know?"

Deborah tensed but said nothing.

"Did you hear what I said?" he added, still quite calm, adding in a whisper that sounded almost tender, "Jew?"

Then he was balling his fist and drawing his arm back to strike, and she was surging forward, meeting his gut with her head and lunging through him like a spear, thrusting with all the power her legs could muster. His punch glanced off her shoulder. It hurt, but its delivery had left him off balance, and her attack sent him sprawling backward. His head hit the tiled floor with a hollow thud so that she winced, even as she scrambled off him, hoping vaguely, horribly, that the impact had killed him.

For a second he lay on his back and she stood over him. There was no blossoming of blood from his scalp, and though his eyes had rolled back into his head for the briefest of moments, she knew he would be on his feet in under a minute. She hopped clumsily over him, pulled open the bath-room door, and ran into the bowels of the museum.

Get to a phone.

She ran unsteadily toward the office, fumbling for her keys as she did, her great loping strides uneven as her ankle began to twinge.

Not now, she thought. *There isn't time for pain.*

She was in the lobby when she heard the bathroom door crash back against the wall. He was coming.

She hesitated. If she went into the office now, there would be nowhere for her to go. He would probably smash his way in before she could make her call, certainly before anyone arrived in response. The call would have to wait. She needed to get out into the grounds. The road was only half a mile away, and she knew the area better than he did.

She turned to cross the lobby, and there he was, on the other side of the ghastly ship prow, making for the lobby doors, shambling past her and leaning to one side like a listing galleon. Maybe the whack to his head had concussed him a little.

Good, she thought.

He thought she'd already made it out. Maybe he had lost some blood after all. Maybe he had blacked out for a second and lost track of time.

Good.

But not good enough. As she held her breath in the shadows, hoping he would blunder out into the rain and she could lock herself in and make her phone call to Cerniga, he slowed and stopped, considering the closed doors, animal-like. Then he pivoted and stooped. He seemed to be looking at something on the ground. She peered around the greenish snake-woman who was grinning out at him, and her heart seemed to leap. He was reaching down to a white plastic bag on the floor, touching its side with the flat of his hand.

Distantly, as if echoing back from a nonsensical dream, she realized what it was: The Chinese food.

He's seeing if it's still hot.

Only minutes ago that was to be their dinner, their shared experience, their foreplay. The memory was so grotesque that it took her a second to realize that he was trying to decide how long he had been out, how far she might have got. He reached into his pocket, withdrew his cell phone as he straightened up, and began pushing buttons.

At the first sound of his muted voice, Deborah began to move back and away. Two silent steps, three, then her ankle turned underneath her, and she stumbled clumsily, her eyes still turned toward the man muttering into his phone. The sound echoed briefly, and he turned, finding her across the darkened lobby as she scuttled back the only way she could go, down the corridor to the double doors and into the museum proper.

She knew the museum like the back of her hand. She could hide. She could double back. She could get to the residence and out that way . . .

The double doors in front of her cannoned open.

In between them, arms outstretched, phone squashed under his chin, was the skinhead kid with the tattoos who she had left unconscious in the subterranean stairway under Mycenae. The White Rabbit.

"Yeah," he said into the phone as he took another surging stride toward her, "I see her."

From behind his back, flourishing it like a magician or a striptease artist, he drew his knife. It was a different knife from the one he'd had in Greece. This one was long and slender, its hilt curved down slightly, a tiny swastika on its pommel. This was the knife which had killed Richard. This, she thought with a stab of deep, hollowing grief, was Calvin's knife.

CHAPTER 72

There was nowhere to go. Calvin was behind her and closing fast, the kid up ahead, humming to himself and watching her. She could run at one of them, but she didn't like her chances; there would be no element of surprise, and the other would be on her quickly enough. She had no weapon, no means of escape, no chance.

From her purse she plucked a vial of perfume, Chanel No. 19. For a second she aimed it at the skinhead, and he faltered, not out of fear for his eyes, but because he actually laughed.

"Drop it," said Calvin. He sounded more cautious, as if he thought it might be mace. "We're not going to hurt you. I want to ask you a few questions."

"Like what?" she said, managing a little defiance still.

"How long you've known," he said. "And who else knows."

"Bite me," she said.

"I don't think that this is the time for your patented feminist posturing," he said.

He reached down to his shins. There was a brief tearing sound, like Velcro, and then he was upright again, training a small pistol on her.

She turned to consider him and pointed the bottle's atomizer head his way.

"Bitch," said the kid, still grinning disdainfully, "that's so pathetic."

He took two quick steps toward her, and Deborah, capitulating dramatically, let the vial fall to the ground. It exploded in a tiny nova of glass and aroma, part flowers, part musk.

In three long and hurried strides, Calvin was next to her and grasping her arm.

"Come with us, do as you're told, and you might live out the night."

Even if that's true, she thought, *that's as far as it goes. Once he's satisfied that he knows all you do, earlier if he figures out that no one knows you're here, you're dead.*

It's hours away now, maybe less.

The kid half led, half dragged her through the museum to the residence, then out through the back door into Richard's private lot. There was an old blue van, dark and windowless except for the cab, parked there by itself, the engine running. She recognized it at once as the van which had tried to force her off the road the day she had fled to Greece. The windows were heavily tinted, but there was a light on inside, and she could see somebody turn to stare out, another skinhead kid.

Great, she thought. *He has a private army. His own little Hitler Youth movement.*

"Here's a treat you don't deserve," Calvin said to her. "You get to ride in the back."

"That's supposed to make me happy?" she answered

"Sure," he said. "It's what you've been looking for, isn't it?"

Even now, even staring at the imminence of her own death, she felt a stirring of something like curiosity.

It's in there!

They had strapped her hands behind her with slick, gray duct tape. The kid pushed her inside roughly and slammed the door, locking it with the key from outside. She was doubled up on the floor of the van, the seats of which had all been removed. As they got in the front and started the engine, she twisted round to consider the crate beside her.

It was quite unremarkable, or at least it was from where she was lying: a large, casket-sized box of black-painted wood. She couldn't see the top which was, presumably, glass, and the only thing which broke the object's blank regularity was a power cord which snaked a few inches from within. A heavy dark blanket had been thrown over the top.

She lay there, feeling the presence of the thing beside her, as the van began to move.

They drove for about fifteen minutes, she thought. For a while at the beginning and end of the journey they moved relatively slowly through darkened areas and winding roads, but in the middle they went faster, and the buildings outside cast distorted reflections of flickering lights through the cab windows onto the ceiling. It rained constantly, and the windshield wipers droned and squeaked throughout the journey.

When they stopped, the kid got out first and was gone at least a minute before the creak of the rear doors made Deborah raise her head.

"Slowly," said Calvin from the front seat. "Get out. And do anything stupid, and I'll put a hole in your head. Got it?"

He's not kidding.

She said nothing, but shifted back until she could get her legs down to the gravel outside. The kid was waiting for her, knife still drawn, looking at her through the rain with malicious amusement.

"You hurt me back in Greece, Jew," he said.

He had a petulant voice tinged with the nastier side of rural Georgia. It was boyish and might have been absurd—a mere stereotypical cartoon—if it hadn't been so hard and full of hatred.

"That's 'cause you tried to kill me, hick," she said.

He lashed his hand against the side of her head, and it popped so loudly she thought he'd ruptured her eardrum. Tears started to her eyes, and she bent over involuntarily, biting her lip to stifle a sob.

"You watch your mouth," he said.

She said nothing, but straightened, sensing Calvin had moved around to the back of the van.

"Get the ramp set up," Calvin said. "I'll watch her. Give me my knife."

He met her eyes impassively, but at her look of contempt, he shrugged and smiled a little.

"Nice, isn't it?" he said, showing the weapon with its slender blade. "A Third Reich Luftwaffe dagger. I got it from *my* mentor."

"Edward Graves," she said.

Calvin's face tightened.

"Now, how did you know that?" he said. "Tell me what you know and who else knows it, and we'll make a deal."

"Like you did with Richard?"

"Richard was a lousy businessman," he said. "I'm sure we can do better."

"Don't bet on it."

He shrugged again.

"You want to be a martyr, who am I to stop you?" he said. He held up the knife and let her see it. She caught her own face reflected in the blade. She looked far away, a dream image, bright and strange like a mermaid rearing from the surf.

"Give me a hand with this," said the White Rabbit. He was shunting the great black box down the plank ramp he had set against the rear doors. It was still covered by the dark blanket.

"Don't run," said Calvin.

He needn't have warned her. They were parked behind a large stone building, in a walled courtyard with a wrought-iron gate through which they had driven but which was now closed and, presumably, locked electronically. There was nowhere to run. He'd shoot her down in seconds.

Bowers turned and braced his weight against the wheeled box as the kid guided it down to the gravel.

"We need to get this inside," said the kid. "What about her?"

Deborah felt a sudden urgent need to speak, to delay whatever decision he would come to.

"You want to know how long I've known?" she said. "A long time. Remember the night we spent in Athens, when you said you knew what I meant about how Richard looked? The first time we met you said you had never met Richard. And you think it never occurred to me that the only person other than me who had seen the address the lab was going to send the results to was you? Do you think it never occurred to me that while I was e-mailing you details of my movements in Greece, some maniac was trying to kill me? You think it never occurred to me that whoever that maniac was thought I knew something, something he had seen me studying on Richard's computer, or that you were the only person who knew for a fact that I would have seen the letter you had sent to Richard at the museum? Actually, Calvin, it was earlier than all those. It was the first day we met, when you said that that 'barbaric' tomahawk was evidence of Manifest Destiny. You think those things didn't add up in my head to your being a white supremacist moron?"

They didn't. Not really. They should have, but they didn't. Not till you saw the tattoo. If nothing else, you should have known that men who look like him don't date women like you.

Yeah? Their loss.

Now you recover your antiromantic defiance. Too bad you didn't have it before when you were talking to Cerniga and said absolutely nothing about all the clues you were starting to string together, all those rancid little bread crumbs that led straight to Calvin Bowers's door.

She hadn't known then. Not for sure.

Calvin considered her. The rain was streaming down his face, but he seemed quite unaware of it.

"So who else did you tell?"

Deborah said nothing, staring into his face with all the defiance and contempt she could manage.

He smiled slightly, an amused, doubtful smile that said he didn't trust her, but that was OK. For now.

"We'll lock her up with it," he said. "Until she's ready to talk. If she has any doubts about our seriousness, I think she's about to see something that will convince her otherwise."

CHAPTER 73

It was a house, she supposed, or had been once. But it didn't really look like any house she had ever seen. It looked more like a temple, an ancient Greek temple made of white stone and fluted columns. Cerniga had suggested that Atreus might have inherited a lot of money from their founder's shady business dealings during the war. This house was probably built out of that money. Beyond the courtyard wall she could hear the erratic hum of traffic fairly close by, but she had no clear sense of where it was coming from.

"It was built by my predecessor," said Calvin, propelling her forward by her elbow, "the man who set all this in motion fifty years ago. Mr. Edward Graves. A great man and a great friend to me. A kind of father, almost. I wish he'd lived to see it. I maintain it as a ritual hall for our little organization, but the legal connection is very circuitous."

"It's a bourgeois monstrosity," said Deborah.

"I didn't mean the house," said Calvin, "though he also built that. The house is unimportant, however. It's merely a shell."

"Protecting what?"

"You are about to find out," he said, sounding pleased, even a little excited.

There were a set of large double doors atop a flight of shallow stone steps, and Deborah began to walk toward them as the kid moved the makeshift ramp from the back of the van to the stairs.

She paused, waiting for Calvin to unlock the doors, inching away from the White Rabbit with his leer and his unfeeling eyes, and wondered if she should run for it. Could getting shot down out here be any worse than what awaited her inside?

"In you go," said Calvin, gesturing like an eighteenth-century nobleman.

They walked into a square lobby and then a hallway with dark hardwood floors and framed pictures, athletic male bodies, rugged landscapes, and studies of ancient weapons. One wall showed black-and-white photographs of classical—or reproduction classical—statues on display in a museum hung with swastikas, all dated prominently to the late 1930s and marked simply "Berlin." One showed the Nazi high command in full dress uniform inspecting a famous marble discus thrower.

Then, one eye and the pistol still on Deborah, Calvin stooped and dragged aside an Oriental rug, revealing a rectangle of wood less faded than the surrounding floor. He flicked a pair of recessed brass catches, and the floor dropped slowly away: a hatch revealing a stone ramp sloping sharply down into the bowels of the house.

"Down here," said Calvin, still more pleased with the look on her face.

She edged forward and peered down uneasily. There was something familiar about the large stone blocks that made up the walls.

"Go on," he said, nudging her with the gun barrel.

She tensed, then began to descend as Calvin behind her picked up a large flashlight and switched it on. She stooped to get under the wooden floor, and for a moment she smelled the warm, cut timber of the house, but as she walked down the stone ramp, that scent was replaced with the aroma of cool, damp earth. The light flashed off the stone walls, and she felt the temperature drop as they advanced cautiously. They were halfway down before she could see what was at the bottom of the walled ramp.

"Oh my God," she said.

"Exactly," said Calvin. "Impressive, isn't it."

At the bottom were a set of heavy doors between two sturdy columns. Above the massive lintel was a triangular stone carved with a pair of imperial lions. It was the Treasury of Atreus from Mycenae, reproduced as it would have originally looked, transported into the heart of Atlanta and hewn from Georgia granite.

Deborah faltered.

"It's an exact replica of the original," said Calvin, "built to one-third of the original scale. It was constructed secretly over ten years by private contractors. Very private. Our own people did most of the work. It exists on no blueprints or plans of the house. Search the building from top to bottom; no one would find it."

Behind her the kid was laboring to ease the box on its casters down the ramp.

"I don't understand," she said. "I thought . . . I don't understand."

Calvin just smiled that bland, knowing smile of his, took a heavy key from his pocket and a flashlight from a bracket on the wall.

"I thought not," he said, as he fitted it into the lock. The mechanism clicked in several places up the massive doors, and as he wrenched the latch and cracked them open, revealing an impenetrable darkness beyond, she heard a resounding echo from inside.

"You thought that seeing this would make me think you were serious about killing me?" she said, recovering a little of her poise. "This just convinces me that you're a lunatic."

"Not this," he said, pushing the thick, studded doors open and flicking on a light. "This."

It was exactly like the tholos tomb in Mycenae, a great beehive of Cyclopean masonry, grayer in color, but otherwise the same, the great vaulted dome, the chill emptiness. There were differences: the huge torch brackets, the angry red banners daubed with swastikas, but the only one that mattered, the only one Calvin's flashlight picked out and held, was the body on the ground.

It was sprawled on its back, one arm flung out as if in supplication.

Deborah closed her eyes tightly and locked her teeth together so that she wouldn't sob aloud.

There was a broken tobacco pipe on the ground at her feet. Marcus had met the same fate as his father.

CHAPTER 74

"We'll lock you inside for a little while," said Calvin, "while we adjust our plans, and then we'll talk."

"You killed him in Greece and then brought him back here?" she said. "Why?"

She didn't care. She was just talking because she didn't want to be locked in the dark with Marcus's murdered body.

"Of course not," he said. "He came back looking for me. Found me, in fact."

"And you killed him," she said.

"Obviously," he said.

"Why?" she said, swallowing back the unsteadiness in her voice. "He was just an enthusiastic collector like Richard, who thought he had found the body of Agamemnon."

"He was," Calvin agreed. "Till he met me. Somehow he connected me to my predecessor and discovered my little tomb, his tomb as it turns out. For a little while."

He grinned at his joke.

"Once he had discovered my"—he looked for the words— "philosophical orientation, he started doing research of a very different kind. By the time I found him, he had done what you apparently have not."

"What's that?" she said, still not caring.

"He had discovered what is contained within that box."

As he said it, the kid, who had been pushing the display case into the center of the chamber, looked up.

"It's nearly ready," he said. "Hold on."

Deborah thought quickly. The more she seemed to know, the more she could have told other people. That might keep her alive.

"I know everything," she said.

"Right," said Calvin, scornfully. "Of course you do."

"I know that if the police run a ballistics check on your gun they'll nail you for the death of Sergei Voloshinov, an MVD agent who you killed because he knew as well as I do what you have in that box."

That stopped him. He looked genuinely surprised for a second, but then he began to smile.

"You want to know what else I know?" said Deborah, challenging his silence, his smugness.

Bowers ignored her, turning to the kid as he felt underneath the box, located the power cord, and slotted it home. From under the blanket came an unearthly glow that threw the contours of the rough-hewn boulders into sharp relief. At the same time, a panel of soft lights that had been invisible till this moment flickered into life directly above. The kid scuttled back toward the wall and watched, his face drawn and anxious, even a little fearful.

"The moment of truth," said Calvin.

He took a step over to the foot of the casket and slowly, reverently drew back the blanket.

The box contained the wizened body of a man, roughly preserved, though largely invisible beneath the gleaming gold mask and the weather-stained banner, which was a faded red overlaid with a stylized black eagle.

"You should have left him to stink in Berlin," she said.

The kid snapped his head round to stare at her, and for a second she thought she had gone too far. But Calvin was smiling his oily, self-satisfied smile, and that seemed to quell the boy.

"Our general is home at last," Calvin murmured, a light in his eyes that she had never seen before, "and Atreus's mission is fulfilled. We have brought the mortal remains of Adolf Hitler to America, and to his bones our people will flock. Who will stand before such an army?"

So she had been right. It wouldn't save her, not now, but she had, at least, been right.

CHAPTER 75

"She knew," hissed the kid.

"It doesn't matter," said Calvin, still smiling over his trophy.

"Man, we have to talk. Now."

Calvin's unblinking gaze finally slid away from the half-mummified corpse and found the White Rabbit's face. For a second he just looked, reading the kid's anxiety, and then he nodded and took a step out of the tomb.

"What about her?" said the kid.

"Lock her in," said Calvin, turning his smile on Deborah. "For the moment."

Deborah sat in the beehive tomb, as far from Marcus's body as she could get, staring at the glass-topped casket which was the focus of the chamber's only light, and thought. She had kept her half suspicions about Calvin under wraps in the vague hope that if he was involved, she might learn from him where the weapon was and what it was. Well, now she knew, and it would avail her nothing.

But that wasn't the only reason you ignored your doubts about Calvin, was it?

She had ignored them because if they weren't true . . .

If you could convince yourself they weren't true . . .

. . . then maybe they would settle down in a cottage with a picket fence and raise their allocated two point two children?

Ironic, wasn't it? She had stifled her unease to make the *relationship* work like some paper-thin heroine in a TV movie, and now her beloved (and his White Rabbit henchman) would kill her. They would torture her till she told them that she had not in fact told the Feds, and then they would kill her, and sprinkle her blood in some quasi-primitive funerary rites for the goose-stepping butcher of millions. It was almost funny. Almost.

But she wasn't done quite yet, and as she had been mulling over her "relationship" with Calvin, she had been teasing the slim nail file out of her back pocket with the tips of her fingers. Now she guided its tip into the silver duct tape that bound her wrists and pushed until she felt it puncture. Gripping the metal tightly she sliced up and down, feeling the webbing of the tape tear, till she could slough it off, and toss it into the shadows.

She stood up and moved to the glass case, feeling with her fingertips for a latch. She found two, one at each end, unsnapped them, and raised the lid. The body smelled of nothing except a faint whiff of formaldehyde perhaps, though she might have imagined that. She reached over, took hold of the mask in both hands, and lifted it free.

The face beneath was wizened but recognizably male. There was a small, bristly mustache and a lock of thin black hair over the forehead, straying across what looked to be a bullet hole. The eyes were closed and sunken.

How many deaths had this man caused? How many more might these half-rotten bones still cause?

She looked for a weapon, a loose rock with which she could smash the thing to pieces: her final act of defiance.

Or you could try something else.

She considered the idea, pacing around the casket. There was nothing else to be done. She may as well try.

It took her perhaps fifteen minutes. When she was done, she pulled the one electric cable she could see until she tore it out of the wall and, without flash or sound, the lights died, and she was left in darkness. She sat against the chill stone, listening to the muffled rumble of thunder, her eyes trying—without success—to make shapes out of the blackness. She had been there no more than a few minutes when she heard the locks snap back and the latch click. She got to her feet, snapping her hands behind her back as the doors swung open.

Maybe it's Cerniga.

But it was the White Rabbit, and Calvin was behind him.

"Bitch broke the lights," said the kid.

"Doesn't matter," said Calvin.

"I can't see what I'm doing," said the kid, his hard little eyes peering into the darkness.

Deborah thought they looked agitated, a little panicked, and was glad. They were worried that she would somehow lead the police or the Feds to them here.

"Change of plan," Calvin said, and he was quite calm again.

As the kid threw the blanket back over the top of the display case and started wheeling it out, Calvin aimed his pistol at Deborah's face. Then he smiled a small, brittle smile and said, "Good-bye Deborah."

CHAPTER 76

She didn't hesitate. The moment she saw the gun she took a step backward, then another. He was still well lit, but she could see from the look of irritation on his face that he had lost her in the shadows. He hesitated, the gun moving fractionally from side to side, and she took two more silent steps and dropped quietly to the floor, making herself as small as possible. Her eyes still on the light space beyond the doors where Calvin stood immobile, she slipped out of one shoe and tossed it gently. It landed softly three yards away, and the sound was just enough to give Calvin something to aim at. He fired once, then twice more, the gun booming in the confined space.

Deborah heard the ricochet, and she clenched smaller still, her breath sucked in tight, as the bullets zipped around the stone chamber.

"Come on," said the kid outside, clearly impatient now. "We've gotta move."

Deborah looked up, moving as minimally as possible, in case Calvin's eyes had grown used to the darkness. He was still peering in, the gun raised. He didn't know if he'd hit her or not.

"Did you get her?" said the White Rabbit, looking up from the box he was shoving back up the ramp. He sounded jumpy. "I need a hand with this. There isn't time—"

"Right," said Calvin. "I think so."

"You *think* so? Get in there and make sure."

"So she can slip past me in the dark like she got past you in Mycenae?" said Calvin, finally lowering the gun. He looked at the kid now, and Deborah could tell from the rigidity of his body that he didn't like being told what to do. "It doesn't matter," he said. "She's dead anyway."

Not yet, you son of a bitch.

He backed steadily out, and then the heavy doors were closing, latching and locking. The tholos was plunged into total darkness.

Deborah exhaled and wondered if, as the bullets had been flashing from stone to stone, she had been praying.

A little, perhaps, yeah. Part of you still is . . .

So now what? It felt like they weren't coming back— which seemed like good news—but they seemed confident that she was no longer a danger to them, and that was odd. They didn't want a hostage and didn't want to drag her along, but could they think she would merely starve to death, locked in this chamber with only a corpse for company?

"She's dead anyway," Calvin had said.

Bravado, or did he really believe it?

The thought alarmed her. How long before Tonya found the perfume? That had been the code she had left on her answering machine. If her vague, half suspicions about Calvin were right, she would leave a sign which Tonya would stumble on during her cleaning. It was to be something feminine which Deborah wouldn't usually use. Something "girly," as Tonya had put it: a slush of lipstick across a mirror, a carefully placed earring, a puddle of Chanel No. 19 that any woman would detect the moment she stepped into the building. These were signs of her discovery . . .

And of another failed effort to be . . .

What? Female? Nonsense. She needed no doting man to prove her femininity.

So you keep saying.

And will continue to do so.

Any loss, any pang of regret that there would be no further flirtation with Calvin Bowers was dwarfed, was rendered laughably insignificant, by the look in his eyes when he had called her—so carefully, with such exquisite deliberation— *Jew.*

Goddamn him straight to hell.

She had known she had been right, and if any part of her

wished she hadn't found out, she should find where it lived
and cut it out—even from her heart—because it was prepos-
terously sentimental, stupid, and self-destructive. Cut it out,
and let it burn with him.

Let it burn . . .

As half her mother's family had been burned at Auschwitz
by the likes of Calvin Bowers, by the ragged huddle of bones
that Atreus was so keen to preserve.

Let it burn.

It was some time before she realized that the chamber
didn't feel as cold as it had done, longer still before she realized the precise way they had intended to accelerate her death.
She was inching her way hopelessly around the darkened
chamber, feeling around the walls for any sign of looseness in
the masonry, when it struck her that the stones were warm.

Let it burn.

You're imagining it.

But it was quite plain, and the longer she went, the clearer
it was that the stones were getting hotter by the second. After
another minute or so, she was fairly sure she could smell
smoke. She fumbled her way round to the doors and listened.

She heard a distant crash and a rush of something dreadful
and familiar, something very like the hungry surge of spreading fire.

"She's dead anyway."

Oh, God.

The house was ablaze, and the stone tomb was nothing
more than a great oven. Long before the solid cedar doors
burned through, long before the fire department got the inferno under control, she would be dead, dehydrated and
baked like a mummy interred in the baking fires of the Sa-
hara sand. And for a moment, for one moment that looked in
the pitch-blackness of the tomb very like despair—not depression or hopelessness but despair in its true, soul-sucking,
annihilating horror—the phrase came back and lingered . . .

Let it burn.

CHAPTER 77

No, she thought. She would not give up. Not yet.

She pounded on the door and shouted for help till the strain on her throat made her retch. The air was drying fast, and she could taste the smoke she couldn't see. She inched around the chamber walls, clawing again, feeling the mounting panic as the air grew thick and acrid. She forced herself to stare into the blackness, in case the flames outside would reveal a crack in the masonry, but she knew that the tomb had been hollowed out of the ground itself; if she were able to move the rocks at the back, she would find only the impervious Georgia clay stacked dense and thick.

Think!

She considered trying to climb, but the bell jar shape of the tholos made that impossible, and even if she could get up to the top, there was no way out. The smoke would be thicker up there anyway, the air hotter, doubly so if—as seemed likely—the entire structure above it was ablaze.

Quite the hellish little clambake, she thought. *The flames don't need to get in for you to cook nicely.*

Tonya wouldn't detect the perfume till morning, and even if she did, the police wouldn't know where to go.

Think.

There was nothing *to* think. She couldn't get out and couldn't sound an alarm. The fire department would come eventually when some neighbor spotted the blaze—assuming there even *were* neighbors—but by then it would be too late.

The stones closest to the door were the hottest, and she instinctively backed away from them. That made sense: The fire was burning in the house and basement, but the rear of the tholos backed into dirt and rock. In this great oven, of course, it made little difference. She might take a little longer to die back here, but the difference would be measured in minutes only.

And then something struck her.

"It's an exact replica of the original," Calvin had said.

OK. What do we know about the original that might help?

Nothing. There's nothing to know. It's a stone chamber with wooden doors that will take longer to burn than you will to roast.

No. There's something else.

She ran forward toward the door and spread herself against the warm stones to the left of the great doorway.

This is crazy. It's cooler back there.

She began to feel for handholds in the rock.

You can't climb. It's concave.

"The first ten feet are vertical. I just have to get a little way up."

She found a niche with her fingers and began to pull. Slowly, first one foot then the other left the dirt floor and scrabbled for a purchase on the rim of one of the Cyclopean blocks. Her fingers ached as she searched the stone with her toes. Nothing.

She dropped, coughing, to the dirt.

It can't be done.

She moved to the other side of the door, conscious to avoid the huddled body against the wall.

Again she reached up, probed with her fingers and dragged herself up. This time her feet found a ledge, and she was able to push up another two feet, high enough to reach the lintel above the door. Half reaching, half falling, she grabbed at the square edge and let her body swing sideways with a cry. For a second she hung by one hand, flailing, then she reached up and made a grab with her other. She knew as she did it that if she couldn't pull herself up with this lunging stab of her arm, she would fall.

She caught it, felt the sharp edge biting into her palm like relief, and pulled herself up.

The lintel was a foot and a half wide, just enough for her to crouch against the great triangular slab. She put her hand close to it, feeling its heat, hardly daring to hope.

"You said it was an exact replica, you son of a bitch," she muttered. "Now let's see."

She rose slowly to a standing position, hugging the stone blocks on either side of the great carved triangle, the angle of the dome pressing her to lean backward into black space. Then she drew back one foot as far as she dared, poised to kick forward at the hot stone panel, carved on the outside with its imperial lions.

"A replica," she spat. "One-third size."

Which means that this stone slab should be no more than an inch thick, the originals being designed to spare excessive weight on the lintel . . .

Well. Let's see.

She kicked hard.

Nothing but a jarring of the bones in her leg that made her shout out, so that her concentration wavered, and she almost fell back into the tomb.

She kicked again, harder, shouting out as she made contact.

A pause, then again, harder still, throwing her whole weight into the kick, knowing it might shatter her leg.

It didn't, and this time the jarring, unyielding rock seemed to give fractionally. She kicked again and heard the tiniest crack. Deborah grinned wolfishly.

Two more kicks, and she heard splinters of stone falling. A third, and she could see light: red, flickering, angry light, admittedly, but light all the same.

She returned to a squat on the lintel and began pushing and hammering with the heels of her hands. Another crack appeared, amber in the dark, like lava pouring down a volcano crater at night, and then a slab the size of her head popped out. Exhilarated, she put her shoulder to it, swung out and then back with a heavy thud against the hot stone. It gave a little, the panel grating like a broken molar as she tested it. She repeated the action again and again, till the triangle split raggedly and the top two-thirds yawned wide.

Deborah pushed it free and heard it fall below, shattering. She could just about get through the hole now, she thought, though the sight of the inferno raging on the other side gave her pause. It looked like the entire timber framing on the underside of the house was ablaze. Eventually, it would collapse, and whether or not it brought the tholos tomb crashing down with it was a moot point. If she didn't get out now, she wouldn't get out at all. She took one last look into the burial chamber, lit now by the dancing firelight without, and clambered out onto the external lintel.

The heat on her skin was tremendous. She squatted, turned to face the building, and gently lowered herself as far as she could before dropping to her feet and rolling, to take the shock out of her knees and ankles.

The stone ramp was the only thing that wasn't burning. What had kept her alive so far, she thought, was the fact that she was below the worst of the fire and smoke, not above it, but she would have to go up and through it to get out. She put her head down and ran. As the ramp shallowed to nothing, the heat increased exponentially. There was a small lever at the top. She pulled it, and the ceiling trap swung down with a sigh of grateful flame as the air from below was sucked into the conflagration.

She put her head through, feeling wisps of her hair frizzle and shrink in the heat. The way she had come in was a wall of fire. There was no getting out that way. There was also no getting out if she stayed where she was. Without giving herself time to think, she climbed up, out, and skulked low and fast down the corridor with its burning walls, her shirt over her mouth, her breathing shallow.

At the end of the corridor she came to a door and put her hand on the handle. It was so hot that she heard the skin of her palm sizzle before she felt the searing pain. She pulled back and ran on farther, coughing now as her breathing roughened. The next door handle was cooler, but on opening it she found it led only to a closet. She gasped, crumpled, and sank to her knees, pressing her face to the floor to inhale the cooler, cleaner air. Compared to what she had been breathing it tasted like a mountain spring. She got up and ran on, rounding a corner at a stumbling trot. Suddenly, up ahead were doors, doors to the outside.

There was a great crash above, followed by a groaning of timber as part of the ceiling gave way in a shower of sparks. Deborah put her head down and ran for the doors as a beam above where she had been standing exploded as if it had been stuffed with dynamite. Then the doors, their hot bolts and fiddly, maddening latches, and then the cool, moist night air.

She bolted out of the front and onto an expansive driveway lit not just by the fire which raged impressively behind her but by the lights of three fire trucks whose crew, several of whom were connecting hoses, stared at her openmouthed. As the first of them came sprinting heavily over to her, oxygen mask at the ready, she heard one of them exclaim, "They said there was no one inside! They said . . ."

"Is there anybody else in there?" said the firefighter with the mask, helping her down the steps, cradling her like an infant. She felt suddenly weak, almost beyond speech let alone walking, and leant into him gratefully.

"Any *body*?" she said.

"Is there anybody else still inside?" he repeated. "We can't get it under control. We were just going to make sure it didn't spread. Let it burn out. There's no one else still inside, right?"

She thought for a moment and then shook her head.
Let him burn.

CHAPTER 78

It was morning. Deborah had spent the night in Grady Memorial Hospital as a precaution, had been given a few hits of oxygen, and had her cuts, burns, and bruises poked and treated by various nurses till they pronounced her fit to go at dawn after a short and fitful sleep. Cerniga and Keene came by personally at six.

"Busy night?" said the federal agent.

"Average," she said.

"Wanna tell me about it?"

"Not here," she said. "On my turf."

"Home?"

"The museum," she said.

The traffic was still light at this time, and they were inside in under twenty minutes.

"Can we do this in Richard's room?" she said.

"Sure," said Cerniga. "Why?"

"I don't know." She shrugged. "Closure, I guess."

Cerniga sat at Richard's desk with his notebook in front of him. Deborah sat in the one armchair with her back to the bookcase, feeling the tenderness of the skin on her arms and hands, one of which had had to be heavily bandaged. She had been given various creams and lotions for her burns, but the skin still felt papery and sensitive, tingling when the air so much as shifted. Keene watched, looking abashed and saying nothing.

"This *is* closure, I take it?" she said.

"As far as I'm concerned," he said. "It will drag out for

months in paperwork of one kind and another, but I'll do what I can to keep you out of that."

"You're sure it was him?"

"Bowers?" said Cerniga. "Yes. The van was found burning in a gully near Virginia Highlands."

"It crashed?"

"Hard to say," he said. "It looks more like it was torched."

"Torched?"

"Self-immolation is a favorite with these political martyr types," he said. "Though we don't understand why they would do it when they had apparently gotten away with what they had been looking for. Two bodies were removed. One was clearly the tattooed skinhead you described. The other, the driver, was, presumably, Calvin Bowers. We'll have to wait on dental records, but it seems a safe call. There was a third body in a box in the back. Is that what I think it was?"

"No," she said. "They didn't get away with what they had been looking for. That's probably why they torched it and themselves. The third body was Marcus. I switched the corpses and left the other to burn in the Atreus tomb. At the time, they were in a hurry and didn't look too closely, but I expect they realized soon after they left."

Keene gave a low whistle.

Cerniga looked at her. He said nothing, but she thought he looked impressed. She looked away, not wanting his admiration or his pity, anxious to get this all over.

"Did the death mask survive the fire?" she asked suddenly.

"Not in a way you'd want to display, sorry."

"It's OK," she said. "Marcus would have liked to be burned on a funeral pyre in the grave mask of Agamemnon. Or," she added, smiling sadly, "something like it."

"You know that when the Germans invaded Greece," said Cerniga, "Hitler gave express instructions that Athens should not be bombed. He saw it as his spiritual home. They say that World War Two was a modern war in terms of its technology but an ancient one in terms of its objectives."

"The annihilation of the enemy," said Deborah. "The

eradication of alien cities, cultures, people that were considered inferior."

"Pretty grand goals for Atreus, considering they never had more than a couple of members," said Cerniga. "I guess that's the price of secrecy and paranoia. You can't exactly recruit outside Wal-mart. Still, they had a ton of money evidently."

"From Graves?"

For a moment Cerniga looked baffled.

"*Graves,* capital *G*," said Deborah. "Edward Graves, the military policeman."

"Right. Yes. It seems he raised a lot of money while he was in France and put it to good use once he got Stateside. Quite the entrepreneur and businessman. Respectable too."

Deborah snorted wearily. She saw no paradox there.

"Now that we know who was running Atreus," said Cerniga, "we'll be able to get access to his bank accounts. I expect we'll find Calvin Bowers had a rather substantial fortune. He would need it to orchestrate a plan of this scale."

Deborah looked away. She had, she thought, been briefly fascinated by Calvin's aura of confidence and power, attracted to it even. The thought unsettled her. She had always assumed she was immune to such things.

Maybe that's not possible. Not really. Better be on your guard against it . . .

"When you went back to see Bowers," said Cerniga, cutting off her train of thought, "did you know?"

"What?" said Deborah, shifting under his steady gaze.

"Did you know he was the guy, the Nazi, the one who killed Richard?"

For a second she didn't say anything, then she looked away as if distracted and shook her head.

When Cerniga and Keene left her, she sat exactly where she was for ten long minutes, thinking about Marcus and about Richard, even a little about Calvin. She had thought that the mask of Atreus was the gold faceplate placed over an ancient body, but it wasn't. It was the face that Calvin—and people like him—wore on a daily basis, the constant lie that allowed them to live in the world unrecognized, untouched by the panic, horror, and disbelief that their true faces would produce. How many more of them were there today, in Georgia, in America, living the lives of ordinary people, privately hating, despising, wishing for the utter destruction of all who didn't look like them, or believe like them, or love like them? The thought chilled her and depressed her, like an iron gauntlet tightening about her heart and lungs.

Children and their fathers, she thought.

That's what it was all about. Deborah and her father, Tonya and hers, Marcus and his, Alexandra and hers. Less literally, Richard. Maybe even Calvin and Graves, the fascist MP who had mentored him in Atreus. Atreus himself and Agamemnon, Agamemnon and Orestes, who revenged himself on his murderous mother . . . Priam and Hector. Achilles and Pyrrhus. The countless—and, to her, nameless—victims of the death camps, parents and children all. The curse of Atreus had been the repetition of murder and vengeance visited upon his successors. Sitting there in silence now, she saw it had spread like blood through fabric, like contagion, corrupting anyone who touched it. She turned to her book: *The Rise and Fall of Nazi Germany.*

Calvin was dead, a suicide unable to live with his failure. Pending dental records, of course. But who else could it be? Atreus had been two people. Pathetic really. But the amount of hatred those two carried with them was disproportionate and therefore quite lethal.

She paused, suddenly distracted.

Two? No. There had been a third man, someone she had only glimpsed once as he sat in the van which had driven her to Calvin's little funerary monument . . .

Which means . . .

She had to call Cerniga. She turned in her seat, and at almost the same moment she heard the telltale click of the latch as the bookcase behind her began to swing slowly open.

CHAPTER 79

She didn't think the space behind the bookcase could be any colder than the rest of the room, so the chill she felt on the back of her neck and running down her spine had to be in her mind.

"Hello, Calvin," she said without turning round.

He walked past her to the door and turned the sneck on the lock. He looked haggard, his easy composure gone, his suit now far beyond the fashionably rumpled look he affected, his hair awry, his face smeared with dirt and grease and blood. He was holding that long Nazi dagger again, though it dangled from his hand as if he didn't remember it was there. It gave him a new and psychotic unpredictability which Deborah didn't like.

"You are not surprised to see me?" he said.

"Hardly," said Deborah. "This last creep-show scare is about your level of imaginative vision. I've been reading about the great Nazi aesthetic: beauty and purification through genocide. If it wasn't so repulsive it would be laughable. I assume the police will find bullets in the bodies you left behind in that burning van?"

"My last bullets, unfortunately, yes," he said. "Though this," he added, remembering the dagger, "has a certain poetic justice, wouldn't you say?"

She looked at the knife but kept quite still.

"Justice," he persisted, taking a step toward her and speaking more insistently, "because of what you did last night. What you did to—"

"*Der Führer?*" she said, a note of contempt forcing itself through her caution. "Good. He finally got the ignominious torching he deserved. And you know the best part? You set the fire yourself."

"Shut up," he said, raising the knife.

What are you doing?

She didn't know. She was pissing him off on purpose, perhaps because it might throw him off balance when he made his inevitable attack, but maybe because he was just a stupid, stupid man who had gotten too much admiration for too long.

"You people are idiots," she spat. "White supremacists!? That's a joke."

"Shut up, Jew!" he shouted.

"You can't hurt me," she said, getting to her feet and squaring her shoulders, "you infantile little prick, with your banners and your slogans and your moronic, half-baked ideas, and your—"

He came at her then, lunging savagely, and that little reptilian part of her brain was thrilled with a wild delight as she dodged and parried and kicked. She didn't slap or claw, but balled her fists and smashed at his face, so that he came in close like a boxer, hugging her to his chest to keep her from making contact. She brought her knee to his groin, sharp and hard, but he anticipated and rolled left, twisting her backward so that she fell heavily onto the bed. He went after her, pinning her there, fighting to control her hands while he raised the dagger.

Then there was a knock on the door.

"Miss Miller?"

It was Tonya. Calvin's eyes widened, then one hand closed around Deborah's throat. She fought it, and he released the knife to restrain her, but she couldn't speak, couldn't make a sound. She struggled, catching the muffled sound of Tonya's voice through the door.

"I just got in and didn't know if you were in there?" she said.

Calvin paused, his grip firm around her windpipe. Then his face began to grin.

"She doesn't know," he whispered. "Shh . . ." To Deborah's surprise he called out, "Give us a few minutes will you, Tonya? You've caught us . . . er . . . *indisposed.*"

"Oh I *am* sorry, Mr. Bowers," said Tonya, respectful and embarrassed, from behind the door. "I'll come back later."

"That's OK," he called back.

No! Don't go! Come back!

He listened to the silence for a moment and then smiled that lurid smile she had glimpsed earlier, and then whispered, "We'll consummate our relationship yet."

"I really don't think so."

It had been Deborah's thought, but she had not said the words. Tonya had said the words.

She was right behind him. He rolled and twisted as she dropped the key, but not before she had brought the antique tomahawk hard across the side of his head. As he sagged and tumbled into a heap on the floor, Deborah sat up, gasping and clutching her throat.

"For a barbaric weapon, that thing works pretty good," said Tonya.

Deborah stared at her.

"Just tell me," said Tonya, "you didn't spill that perfume by accident."

CHAPTER 80

Two Months Later

The fund-raiser was almost over. The food (significantly improved over last time) had been served, and the staff of Taste of Elegance had begun busily—some might say conspicuously—cleaning up. The only thing still to do was for Deborah to give her closing toast.

She stepped up onto the podium and glanced over at the string quartet, who had stopped playing and were taking the opportunity to quench their thirsts. She looked out over the crowd of faces, some of whom were starting to focus on her, and caught Tonya, at the back, brandishing a showy smile, a prompt to Deborah who promptly snapped one on. Someone began tinkling the side of their glass with a spoon, and the museum lobby fell silent.

"Good evening, ladies and gentlemen," said Deborah. She paused, waiting for all traces of conversation to finish. "I don't want to spoil the evening with a lengthy speech, but I would like to make a few announcements. First, on behalf of the museum, I want to thank you all for coming and for offering assistance after what has been a very difficult time. Your support—moral and financial—has been invaluable to us over the last few weeks and will go a long way to ensuring the success of the museum in the future."

A pattering of applause. She waited for it to die down, smiling and nodding.

"I wanted to take the opportunity to introduce you to one of our new staff members," she said. "Tonya Mulligrew has been with us for several months now, but her role has changed, and she will now function as the museum's communications director, a catchall title covering matters of publicity, community relations, and whatever else I can think of to dump on her. Tonya?"

The crowd pivoted, and Tonya, smiling humbly, raised a hand, half greeting, half admission of guilt. The fact that the sea of faces was larger than usual and broadly diverse of color was testament to the work Tonya had already done, something Deborah and Richard's best efforts had been unable to achieve.

"I also wanted to announce two new exhibits, one permanent, one visiting, which will come to Druid Hills in the next twelve months. The permanent exhibit will concern Georgia's nineteenth-century slave culture: an exciting and moving study of the region's African American heritage, including a narrative documentary to be shown in a purpose-built auditorium, and exhibits combining artifacts, photographs, and documents detailing everything from the capture and trade of slaves in Africa and the slave ships themselves, to plantation life and the Underground Railroad. We hope to gather pieces from small, underfunded museums and from private collections from Savannah and elsewhere in the state as well as presenting materials on life in Atlanta before the Emancipation Proclamation."

Another patter of applause, longer, more heartfelt this time.

"The temporary exhibit will be here for the first three months of next year-and presents a unique opportunity to glimpse ancient Greek antiquities in North America. Thanks to Dimitri Popadreus, director of the National Archaeological Museum in Athens, the Druid Hills Museum will be the first non-European museum to display a special traveling exhibit of Mycenaean gold, bronze, and ceramics. This will be, as you can imagine, an extraordinary exhibit, unlike anything seen in the area, perhaps even in the country, and we are delighted to be able to host it."

More applause.

The exhibit was, of course, Popadreus's tribute to Richard's goodwill and Deborah's tact, but it was still astonishingly generous. The call had come, unsolicited and unexpected, only three days before, the Greek's languid tone echoing down a crackling line like a voice from the ancient past. The thoughtfulness of the gesture had brought tears to her eyes. In some corner of her heart she felt that Richard would have thought it all worthwhile just to be able to show the people of Georgia the culture which had inspired Homer and, in turn, him. He might even have thought it was worth dying for.

"Lastly," she said, "I want to offer a toast to a man without whom none of this would have been possible, a man we miss sorely this evening . . ."

Her voice warbled and cracked. She paused, opening her mouth again and pressing a smile, as the crowd waited, patient and understanding. But the words wouldn't come. She had prepared several minutes on what Richard had meant to the community and to her personally. She had anecdotes on his courage as a leader of the arts, on his sense of humor and his compassion. She had sat up half the night trying to find a way to express her love for the man who was gone, but now the words stuck in her throat.

"I'm sorry," she managed.

She paused, composed herself, still smiling in an apologetic and self-deprecating way, and then she opened her mouth to say something, anything. Tears broke from her eyes and streamed suddenly and unstoppably down her cheeks. No words came.

Somehow, her vision blurring fast, her eyes found Tonya at the back and saw her silently raise her drink. Deborah did the same, and the room as one lifted their glasses and said, "Richard Dixon."

"A touching speech," said Harvey Webster. "I didn't think you had it in you."

"You are the master of the backhanded compliment, Harvey," said Deborah, smiling.

Five more minutes, and they would all be gone. Five

minutes, and she could go home, sleep, get back to running the museum and to some version of normalcy. Five minutes of enduring the condescension and lechery of this bloated old goat.

"There is one other thing you might have announced," he said, "but I thought it best to bring it to you privately."

Deborah tensed. *The board was going to try to oust her, or cut her fundings or . . .*

"Go on," she said, taking a steadying sip of her gin martini.

"The League of Christian Businessmen is disbanding," he said. "We feel its time has passed. We will, as our last philanthropic act, be donating a significant lump sum to the museum."

"That's very generous of you," said Deborah, feeling a tide of relief. Getting the League and its dubious interests off her back would give her untold freedom with the museum, simultaneously eliminating a growing suspicion, suspicion that would be touched with guilt so long as the museum was receiving their support.

"It was the least we could do," said Webster, smiling, showing that wet, sluggish tongue of his.

"Interesting timing," said Deborah. "Why break up the League now?"

"It just seemed right," he said, his eyes fixed.

"The FBI believed that Atreus was linked to other more legitimate business concerns," said Deborah, apropos of nothing. "They thought that they provided a kind of hard-core hit squad for more respectable organizations which shared white supremacist assumptions."

"Really?" said Webster. "I am not familiar with that organization."

"I'm sure you're not," she said. "They were a cell of what might be considered a terrorist organization. We thought they had gotten hold of a particularly powerful weapon, but it turned out that the weapon was more ideological than practical."

"Indeed," he said, still smiling, still simulating polite curiosity, still playing along. "Atreus, you said? Sounds Latin."

"Greek," she said, still smiling. "He was the father of a doomed house, responsible for the most appalling acts of brutality against members of his own family, for which his descendents were cursed to fight pointless wars and die violently at the hands of their spouses and children. As a figure of violence and hatred, tied to Greece's ancient glory, these neo-Nazis made him and his descendents their emblem, a representation of all they wanted to accomplish, particularly against people like Tonya and me."

"Extraordinary," he said.

"Yes."

He shaped a bleak, hard smile.

"It will always be something with people like you, won't it?" he said. "There will always be some cause, some wrong to be righted."

"God," she said, "I really hope so."

"Crusades," he said, avuncular now, "can be *very* expensive."

"I know," she said. "But they are always worth it. There was a homeless man killed a few months ago. A Russian. He was a crusader. His fight, his obsession, cost him everything."

"Well, there you go," said Webster, smiling.

"I got a letter from his daughter yesterday," she said. "His government has reinstated all the awards he won and given him a special posthumous medal for service to his country."

"He's still dead though, right?"

"Yes," she said. "But his daughter loves him again, and you can't beat that."

As she walked away, her phone rang.

It was Cerniga. He said he had wanted to be there for the fund-raiser—as a show of support—but he had had to work. He said he was glad she seemed to be doing OK and that the museum was back on its feet, and maybe she would like to join him for a drink sometime, "to catch up."

Deborah considered the throng of people milling around beneath the great greenish ship prow with the dragon-lady (now proved authentically sixteenth-century) bestowing her glazed smile on the sea of people. It had grown on her. She still thought it ghastly, but it had a kind of wit, like it was Richard's last wry joke at her expense, and for that, she rather liked it.

"Thanks," she said to Cerniga. "I appreciate the offer."

"And?"

"I have your number," she said.

"OK," he said, uncertain.

Deborah hung up and started surveying the crowd for Tonya. Despite the promising behavior of the caterers earlier, they had still left an entire table heaped with napkins and discarded plates. She needed to get these people out of here, politely but firmly, so she could get to work, and get to bed at a reasonable hour. Tomorrow was Saturday, and she had decided—as she had told her astonished mother on the telephone the night before—to attend Shabbat Balak for the first time since moving to Atlanta at Havurat Lev Shalem, a reconstructionist chavurah she had stumbled upon online. Whatever else it was, it would mark a new start, and that she found immensely appealing, better at least than the lipstick and perfume she had returned to the cabinet under her sink for the immediate future. She would say good-bye to Richard, to Marcus, perhaps even to her father and the nameless dead of her grandmother's family in the words of the "El Moleh Rachamim," whispered privately to herself:

O, God, full of compassion, Thou who dwellest on high, grant perfect rest beneath the shelter of Thy divine presence among the holy and pure who shine as the brightness of the firmament to the soul of my beloved who has gone to his eternal home.

Mayest Thou, O God of Mercy, shelter him forever under the wings of Thy presence, may his soul be bound up in the bond of life eternal, and grant that the memories of my life inspire me always to noble and consecrated living. Amen.

Did she believe it yet? Not really. But she might, in time, because a part of her felt that she might have to say the words to make them true, that if she *could* say them in the presence of others who wrestled with the same world, the same hard truths, the same balance and paradox, then the new beginning she looked for might yet be within her grasp. There was at least hope, and that, she thought, was worth so much more than she had imagined.

SOURCE MATERIAL

While all novels inevitably draw on fact, *The Mask of Atreus* does so more than most, and while the core story and its characters are fictional, I thought it worth directing the reader's attention to some of the material I consulted in constructing the story. The list of source materials that follows (some of which are referenced directly in the novel itself) may help the curious to discover for themselves some of the historical or otherwise factual bones which hold the tale together.

—A. J. Hartley

On Greece and Its Archaeological History

The Rough Guide to Greece, Mark Ellingham, Marc Dubin, Natania Jansz, and John Fisher. Sixth edition. London: Rough Guides/Penguin, 1995.

Also, the 10th edition (2004) by Lance Chilton, Marc Dubin, Nick Edwards, Mark Ellingham, John Fisher, and Natania Jansz.

Memoirs of Heinrich Schliemann: A Documentary Portrait Drawn from His Autobiographical Writings, Letters, and Excavation Reports, Leo Deuel. London: Harper and Row, 1977.

Schliemann's Discoveries of the Ancient World, Dr. C. Schuchardt, trans. Eugenie Sellers. New York: Avenel Books, 1978.

Lost and Found: The 9,000 Treasures of Troy, Caroline Moorhead. New York: Viking, 1994.

Minoan and Mycenaean Art, Reynold Higgins. London: Thames and Hudson, 1997.

The Greek Myths, Robert Graves. London: Penguin, 1964.

On WWII and Its Aftermath

"Of Flowers and Murder—Mass Grave Found in Magdeburg, Germany," *Discover*, February 1999. Copyright © 2000 by Gale Group. www.findarticles.com/p/articles/mi_m1511/is_2_20/ai_53631736.

On Nazi body-doubles: www.blackraiser.com/nredoubt/identity.htm.

World War II Tanks, Eric Grove. London: Orbis, 1972.

Brothers in Arms: The Epic Story of the 761st Tank Battalion, WWII's Forgotten Heroes, Kareem Abdul-Jabbar and Anthony Walton. New York: Broadway, 2004.

The Architecture of Doom, dir. Peter Cohen. First Run Features, 1989.

Miscellaneous

Garlikov, Rick. "Jewish Beliefs As Found in Jewish Prayers." www.garlikov.com/sundayschool.html.

Southern Poverty Law Center. www.splcenter.org.

CAIS (Center for Applied Isotope Studies). www.uga.edu/~cais/.